THE FIFTH SEASON

(Pancaroba)

KERRY B. COLLISON

Published by: Sid Harta Publishers

P.O. Box 1042
Hartwell Victoria Australia 3124
email: author@sidharta.com.au

Phone: +61 3 9650 9920
Fax: +61 3 9545 1742

Internet sites: http://www.sidharta.com.au
http://www.publisher-guidelines.com
http://www.temple-house.com

Revised: February 2003
First Published: December, 1998 as *The Fifth Season*

Text: Kerry B. Collison
Cover design
& Typesetting: Alias Design

Collison, Kerry B.

ISBN: 1-877059-17-X

Printed by: Shannon Books

Dedication

In memory of those who lost their lives as a result of the tragic Bali bombings in Kuta, Saturday 12 October 2002.

In spirit, you will always be with us.

Kerry B. Collison followed a distinguished period of service in Indonesia as a member of the Australian military and government intelligence services during the turbulent period known as 'The Years of Living Dangerously'. This was followed by a successful business career spanning thirty years throughout Asia.

Recognized for his chilling predictions in relation to Asia's evolving political and economic climate through his books, he brings unique qualifications to his historically-based vignettes and intriguing accounts of power-politics and the shadowy world of governments' clandestine activities.

Further information is available on the Internet site: http://www.sidharta.com.au

Photo: Courtesy of Dominion Newspapers, N.Z.

Postscript 2003

Subsequent to the events of Bali, Saturday 12 October 2002, I revisited this story and discovered, sadly, that many of the predictions contained in the original edition had come to pass. We have witnessed the emergence of powerful, influential militant Moslem groups, such as the *Laskar Jihad* and *Jemaah Islamiyah*, both linked to Osama bin Laden (spelled bin Ladem in *The Fifth Season*) and responsible not only for the slaughter of many thousands of Christians in the eastern Indonesian provinces, but the incomprehensible attack on innocent tourists and Balinese which resulted in the loss of so many lives, many of the victims Australian.

It is now an accepted fact that Osama bin Laden and his *Al Qaeda* had established a sound network throughout Indonesia, parts of Malaysia, and in the southern Philippines, with the intention of supporting the realization of an Islamic state that would embrace all of these nations as one.

Today, in Indonesia, hardly a week goes by without another bombing or news or yet another massacre in Aceh, Maluku, West Papua, the Celebes or Indonesian Borneo, Kalimantan, and, sadly, the burning of mosques in Lombok or the desecration of temples in Bali. Mass graves have recently been discovered containing thousands murdered by the brutal Indonesian Special Forces, whose American trained leadership will, undoubtedly, escape judgment by international tribunals such as those established to prosecute Balkan war criminals.

Over the past two years Australia's own political landscape has changed, influenced by the threat of a flood of refugees entering its waters via the vast Indonesian archipelago to the north. *The Fifth Season's* premise that one day Australia could, as a result of the destabilization of Indonesia, be inundated with a massive wave of refugees seeking asylum is no longer a matter of fiction, but an event which has become inevitable as that great country continues to disintegrate socially, politically and economically.

In 1998, when Indonesia's political climate became confused, then convulsed violently, many of the Archipelago's two hundred millions sensed that the long-awaited winds of change carried the elusive promise of reform, and a political shift towards democracy.

Pancaroba, the brief and often erratic time which conjoins the tropical Wet and Dry, is accepted in Equatorial Asia as the Fifth Season, and is known as the transitional climatic period when weather patterns become confused and turbulent.

Often, during these uncertain periods omens become apparent, tempting people whose cultures have been so deeply rooted in mysticism, spiritualism and animism through the millenniums to succumb to even greater superstition than would be their norm.

This is an account based on factual events, and the men and women who struggled to survive the bitter turmoil of Indonesia's Fifth Season.

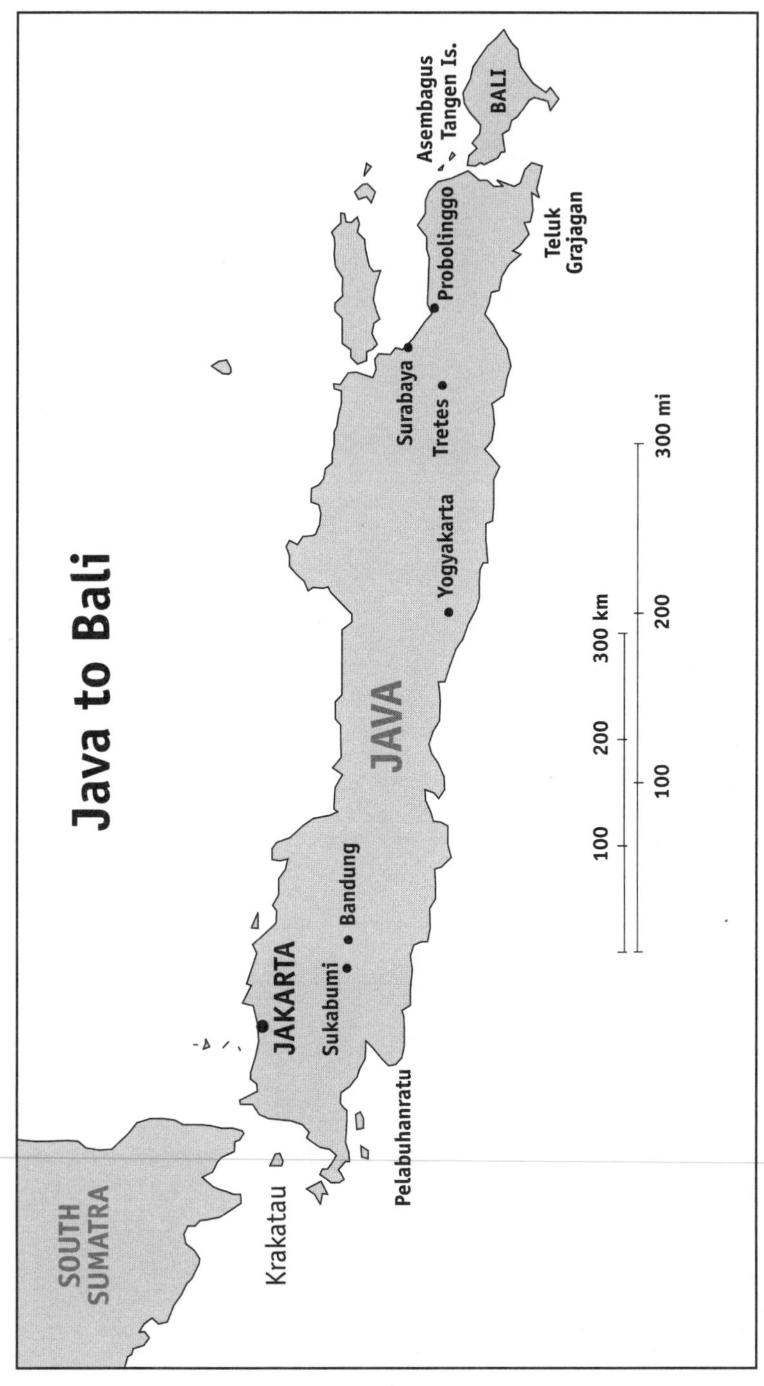
Java to Bali
SOUTH SUMATRA
Krakatau
Pelabuhanratu
JAKARTA
Sukabumi
Bandung
JAVA
Yogyakarta
Tretes
Surabaya
Probolinggo
Asembagus
Tangen Is.
BALI
Teluk Grajagan
100
200
300 km
100
200
300 mi

Glossary of Terms

This simple glossary includes *Bahasa* Indonesia words used throughout the novel and may assist readers who have not yet been fortunate enough to visit the beautiful archipelago and become familiar with its multi-faceted culture and language.

ABRI	Indonesian Armed Forces
ADRI	Indonesian Army
ALRI	Indonesian Navy
AURI	Indonesian Air Force
Allahu Akbar	God is Great - (Moslem chant)
Allah	God
ANZUS	Australian, N.Z., U.S. Defence Treaty
ASEAN	Association of South East Asian Nations
Asalamalaikum	welcome greeting
babat-pedas	chili tripe
Bahasa	language
bangsat	arsehole, bastard
Bapak	respectful address to an older male, father
batik	printed cloth
becak	three-wheeled pedicab
bule	derogatory name for white people
CIA	Central Intelligence Agency
COMINT	Communications Intelligence
cukong	middle-man, broker
DIA	Defense Intelligence Agency

dukun	unlicensed herbalist who casts spells
El Nino	devastating weather pattern.
Fatwah	religious statement of condemnation
Golok	field knife of sword length
ha-Mossad le-Modiin ule Tafkidim Meyuhadim	Institute for Intelligence and Special Tasks
Haji	one who has completed the pilgrimage to Mecca
hati goreng	fried liver
Ibu	mother, respectful form for older woman
kain batik	sarong
Kalimantan	Indonesian Borneo
KOPASSUS	Indonesian Army Special Forces
KOSTRAD	Indonesian Army Strategic Forces
kretek	clove cigarette
La Nina	El Nino's twin sister - opposing weather pattern
Lohor	one of the five prayer periods, around 1330 hours.
magrib	sunset
mas	friend, you
Mufti Muharam	Islamic religious/political party
nasi	rice
nasi goreng	fried rice
NSA	National Security Agency
Nusantara	early name for Indonesia (Java to the east)
Ombar-Wetar	deep submarine trench off Timor
Oom	uncle - idiomatic term for older male
Ora Et Labora	a school in Jakarta
Pancaroba	The Fifth Season
Pak	abbreviation of Bapak
Pancasila	the five basic principles underlying Indonesian life
paru-paru	lung

pribumi	indigenous person - son of the soil
Perkarya Party	(Perkumpulan Karya) Workers' Party
rakyat	the people, the masses
sambal	sharp spice
sate	meat, chicken, cooked on skewers
Selamatan	blessing ceremony
Selamat Pagi	good morning
selamat datang	welcome
sialan!	damn!
surat-kaleng	anonymous note
terima kasih	thank you

The Fifth Season

(Pancaroba)

'Kemarau setahun dihapuskan oleh hujan sehari.'

A year's drought can be washed from the memory by just one day of rain.

INDONESIAN PROVERB

Prologue

A hushed calm permeated the eager assembly, silencing soft whispers of disbelief that the rumors had any substance. The President moved forward slowly, his fatigue apparent as he removed his glasses and gently rubbed troubled eyes.

From Jakarta to Washington and across the Atlantic to Europe, tens of millions sat transfixed to their television screens mesmerized, as another ancient prophecy was fulfilled, when the former general announced that he would step down from office immediately, ending his thirty-two year reign over the world's largest Moslem nation, the Republic of Indonesia.

Moments later, with the world as his witness, the Javanese ruler stepped back from center stage, smiled tiredly, and surrendered the country to his deputy.

Holding the Holy Koran and clutching his over-sized pici nervously, Mr. L.B. Hababli was sworn in and became the Indonesian President, rendering most observers speechless at the speed with which the transfer of power had been effected.

The seeds had been sown; the bitter harvest inevitable. Indonesian women of ethnic Chinese origins would learn to mark this day as the beginning of their journey into hell.

* * * *

Chapter One

May 1989

The False Prophet

Shimmering, layered-mirages accompanied the windless, cloudless sky as the land below surrendered to the heat of the day, the once-fertile, but now cracked and spoiled paddy-fields silent evidence of the pestilence which had overtaken the scorched countryside. Rodents, grasshoppers, snakes and other unpleasant residents occupied their temporary haven, revelling in the absence of their natural enemy, man, content to feed in the shadows of his disaster.

Blistering sun burned its way through the dry, volcanic soil, leaving fields of desperation, barren because of nature's irreversible effects. The land had become desolate; the farmers feared the one responsible they had come to know as *El Nino* as they struggled to preserve their beliefs, praying that this unwelcome stranger would soon depart their land, and permit their lesser gods to return. It was as if some angry stranger had cast a giant, unyielding, suffocating net across the nation. It would seem certain that they would all perish.

The seasons had become confused. Without warning, persistent, dry, equatorial skies tormented when there should have been rain. Evening storms, which once signaled the *Pancaroba,* mysteriously vanished, taking with them their thunderous cries which heralded the fall of life-giving rain. These ominous signs cast doubt, then fear, as the fertile valleys of Java became dry, and the descendants of those who had migrated to the tropical paradise millenniums before, suddenly became afraid as their beliefs failed, and their gods deserted them.

As the winds of change swept through remnants of these ancient Javanese kingdoms once known as *Nusantara,* there were those who were reminded of the Twelfth Century prophecies of Joyoboyo, and his predictions of the five kings.

"The kingdom of Java would be subjected to claim by a fair-skinned race. The first of two kings would rise and lead his people from their four centuries of serfdom. Another would be born at that time to release the people from their spiritual bondage. A third would appear from the shadows, as a thief in the night, and feed his family from the fat of the land. Then, in chaos, a weak prince, not of their blood, would be anointed by others to stand in their place.

As the kingdom languished in its abyss of darkness, a fifth king would emerge, demanding his rightful place to lead his people through their troubled times. And with his presence, Nusantara would suffer great pestilence and sorrow, and the people would flee, the skies behind filled with a light so blinding, none but those who were evil would even consider remaining behind, in the once promised land."

* * * *

Haji Abdul Muis

In contemplative mood, Haji Abdul Muis examined the withered stalk, the half-formed husk evidence of another failed harvest. The Moslem leader cast his eyes slowly across the neglected fields, the midday heat distorting the scene with false promises of water, as a broken-layered mirage danced tantalizingly above the land. His land.

He remained sitting on the dry, cracked mound, the pile of overgrown earth designating the boundary to his property. In the distance, settled half-hidden amongst a copse of coconut trees, sun-bleached, clay roofing-tiles indicated the presence of a house. His house.

Surrounding hills, in days past covered with tall, majestic stands of teak timber, now stood denuded of their former glory, casting shadows of despair across the desolate farmland, and those who had stubbornly remained. Once, on the other side of the spur, a tranquil lake had nestled, filled with flocks of pelicans, visitors on their annual pilgrimage from distant lands. There wildlife had thrived amongst the wetland, fed by rivers filled by abundant rain. Then, when the population had finally reached unsustainable levels, and the effects of El Nino had burned, the water disappeared, lost to the sun and dry earth.

* * * *

Somewhere behind an engine came to life and Haji Abdul Muis instinctively glanced over his shoulder in the direction of the waiting Mercedes, aware that his driver would have engaged the air-conditioner in readiness for his return. He ignored the engine's low, mechanical hum, turning back to savor this special moment in his life, observing the fields of promise spread out subserviently before him. He removed the deeds from inside his safari jacket, and read the contents aloud to his absent audience, his ears filled with the silent drum pounding heavily in his hate-filled chest.

Abdul Muis had not set foot on this land in more than three decades. His acquisition fulfilled a promise sworn many years before, when his family had been evicted, and their lives destroyed by manipulative local traders.

* * * *

Born in the small, shanty-style house, now standing derelict in the distance, Muis had been the youngest of five children, his parents indigenous farmers of some substance. They were *pribumi*, sons of the soil, whose forebears had occupied this land even before the Prophet Mohammed had walked the earth. Their holdings covered more than ten hectares of fertile fields, which in memory had rarely failed to produce two generous crops of rice each year. He remembered how laboriously his father and elder brother had toiled, and how envious their neighbors had been whenever harvests were completed. His family's land had been blessed with rich, black, volcanic earth, their acreage greater than most other holdings in the district, including those belonging to local, and covetous, party officials.

Muis' family had been deeply devoted to their Moslem faith, their lives governed in every way by the teachings of the Prophet, Mohammed. Each day, his parents would rise with false dawn, and complete their ablutions before attending to the first of their five daily prayer rituals. The children mimicked these habits without question, eagerly falling into line and habit while emulating their parents, as had generations before them. With religious rituals absorbed into routines, Muis' life became totally immersed in faith and traditions, even when this subservience sometimes brought pain.

Custom dictated that all Moslem children be circumcised. Muis' three sisters, who had all been cut not long after birth, remained chaste until fourteen, and were married and nursing their own children before achieving their fifteenth birthdays. Muis' own circumcision ceremony had been a most painful affair. Taunted by the other children as to what he might expect, he would never forget his bloody sixth birthday when he and two other children were held, wide-eyed, their foreskins publicly removed according to Moslem tradition.

But generally, Abdul Muis' early childhood had been idyllic in the isolated village community. He could always be found playing in the fields with the other children, catching tadpoles and dragonflies, or flying colorful kites, the seemingly endless summer days a young boy's dream as Muis' mind learned about life in this paradise setting.

At night he often lay awake listening to his father read from the Koran, or sit silently at his feet listening in awe to the captivating folklore he knew so well. Occasionally, he would accompany his sisters into the village proper, where they would sit through the night on hand-woven mats spread neatly under huge banyan trees. There, they would remain, engrossed, as visiting puppeteers related tales of the creation, of white and red monkeys, of evil and good spirits, all given meaning through their slow-dancing, *wayang kulit* shadow puppets. For Muis, life could not have been better.

* * * *

The village school was some distance from Muis' home, accessed by walking carefully along slippery, narrow paths which meandered between lush, green rice paddies where he would often stop along the way, catching grasshoppers, or beetles, examining those things of interest which so easily satisfy a child's inquisitive mind.

The inadequate, post-colonial Indonesian school system offered a basic curriculum in village schools. Lessons were presented by poorly-equipped, and grossly underpaid teachers, often in shanty-style buildings erected over meticulously-swept, foot-hardened dirt floors. The children were required to sit cross-legged on *tikar* mats, those with writing pads obliged to hold these in their laps as they scribbled or drew.

While the country's population continued to grow at an alarming rate, adding millions to the already over-crowded system with each new year, schools operated morning and afternoon sessions to accommodate the rising demand. Muis was an attentive child, quick to learn and eager to add to his knowledge, these attributes soon coming to the attention of others in his environment. For many in this rural community, a formal education was not considered necessary, as empiric knowledge carried more value when tending matters of the land.

With an abundance of leisure time to fill and not particularly interested in returning home to assist his brother with the chores, Muis found other interests to occupy his mind. Encouraged to do so by his father, he filled in the empty hours reading that most precious of books, the Holy Koran. It was not long before the young man earned the interest, and respect, of his elders, including the local *ulamas*. In a devoutly Moslem atmosphere Abdul Muis' star first commenced its ascent, the influence of the Prophet

Mohammed over his young, and receptive mind, most potent.

Muis continued to excel at school. At the age of ten, he was selected by the *gurus* to attend religious classes, a decision he would never regret. As the years progressed, Abdul Muis became increasingly absorbed in his religion, determined by the age of fifteen, to dedicate his life to the study and advancement of Islam.

His father had never attended school, and although well versed in the Koran, the farmer was ambivalent towards his youngest son's persistent pleas to be permitted to continue his Islamic studies. Muis sought the support of the local *ulama*, who interceded on his former student's behalf, successfully convincing Muis' father that his money would be well spent. The older brother displayed no resentment whatsoever when Muis was granted his wish, and in 1965 they parted company, the family proud of their youngest as he bid farewell, and departed for the provincial capital of Surabaya. There, Muis had settled down, diligently pursuing his quest at the Faculty of Islamic Studies. Then, as the year entered its final quarter, disaster had struck when Indonesia had plunged into darkness as word of the failed October Communist *coup d'etat*, spread through the country.

The President had come under pressure to resign. Rumors suggesting that Beijing had sent weapons to support the communist cadres, galvanized the army into action. The deaths of five senior *ABRI* officers shocked the nation and, as their slaughter took place on China's national day, innuendo soon turned to accusation, and the Indonesian ethnic Chinese became victims of ignorance yet again. They were attacked on the streets and in their homes, their shops were burned, these events precipitating a mass exodus to Singapore and Hong Kong. For those unfortunates who were obliged to remain behind, their world was constantly filled with fear.

In the ensuing leadership vacuum, opportunists seized control of the military and commenced their reign of terror. Supported by an American Administration eager to see Indonesia cleanse itself of Communism, General Sarwo Eddie, the Butcher of Java, swung into action, his troops conducting their own cleansing campaign throughout the island, resulting in more than five hundred thousand being murdered. The general's putsch through rural communities cost the country dearly as villagers were indiscriminately targeted, and families turned on each other, settling old scores in the most brutal way. With the annihilation of entire communities, century-old villages disappeared, unfounded accusations of complicity with communist groups sufficient to warrant immediate dispatch, with no mercy shown even to children.

As well established farmers, Abdul Muis' father and brother often had cause to deal with local Chinese traders. They were also members of the village land committee responsible for arbitration over local disputes. The village *lurah*, or chief, had innocently listed their small association with the powerful *Partai Komunis Indonesia*, hoping for their support in land-related matters. As a consequence, when the blood-letting commenced, envious neighbors informed the newly established anti-Communist vigilante squads that the wealthy farmers who controlled the fertile lands in their midst were, in fact, communist sympathizers and friendly with the Chinese community.

An early morning raid left Muis' father, mother, and brother dead, their headless bodies discovered dumped down a well. His three sisters, together with their offspring, all perished when Sarwo Eddie's butchers arrived and cleansed the area of any remaining signs of communist roots, or ties.

Two months passed before Muis was to learn of what had transpired in his village. He had written, asking for his father to send more funds, and when his second request also went unanswered, he caught a bus and returned home. The discovery of his family's demise sent Muis into shock. By then marauding gangs had taken control over the countryside, as the Republic teetered on the brink of anarchy. He went to the local authorities but was shunned. It was then that he was informed that his family's land had been seized by the government. When he complained, the self-proclaimed local military head had ordered Muis to return to Surabaya or face charges of sedition. Without compensation, and without any form of income, Muis returned to college and laid his case before the faculty head who, out of consideration for the brilliant young student's talent, took him under his wing and nurtured Muis though his remaining days at the university.

The following three years did little to ease his pain nor relieve the festering hate which dominated much of his conscious mind, growing in intensity, while the rest of his countrymen struggled with their own demons and ghosts and the legacy of those horrific times. Muis became inflamed as the country emerged from its perilous era, disgusted that the United States-sanctioned New Order discouraged the growth of Moslem unity through political representation, and was incensed with the rapid spread of Catholicism and other religious faiths throughout the archipelago.

It did not go unnoticed as he became more radical in his views, that the Christian religions were making startling inroads into what were predominantly Moslem communities. He seethed when he witnessed foreign missionaries, mainly youngsters of U.S. origins blatantly canvassing the country's streets with bibles in hand, their insidious intrusion adding to his hate for all things American. He observed that the majority of Christians were of ethnic Chinese descent, and Muis clearly felt their presence, their beliefs and customs, a direct threat to his own, and in his confused mind, responsible for his family's demise.

Devoted, Muis totally immersed himself in his religious studies. The more he learned, the more he became convinced that Indonesia would never have suffered the calamitous events of recent years had the country followed the teachings of the Prophet and believed in *The One and True God* and remained pure to *His Ways*. Muis became determined that the *lintah-darat*, the blood-sucking, usurious Chinese bankers who conducted their business in contradiction to Islamic teachings, should all be destroyed.

Upon graduation, he had revisited his village. There, he discovered that ownership of his father's fields had changed hands yet again, and was now the property of the local loan sharks. He was mortified to learn that these were not only Chinese, but members of the flourishing Christian community now well established in the nearby town where they had recently constructed their church. Overcome with anger, he had returned to Surabaya where, under his mentor's guidance, he established his own religious forum for others as disgruntled as he, and within that month, declared the existence of Indonesia's newest Islamic organization, the *Mufti Muharam.*

Abdul Muis now had his vehicle to drive Indonesian Christians into the sea, and extract retribution for what he believed those associated with the Church had done to his family. He roamed the countryside speaking at Mosques and schools, his messages of hate cleverly disguised, but warmly received. Muis' following grew at an alarming rate, reaching five hundred thousand within the first year, five million during the next, the exponential growth continuing until the *Mufti Muharam* finally achieved a membership of thirty million Moslems. His dream of an Islamic state finally within reach, Muis set about cultivating a relationship with the Indonesian leadership.

* * * *

The country was clearly controlled by *ABRI,* the nation's military. They in turn, followed the dictates of the aging President, Suhapto. Muis made several approaches to ingratiate himself with the First Family, but was rebuffed, his chagrin such, Muis swore he would one day settle that score. Patiently he waited for his opportunity to strike, and this, ironically, was delivered to him by the President's ambitious, and impatient son-in-law, General Praboyo. When it became quite clear to all that President

Suhapto had never intended relinquishing his crown, Muis moved to position himself for the day when Suhapto's indisputable and powerful grip on the country finally passed to another.

Abdul Muis understood the importance of securing international support for his strategies. An Islamic state would require recognition from the Arab nations and although he believed this would be forthcoming once he had demonstrated his strengths, he examined the possibilities of establishing dialogue with Middle East leaders, arranging frequent visits to their shores. It was during one such visit to Iran, that Abdul Muis fell under the influence of the *Ayatollahs* and their militant persuasions.

He became convinced that Indonesia, as the world's largest Moslem community, should never have fallen behind other nations technologically. He sincerely believed that his country would one day be threatened by its giant neighbors, Communist China and India, both nations boasting populations in excess of one billion, both countries possessing nuclear capabilities. Muis had also come to learn that it was United States' vested interests which had prevented Indonesia from developing its own, defensive nuclear capabilities.

Under his leadership, Abdul Muis would ensure that the Indonesian people would enjoy freedom from the fear of nuclear attack, simply by arming his nation with the technology offered by his new allies, Iran, Iraq and Osama bin Ladam.

* * * *

As Muis sat pondering the future, his thoughts were interrupted by the distant cry of a bird as it winged its way across his field of vision. He looked up, surprised, and identified the fierce, black shape, then stood, waving his arms and shouting as the crow balked and changed direction. Although devoutly religious, Muis' childhood had been peppered with village superstition. The despised crow not only wreaked havoc during harvest, and terrified children with their deep-throated cries, their presence was associated with evil and peasant folklore warned that these black couriers carried messages from the damned.

Unhappy with the ominous sign, Muis frowned, undertaking to have the local *dukun* conduct a *selamatan* to cleanse his property of any evil spirits before the first stone to his retreat had been laid. With that, Haji Abdul Muis strolled back to the waiting car and returned to the splendid mansion that was his in Surabaya.

Chapter Two

New York – April 1996

Mary Jo Hunter

'Where ya goin, Lady?' the cabby asked, stretching to catch a better glimpse of Mary Jo's long, fine legs as she climbed into the back of the vehicle, her nostrils immediately offended by the stale, lingering odors of those who had gone before. Her baggage had been flung carelessly into the trunk, the sloppily dressed driver's smirk already annoying Mary Jo from the moment he had arrived to take her to the airport.

'Hong Kong,' she answered, checking her carry-on case again for reassurance. Her hand settled on the document folder containing her passport and she relaxed slightly.

'First time?' he tried, his eyes glancing into the rear vision mirror admiringly.

'Yes,' Mary Jo responded, hoping the conversation would stop there.

'Traveling alone?' he inquired, impertinently, but she took no offense, half-expecting the driver to make small talk. Having lived and worked in New York's aggressive environment for several years, Mary Jo had soon fallen into step with other residents, her smooth, well-mannered, small-town response a thing of the past.

'Maybe,' she said, the driver's eyes darting to the mirror again, wisely accepting the hint. Mary Jo leaned back as the taxi jerked its way through the Midtown traffic, contemplating what lay ahead. She was on her way to JFK and her posting to the S.E. Asia bureau. She thought about the long haul, eager to get under way, in no way daunted by the twenty-four hour flight on United to Hong Kong.

Mary Jo's thoughts were distracted by the occupant of a car traveling alongside and she smiled, observing a young woman sitting confidently alone in the rear, her appearance reminding Mary Jo of when she had first left home in pursuit of her dreams. Then, she frowned as the image of her mother waving goodbye intruded and she recalled with some sadness that there had been no tears, only excitement and relief that she had finally managed to escape her suffocating surrounds.

This brief recollection triggered other memories sending Mary Jo back to early childhood and, as the cabby fell into silence, her mind wandered back in time.

* * * *

Mary Jo had been an only child. The exhilaration of the *Sixties* and her mother's determination to maintain her liberated status, had resulted in her parents separating before her sixth birthday. She had remained with her mother in Ohio, the memory of her father's departure deeply affecting her mind.

Mary Jo had been thoroughly confused by the absence of her father, her mother refusing to acknowledge any questions as to where he had gone. She missed him greatly, the void in her life immeasurable after he had left. The memory of him sitting on her bed at night, holding her hand, reading stories of faraway places and filling her mind with wonders as she drifted off to sleep, filled her eyes with tears. Mary Jo yearned for the warmth of his strong, comforting arms she remembered so well and his deep, but soft, reassuring voice.

For months after his departure, Mary Jo had cried herself to sleep at night, brokenhearted that he could have abandoned her so. Alone with her strong-willed mother, she had done little else but cry. Then, after what seemed to have been an eternity, he returned.

On that day, Mary Jo had arrived home early from school to find her father sitting in their kitchen. Her heart had skipped a beat, and she had run across the small room banging her knee painfully against the door of an open cupboard. She remembered throwing herself up into his strong open arms and burying her head deep into his chest, his reassuring words comforting the pain of her bruised limb.

But he had not returned to stay. When Mary Jo overheard her parents argue, she had feared the worst. Suddenly he was gone again, the overwhelming, fearful emptiness which followed even greater than before.

Another year passed, and Mary Jo had come to believe that her father had deserted them forever when, unannounced, he amazingly reappeared. Against her mother's vitriolic protestations, he had carried Mary Jo off to the movies, his unforgivable absences immediately forgotten as she hugged him close, in a moment filled with joy.

That night, her father had tucked her into bed and read as he had done so many times before. With his hand gently stroking her head, his voice carried Mary Jo away on a familiar journey, the story of the Great Wall amongst her favorites. She remembered how she had visualized herself as part of the scene, walking hand in hand with her father along the forever-winding, man-made miracle through the mountains, the familiar resonance of his voice a delight, the images of Genghis and Kublai Khan no longer of frightening concern. She recalled begging him to promise to stay, his response, another hollow commitment to return. When she awoke the following morning, he was gone.

Two more years passed before Mary Jo saw his face again; this time, as he was passing through. She found the painful infrequency of her father's visits bewildering, recollections of how he looked slowly fading in her mind, until his face eventually resembled nothing more than a blur in an occasional dream. Finally, her father disappeared from their lives forever. Her mother refused all mention of his name, and with time, Mary Jo learned not to care, and accepted that he would never return.

* * * *

At first, Mary Jo had not really excelled at school, lacking motivation and the necessary concentration. Often, as the teacher's lulling, monotonous tones would cast their spell, her mind would wander, day-dreams carrying her away to distant lands and peoples, whose faces she had seen captured in still-life photographs. Her favorites were those found amongst their neighbor's National Geographic magazines, the reason she spent more time there than in her own home. Mary Jo would often sit for hours examining their collection, her hands moving across the amazing photographs, touching mountains and valleys as she imagined herself part of the wondrous scenes.

At fourteen, when their neighbors moved to California, Mary Jo joined the local library to satisfy her inquisitive mind. There she discovered an even greater world, the science of photography, her interest in still-art forms leading her to an inevitable conclusion. Having pestered her mother for months, Mary Jo received her first camera on her fifteenth birthday, and her life changed forever. After that, there was no doubt in her mind what she wished to do with her life, already consumed by the dream to become a photojournalist, and travel the world.

As fate would have it, her mother's timely remarriage provided Mary Jo with the means to attend college. With her step-father's encouragement and financial support, she applied to attend the Rochester Institute of Technology, and was accepted into the School of Photographic Arts and Sciences, one of the four schools within the College of Imaging Arts and Sciences at R.I.T. For Mary Jo, it was a dream come true. Although her mother was not overly keen about the prospect of sending her off alone, she acquiesced, and Mary Jo bade farewell, moving to Rochester to commence her studies.

Her first impressions of the bleak, red-brick architecture to be her home for the next four years were less than favorable, immediately understanding why students irreverently referred to the sprawling edifices as Brick City. But it was not until Mary Jo first experienced the infamous quarter mile walkway between the dorms and the academic buildings during her first Winter, that she appreciated the derogatory comments regarding the campus architectural layout.

As a freshman, Mary Jo was obliged to share accommodations with fellow students. She elected to dorm with others in what was known as Photo House, as there were special interest floors which provided darkrooms and studios for the students, where Mary Jo came to spend endless hours, engrossed in the practical applications of her studies.

Mary Jo had selected this college after considerable examination of her own expectations. She had learned that R.I.T. had earned national prominence in her field of choice, and was greatly impressed when she read that so many of the college's graduates in photojournalism had won prestigious Pulitzer Prizes for their work. This, in association with the fact that Rochester had achieved recognition as the Image Capital of the world, with such established names as Kodak, Xerox, and Bausch & Lomb head-quartered there, left little doubt in Mary Jo's mind that she had made the right choice.

At R.I.T., Mary Jo threw herself into her studies. The demanding four year degree course program in contemporary journalism provided her not only with practical experience in documenting real-life events, but a depth of knowledge in the mechanics and history of photography as an art.

For Mary Jo, life outside class had also been fulfilling. R.I.T. offered fraternities, sororities and organizations which catered to the multi-cultured student body's interests, and Mary Jo found herself at home within this new, and exciting environment, expanding her interests and circle of friends both on, and off campus.

Her extra-curricula activities in no way affected her studies. If anything, these enhanced her view of the world, providing Mary Jo with a sound perspective of the social and political environment in which she lived. She enjoyed participating in most sports, but her preference for the swimming pool consumed the greater part of her leisure hours.

When her mother visited Rochester, Mary Jo had taken her to the world-famous George Eastman House, the mansion having been turned into an international museum of photography and film. Mary Jo wanted to explain something of her love for this science. Unfortunately, her mother did not share Mary Jo's enthusiasm, or interest, strolling away out of earshot before her daughter had the opportunity to explain something of what she had learned of the wonders and technological leaps her field had seen in her lifetime. Mary Jo had been deeply disappointed. She had wanted to share, but her mother's obvious disdain turned the visit into disaster, and they had fought, the exchange raising eyebrows with those within range. Subsequent to this visit, outside semester breaks and an occasional birthday call, Mary Jo rarely communicated with her mother, both gradually growing indifferent to the other's needs, each content with the waning relationship which had crept, unobserved, into their lives.

Mary Jo's leisure time was mainly spent alone, wandering around the historical centers of the Woodside Museum and the Gothic cottages district with her camera in hand. It was during one such outing that she met a young research science graduate and experienced her first affair. It had been a brief and disappointing relationship, leaving her feeling empty and used. During their second date, they had driven to Niagara Falls where, consumed by the magnificent spectacle and overpowering force of nature's work, she had willingly surrendered herself to his eager hands, their coupling completed and her date half-dressed, before Mary Jo had even recognized what had transpired. For a time, she retreated to her studies, satisfied to bury herself in activities associated with the demanding, practical applications of photojournalism studies.

Mary Jo had chosen to remain in the dorms right through to graduation. If anything, she felt a little guilty that her step-father had never once questioned her seemingly endless requests for funds, and decided to apply for a position as a resident adviser in her third year. The quid pro quo required that in consideration for her board, she helped take care of students on her floor. Mary Jo found offering advice, even counseling students not much younger than herself, thoroughly rewarding. The small stipend she received provided her with a sense of accomplishment, knowing that this lessened her dependency on others, and in her final year she took on tutoring.

It soon became apparent to R.I.T. staff that Mary Jo had a most promising talent and they encouraged her in every way. Her practical achievements attracted considerable praise and upon graduation, the Dean arranged a position for her with a mid-western daily. But it was her childhood dreams of travel that continued to drive Mary Jo forward, her restlessness resulting in a reluctant chief-of-staff agreeing to introduce her to an associate in New York, who placed her on probation for three months at the respected news agency. To Mary Jo's great satisfaction, she excelled and flourished in the Big Apple's exciting and challenging environment. Mary Jo's dedication and skill firmly ensconced her within the media corps, and soon became recognized as one of the finest journalists in her profession.

At twenty-three, Mary Jo's reputation was already well established. Her circle of acquaintances and friends revolved around the competitive media industry and, although she enjoyed a number of brief, sexual skirmishes, she had no real desire to settle down. It therefore came as some surprise to Mary Jo when she fell passionately in love, the whirlwind romance leaving her giddier than even she thought possible. When Eric Fieldmann entered her life, the high-profile, foreign correspondent had swept her away, and Mary Jo gave herself completely, convinced that he was the one.

Her world took on an entirely new meaning. Mary Jo's friends smiled knowingly whenever she spoke of her lover and their moments together, observing the young, love-stricken woman's metamorphosis most had experienced whilst still in their teens. Mary Jo's demeanor softened, her perspectives acquired new dimensions and her attitude towards her career took an unexpected turn. She was earnestly in love and did not care who knew it. To her, Eric Fieldmann was everything she could possibly want in a lover and companion. He was handsome, witty and highly respected by his peers. His voice, smell and their lovemaking constantly invaded her thoughts, every minute of the day. Mary Jo moved her things into his Soho apartment and canceled the lease on her own. She was deliriously happy, and ecstatic when her lover announced that he had decided to settle down.

The affair lasted six months, ending only when distance finally took its toll during a prolonged separation. Fieldmann accepted a position as bureau chief in Rio, and although he had asked Mary Jo to accompany him, the invitation did not come with a ring. Had he proposed, she would have willingly sacrificed her career and followed Eric to South America. Instead, she declined, deeply distressed that their relationship would end, bitter when he left, without a promise that he might return.

She became introspective and moody. Depressed, Mary Jo often stressed herself beyond acceptable limits and her work suffered, the symptoms easily recognized by friends and workplace associates. Sometimes she would phone Eric at home in Rio just to hear his voice, wishing that their conversations might occasionally lead to something more meaningful than the light-hearted banter which invariably dominated their exchanges. Once, when she identified a woman's voice answering, Mary Jo had hung up, startled and embarrassed. The realization that she had become an intruder into her former lover's life prevented Mary Jo from calling again.

When Eric sent cards on her birthdays and at Christmas, she reciprocated, but after a time, even these communications slowed, trickling to an occasional, hurriedly-scribbled note, until finally ceasing altogether as both moved on with their lives. Then, without understanding why, Mary Jo had taken up smoking.

Her chief-of-staff watched Mary Jo with increasing concern, as her performance at work failed to achieve the same high standards she had produced in the past. He took Mary Jo aside and warned her to pull herself together or risk losing her position and the respect of others in the industry. The ultimatum was sufficient to galvanize Mary Jo back into action, heeding the chief's sound advice. The quality of her work improved, and she threw herself back into her profession with renewed vigor. The change was significant, even startling. Her confidence returned once she managed to put her personal problems into perspective, and behind her. Soon, Mary Jo was back in the air, covering North American events with even greater energy and dedication than before.

Alone, while resting in her apartment at the end of a long tiring day, Mary Jo often questioned her independent nature and the sacrifices she had made. Fortunately, these rare journeys into the murky world of self-pity quickly passed. She came to terms with what had happened, accepting that the final choice not to proceed to Rio, had really been hers. Jaundiced, but not hardened by the experience, Mary Jo promised to be more careful in her future relationships.

Throughout the following two years, she spent most of her life on flights jetting to destinations even her chief-of-staff had difficulty spelling. Bosnia, Chechnya, and many of the former Soviet satellites whose names were a linguistic nightmare, were all reported in depth, her skillful coverage recognized as amongst the finest journalistic efforts in that year. Her knowledge of peoples and cultures grew, but only partially satisfying her insatiable appetite for more. Mary Jo's coverage of the brutal Central African slaughters earned her a Pulitzer nomination, although she was greatly disappointed not to be awarded the prize.

Occasionally there were moments of doubt when she wondered how life might have been, had she followed Eric to South America, but these moments of lapse and self-indulgence were easily dismissed when Mary Jo reminded herself of the fulfilling experiences she continued to enjoy, due to the choices she had made. The satisfaction of knowing that she still had control over her own life, brittle as it sometimes seemed, spurred her forward. Her confidence returned, and she ceased smoking, determined not to fall into *that* trap again.

The following Spring, her life suddenly took a new and promising turn. She was offered a senior photojournalist's position in Hong Kong. Mary Jo had not hesitated, thrilled with the chance to be based in the Far East on permanent assignment, the opening providing her with the opportunity to fulfill a lifelong dream. Her self-esteem completely restored, Mary Jo became impatient to get under way.

* * * *

'We're here, lady,' the cabby announced, bringing Mary Jo back from her reverie, immediately amused that she had been daydreaming. She waited until the driver unloaded her baggage, then followed the lines of other passengers into the main terminal, and onto the shuttle. An hour later, Mary Jo took a final glimpse of the World Trade Center towers and boarded her flight for Hong Kong, her mind filled with anticipation and excitement, the memories of her relationship with Eric Fieldmann now comfortably washed from her mind.

* * * *

Israel - Tel Aviv

Mossad

Major General Shabtai Saguy sat contemplating the recommendations before him, confident that the Prime Minister would now support the initiatives proposed. The General Staff had approved the covert action, convinced that they had no choice but to proceed. Israel's ultimate survival depended on neutralizing the growing threat of an Islamic bomb.

The responsibility for ensuring secrecy over Israel's complicity in this deadly game weighed heavily, and the Mossad Director sighed, accepting that any disclosure would not only be harmful to the Middle East Accord, but could also wreck Israeli-American relations. He considered the ramifications of discovery, believing that the imminent nuclear threat to his people greatly outweighed these risks. The possibility that Israel could be destroyed in a Moslem nuclear holocaust only strengthened his resolve; the general had mobilized Mossad's powerful resources in anticipation of a favorable response from the Prime Minister's office.

He was reminded of earlier operations conducted under his predecessor's leadership, and the secrecy which surrounded Mossad and its clandestine activities. The Director frowned, unhappy with recent revelations which he believed undermined the organization's operational capabilities. Traditionally a state secret, the identity of the Mossad director was not widely known until the government had announced his appointment. He was gravely concerned by the gradual deterioration in the level of secrecy surrounding the Institute for Intelligence and Special Tasks, more commonly known as Mossad.

When Director Saguy was appointed, he had inherited a sophisticated intelligence machine second to none, with a staff in excess of fifteen hundred specifically trained and highly skilled men and women. Upon reading Ben Gurion's words at the time he had first established the organization back in 1951, Shabtai Saguy wondered if Israel's elder statesman had ever envisaged a Mossad, such as his creation had now become.

The director reflected on how the original concept had evolved over the years into a highly sophisticated tactical arm, dedicated to Israel's defence. Details of earlier successes attracted unnecessary attention, although the agency's funding benefited from such celebrated operations as the kidnapping of Nazi war criminal Adolph Eichmann from Argentina in 1960. Saguy was reminded of Israel's current dilemma as Mordechai Vanunu's name crossed his thoughts, and how his organization had kidnapped this man and brought him back for trial, charged with revealing details of Israel's nuclear weapons' program to the London tabloids.

And then there were the successful assassination operations which removed a number of Arabs connected to the Black September group, and executed Arafat's deputy, Abu Jihad, who at that time was considered to be the section chief responsible for all PLO military and terrorist operations against Israel. But it was the Brussels murder of Gerald Bull, the Canadian scientist who had developed the infamous 'Super Gun' for Iraq, that had focused media attention on the existence of the Mossad assassination teams, resulting in more accountability. Although there had been substantial changes to the organization's structure, Saguy knew that Mossad would always be surrounded by controversy.

The new and more streamlined Mossad with its eight departments would continue to provide his country with intelligence resources of the highest caliber, although Saguy admitted that the institute had not always been successful in its endeavors. He recalled his government's embarrassment when Mossad mistakenly assassinated a Swedish national. Then, there was the failed attempt to eliminate Khalid Meshaal by injecting the Palestinian Hamas leader with poison. But it was Mossad's failure to provide adequate protection to Prime Minister Yitzak Rabin against Yigal Amir's deadly attack that had resulted in leadership changes which, in turn, had paved the way for Saguy's ascent to his current position and the unenviable task with which he was now faced.

Israel's enemies had continued to arm, the threat of a nuclear war becoming more real by the day. Mossad became increasingly preoccupied with the necessity to maintain intelligence access by penetrating its neighbors' defenses, and it was the success of these missions which had provided the information revealing the growing nuclear arms build-up amongst the Moslem nations. The director did not need to refer to his database to refresh his mind. The Iranians, he knew, now boasted their new *Zelzal-3* missiles could destroy any target within fifteen hundred kilometers with a one thousand kilogram warhead and would soon test the first of their North Korean *Nodong-2's,* capable of delivering their deadly payload as far as Germany and Western China.

Of even greater concern was confirmation that Iran now had at least fifteen nuclear material sites. The list went despairingly on; Saddam Hussein's arsenal contained not only deadly nerve gases and chemicals, but also eleven confirmed nuclear facilities left undestroyed by the Gulf War.

Now, it would seem, Indonesia, the world's largest Moslem nation, wished to enter the Arms Race. Mossad had become alarmed when the Indonesians acquired all thirty-nine warships from the former Soviet-backed, East German Fleet. Alarmed by this shift in policy, and unable to penetrate the Jakarta-based government with his intelligence teams, Director Saguy had depended on other Israeli resources to gather information regarding the Indonesian's long-term strategies and military ambitions.

This had not been so difficult. Indonesia remained heavily in debt to both the World Bank and International Monetary Fund. Conditions precedent in all financial loan agreements required transparency in the debtor nation's fiscal policies and, through Mossad-related resources, Saguy had managed to obtain the information he required. Senior officers within both the World Bank and the IMF reported directly to Mossad, and this provided Saguy with a clear overview of Indonesia's future military intentions through the monetary monitoring processes.

He had become further alarmed with the growth of militancy amongst the powerful, and previously apolitical, Indonesian Moslem movements, the Director's concerns growing even further with the discovery of a developing relationship between Islamic terrorist groups, headed by the Saudi, Osama bin Ladam and the powerful Indonesian *Mufti Muharam* movement. Saguy had flown to Washington with evidence of bin Ladam's plans to expand his terrorist movement's activities to include Indonesia and Malaysia, where training camps could be conveniently disguised by Moslem elements within those nations' military hierarchy.

Saguy had been convincing in his arguments. Mossad teams had infiltrated a number of bin Ladam's terrorist training camps in Afghanistan, close to the Pakistani border where the Saudi tycoon frequently recruited guerrillas from amongst those fighting against the Indian army in Kashmir. Saguy revealed to the Americans that his agents had observed Osama bin Ladam hosting meetings in his mountain stronghold with Chinese and Pakistani officials. The Mossad Director had extrapolated his theory that the wealthy bin Ladam was already well advanced in his strategy to develop an international terrorist organization with training camps already established in most Moslem nations.

Armed with an adequate flow of funds, Saguy had argued that bin Ladam would soon be capable of threatening both Israel and the West with Chinese manufactured copies of Soviet missiles. He firmly believed, although the CIA had scoffed at the time, that it was the terrorist's intentions to test such weaponry in Pakistan, for any such trial detonation in Iran, Iraq, or other Middle Eastern Moslem states, would result in an immediate United States response. The Israeli had, unfortunately, been unable to convince all those present during the Washington visit, how his intelligence justified these conclusions.

When he suggested that the successful testing of a nuclear device by a Moslem nation would act as a catalyst for unification amongst the Islamic world, the American Defense Secretary, Steven Cohen, had disagreed, citing Indonesia's Moslem community as being non-aggressive and committed to their government's policy of non-alignment. It was when Saguy suggested that elements within the Indonesian Government actively supported the terrorist organization, that the Americans became indifferent to his theories.

Saguy had insisted that China's willingness to provide technology to Moslem states would eventually lead to confrontation. Members of the Israeli Cabinet who were also present, urged the American Administration to act quickly before even the less powerful Moslem countries acquired nuclear technology and missile weaponry from the Chinese. It seemed that the Mossad-proposed hypothesis was to be rejected. The Americans were not convinced, unable to accept that countries such as Indonesia would ever desert their lucrative pro-Western alliances in the interests of international terrorism.

Saguy and his fellow countrymen had returned to Tel Aviv, without any commitment from the United States. The Director had gone directly to the Prime Minister to seek his support for Israel to act alone. He firmly believed that for Israel to vacillate, would ultimately place their country at extreme risk as Israel had insufficient retaliatory capability to survive an Islamic-led nuclear attack.

The director felt the despair of impotency this knowledge carried, his concern that Israel's own facilities could not provide the defense his country required. Names such as Dimona, Eilabun, Nevatim and Be'er Yaakov came to mind as he considered the nation's nuclear and missile facilities, wondering just how much more of the country's budget would be consumed by these demanding capital intensive projects.

The thought of the many billions raised in the United States via their Swiss-based banking operations warmed his heart. He prayed that Israel could always depend on her powerful American lobby without which his country might not survive. It had been imperative that Israel manage its off-shore funds through Geneva for, ironically, many of the country's investments had been conducted in Moslem nations such as Malaysia and Indonesia, where oil and other precious resources were found in abundance. Major General Saguy's eyes dropped back to the folder lying almost innocently on his desk.

As he further considered the file's contents, the director's fingers tapped a silent beat on the plate-glass-topped desk, his mind preoccupied with the one report which had first alerted Mossad to China's provocative intentions. He remembered reading that it had been as early as 1985 when *Lekem*, Israel's Bureau of Scientific Relations had identified the increased flow of technical information from the Chinese to a number of Moslem nations. *Lekem* agents located in Israeli embassies throughout Asia and the Sub-Continent had stumbled across Beijing's first transfer of nuclear technology to Pakistan. Alerted, Mossad worked together with its sister agency in the covert collation of all material which fell into their hands. Now, with more than ten years of data to substantiate their intelligence, it was clear that China's efforts were soon to bear fruit.

Shabtai Saguy closed the highly classified file stamped '*Most Secret - ha-Mossad le-Modiin ule-Tafkidim Meyuhadim*', removed his glasses and rubbed his tired, gritty eyes, while wondering how other intelligence chiefs always managed to find time to play golf. He then stared down at the document cover before him and a thought crossed his mind, causing a thin, mirthless smile to crease his lips, as he visualized Saddam's mocking face collapsing into shock once the game unfolded, revealing his weakened flank. Buoyed by this image, Major General Sabtai Saguy left for the Prime Minister's office where he expected to receive confirmation that Israel would send its scientists and engineers to New Delhi.

If Pakistan was to have its Islamic bomb, then India's one billion Hindus would receive Israel's assistance to discourage the further spread of Chinese nuclear technology. Israel's contribution would prevent, hopefully, the world's largest Moslem nation, Indonesia, from acquiring such weapons of mass destruction through their new companion, Osama bin Ladam, the man now recognized by the Jewish community worldwide, as their most serious threat since Adolf Hitler.

* * * *

Indonesia - Surabaya – August, 1997

The white Mercedes 300 carrying General Praboyo's mother was last to arrive at the compound, and even before her driver could assist the aging woman from the vehicle, heavy-duty reinforced steel gates slid into place with an ominous grating noise, momentarily startling the seventy- year-old.

The woman's frail figure belied her true strength as she shuffled slowly past tall, white-washed walls towards the colonial villa's entrance. Her well-armed driver followed closely, ready to spring to her aid should the need arise. As they moved slowly along the crushed stone path she hesitated, then reached out and picked a small bunch of white and yellow frangipani which hung low on the tree. The aroma obviously pleased her as she turned and smiled, before passing the flowers to the driver. They continued towards the entrance where a number of men waited, their hands clasped in traditional welcome gesture. Satisfied that she was in safe hands, the driver returned to stand by the limousine.

'Selamat datang, Ibu,' the men greeted, edging aside as she stepped through the doorway, nodding courteously. They moved, with solemn gait, into the main guest lounge area where a number of white-clad, male servants fussed over the guests, before discreetly retiring to their own accommodations. It was not until the customary pleasantries had been observed and tea taken that the host, one of Indonesia's most prominent Moslems and senior adviser to the *Ulama Akbar* leadership, addressed those gathered, in sotto voce.

'We welcome you back, Ibu,' he commenced, smiling at the elderly lady who sat comfortably, in the well-cushioned rattan chair. *'It is regrettable that this meeting has required you to travel alone, and so far from your home. It would seem however that your efforts are to bear fruit, subject of course to your son's agreement concerning our requests, as discussed during our last meeting.'*

The General's mother returned Haji Muhammad Malik's smile, but there was little warmth in her heart as she did so, for this was the meeting about which she had agonized for so many months, before finally agreeing to her son's request. His image came to mind, and she paused, sipping from the thimble-sized teacup before responding.

'Pak Malik,' she commenced, looking at each of the four men in turn, *'we have given a great deal of thought to what you have proposed. I am pleased to inform you that the General accepts your kind offer.'* She hesitated, as if reluctant to continue. *'But to be honest with you, as a mother, I am not entirely at ease that this alliance will be without risk to my son.'*

She could see from their expressions that her candor was unexpected. *'Then, of course, the issue of my personal religious differences, must still be resolved.'* She had prayed that they might reconsider earlier demands and would not still insist that surrendering her own faith remain a prerequisite to their agreement. But, she knew in her heart, that these hard-line religious leaders would not consummate the relationship unless she converted. Had it not been for her son, she would never have considered such an unreasonable request. Habit directed her fingers gently upwards where they touched her neck in search of reassurance; the platinum cross she had worn since childhood had been removed, whilst dressing in preparation for this meeting, and placed in the safety of her purse.

'Madame, we ask your understanding in this matter. Your current position has presented us with some resistance amongst our colleagues,' Haji Abdul Muis advised, his soft voice almost inaudible to her ears. *'The question must then be, would you accept embracing Islam?'* The General's mother turned her head slightly, and looked directly at the aloof and unsmiling figure. She knew that

the support of Abdul Muis's following of thirty million was essential to her son's success. She would need to show subservience to this man.

'Yes,' she said, with rehearsed conviction, *'if that is the price to be paid, then yes, I would convert to Islam.'* The *Ibu* observed from the immediate change in their demeanor that they were all pleased, albeit surprised, at her commitment to abandon her Christian beliefs. Previously, she had been adamant, and stubbornly refused to even consider such a notion.

'Then you may inform your son that when the time arrives, he may count on both the Ulama Akbar and the Mufti Muharam,' Malik declared, his statement accompanied by confirmatory nods from the others. The Haji rose slowly and held her hand warmly, signaling that he understood the sacrifice she had agreed to make, a sacrifice which would guarantee their support for her ambitious son.

Satisfied, General Praboyo's mother departed their company, saddened by the knowledge that she must fulfill her pledge to abandon her own faith, and embrace the teachings of Islam in order to secure the support of the country's powerful Moslem parties.

As her Mercedes drove slowly away, she stoically accepted that her actions that day could easily precipitate the beginning of the end of the current Indonesian leadership.

She sighed, dabbing at the dry corners of her eyes, wondering why it was so difficult for an old woman to cry. She dismissed the cloud of depression which threatened, closing her weary eyes to again consider the consequences of the new alliance.

With frail, shaking hands, she opened her well-worn purse and retrieved the delicate cross hidden there. General Praboyo's mother then lowered her head, and prayed for forgiveness; and for what she knew in her heart, would most surely now transpire.

* * * *

EAST JAVA - SITUBONDO – DECEMBER, 1997

Second-corporal Suparman waited impatiently for the signal to move. His hands moved nervously in the darkness and found the haversack containing the deadly cocktails. Reassured, he continued to listen for the others' voices as he lay hidden at the edge of the field. Rain filled clouds moved silently across the evening sky blanketing the moonlight and Suparman sensed that the attack was imminent, as darkness enveloped their surrounds. Habit forced his hands to check the lower leg pockets of his battle-dress, but then he remembered that they had changed out of their uniforms as the mission directives required.

This would be a civilian raid.

'Let's go!' his Sergeant hissed, sending eight half-crouched men running along the soggy rain-water drain towards a number of barely visible buildings, the structures' silhouettes confused to the marauders' eyes, in the absence of light. They had covered more than a hundred meters when their leader's voice snapped again.

'Get down!' Suparman heard the NCO's command and the team threw themselves against the embankment, waiting for whatever it was that moved towards them along the narrow, bitumen road. Moments passed before they continued cautiously towards their target in file, listening for sounds which might be out of place here in the dark. Frogs croaked, a worrying sign that rain might interfere with their mission, but Suparman was more concerned with the filthy, slimy, colorfully ringed, deadly poisonous snakes which slid around in the night, preying on the noisy creatures.

The soldiers hurried across the road and came to rest less than fifty meters from the buildings, where they spent several more minutes determining where the civilian security guards slept.

'To the left of the smaller building,' a corporal indicated, pointing to where a soft, fifteen watt globe burned inside what they knew to be the sleeping quarters. Sergeant Subandi squinted, concentrating on the buildings, then cursed silently, swatting whatever insect had attached itself to his face.

'Suparman,' the NCO whispered for all to hear, *'take Dedi and two others, and hit the church from there.'* He pointed to the walls farthest from where the tenants slept. *'You,'* he ordered, placing his hand on the corporal's shoulder, *'take the others and approach from behind.'* The corporal raised his eyebrows questioningly, but this went unseen in the dark.

'What about them?' he asked, moving his free hand closer to the sergeant's face while pointing at the dim light. Over the past month, they had razed almost a dozen other churches and not once targeted those inside. During those operations, the inhabitants had fled in terror, encouraged by their attackers to do so. He sensed that the sergeant had moved outside the operation's parameters, and wanted confirmation that this time, they were to kill. He could not see the cruel grin which marked the team leader's face.

'Burn them,' he ordered, and rose to his feet clasping one of the Molotov cocktails in his right hand, simultaneously extracting a lighter from his jacket pocket with the other. The men followed suit, opening their own

sacks containing the highly inflammable contents, and taking their positions as instructed.

Within minutes the church was ablaze. Tall dancing flames licked at the sky, casting light for hundreds of meters. Then the soldiers turned their attention to the adjoining buildings, hurling their deadly gifts into the air to smash against the buildings' roofs, releasing burning fuel which spread through the ceiling and into the meager quarters where the minister and his wife remained, clutching each other in terror.

They cried out for assistance, and were dismayed when none came to their rescue. The ceiling above burst into flames, the heat and smoke unbearable. Finally, overcome by asphyxiation, the couple died, only minutes before the arsonists' deadly fires could engulf their bodies.

The soldiers regrouped, then disappeared silently back through the fields to where their vehicle waited. By the time any of the local population had found the courage to investigate the carnage, the entire American-trained squad had driven more than fifty kilometers back to their station, where they changed back into uniforms bearing the insignia of the 21st Battalion, before returning to their provincial *Kopassus* headquarters in Surakata, Central Java.

Chapter Three

EAST JAVA – DECEMBER, 1997

Lily Suryajaya

As custom required, Lily worked together with the older women in silence, their grief not evident as they washed the bodies in preparation for the funeral. Tears would flow later, when their work was done; when their minister and his wife had been laid to rest in the sacred ground within sight of the fire-gutted church.

Other non-Christian townspeople had demonstrated their deep-rooted apathy, electing to ignore the significance of the attack, silently pleased that the Chinese community had been punished for their apparent greed and commercial successes. Overwhelmingly, it seemed, even Christians not of Chinese extraction had elected not to attend their churches. They all now lived in a world filled with fear.

The church's destruction had been the twelfth in a series of mysterious events which had, until the evening before, not claimed casualties. With the death of the two whose bodies now lay before them, these provincial Chinese had legitimate reasons to become even more deeply concerned with the escalation in violence, which they believed to be part of some concentrated campaign to further intimidate their race. Although there was no evidence to support the wide-spread rumors, the Christian community feared that the provocation had been initiated by Moslem elements, and that the orders had come from those in Jakarta who wished to create civil unrest to support their own secret agendas.

Whispered innuendo suggesting that men sporting typically military style haircuts had been seen at several of the churches before these were torched, had added to their fear. Such rumors were of great concern to the Chinese who suspected what this might mean to them, as it was common knowledge that the Indonesian army had often been deployed in the past, when the need arose to terrorize specific ethnic groups, for political gain. But the Chinese were confused as to why suddenly churches had become the target of marauding bands of arsonists. Could it be, they asked each other, that the attacks were really the responsibility of militant Moslem groups? After all, the Chinese communities only accounted for a small percentage of the Christian population. Surely, then, some argued, it was not the Chinese who were being specifically targeted, but Christians in general?

Although graffiti found at the scene of each desecration indicated that this sectarian violence had been instigated by Moslem raiders, the Christian communities questioned these attempts to fuel existing animosities between the rival groups. Bewildered by the escalating violence, the general consensus grew to support the belief that Jakarta elements were behind the civil unrest in the area. And now these subversive actions had resulted in the loss of the minister and his wife to the small Christian community.

* * * *

When the alarm was first given signaling that the Church and its adjoining accommodations were burning, not one from the congregation went to the scene, fearing that the gang responsible might still be present, and would confront any foolish enough to intervene. Besides, they had justified, those inside would surely have already fled to safety.

It was not until the following morning that evidence of the evening's horrors became evident to all. The minister and his wife had perished, their remains found clutched together in scorched embrace. Too terrified to leave their premises, they had been overwhelmed by the heat and smoke and died. Their partly-charred bodies had been discovered amongst the smoldering ruins and taken to the rear section of the *Apotik*, the local, Chinese-owned pharmacy, until the authorities would agree to their burial. There, a number of local female parishioners had gathered, to prepare the bodies for burial.

Lily's mother had been amongst the volunteers, and had insisted that her daughter accompany the women whilst they carried out their traditional preparations. The corpses were washed and cleaned where practical, injected and painted with formaldehyde, then dressed in cloth. When Lily first entered the chemist's storage room she avoided looking at the bodies. The acrid smell of chemicals assailed her nostrils, but she resisted the temptation to flee. As the minutes dragged by, her stomach settled and Lily reluctantly went about assisting her mother, surprised with herself that she had found the strength to remain. Within the hour, the experienced women had managed to complete their tasks and stood by the corpses, admiring the results of their labors.

Lily wiped her forehead with the back of her wrist and, glancing across the room at her mother, she sighed. Lily desperately wished that her parents would now leave this hostile environment and travel with her to Jakarta, where she lived with her uncle while preparing for university. Sadly, she realized, they would not leave their community, unwelcome as they might be. Generations of their family had lived in East Java since fleeing China more than two hundred years before and had developed strong ancestral ties with their new land.

* * * *

Originally, Lily's family name was Ong. They had been obliged to adopt an Indonesian name as part of the assimilation process required by the New Order regime, which had come to power in 1966. Although born more than ten years after the holocaust, Lily knew that some half a million people had died during the two years following the abortive coup. She also knew that her race had been cruelly targeted by the indigenous people, who accused the ethnic Chinese of involvement in the communists' attempt to take control of the government.

Vicious rumors had spread claiming that her people were responsible, at least in part, for the kidnap, mutilation and murder of the nation's leading generals. The resulting cleansing campaign spread through the archipelago, striking fear in the hearts of all who were of Chinese extraction. Eventually, once the new President had been firmly ensconced at the nation's helm and the blood-letting ceased, many of the Chinese who had fled the horrors of the Sixties returned, bringing with them capital the new government so desperately needed.

Lily accepted that the Chinese had prospered under the New Order and, softened by time, there were occasions when stories relating to events of more than thirty years ago often seemed exaggerated; almost fabrications. Having moved from the rural community to the exciting, sprawling metropolis of Jakarta to further her studies, she could see no evidence anywhere to support such stories. There, she discovered, the Chinese were influential, and extremely successful. She was delighted to learn that even the First Family had developed close ties with her race, and Lily, as did her peers, believed that this relationship virtually guaranteed all Indonesian Chinese their ongoing safety.

In Jakarta, Lily discovered that racial discrimination, although evident, was generally ignored due to the realities of commerce, and she had eagerly assimilated to the exciting conditions, captivated by city life and the metropolis' amazing entertainment facilities. Pleased to have left her provincial surrounds of Situbondo, and the growing ethnic tensions now prevalent throughout the countryside, she undertook to work diligently, hoping, that upon graduation, her uncle would provide the opportunity for her to remain in the capital.

Now, she regretted having returned home for the Christmas holidays. Memories of her childhood and school, when she had been subjected to fear and humiliation at the hands of discriminatory groups came flooding back the moment she had stepped down from the train. On those all too frequent occasions, she would return home from school, her face wet with evidence of tears. It had been difficult and demeaning to follow her mother's advice, to ignore the insults. Lily found it impossible for the hurtful racial slurs and intimidating language so often encountered in this small, isolated community in East Java, not to leave some scars.

For Lily, shocked by the minister's death, the evidence before her only reaffirmed her belief that racial hatred for the Chinese was more than a passing phenomenon. This perilous culture of envy had spread over the centuries, its origins dating back in Indonesian history to a time when her people had been given special status over the indigenous by the Colonial Dutch. Now, that legacy had all but disappeared, displaced by deep-rooted tribal animosities which lurked dangerously close to the Indonesian society's fragile surface. It would seem, she felt disconsolately, that contrary to what the nation's leaders would have the international community believe, there was, in fact, no unity in diversity; at least, not in this nation of more than three hundred ethnic groups, each clamoring for recognition and autonomy from the Javanese.

* * * *

Lily glanced over once again at her mother and smiled weakly, wishing she could escape the demanding duties and stuffy conditions. Since word of the carnage had swept through the small country town, not one Chinese family dared venture more than a few steps from their homes, most of which were situated above the endless rows of shops they controlled. Even the iron-barred windows had been locked firmly shut and, for a fleeting moment, Lily feared that she might faint, struggling to control her rising fear in the hot, humid, suffocating atmosphere where the bodies now lay together, awaiting burial.

'Lily, go outside and get some air,' her mother demanded, and she did so, not wishing to spend any more time in the room than was necessary. The smell of formaldehyde had permeated the room, her clothes and hair, causing her discomfort.

'I won't be long, mother,' she replied, thankfully, then smiled weakly before escaping the smell of death which she knew, would require time to wash from her memory.

Once outside Lily squatted on the footpath, bent her head forward, and drew long, deep breaths filling her lungs until the giddying effects threatened to exacerbate her nausea. Slowly, with one hand against the concrete wall to secure her balance, she rose to her feet and remained still for some minutes until assured that the panic attack had passed. At that moment, a truck rumbled past, the driver blowing the horn unnecessarily just as the vehicle reached the point where Lily stood recovering her composure, choking in the wake amidst billowing clouds of dust.

Her pale face in no way reflected the anger she felt inside, not just towards the inconsiderate driver, but also with having to live in constant fear simply because she and her family were of Chinese extraction. Lily had wanted to wave her fist angrily, but instead, had merely wiped her face with her hands. Remembering, suddenly, where these had been, she struggled to prevent the flow of tears which threatened and quickly wiped her face again, this time with the back of her arms.

Lily Suryajaya peered down through the provincial backwater's commercial district. The pot-holed, dusty street, lined on both sides with aging two-story multi-purpose shops and dwellings, caused her to sigh. She counted the number of days remaining before she would return to Jakarta, wondering if she could last. She was anxious to leave, and this impatience was further fueled by the knowledge that her uncle there planned to move into new accommodations within the following weeks, where they would all enjoy access to the condominium's private facilities. For Lily, this meant time in the swimming pool. She tried to remember when she had last been swimming, and was surprised to discover that it had been more than three years.

Depressed by her surrounds and too frightened to walk down the street alone, Lily remained sitting outside the chemist's shop, and passed the time contemplating her future. She prayed that her education would provide the means for her to escape her humble origins, and find permanent employment away from the angst and racial discrimination evident in the provinces.

Sitting alone on the footpath she suddenly became anxious and decided that it would be best she return to her parent's shop further down the street. Although reasonably confident that she would be safe to walk the distance alone, considering events of the past days, Lily decided not to take the risk. Reluctantly, she took one, long, last breath of fresh air and strolled back inside to see if her mother had finished and would accompany her home.

Within the hour Lily stood scrubbing her hands and body until the pale skin turned red under the fierce attention. Satisfied that nothing remained from that morning's visit to assist in attending to the dead, she wrapped herself in a cotton towel, then wearily climbed the steep, concrete stairway to her cramped quarters. There Lily locked herself inside the window-less room and lay down, miserable with the knowledge that it would still be some time before her brief holiday was over, when she could flee these surrounds and return to the dream city of Jakarta.

* * * *

WEST JAVA

Hani Purwadira

'Allahu Akbar, Allahu Akbar,' Hani cocked her head, waiting for the third call, *'God is Great!'* to follow. Without checking, she knew what the time would be, as one could set one's watch to the ritualistic summons to attend prayers. She finished washing her face and hands, then went to the privacy of her bedroom to pray. She covered her head with a lightweight *mukenah,* permitting the cloth to fall gently over her shoulders. Hani then unfolded the colorful prayer rug, placed this on the floor, and knelt as she had been taught as a child.

Hani could hear her younger sister, Reni, in the adjacent room, and had no doubt that their mother would already be on bent knees in her own chamber. She expected that her younger brother would have accompanied their father to the Mosque, a privilege enjoyed only by males. That women were not permitted to attend the *Mesjid* in no way bothered Hani, having been immersed in Moslem tradition since birth. In what was still basically a polygamous society, women were relegated to a lesser position by virtue of their faith and a culture which resisted social reform at the village level. Fortunately, President Suhapto's doting wife had persuaded her husband to discourage government officials from their polygamous ways, the reason, Hani believed, her father had not been successfully seduced by the many offers she expected he would have received.

The Palace's unofficial instruction had not, however, dissuaded the lower classes from continuing with the practice of filling their allocation of up to four wives, the relatively uncomplicated procedure for divorce, permitting even more. In villages across the nation, girls often produced their first child before reaching fourteen, in many cases becoming grandmothers before the age of thirty. In a country where life expectancy had climbed to above fifty years only the decade before, Hani knew that early marriage, and propagation, were encouraged. It made sense to her; the children would provide for their parents, and grandparents, once the elderly became too old to fend for themselves.

Hani's family was well insulated from many of the daily problems which so dominated the lives of others within their community. Her father's star had commenced its ascent, and his family now enjoyed the benefits of his position as senior police commander in the mountain city of Sukabumi. Colonel Purwadira had held this post for nigh on three years, quietly accumulating wealth and power, his wife and children clear beneficiaries of his success.

Hani's mother had become actively involved with the local women's association, much of her time engaged in raising funds for charities which, unfortunately, received but a fraction of the donations extracted from the wealthy, Chinese donors. The Purwadira family were respected citizens, the children's futures guaranteed. *Ibu* Purwadira had recently acquired a new Honda Accord and, although she could not drive, she managed to spend a great deal of her time in her prized possession, driven around by one of her husband's soldiers. Life had become kind to the Purwadira family and it appeared that it might even get better.

The Indonesian economy had grown at an incredible speed, and although some said it may be slowing down, middle-class Indonesians' pockets were still full. Local shops were crowded to capacity, shop-windows displayed the finest clothes, parabolic satellite dishes covered the already congested rooftops, and most homes now boasted video-recorders, refrigerators and, in some, even washing machines. It seemed that it would go on forever.

As school was taught from Monday to Saturday, Hani looked forward to her one day off from study. Usually, after their morning prayers, her mother would permit the children to go to the movies with friends, or attend the Sunday soccer matches but, on this day, she had insisted they remain at home to honor their father's wishes. He had something he wanted to discuss. Hani knew this had to be important; the other occasions he had insisted they gather in such fashion had always resulted in announcements relating to his career. Having completed her prayers, Hani gathered her rug, removed her shawl, and placed these neatly away before wandering out to stand on their three-bedroom home's porch.

While waiting for her father to return from the Mosque with her brother, Hani lowered herself cautiously into the hanging rattan chair, bolted to the ceiling by the servants, just days before. That day, she had tried the swinging seat within minutes of arriving home from school but, to her dismay, had lost her balance and spilled onto the hard, concrete paving under the watchful eyes of her friend, Budi. Recalling the incident, Hani's hand went to one elbow, finding the crusty wound with her fingers.

She had been annoyed with her friend, fighting back tears as he helped her regain her feet, but Hani knew she could not remain angry with Budi for very long, except for that one time, when he brought a Chinese girl along to a mutual friend's party.

Hani had avoided Budi for an entire week after that, not understanding how he could even consider doing such a thing. The girl looked gangly and wore no makeup, her hair was far too long and, in Hani's opinion, she displayed very little breeding, flashing those gold bangles for everyone to see!

Although a number of ethnic Chinese attended her high school, most kept to themselves. Not that this bothered Hani in any way as they had so little in common. She had overheard many of her parents' conversations through the years, learning from their convictions, and adopting their distaste for their fellow citizens. She knew that her father often met with the local Chinese business community. What Hani did not know, was that most of the fine ornaments, and other expensive acquisitions which lay around their house, had been gifts from those soliciting the colonel's favors. Even her mother's Honda Accord had derived from her husband's commissions, received from grateful Chinese traders for the police supply contract he had channeled their way.

As she waited for her father to return, a group of teenagers rolled past on their bicycles and waved, amongst them, Budi. He called out but his voice was drowned by a passing bus, and she watched as he pedaled away.

They had been friends since early childhood, but Hani had noticed that their relationship had taken a shift recently, and she was unsure of what to do. She liked Budi, but only as a friend. Along with others in their age group, Hani would often play badminton on Sundays once they had returned from the movies, or gather back home under her mother's watchful eyes to listen to music, or catch a programme on TV. Hani had never been on a date, alone. At least, not with Budi.

Many of her friends were planning on marrying that year, having completed high school. Hani thought that was a wonderful idea, wishing she too could meet someone and fall in love, now she had so little else to do. Sukabumi was not the most exciting place to live, but she had roots there, and wanted to have her own home and family, just like her friends. She often fantasized about being married to one of the tall officers she often saw in her father's company. A thought crossed her mind and Hani giggled privately, imagining herself with child, her oversized stomach held between her hands for support, as she had so often seen pregnant women do when approaching term.

A horn sounded, signaling her father's return, and Hani climbed out of the rattan seat to greet him.

'Hi papa,' ignoring her brother, she moved to the colonel's side, waiting for the customary squeeze.

'Hello, my sweet,' he said, placing his arm around Hani's waist, *'Are your mother and sister inside?'*

'Waiting for you to return, papa,' she answered, stepping in front of her brother to block his way. His hand shot out to pinch Hani's arm, but she pulled away, just in time, poking her tongue as she did so.

'Come on, then, I have something to tell you all,' with which, they all filed inside, where they were joined by her mother and sister. Once they were all settled comfortably around the family dining table, the colonel made his announcement.

'How would you like to live in Jakarta?' he asked, his face breaking into a wide smile.

'Jakarta?' they shouted, in unison. *Could it really be possible?*

'You received the promotion?' Ibu Purwadira's face was just as surprised. Although she had been given advance warning of the pending decision, she had not dared hope that it would come true.

'Yes, it was confirmed by General Sutjipto this morning. He rang from Jakarta.'

'You've known since this morning?' his wife asked, too overcome with excitement to be annoyed.

'Yes,' the colonel replied, his eyes dancing mischievously. *'I wanted to be sure that you would all be awake.'* Hani pouted, knowing this not to be true. She watched her mother smile lovingly at her father, all present aware that the colonel would first have given thanks at the mosque, before discussing

his appointment with the family. Her mother then reached across the table and pinched her father's arm affectionately.

'When?' she asked, and Hani became even more attentive.

'Next week,' the colonel advised. *'They want me there before the fasting starts, and I agreed.'*

'Ramadan in the capital? Wonderful!'

'Will we return to Sukabumi for the holidays?' Hani was concerned that she would miss the celebrations with her friends. These followed the demanding month-long fast, and were the highlight of the Moslem calendar.

'No, Hani, we will have many obligations to consider in Jakarta. Also, you will all have new friends to make, and your studies to prepare for.'

'Studies?' Hani looked at her father, confused.

'Yes, Hani. You will now be required to attend university.' This announcement surprised her even more. *'And there will be no argument,'* he added, confident that she would obey, *'after all, a general's children should have the best education.'* For a moment there was silence as the import of what had been said, hung in the air. Ibu Purwadira's eyes filled with tears, and she rose and moved around the table to embrace her husband. Her dream had come true! He had been promoted in rank, and would become the new Jakarta Garrison Police Commander. The three teenagers broke into excited chatter, overwhelmed with their father's wonderful news.

That night, Hani lay quietly conjuring up in her mind, visions of things to come. She would attend a fine university and have even finer clothes than those now hanging in her cupboards. She would be given her own car, and who knows, she might even find the right suitor to marry, in time.

With her head resting comfortably against the soft, feather pillow, Hani fell into a deep, restful sleep, her last thoughts centering on the promise of things to come, in the national capital, Jakarta.

* * * *

EAST JAKARTA - CIJANTUNG

Kopassus (Special Forces) Command HQ

General Praboyo

Major General Praboyo raised the baton, touching his beret in arrogant style as the command vehicle swept past his father-in-law's home on *Jalan Cendana*, the Presidential Guard already at attention for this morning ritual.

His driver slowed measurably, maneuvered the vehicle around the barbed-wire blockade and around the two armed personnel carriers, before accelerating away through the elite suburb of Menteng, Jakarta's central residential district. The traffic was typically slow. Praboyo used the time to prepare for the morning's scheduled appointments, ignoring the city's undisciplined drivers as they angrily flashed headlights, braked unnecessarily and constantly blew their horns contributing to the early morning cacophony and suffocating pollution.

The general glanced at his wrist, and decided that he would not be late for his first appointment. The gold Piaget watch, a gift from his wife to celebrate his forty-sixth birthday, caused him to smile as he was reminded of the gift his mistress had also pleasured him with just a few hours later. Praboyo made a mental note to ring the beautiful Menadonese girl later in the day and arrange a quick visit to the home he provided in Tebet Village.

His thoughts then turned to Colonel Carruthers, and the American's terse call the day before insisting they meet. Praboyo had been concerned with the officer's tone, conscious that Carruthers was one ally he could not afford to lose, particularly at this point in his career. The United States had been particularly supportive, and although he recognized that the origins of their relationship related directly to his marital situation, nevertheless Praboyo believed that he was deserving of the accelerated promotions he had enjoyed since marrying the President's daughter. After all, he mused, had he not acquitted himself admirably in a number of campaigns, such as in East Timor?

Praboyo recalled his first exposure to the Americans' involvement in training the Special Forces anti-terrorist squads, and how their ongoing relationship with the Indonesian military had survived the purge which followed President Suhapto's successful 1966 *coup d'etat*. Although still in high school at the time, he had already decided to enter *ABRI*, the Indonesian Armed Forces, once he had graduated, and make the army his career. He had first become interested in *Kopassus* when it was still known as *Kopassandha*, the Covert Warfare Forces Command, and boasted three battalion-sized para-commando units and a support battalion specializing in covert warfare.

It was obvious to the young officer, even then, that the Special Forces enjoyed privileges not afforded to others, and he had decided to work towards achieving a position within the well-funded command. When the United States covertly organized the formation of Detachment 81, an anti-terrorist unit comprising some 350 highly trained soldiers, Praboyo was overjoyed to be posted to this *Kopassus* unit. Just two years later, his team was flown to Bangkok when an Indonesian domestic flight had been hijacked from Sumatra, and flown to Thailand. In the resulting confrontation, they killed all but one of the hijackers, several of the airline crew, and left a trail of blood across the international airport's tarmac that still sent chills through officialdom, whenever the mission was mentioned.

Praboyo was most proud of his achievements during the East Timor campaign. When the former Portuguese colony was invaded on 7th December, 1975, the Special Forces were the first troops to enter Dili where they systematically annihilated most forms of resistance. Throughout the following two years, his teams were sent also into North Sumatra in operations against the Aceh Liberation Movement, utilizing the very tactics rehearsed under the watchful eyes of their American instructors during their training programs in the United States. General Praboyo appreciated the significance of that training, and the necessity for the alliance.

Ambitious to the core, he used the capture of the East Timorese Resistance leader, Xanana Gusmao, to further ingratiate himself with the Palace. Praboyo clearly understood the power he had acquired as Commander, Special Forces, and the assumption that his star would continue its accelerated ascent due to his father-in-law's sponsorship. Although his status within military circles still necessitated frequent displays of humility, he had little doubt that his future included the strong possibility that he just might succeed the President, once he had been appointed Chief of the Armed Forces.

Even a near miss with a speeding cement truck failed to ruffle the young general on this day. Foremost on his mind was not the imminent meeting with the American officer, but the success his assassination teams had recently achieved in East Java; missions he had personally planned and directed. Praboyo cared not that responsibility for the destruction of these churches would be laid at the feet of Moslem extremists. That was part of his strategy. Now, he believed, it was time to cease the attacks and demonstrate once again how effectively he could control such outbreaks of violence and insurrection in the provinces.

He would be applauded by all. His allegiance with the powerful *Mufti Muharam* would be strengthened by preventing these baffling attacks, which had so inflamed anti-Moslem sentiment, and the Chinese would admire him, for having interceded on their behalf. He could not lose.

The general recognized the familiar sign as they turned onto the Cilitan-Bogor arterial road. He examined his beret as they continued down through the Pasar Rebo intersection and turned right, arriving at the Special Forces Command Headquarters only minutes before his first visitor was expected. Praboyo barely had time to be briefed by his adjutant when the American Attaché's arrival was announced. Colonel Carruthers was immediately ushered into Praboyo's office.

'General,' the American saluted, then extended his hand. The *Kopassus* commander returned the salute, almost idly, then accepted Carruthers' firm handshake as he examined the foreigner's four rows of campaign ribbons, arranged in orderly rows above the man's left breast pocket. Praboyo knew from earlier conversations that his visitor had served two tours in Vietnam, and wondered if this soldier had actually killed any enemy in combat, as he had during anti-guerrilla sweeps.

'Jean sends her regards, and this small gift for Tuti.' Carruthers spoke in *Bahasa Indonesia*, placing the delicately wrapped box of mints on the teak table. His secretary had organized the present as his wife Jean despised everything about this country, and would never have considered sending a gift to one of the Indonesian wives whom she found distasteful at the best of times, or at least stated so, in her correspondence to friends and relatives back in the States.

In reality, the Attaché's wife was unable to compete with the obvious wealth the Indonesian officers' wives flaunted, and was irked by their natural beauty, convinced that her husband would have no hesitation leaping into bed with any of these attractive women, should the opportunity arise.

'Please thank your wife, Colonel. Has she recovered from her recent illness?' Praboyo asked innocently. The woman had feigned ill health to avoid attending a function organized by *ABRI* wives, and was sighted the following morning by one of the Indonesian ladies, playing tennis at the Embassy compound.

'She's fine, thank you, General, just fine,' Carruthers answered, then wishing he had left the damn chocolates behind.

'Good,' he said, *'then I hope she remains so, and that we might soon see her at one of our Indonesian ladies gatherings.'* The American nodded, crossed his legs, and moved the conversation to the reason for his visit.

'Speaking frankly, General,' he began, having rehearsed what he needed to relay to this influential officer, *'the DIA is quite concerned with what is happening in East Java.'* For a moment, the commander expected his guest to continue, and elaborate. But when he remained silent Praboyo too decided to play this evasive game.

'East Java?' he asked, knowing full well what was on the American's mind.

'Yes, General, East Java. Washington is becoming quite agitated with these organized attacks against Christian groups and their churches. What do your intelligence sources say? Are you in a position to shed some light on what's really happening?'

Without hesitation, anticipating that the Americans would want some sort of explanation, Praboyo offered his prepared explanation.

'Moslem radicals,' he lied.

'Are you sure?' Carruthers wanted to be convinced. He needed something concrete to take back with him, preferably evidence that the military had no involvement in the attacks. The heat had come from church lobby groups back home claiming that humanitarian agencies had reported sightings of soldiers participating in the violence. The Defence Aid agreements between the two countries would come under scrutiny again, and the Pentagon didn't need any more pressure from civil liberty groups, nor could the senior brass afford discovery of the covert training provided to the Indonesian Special Forces. *'Have the police been able to come up with anything yet?'*

'No, but we caught two,' Praboyo lied again. The American raised his eyebrows in surprise.

'And?' he waited, observing the Indonesian for any sign which might give the man away, but there was nothing.

'They were taken to Serang and interrogated at 12 Battalion headquarters. They didn't have a great deal to reveal, just that they were part of a local group of dissident Moslems youths who felt that the churches in their area had encroached on what has been traditionally Moslem communities.'

Carruthers was aware that the Indonesian Government did not permit the churches to expand their congregations by attracting converts. The story was believable, and basically what he had expected to hear.

'Any chance that we might have an opportunity to interview these two?' he asked, expecting that this would be unlikely. General Praboyo smiled, and shook his head.

'A D18 team conducted the interrogation.' He paused, then crossed his arms, a gesture he would have found insulting in others. *'Apparently, the team was a little over enthusiastic.'*

'They're dead?' The Colonel queried, with incredulous surprise.

'Yes,' he replied, chuffed that he had handled the matter so easily. *'We have had the local military commanders call on the Moslem religious leaders, the*

ulamas. All have given an undertaking that they will endeavor to prevent any further violence against the minority communities.'

Carruthers knew then it would be futile pursuing the matter unless further incidents occurred. He seemed satisfied, then steered the conversation towards other matters relating to the U.S. Defence Aid programs responsible for funding the ongoing training of *Kopassus* soldiers in the United States.

They remained in conference for another hour, after which the Defense Intelligence Agency Attaché returned to the United States Embassy where his written recommendations concerning General Praboyo were encoded, and electronically mailed to his Director in Washington. For the moment, the Indonesian President's ambitious son-in-law would remain safe.

CHAPTER FOUR

JAKARTA – JANUARY, 1998

The President's daughter

Tuti Suhapto reflected upon her marriage to Praboyo and decided that she had never really been in love with the man, and now accepted that had their union not been arranged by her dear, departed mother, then she would most probably have found another, and more caring suitor to marry.

Tuti recalled her first meeting with the young officer, and how she had admired his proud bearing and confidence, interpreting his arrogance as bravado. It seemed that he was not to be intimidated by her surroundings, and this particularly pleased Tuti, accustomed to earlier beaus who all seemed betrayed by their nervousness whenever her parents appeared.

Her father had served the nation as President for more than thirty years. Tuti recognized that when she first commenced dating, being a member of this select household virtually endowed her with the opportunity to select any man of her choosing. As this thought crossed her mind, she looked at the row of photographs which had been placed along the living-room shelves and frowned. In all but two of these, the handsome Javanese features evident in the elegantly framed pictures were those of her husband's and, as Tuti's forehead wrinkled even further, she was swept by waves of loneliness, then anger, because of Praboyo's capricious ways and blatant indifference to her pain.

Knowledge of his promiscuous behavior had set the Jakarta circles chattering. Even amongst her closest friends there were few who enjoyed the courage to expose Praboyo's extra marital relationships to Tuti. This task willingly fell to her brother Timmy whom, she recalled angrily, actually relished in relaying some anecdote that was circulating, concerning her husband's most recent conquests. Tuti had endeavored to discover the whereabouts of her husband's current attention, but had been unsuccessful. This had only added to her frustration and anger, and the temptation to reveal Praboyo's transgressions to the President grew daily. But Tuti knew that she would never inform her father as to her husband's indiscretions, for he would be saddened by her inability to keep her man in line. Instead, Tuti decided to continue with her search for Praboyo's latest beau, and deal with her in a manner which would at least discourage others from offering their favors too freely to Major General Praboyo.

Tuti wondered what would happen to their considerable joint wealth if they were to separate, even divorce. These thoughts brought another frown and immediately she attempted to recall which of the larger enterprises they controlled were majority owned by her husband. Annoyed that Praboyo enjoyed considerably more wealth than she thought should be his entitlement, Tuti decided to speak to her eldest brother concerning her demise. Perhaps he could help force her husband to toe the line.

Tuti preferred not to discuss her problems with Nuri, her older sister. As first born, she had enjoyed a special relationship with their parents and, once their mother had passed away, this sister had assumed many of their mother's duties, including that of confidante to their father. Tuti acknowledged privately that she was jealous of their relationship, but even more, she had become deeply envious of her sister's new role as chairwoman over the many foundations and charity organizations which were responsible for generating, and hiding, so much of her family's wealth.

Tuti understood the extent of the enormous fortunes the Suhapto's had amassed, and never once considered the possibility that her brothers and sisters, the family gatherers, would ever cease searching for new opportunities to increase their wealth. The family firmly believed that the *Bapak*, their father, was deeply loved and respected by all the Indonesian people and accepted that his role was more that of king than President, and was therefore entitled to the riches and spoils which accompanied such power. It seemed obvious to the Suhaptos and their close associates, that the First Family's involvement in commerce should be applauded, as their efforts had greatly benefited the country.

They had all been pleased when their father had publicly acknowledged that without his children's involvement in many of the major ventures undertaken throughout the nation then, in all probability, the foreign investors would not have committed their substantial capital to developing the country. Even the world press had commended the Suhapto Government's efforts in raising living standards, literacy, and longevity throughout the archipelago. That many of the infrastructure projects now belonged to the family's extensive financial empire was, in their opinion, a clear demonstration that without their continuing involvement in the country's industrial growth, the nation would flounder.

Nepotism, cronyism, and other distasteful utterances were not part of their vocabularies; neither did these words ever appear in the Indonesian Press.

With this thought, Tuti reached down and retrieved a copy of *Femina* Magazine and flipped through the pages, deciding that she would occupy the rest of her day with a change of wardrobe. She knew that most of the famous European houses' fashions were available in Jakarta within days of their first being displayed along Paris catwalks, and decided that she would have her staff phone ahead to alert the managers that she would visit their boutiques. Tuti thought she might also take time to inspect the latest jewelry shipments, before returning home for tea.

Hopeful that an afternoon of extravagance might assist to distract her mind from the problems at hand, Tuti called her secretary to make the necessary arrangements, then went out on her shopping spree, spending tens of thousands of dollars throughout the afternoon at Jakarta's largest, and most modern mall, unaware that the warm reception she received from the management was not only in response to her substantial purchases. For the extent of the President's family holdings were so great, even Tuti had no idea that the complex she had visited also belonged to one of the Suhapto family subsidiary enterprises, and that the money she had spent would simply be recycled, eventually reappearing in the collective Suhapto coffers.

* * * *

Bank Negara Indonesia

The Indonesian Central Bank's Governor looked at the hourly report nervously, wondering how events in Malaysia would compound the regional monetary concerns since Thailand and Korea's currencies had all but collapsed. The Malay Ringgit's demise would most certainly affect the Rupiah, and Indonesia's current negotiations with the International Monetary Fund and World Bank representatives.

The Governor's concerns were real. The Republic's staggering private sector debt which had accumulated just over the past decade was choking the banking system and threatened to cause a further downgrading by most international financial institutions. *Who in the hell was this international speculator Soros anyway?* he worried.

Governor Sutedjo agonized over informing the Minister whom, he knew would simply tell him to continue with business as usual, ignoring the cold reality that the Indonesian economy had begun to show dangerous signs of stalling, due to the excessive private sector and government debt held in foreign currencies. He estimated this figure to now exceed one hundred billion dollars. The enormity of the problem threatened a wave of panic; several of the smaller banks had failed during preceding weeks directing unwanted attention towards questionable practices exercised by the banking fraternity.

The Governor was most concerned as to how the international community would react when they realized that the aggregate debts represented an impossible sum to repay. The Indonesian economy outwardly appeared healthy, with foreign investment once again exceeding expectations. The resources sector had continued to perform well, although he knew that the government would have been in a stronger position had oil prices been maintained at the higher levels. *Why had the money speculators moved on the Asian currencies?*

As if the flow-on effects from what had already commenced in Bangkok and Seoul were not enough, *now* the country had to contend with one of the poorest rice harvests on record. The Governor muttered to himself as he recalled the latest statistical reports forecasting extreme shortages across the country. The prognosis was that the island of Java would be worst affected by the drought. *Sialan! Damn!* he cursed silently. Until six months ago he had never heard of this calamitous climatic event the world knew as El Nino.

The New Year had presented Sutedjo with the most formidable task. Within days the country's Moslem community would commence their fast which, he feared, would accelerate the inevitable. Sutedjo wondered what would happen in weeks to come when the country's one million public servants, and half a million members of the armed forces discovered that they would not receive the mandatory additional month's salary, nor the traditional bonuses and gifts once their month-long fast had been broken. The Governor shuddered. He was tempted to agree with the Minister that they could temporarily resolve the problem by printing more money, but knew that this would, undoubtedly, further exacerbate their problem downstream. He also believed that such action would deter both the IMF and the World Bank from initiating steps to assist propping up the failing Rupiah, restarting Indonesia's comatose economy.

Governor Sutedjo looked out through the pollution-stained windows and down at the seemingly endless lanes of cars, buses, trucks and motorbikes moving in miniature along the city's main thoroughfares and admitted that fiscal and monetary policies had not been overly clever under the New Order's leadership.

Not that the Central Bank could be considered blameless, he admitted. When the President's son had demanded a bridging loan in excess of two hundred million dollars to assist in recovering his situation with his disastrous foray into the traditional clove market, the former Governor had refused. Sutedjo had been appointed successor and immediately went about arranging the loan. Now, he realized, such loans contributed towards most of the country's banking dilemma.

Sutedjo knew that he could no longer procrastinate, and called his secretary to invite the IMF Jakarta-based representative for further discussions. The International Monetary Fund's current offer would not be sufficient to prevent further deterioration in the local currency, but perhaps an immediate injection from the World Bank might just provide sufficient funds for the Government to overcome its immediate dilemma regarding the traditional payments due to members of the military and public service. Encouraged by this possibility, Governor Sutedjo leaned back in his chair, closed his eyes, and commenced formulating some ideas he would suggest to the World Bank officers later in the week, while considering how he could personally benefit from the current situation.

* * * *

United States of America – Washington, January 1998

The President leaned forward and placed both hands dominantly on the historic table as he glared at his advisers. *When would they ever get it right?*

'George Bush had the perfect opportunity Mr. President, and he blew it.' The speaker turned to others in the room knowing that the general consensus supported his position. 'We had Saddam by the balls, but let him get away. We should have gone all the way and destroyed anything that even resembled a factory or warehouse while we still had world opinion on our side.' The Secretary of State then sighed heavily, more out of frustration than tiredness, and shook his head.

'Sanctions?' the President asked, looking at no one in particular.

'The Press believes that we should reconsider some aspects of these, Mr. President,' It was Dean J. Scott, the President's chief of staff who offered this opinion. Although the Middle East, with its complicated political, ethnic and religious rivalries had continued to dominate American foreign policy for more than half a century, it was the President's popularity which had prompted Scott to suggest that, by removing sanctions which directly affected the flow of medical and other humanitarian supplies, the Press would look more favorably on the current Administration. The President's sexual indiscretions continued to consume an excessive amount of Oval Office time and he was the one responsible for taking most of the heat out of the media.

'If anything, we should squeeze him even more,' Admiral Colin Brown, insisted. The Joint Chiefs were impatient for another action against Saddam to field test new technology under actual combat conditions.

'These sanctions are hurting him seriously, but not enough to bring him down.' The Defense Secretary took control of the conversation. He too believed that President Bush had erred by not finishing what he had started. 'His organized mass rallies are starting to work for him, with human rights activists screaming bloody murder about the interrupted flow of medical supplies. If we don't act soon, public opinion might prevent us taking any pre-emptive action against Baghdad this time.'

'How much time do we have?' The President asked. Somewhere in the back of his mind he remembered having been told but, with the incredible pressure he had been under lately he just could not recall the information. He resisted thinking about the Press, and how they continued to paint him as a sexual predator.

'Six, perhaps even eight months Mr. President,' the Defense Intelligence Director stated. 'We must assume that he has successfully hidden some of the completed stages within the palace grounds. Also, we still have not been able to verify delivery of the current Chinese shipments.' Those present were all painfully aware of China's role in the destabilization of the entire region running from its own borders, across Pakistan, Afghanistan and into the powerful oil economies of Iran and Iraq.

This was of major concern to all her neighbors. China's incredible industrial growth over the preceding ten years had seen the country become a net importer of oil, most of which originated from Iran and Iraq. As an additional incentive to those two hostile nations, China provided highly sensitive weapons technology via the Great Wall industries group, and successfully encouraged North Korea to participate in these Middle East missile programs. This, to the dismay of many intelligence observers, included the *Shahab-5* Intercontinental Ballistic Missiles which, with their five thousand kilometer range, would give Saddam strike capability throughout all of the Middle East and Europe, once the project was realized.

'Do we have the numbers now to proceed?' The President looked directly at the American Ambassador to the United Nations who, having already commenced lobbying those representatives whose countries were ambivalent to the West's concerns, seemed quite unhappy with the question.

'If China abstains without veto in the Security Council, we should have no difficulty there. What concerns me most is the amount of growing resistance to another strike against Iraq within the General Assembly. Support has dwindled considerably, and with the currency meltdowns occurring in Asia, the United States does not exactly head the popularity lists. There is considerable anti-American sentiment running through Asia, as we are perceived to be responsible for the currency meltdowns in Thailand and Korea.' He then paused, spread his open hands and shrugged. 'If we push for a vote before the Asian situation deteriorates further, my guess is that we will have the support needed.'

The President considered the ambassador's response for some minutes, then looked over at the Admiral.

'When we go in, I don't want any American soldiers on the ground anywhere near this goddamn gas.' He was troubled by the reports that Saddam had amassed stockpiles of the lethal VX nerve gas.

Once the Israelis had discovered the existence of the deadly gas, they had threatened their own pre-emptive strike against Iraq without waiting for any U.N. debate on the matter. Although *'Operation Desert Storm'* had successfully destroyed most of Iraq's armaments, the country had maintained its belligerent course, rebuilding its shattered defenses. Saddam Hussein's refusal to permit U.N. inspectors access to what U.S. satellite intelligence identified as suspected armories for the storage of weapons of mass destruction, only supported the West's gravest fears. The Chinese ICBM's were to be used to deliver the VX as part of their payload.

Admiral Brown affirmed that there would be no ground troops deployed in the action, having already decided to maximize air-strikes to destroy the targeted depots and suspected missile storage sites, including the Presidential Palaces.

The conference concluded and those no longer required departed leaving the President to discuss other matters with National Security Adviser Alex Hastings, the Defense Secretary, Steven Cohen, and John

W. Peterson, Director of the Central Intelligence Agency. The Chief of Staff hesitated at the door expecting to be included in these discussions.

'Thanks, Dean.' It was a clear signal that the President would not require his presence and, although miffed with the polite dismissal, he smiled and closed the door gently behind as he exited, curious as to what might transpire in his absence.

* * * *

The concerns which were to be discussed had arisen out of growing evidence that there had been a substantial shift in Indonesian politics, one which had been discussed over a number of months, and one which had the potential of destabilizing not only South East Asia, but America's efforts to consolidate its position in China. Less than three weeks had passed since these men had last been required to brief their chief. Now, with confirmation that the American President would visit China within the following months, it was essential that events in the Indonesian archipelago in no way influenced negotiations which would take place in Beijing.

'Well?' The President asked, standing to restore circulation. He rubbed the back of his thighs, stretched, then returned to his seat. Director Peterson carried no files, for what he had to impart would not be recorded, not even for future Presidential libraries.

'It's not good news. It appears that our earlier speculations were on track. No matter which way we interpret the intelligence, it would appear that Suhapto is, indeed, considering the acquisition of nuclear-capable missile technology from Iran,' he relayed, his voice devoid of any emotion. 'The general consensus is that he also intends giving the Indonesian Moslem parties a major say in the country's administration.'

'I don't know, John,' the President argued, 'seems like a radical flip to me. Suhapto is a cunning old codger, are you sure we're not misreading what's going on here?'

'Everything we've gathered points to the same conclusion.'

'Are we certain that our judgment is not being influenced because he's been courting the Chinese?'

'That's certainly part of the bigger picture, but for now our prime concern relates to what is happening within Indonesia. A sudden swing towards Moslem militancy would destabilize the region. Considering current economic trends in South East Asia, we believe that the mood amongst lower income communities would support a resurgence of Moslem extremist policies.'

'And these links with the PLO and..,' the President hesitated, looking for assistance.'

'Osama bin Ladam,' Peterson offered.

'Yes, bin Ladam. How does this tie in with Suhapto?'

'At first, we missed what was happening because we had no reason to monitor the external flow of funds from Jakarta to Switzerland. As it turns out, even had we been aware of the transactions, it's possible that these would have been ignored. The amounts were not excessive, and could have been easily overlooked. It's not as if the Suhaptos have never had payments made into their Swiss accounts before. Had it not been for the Israelis, in all probability, we might never have picked up on what was going on.'

'But hasn't this bin Ladam sufficient resources of his own? Why is it necessary for the Indonesians to pump funds into his organization?'

'We're not entirely sure. What it does though, is signal that there are those in Jakarta who are prepared to finance radical elements known for their anti-American sentiments. Perhaps the funds were sent simply as a gesture. The jury's still out on this.'

'What are we up against with bin Ladam?'

'It's highly likely that he already possesses at least one nuclear warhead that could be used on a missile, most probably from the Iranians. Our sources have reported an increase in the frequency of his visits to Teheran.'

'What's in it for the Iranians, or even the Iraqis for that matter?' the President asked.

'That's the China link.'

'Let's go over that again. I don't see how the Indonesian situation is affected by Iran's relationship with Beijing.'

The Director exhaled heavily. 'We all know how events of the bloody Sixties were attributed to Beijing's interference in Jakarta's affairs. After the Indonesians broke off diplomatic relations with the Chinese, relationships continued to sour through the years. Even the Indonesian military promoted the belief that the Chinese were responsible for the so-called communist coup attempt. This unexpected rapprochement caught us all by surprise, particularly as it so obviously had military implications.' Peterson looked over at the National Security Council Adviser Hastings for support, who accepted his cue.

'Mr. President,' he commenced, 'it makes sense. Indonesia is the world's largest Moslem nation. All of China's imported oil passes through the archipelago. This oil originates from Iran and Iraq, both basically fundamentalist Moslem nations. China provides missiles and associated technology to them, and has consolidated its position with yet another Moslem nation, Pakistan. The intelligence points to an ambitious move by the Chinese to identify regionally with those Moslem powers.

We believe that Beijing has been wooing the Pakistanis with the promise of additional nuclear weaponry, for the past two years. Tel Aviv's intelligence claims that Pakistan may even be considering nuclear testing, although we have had no evidence of such developments. It could be that our feisty allies may have some explaining to do themselves with respect to India's growing nuclear potential. In short, we believe that Indonesia is next on China's list and, unless we move to destabilize this relationship, it is conceivable that Chinese manufactured weaponry, particularly ICBM missile technology, could end up in Indonesian hands.'

'Why would China want to give them weapons which, in time, could be turned against them?'

'Well, although Chinese in origin, we believe that the technology and equipment will come from Iran, perhaps even Iraq. By giving Indonesia the weapons directly, they'll ensure an uninterrupted flow of oil to China. In turn, Iran and Iraq continue to receive missile technology from Beijing.'

'And China won't object?'

'China would still maintain control over the technology. It's unlikely they'd permit anything too serious to pass into Indonesian hands. It's most likely we'd see short-range missiles popping up around the country, but nothing which could threaten China directly. Our guess is that Beijing would see this development as another positive step towards loosening American-Indonesian ties. Any diminishment of American influence in Asia would receive a positive response from them. They know we'll do whatever necessary to prevent Jakarta from acquiring such technology and, in their minds, any rift between our countries could only benefit China's influence over the region, in the long term.'

'But why would Jakarta need missiles? They're not under threat.'

'Our concern lies with the possibility of a major shift towards Moslem fundamentalism in Indonesia. This would open the door for the extremists there, whom we all know, are less than pro-American. With President Suhapto's support, we could see a polarized Moslem government in Jakarta espousing anti-American propaganda, providing a forum for Filipino and Malay Muslims to follow.

In Malaysia, this could be a particularly nasty scenario, considering the last ethnic and religious upheaval which pitched indigenous groups against Chinese-Malays. Possessing missile technology would undoubtedly be a major boost to national pride and, as Jakarta has obviously fallen under the influence of the mullahs, we can be reasonably certain that an Indonesian Muslim government wouldn't hesitate to improve its status amongst the world's Islamic community.'

The President recalled how his fellow Americans had once been totally consumed by their anti-Communist zealousness. Subsequent to the collapse of the Soviet Empire, attention had become focused on Islam as the Free World's new threat, the memory of gasoline rationing when the Arabs had held the West to ransom, still fresh in American minds.

'Wouldn't the Indonesians be concerned with China's motives?' the President asked. They had discussed the emerging problem on several occasions over past weeks, and he just did not want to believe that their old ally, Suhapto, was even considering forming an axis with Beijing, particularly one which would undoubtedly result in the reduction of an American presence in Asia.

He was most disturbed with these developments, and experienced a feeling of *deja vu*, recalling that Indonesia's first President, Soekarno, had formed such an unholy alliance with Ho Chi Minh and Mao Tse Tung. This, he knew, was the basis for the American Government's constant but futile attempts to have the man known lovingly by his people as *Bung Karno* overthrown, succeeding finally, when the then General Suhapto came to acceptable arrangements with the United States.

In the weeks that followed his taking office, the American President was moved when reading his predecessor's most secret accounts of the bloodletting which had then ensued, resulting in the loss of more than half a million lives amongst which, were many innocent Chinese.

'Let's not forget that it's been the Chinese who have supported Suhapto thoughout his career Mr. President. There is no doubt that he has delivered the Indonesian economy to them. Banks, flour mills, steel mills, textiles, shipping, timber, property. My god, the list goes on forever!' the exasperated adviser complained. 'These days, the Indonesian-Chinese investment houses can be found anywhere one cares to look; Singapore, London, Sydney, Germany, and in most cities here in the States. Inadvertently, even we've played a major rôle in their rapid growth, by permitting their powerful investment houses to penetrate the Chinese market via our own banking system.'

Alex Hastings then hesitated, not knowing just how far he should go considering the sensitive issues which had emerged over the President's past relationships with the Jakarta-based Chinese who, it had been discovered, had donated huge amounts to his earlier election campaigns. He looked directly at his Chief to determine if he had overstepped the mark. Detecting that he hadn't, Hastings continued.

'Suhapto's overtures towards Beijing caught everyone by surprise, including his senior military officers who agree that this sudden shift in Indonesian politics can only benefit the Chinese. Although China has committed itself to expenditures exceeding fifty billion dollars over the next fifteen years to rebuild and expand its nuclear power facilities, their oil dependency is alarmingly high.

China's economy is growing at an amazing rate, and we can be certain that they would have considered precisely how vulnerable they would be in the event of any interruption to their oil supplies. Indonesia has archipelago status over its shipping lanes. It makes sense that China would be delighted to mend fences with them and even offer to cooperate in other areas, even if this translates into providing their neighbors with limited missile technology to boost Moslem morale.

Should this eventuate, Mr. President, the Japanese people would most probably wake up one morning to discover that China had displaced them as the major trading partner with Indonesia and, subsequently, all ten of the ASEAN member nations. This would represent the world's largest trading bloc, one which would continue to grow at the expense of both the European Union and our own NAFTA treaties.' This was followed by silence as those present considered the ramifications of such an alliance, and the threat of having the doors closed to a potential consumer base which approached three billion people.

'And Suhapto's sudden infatuation with these militant Moslem groups, how does this fit in?' the President left the question hanging for either of the two senior officers to respond.

'We have a man inside the *Mufti Muharam* hierarchy who has confirmed that the Palace has agreed to the proposed shift in policy, one which will provide both the major Islamic groups with a substantial voice in future government. Our source is emphatic that the Palace has agreed to support radical changes in its position relating to minority religious groups, preventing the further spread of non-Moslem teachings. It seems that the aging President senses his end might be near, and is influenced by his approaching demise.

In short, we might be witnessing the beginnings of an Indonesian sectarian state. Ever since Madame Suhapto passed away, the old man has turned much of his attention to studying the Koran, and has spent considerable time with senior members of the Islamic community, both in Indonesia, and the Arab states during recent Haj journeys to Mecca.' He paused for breath before adding, 'and communication traffic between Iran, Iraq and even Libya has more than trebled with Indonesia over the past six months.'

'And what if he suddenly drops dead, where would we be then? Would this resolve the problem?' the President asked. Even he had been surprised at the Indonesian leader's longevity.

'This would depend on the military, and their choice or acceptance of whoever succeeds Suhapto.'

'And this would be?' The President asked, annoyed with his limited knowledge of those who might be considered candidates for the powerful position. It was difficult enough keeping up with the frequent leadership changes generated by political instability in Third World countries.

'Suhapto has been extremely clever. Although his current Vice President, General Sulistio has considerable support from within the army, his popularity will most likely cost him the position. There is no nominated successor, nor is it likely that there would be any challenge to his leadership while he is still alive. It's obvious that he intends remaining at the helm until he dies. Apart from the fact that he believes he is king and deserves to continue, he is discerning enough to realize that the incredible fortunes his family's acquired would be at risk should he relinquish power.'

'And our preferred successor, is he still a viable option?'

'Since our last discussions Mr. President, we have received assurances from General Winarko. Fortunately, we now have two candidates. Both are very pro-American, well educated, and both appear opposed to any emergence of Moslem fundamentalism or moves towards providing the *ulamas* with any majority representation in government. Whatever happens, the military will continue to dominate the leadership, and government for some years to come.'

'And our proposed strategy?' he asked, knowing that whatever scheme his advisers had concocted, it would have its weaknesses, as he had discovered with past forays when his government had intervened in other countries' power struggles.

The Defense Secretary stepped in, taking control once again.

'The Indonesian economy is on the brink of collapse. We have the ideal opportunity to kill two birds with one stone, so to speak.' Cohen coughed, his throat the victim of in-depth discussions throughout the night in preparation for this morning's presentation. 'We could precipitate a change in government leadership, or at least provide the opportunity by refusing to support any further funding of loans to Indonesia through the IMF and World Bank. As he won't step down, we could propose having the IMF insist that Suhapto unwind the cartels and monopolies he has given to family and friends, and present his government with a number of initiatives which would quickly erode his support both from the people, and the business community.'

The Defence Secretary stopped, coughed again several times, apologized, then cleared his throat before continuing.

'It will be the International Monetary Fund and World Bank insisting that changes to the existing financial systems be implemented, and not the United States. We obviously have the ability to direct the IMF and the World Bank due to our substantial positions in both of those organizations. It is most unlikely that the other member nations will balk, as they too recognize that there must be some fundamental changes in Indonesia's economy if it is to have any realistic chance to repay their current debts. We've estimated that the interest alone accumulating on both the government and private sector debt is in excess of one hundred million dollars, a week.

Apart from satisfying our own political agenda in relation to Indonesia, it would be in American interests for the IMF to press for the country's leadership to initiate responsible steps to resolve their problems before U.S. investments are threatened. Should the IMF insist, that as part of any bail-out package subsidies on fuels, fertilizers and other basics be removed, these measures should generate sufficient ground swell along with their depleting dollar reserves, to create the desired environment for change.'

'And if this fails?' the President guessed he already knew the answer. *Why did it so often come down to this?*

'Then our only other option would be to support a coup.'

The American leader listened to the succinct statement, and slowly shook his head. He reached across and lifted the delicately shaped, silver-filigree *keris*, which had been decorated with precious stones and designed as a letter opener. It had been a gift from the Indonesian President, presented during his stay at Camp David the year before. Immediately, memories of Suhapto's visit reminded him of the reciprocal invitation to join the aging Javanese on his ranch outside Jakarta. It would now be an opportunity lost, and he was saddened that the man who had been America's friend for more than three decades, would now disappear from the world's stage.

He recalled listening to a Voice of America broadcast back in time, when he, not unlike many other young Americans who had avoided the draft and left for overseas, suffered severe homesickness and occasionally sat around in London with others in similar situations, wishing they could return home. It seemed, at the time, that his country might soon be fighting a war on two fronts as the violence in Indonesia escalated. *When was that?* he struggled to remember, deciding that it had to be somewhere in the mid-Sixties.

He had not suffered the scars of war, as had so many of his fellow countrymen. Instead, he had only the unpleasant reminder of a wound he had received from falling down the British college steps. This recollection unconsciously sent his hand to touch the soreness which, until this day, remained along the length of his leg.

'Thanks gentlemen,' he said, rising, then moving to look out through the window. 'You know what my preferred option is, of course,' he said, tiredness evident in his voice. The President then turned slowly to face the three men. 'I don't want Suhapto harmed if at all possible. He has been a good friend to this country, and we should let him go as quietly as can be arranged. Understood?'

'Of course, Mr. President,' Cohen answered, the CIA Director and National Security Adviser also nodding affirmatively. There was a brief silence, the Secretary managing to choke another cough. They waited; a few minutes ticked by, then the President nodded, almost absentmindedly, permitting the *keris* to slip slowly from his hand, onto the table.

'Keep me posted,' was all he said, before turning back to peer through the window again, the specter of a Moslem Indonesia loaded with nuclear-capable missiles weighing heavily on his mind.

Unaware that their Indonesian intelligence sources had blundered seriously, the President's advisers quietly took their leave, each returning to his own powerful security realm to initiate steps to remove, and replace, the Javanese born President, believing that these actions would preclude any emergence of an Indonesian Islamic state, and the threat of a Chinese dominated Asian-Middle Eastern trade bloc.

* * * *

THE MIDDLE EAST

Abdul Muis

Haji Abdul Muis was most impressed with what he had observed, relishing the knowledge that very few Iranians, let alone foreigners such as he, had ever been given access to the country's secret installation. The Haji acknowledged that it was his position as leader of the Indonesian *Mufti Muharam* Moslem party which had provided him with this opportunity to inspect these sensitive facilities. This was his third visit to Iran, his efforts to consolidate his relationship with the powerful *ayatollahs*, so far successful.

Situated not far from Semnan, Muis was not aware that this Chinese-built missile plant was, in fact, smaller than the two North Korean engineered installations at Isfahan and Sirjan. These liquid-fuel producing plants would not be on the visitor's itinerary, nor would he visit the Iranian missile test facilities at Shahroud. For it was there that the Chinese M-9 single-stage, solid-fuel road-mobile missiles were stored under cover, away from prying American satellite cameras which crossed this nation on regular, hourly orbits. The Iranians had successfully evaded detection, the United States still believing that recent pressure applied on China had prevented delivery of these advanced missiles. Although they had come to trust their brother from the East, they would need more time before the Indonesians would be accepted into the fold.

The Haji's brief tour was to be treated solely as a public relations exercise to demonstrate to their fellow Moslems how Iran's fundamentalist regime had prospered technologically. His hosts were aware that Muis had little understanding, or knowledge of weaponry and armaments, as Indonesia had yet to acquire such sophisticated systems. They were supportive of Abdul Muis' aspirations, and keen to demonstrate this in a material manner.

Iran's political shift had greatly benefited the post-Shah regime. Although the end of the Iran-Iraq war had seen the United States exert considerable pressure on Russia, China and India to withhold nuclear reactor technology from its former ally, the country continued to receive substantial support from communist nations desperate for foreign currency. And then there was the Iranian chemical warfare capability, developed as a response to Iraq's attacks on Iranian troops during the Gulf War. Now, these neighboring countries both had stockpiles of nerve agents and other deadly chemicals which could be delivered by artillery shells, or as part of a payload on board any of the country's four hundred SCUD missiles. Muis was determined to acquire such weapons, and raised the subject with his hosts during the visit.

Abdul Muis completed his tour through the missile plant and returned to Teheran in time to attend the private dinner organized in his honor, by his friend Osama bin Ladam.

They had first met during Muis' second visit to Iran, the Indonesian immediately impressed, by the persuasive Arab. From the outset, Muis had been captivated by bin Ladam's knowledge and the man's commitment to his long-running holy war, or *Jihad*, against the West. Although Muis suspected claims of his friend's involvement in the recent bombings of American targets to be true, this in no way diminished his admiration for bin Ladam. If anything, from the time of their first meeting, Muis started to emulate his hero in many ways, even in the manner he dressed.

The dinner was attended by a handful of close bin Ladam associates, who had specifically asked to meet with Haji Abdul Muis. Later, the Indonesian was to conclude that the function was to provide bin Ladam's associates with the opportunity to assess Muis for themselves. The two leaders arranged to meet again the following morning, at which time an accord was reached between the two powerful factions.

When bin Ladam had entered his quarters, Muis was again struck by the man's presence. Gaunt features covered partially by a long, graying beard, jutting down from his ears covering most of his face and neck, belied bin Ladam's inner strength. Muis might have been surprised when first meeting the Islamic leader. His movements were slow, stiffened by years of crippling back pain and he carried a cane to support his thin-framed body. But by the conclusion of their early morning *tête-à-tête*, Abdul Muis was left with no illusions as to Osama bin Ladam's strengths, impressed with the forty-year old's clarity of thought, and obvious dedication to his Moslem beliefs. Their discussion was candid, conducted in an atmosphere of Islamic brotherhood, and mutual respect.

'As a token of my respect for you and your people,' bin Ladam had said, with an unsmiling face. Surprised, Muis accepted the unsealed envelope. Inside there was a cheque drawn against a Swiss bank for ten million dollars. He was stunned by bin Ladam's generosity.

'For what purpose?' he asked, silently counting the zeros again, and the international terrorist explained. Muis listened, nodding from time to time, interrupting only towards the end.

'I have just the place!' he claimed, excitedly. 'Ten hectares would be sufficient?'

'Yes. But the facilities must be constructed without attracting too much attention. You understand what might happen if the Americans discover our secret?' he asked, and Muis understood.

'There will be no problem with security. The land I have chosen is in the country, far from prying eyes. We will build a wall around our project. Those who come to know of its existence will believe it is my country estate. I will build a small mosque inside the property. None will dare enter the property of Haji Abdul Muis, I can assure you.'

In that one, brief, historic meeting, Haji Abdul Muis secured a powerful ally, their mutual hatred for the Americans, further strengthening the bond. Muis understood that the United States would do everything in its power to prevent Indonesia from acquiring weapons of mass destruction, the American influence, an obstacle to his success. He received bin Ladam's undertaking to provide the technology, materials and expertise required for the advancement of his cause, the commitment conditional upon the *Mufti Muharam* reciprocating by jointly developing training facilities in Indonesia, similar to those under the Arab's control, in Afghanistan. Sworn to secrecy, Muis was astonished to discover bin Ladam's involvement with the development of Pakistan's Islamic bomb.

Muis left Iran for Switzerland, where he opened a numbered account, deposited the ten million dollars, and made arrangements to draw against these funds via his Singapore bankers. Satisfied that all was in order, Abdul Muis returned to Indonesia, confident that the commitment he had in hand from Iran's rulers and Osama bin Ladam, would guarantee his succession to power.

Once this had been achieved, Muis intended revising the Constitution, declaring Indonesia a sectarian state under his rule. He would raise his fist to the United States and her allies, removing his Islamic state from their sphere of influence. Indonesia would then acquire the sophisticated technology hitherto withheld by the Americans, a technology which would soon be demonstrated in Pakistan's deserts, by those in his new alliance.

* * * *

JAVA, 1998

Mary Jo Hunter

Word that there had been another outbreak of violence sent Mary Jo scurrying to the highland provincial capital, where students from the prestigious Bandung Institute of Technology had ignored a government decree banning off-campus demonstrations, swarming onto the streets to voice their opposition against escalating food prices. Looters had joined the relatively disciplined youngsters parading through the central shopping district, changing the crowd's mood dramatically. Within minutes, the provincial city of Bandung was besieged by rioters determined to use the opportunity to destroy everything in their path as they hunted for opportunities to loot.

Unable to cope with the massive turnout, the police had summoned the military for assistance, but before their presence could influence the outcome, the rioting crowd had left a trail of destruction throughout the garden city. The students withdrew, realizing that they had lost control of the demonstration, anticipating swift retribution from the soldiers as these poured from their trucks onto the streets, brandishing batons, kicking, punching, and firing their weapons into the air. As some looters scrambled to safety, in their panic discarding television sets and VCRs to avoid capture, others continued on their rampage smashing vehicles and shop windows in the ensuing melee.

Mary Jo arrived four hours after the army had taken control of the city and, although most of the rioting mobs had been brutally dispersed, parts of the city remained under siege. Accompanied by her assistant, the American journalist hurried through the devastated city, stopping to take photos of the carnage whilst avoiding antagonizing the over-zealous soldiers.

'Annie, down there!' she called to her assistant, not waiting to see if the younger woman had heard. Mary Jo broke into a run as she attempted to catch up with a number of soldiers dragging a badly beaten looter towards a waiting truck.

'Jo, come back!' Annie cried, expecting that as a foreigner, Mary Jo would not appreciate the dangers of the moment. Ignored, she had no choice but to follow, fearful that her boss's actions might just get both of them killed.

'Get away from here!' a soldier screamed threateningly, immediately bringing the Indonesian assistant to an abrupt halt.

'Jo! Jo! Please come back,' she called, terrified as Mary Jo continued to advance, her cumbersome Nikon F90 recording the moment the soldiers dropped their captive, and commenced kicking him brutally around the head.

'Jo!' she screamed again, warning the woman of an approaching soldier whose raised weapon was aimed directly at the American photographer.

'Stop!' the soldier ordered, reaching for the expensive equipment just as Mary Jo captured the final shot she wanted, and turned, lowering the camera immediately. Suddenly, she froze in her tracks, recognizing her stupidity as the soldier pointed his machine-pistol directly at her face. For a few, brief, agonizing seconds, Mary Jo believed she would die. Then, cursing under his breath, the soldier turned away, yelling at Anne to get the foreigner away before she was harmed. Their hearts pounding, they moved away from the scene quickly, unable to find shelter anywhere amongst the smoldering buildings.

They hurried back along the main thoroughfares, avoiding the determined army teams sweeping the city centre for remnants of the rioting mobs which had all but destroyed the central shopping district. Finally, scrambling over the well-protected blockade surrounding the landmark Savoy Homann hotel, they found refuge inside. They stood, facing each other in the lobby, trembling from the excitement.

'I'm sorry, that was very stupid,' Mary Jo apologized to her assistant, realizing how she had jeopardized their lives.

'I thought he was going to shoot you, Jo,' Anne said, taking the other woman by the wrist and shaking it, admonishingly. 'The soldiers despise us, Jo. You must remember that in future, please?' she pleaded, her small frame starting to shake, suddenly overcome by the gravity of what had occurred. Mary Jo moved quickly to comfort her assistant, placing her arm firmly around the smaller woman's shoulders.

'It's okay, Anne. It's okay,' she offered, encouraging her to follow. Anne permitted the American to steer her across the marble floor through to the Garden Atrium, where they dropped into the comfortable batik cushioned rattan chairs, relieved to be out of harm's way.

While waiting for her assistant to regain her composure, Mary Jo looked around, admiring the art deco design, absorbing the surrounding atmosphere of timeless elegance and grace which so totally contradicted the situation outside. A waiter approached, and she ordered coffees.

She placed her hand on Anne's, and asked, 'Are you okay now?'

The Indonesian journalist smiled weakly, then nodded.

'Will we return to Jakarta now?' Anne was anxious to get back before dark. She had never enjoyed driving along country roads at night, particularly during times of civil unrest. Also, there had been stories of villagers whose land had been appropriated by the government for roads, who sought revenge by rolling coconuts out onto the expressways, turning speeding vehicles into mutilated, twisted wrecks as they speared off the highways into the night.

'Yes. I have a date,' she teased. 'Finish up, then we'll get underway.' Mary Jo knew it would be unwise to delay their departure. Besides, she had a deadline to meet. She looked at her assistant and smiled. 'You okay now?'

'Okay, *terima kasih*,' she replied, thanking the other woman. Mary Jo searched Anne's eyes, deciding that she was fortunate to have her as an assistant. Anne had become invaluable from the outset, and Mary Jo had found comfort knowing that she was also dependable. The job paid well, and the two of them had hit it off immediately three weeks before, when Anne had started as Jo's assistant, *cum* interpreter and gopher.

Often, when they appeared together in the most unlikely places, local children would follow closely, giggling and whispering, the pale-skinned American's corn-colored hair, her height, and soft blue eyes the object of their interest. Mary Jo had laughed when Anne commented on her nose, explaining as she touched the flattened bridge of her own, that most Indonesian girls would die to have such bone structure.

As they sat together, her assistant's eyes remained locked on her own. Mary Jo returned the smile, Anne immediately becoming embarrassed. Staring at another was considered extremely rude, even confrontational in most parts of Asia. Observing the sudden change in her expression, Jo placed ten thousand Rupiah on top of the check, and rose to leave before realizing that this most probably would not cover the coffees. Annoyed with the escalating exchange rate as the currency continued its incredible dive, she dropped another five thousand Rupiah alongside the first, and then placed her arm on Anne's shoulder, leading her back to where they had left their driver. Half an hour passed before they located their vehicle and managed to make their way through the city's barricaded streets, leaving Bandung behind with its smoke-filled sky, evidence of the day's violence.

Neither spoke as they commenced the two hundred kilometer drive, Anne falling asleep as the car's tires hummed monotonously, providing Mary Jo with the opportunity to finish writing the story she would file with her office in New York before attending her dinner engagement. She removed her laptop from its protective case, and went to work. As the car sped along the Cikampek-Jakarta highway, she observed a number of army convoys also heading for the capital. The driver slowed, waiting directly behind the last vehicle for the signal to overtake and Mary Jo looked directly up at the young, expressionless faces belonging to the well-armed soldiers standing in the rear truck, the scene reminiscent of others she had witnessed in former Soviet satellite republics and other distant places.

Momentarily, Mary Jo ignored her notes, her thoughts captured by recollections of other events she had covered during her career, as the names of cities and places flooded her mind. Bosnia, Chechnya, Baghdad, Beirut, the list seemed endless and, she confessed silently, had left her with a seemingly inescapable, haunting emptiness. Mary Jo's brilliant coverage of these wars had established her credentials amongst her peers which, in turn, had resulted in her being permanently assigned to the South East

Asian Bureau, a posting she had sought since first joining the news agency. Memories of her first months as a novice in Asia, came flooding back.

* * * *

Stinking garbage floating down rat-infested canals, snotty-nosed children squatting in the gutters peeing, and rotting, mutilated corpses lying with grotesque, bloated stomachs had soon become all too common sights for Mary Jo, rendering it difficult for her to remain dispassionate, and impartial, when reporting these scenes.

Two years before, when she first arrived in Hong Kong, the colony was gearing up for the hand-over to China. There was an air of despondency everywhere, even amongst the expatriate corps. At cocktail parties and the races, the conversations were mainly the same. Concerns about how China's military would treat democratic gains achieved prior to the takeover, overshadowed all discussion, in every corner of the British colony. Professional Chinese packed their bags and followed their money to Canada, Australia, and America, where they could acquire residency through investments made in those countries.

Mary Jo found the lifestyle exciting, and the travel even more rewarding than she had expected. Her assignments took her to the most exotic, and sometimes dangerous, destinations throughout Asia. She visited Beijing more than a dozen times before finally prevailing on an associate to accompany her to the Great Wall, fulfilling one of her childhood dreams which, at the time, had sadly revived distant and blurred memories of her father.

Mary Jo visited the warrior tombs in China, stood looking across the heavily fortified embattlements separating the two Koreas, and on one occasion, scrambled across slippery, moss-lined rocks to avoid Khymer Rouge soldiers who had appeared, while she was photographing children playing around land mines at Angkor Wat. In her first year she traveled extensively, her reporting and photographic coverage of Asia widely acclaimed by both readers and her peers.

It was towards the end of her two year assignment that she had requested the Jakarta posting, and was delighted when this was granted. Mary Jo had packed up her collections and clothes, posted a sign in the Foreign Correspondents Club just up from Central wishing those she was leaving behind, well, then left Hong Kong to its new Chinese masters. She had arrived in the Indonesian capital as the economy had commenced its meltdown, engaging her assistant, Anne, on recommendations from a friend in Reuters. Mary Jo then went about learning as much as she could about the shaky Republic, and its multi-faceted society.

* * * *

Mary Jo was jolted from her reflections as the driver dropped down a gear and accelerated. She looked up again, sighting a soldier for them to pass, and she acknowledged this with a smile, pleased that they would not be stuck behind the convoy any longer. Returning to her laptop, she concentrated on her account relating to the Bandung riots, relieved that her assistant continued to sleep.

The convoy had not delayed their return to any great extent, and by the time their vehicle had arrived at Mary Jo's small villa in the southern suburb of Cilandak, she had completed her story and was ready to have it filed with New York. Annie accompanied her employer into the villa, where the American had turned one of the bedrooms into an office and communications centre. There, Mary Jo downloaded the information from her laptop and camera, and examined the results of their day's handiwork. Although the shots she had taken had been hurried, she was pleased with the results.

They waited for several minutes before their Internet connection had accessed her agency address, then sent the story, complete with colored photographs, electronically to New York. Finished for the day, Mary Jo sent her assistant home, then climbed into a warm spa-bath and rested, thankful for the bubbling water's therapeutic effects which managed to expel the remorse which had troubled her earlier.

Chapter Five

JAKARTA

Hamish McLoughlin

Hamish checked his watch impatiently, wondering where the hell his friend Harry Goldstein, had disappeared to. He caught the bartender's eye, nodded, signaling for another whisky, then turned to observe the other guests sitting in the magnificently appointed bar. Located on the fourth level, O'Reiley's Pub was patronized by Jakarta-based expatriates and locals who enjoyed the lively evening atmosphere.

He grimaced as the band's sound check got under way, noting that less than an hour remained before the American band commenced playing. Then, he remembered, conversation would become impossible. He glanced over at the giant screen which was so popular with the lunch trade, as regulars filled the pub to catch the live CNN news and sports broadcasts. As he waited, Hamish McLoughlin observed how quickly O'Reiley's had filled, single guests occupying most of the seats around the island-shaped bar.

The financier sighed. There was a time when one could have recognized most of their faces. Numerous waves of foreign investors inundating Indonesian cities had established pockets of Western communities across the expansive country, and it was now possible to meet other foreigners for the first time who had lived in-country for years without having once crossed paths. The booming resources and energy sectors had attracted multi-nationals, and Indonesia's rapidly growing consumer market continued to escalate, or had, until the local currency suddenly came under pressure.

* * * *

Hamish McLoughlin was completely *au fait* with how precarious the monetary system had become. It had been his business to understand the mechanics of money, and how funds flowed, for more than twenty years. Having graduated with honors from Cambridge University in England, Hamish was recruited by Morgan & Morgan as part of their British team. Encouraged to continue his studies whilst in their employ, he forwent the many leisure opportunities and relationships which came his way, dedicating his time instead to furthering his career. Four demanding years passed and, armed with his Masters in Business Administration, Hamish McLoughlin was delighted to accept a newly created position with the international fund management group, as their Hong Kong based representative.

It was there, during his three years dealing with the financial wizards of Asia that the relatively young financier attracted the attention of the International Monetary Fund. Two years later he moved to Washington where he consolidated his position and reputation, amongst some of the world's most powerful financiers as a skillful negotiator and lateral thinker.

It was during this time that he had met and married, the daughter of a prominent Boston banker. Unfortunately, his expertise could in no way have prepared him for the bitterness which would then occupy his life. Eight months into their marriage, during one of Washington's typically bleak winter mornings, black ice sent his inexperienced wife's car skidding sideways through an intersection and to her death, when her vehicle lost control. Desolated by his loss, Hamish had struggled to recover emotionally, but found this impossible surrounded by constant reminders of his brief happiness and, quite out of character, packed his clothes one morning and left his world behind.

Eighteen months flashed by quickly. He started in Mexico, consuming excessive amounts of alcohol, his days spent sitting alone in dark bars, his nights lost wandering through an alcoholic mist. He continued in drunken stupor, often awakening in accommodations with no recollection of where he might be. Awash with tequila, he dragged himself and his self-indulgences through Panama, down to South America and through the tourist traps until copious amounts of alcohol necessitated a stint drying out in a Brazilian clinic. When he resumed his travels, Hamish found himself in Africa where again he was hospitalized with suspected alcoholic poisoning, still drowning in his own self-pity, still looking for closure over his past.

In hospital, while recovering from the abuse his liver and other vital organs had endured through two years of punishing drinking bouts, he finally accepted that he must live with his loss, recognizing that failure to come to terms with what had happened might cost him his own life. Recalling how he had enjoyed earlier years in Hong Kong, Hamish McLoughlin decided to return there and re-establish himself as a financial adviser, offering his expertise to the growing financial markets found amongst the emerging tigers of South East Asia. Emaciated by prolonged abuse, Hamish set about restoring his health, undertaking a rigorous fitness campaign. Slowly and painfully, his condition returned, as did much of his self-esteem. Several months passed and, satisfied that he had successfully exorcised his ghosts, Hamish flew to the British colony, and commenced the next chapter in his life.

Occupying one of the newly constructed condominium apartments perched among Hong Kong's Mid-Levels, Hamish used his remaining funds to establish a finance consultancy, taking advantage of the British colony's favorable corporate and taxation laws. Within two years, his company, Perentie Limited, had achieved considerable success, and the company's reputation for writing deals already legendary.

Offered a staggering amount he believed to be grossly excessive, McLoughlin willingly relinquished control of Perentie to a group of British investors, agreeing to remain on the board only until the transition to new management had been successfully completed. At that time, Hamish resigned his position and commenced trading currencies in his own right, achieving spectacular results. It was during this period that a run on the Thai Baht triggered a series of events creating extreme panic from Bangkok to Seoul, then down to Indonesia where Perentie had overly exposed themselves. As a result of liquidity problems, Hamish's expertise was sought by his former company's new directors.

Perentie's British Chairman's bullish approach to Indonesian investments had attracted representatives from all levels of Jakarta's business community through the company's doors. The chief executive of the Cendrawasih Taxi company was no exception. Once it had been revealed that this organization was, in fact, a subsidiary operation belonging to Nuri Suhapto, the Indonesian President's oldest daughter, Perentie's directors did not hesitate. They plunged in wildly, committing two hundred million dollars to finance the proposed fleet expansion for what they expected would become, another First Family monopoly.

Press announcements revealing that the deal had been consummated brought accolades from afar, and suddenly, within capital investment markets, Perentie Limited seemed incapable of error, resulting in a flood of new capital flowing into his company's coffers. Then, with pressure exerted on the local currency, it became apparent that Perentie might have been overly bullish in Indonesia, causing the new directors to become concerned with the extent of their investment exposure. They retained Hamish McLoughlin to visit Jakarta, and advise what steps might be taken to reduce the company's risk.

The wavering Rupiah was not the only inducement which had encouraged the financier to visit Jakarta. He sensed the imminent chaos collapsing money markets would surely bring. Concerned with the liquidity of Cendrawasih Taxis and Perentie's two hundred million capital, he suspected that it would not require more than a few hours to determine whether the loans had been utilized as undertaken by the company's board or, as he suspected, a portion simply removed by the major shareholder to be squirreled away somewhere in one of her Swiss bank accounts.

* * * *

Hamish could feel the warming, comforting effects of the whisky working, now somewhat less concerned that his friend was this late. Hamish looked around the pub, observing how it had filled almost beyond capacity, as staff hurried cocktails to tables while the bartender worked furiously to fill orders. The CNN broadcast had been displaced by a band, the noise level within O'Reiley's now reducing conversation to inaudible levels.

A group of young expatriates, obviously out for a good time laughed loudly, attracting his attention. He looked over in their direction, and was immediately stung by envy. The young men were accompanied by beautiful Indonesian girls, whose stunning features and elegance were difficult to ignore. Someone yelled out, drunkenly, turning heads in his direction as a roar of laughter followed. Hamish returned to his drink, in quiet deliberation. Then, from nowhere, there was a rain of cashew nuts as two well-dressed groups of young, foreign businessmen flung missiles at each other, as they might do back home.

For a while, there was some semblance of order as the boisterous crowd calmed down, now preoccupied with replenishing their drinks with the overly-generous serves of alcohol staff hurried to their tables. Someone else shouted from a dark corner, and this was greeted immediately by catcalls and boisterous behavior. Hamish let his eyes roam around the bar, observing the near-inebriated bunch, wishing he too could put Indonesia's ills behind, once the office doors were closed.

Few of those present would have any real understanding of what was happening, he knew. Fewer still would care, for the life of an expatriate was, in many cases, a generous, ego-satisfying journey through what some considered to be a subservient culture, justifiably relegated to their lesser position in the economic order of things and destined, deservedly, to fail without their generous expertise. Hamish despised the general air of superciliousness, and unfounded superiority some European foreigners carried to these, and other Asian shores, alert at all times, that he too not fall into this trap.

Deep in thought, Hamish heard the chords and, recognizing the tune, turned with others to clap in approval as the talented pianist commenced his solo. He listened, his thoughts delightfully wandering as the entertainer hit his own version of the chorus:

'..You might be one-legged Pianola Man,
But you can sure play well when your tight,
Remind us how young we all used to be,
Never scared of a challenge nor a fight.'

Immediately, the bar burst in unison, singing the only words those in attendance could remember, and Hamish, the alcohol working, could not resist joining in:

'...Tra la la, diddee da, tra la la diddee da,
La da, ...'

By now, the bar was pumping, everyone present singing the original words, some swaying where they sat while others, already too drunk to notice, splashed their drinks over those standing nearby as the mood lifted, erasing from their minds, what might be taking place outside.

As Hamish swallowed the remainder of his single malt whisky he observed Harold Goldstein enter at the far end of the bar, and raised his arm in acknowledgment. The IMF officer spotted Hamish and strolled over, nodding to several other guests as he did so.

'Sorry, goddamn Jakarta traffic gets worse with every visit,' Goldstein apologized, accepting the other man's hand. 'Give us two more of whatever he's drinking,' he instructed the hovering barman.

'How much time do we have?' Hamish asked, his head a little hazy from the whisky, but nevertheless pleased to catch up with his former associate. They had worked together in Washington at the Nineteenth Street IMF offices, before Hamish's life had undergone drastic change.

'Plenty. In fact, we're having dinner together with a charming young woman, you might just find attractive.' McLoughlin raised his eyebrows enquiringly.

'Business?'

'More or less, Hamish. I had a call from Mary Jo Hunter to see if the IMF would give her an update. We've met before on a number of occasions and, as the choice was to bail out on you or have her tag along I thought, what the hell, and invited her to join us.' Goldstein explained. 'Here she comes now,' he added.

'Fine by me,' Hamish shrugged, turning to meet the journalist, immediately taken aback by the physically arresting appearance of the woman.

'Hello, Harry,' she said, stepping forward as Goldstein bent to kiss her cheek. She turned and offered her hand. 'Hello, I'm Mary Jo Hunter. Please call me Jo. And you're Hamish McLoughlin?' she announced, surprising both men. Laughing softly, she explained. 'Your exploits are well known to the media, Mister McLoughlin. In fact, this is a most fortuitous opportunity for me. You see,' she continued, her smile captivating those present, 'I have you on my list for an interview as well.' With this, she withdrew her hand from Hamish's and placed her handbag on the barstool.

At that moment, a group in the far corner started clapping as one of their number finished swigging a half-yard of ale, most of which being spilt over his tie and shirt during an attempt to chugalug the beer. Mary Jo turned her attention back to the two men just as the pianist reluctantly sang a request for another group, the guests failing to understand how offensive some might consider *'Hava Nagila,'* to be, in a predominantly Moslem country. The entertainer played the first few bars, threw his hands in the air, feigning loss of memory and fell back on Billy Joel's *'Piano Man'* again, seeing it had been so popular when he had played it before.

Hamish found himself tapping to the chorus, again, embarrassed when his eyes came into contact with the delightfully attractive woman who had joined them.

'It's always been one of my favorites,' he explained, smiling at Mary Jo, who pounced on the opportunity.

'What about that interview, then, Mr. McLoughlin?' and he laughed, the mix of music and the beautiful woman added to alcohol, lifting his spirits.

'Well, you may have your time cut out for you Jo,' he explained, with practiced charm, 'I plan to leave tomorrow.' Jo pretended to sulk and both men laughed.

'What about a breakfast interview?' she suggested. Hamish considered this for a moment before replying.

'Only if you can make it by six,' he offered, turning to applaud the pianist as he skipped from one song to another, his audience obviously enjoying the medley as he moved from Billy Joel to Elton John, and across a range of distinctive, popular tunes.

'Never happen,' Goldstein interrupted good-naturedly, 'you'd never get him out of bed.' There was a sudden, embarrassed silence, then Mary Jo laughed softly.

'You know what I mean,' he chuckled, gulping the whisky and ushering the others before him. He raised his hand and scribbled in the air, calling for the check. 'Come on, let's get something into our stomachs. I'm as hungry as hell.' The staff hurried to present the bill, and within minutes they were on their way, Hamish waving towards the preoccupied pianist, as if they were old friends.

They walked casually out into the magnificent foyer, pausing and moving discreetly to one side whenever Goldstein stopped briefly to chat with familiar faces.

'He's very popular,' Mary Jo whispered. She stood alongside Hamish patiently waiting for their friend to rejoin them.

'Who wouldn't be? His presence here represents more than forty billion dollars to this economy,' he replied, almost matter-of-factly. She examined his expressionless face, and decided there was no envy in the response. If anything, he seemed a little drunk.

'Will he give it to them?' she asked, with a slight tilt of her head. Hamish McLoughlin admired the combination diamond and blue sapphire earring exposed, as her soft, blonde hair drifted away from her cheek with the gesture. For the first time, he became conscious of her perfume as the delicate fragrance of Nina Ricci's *L'Air du Temps* touched his senses.

'I wouldn't,' was all he said, his thoughts uncomfortably elsewhere.

'Do you think....' she began, but Hamish shook his head, then smiled.

'Leave it for Harry, Jo,' he advised, then wishing he had not been so abrupt. They were rejoined by the IMF representative, who continued to smile at everyone they passed as they exited the hotel.

'Not eating in?' Hamish asked, surprised, as the hotel's restaurants were all five star.

'I doubt we would be left alone,' Harry replied. 'Besides, I know just the place if you still enjoy a good combination Indonesian and Chinese. It's a bit down market, but the food's okay. What do you say, Jo?'

'Sounds okay to me. Where are we going?'

'Down near Chinatown,' he laughed, winking at the other man in conspiratorial manner. 'There's a place I was taken last time I was in town. Food was great and I'm sure they'll remember me.'

'You've got to be joking!' Hamish laughed. 'Don't you know we all look alike to the locals?' Mary Jo remained out of the banter, enjoying their obvious camaraderie.

'No, they'll remember me,' the American assured them, alluding to whatever had taken place during his recent visit. Content to leave it at that, they bundled into a taxi and permitted Goldstein to direct the driver to their downtown destination.

As they drove down Jalan Thamrin the traffic seemed endless. Skyscrapers lined the boulevard, lights blazing as if staff manned their offices around the clock, and colorful bulbs strung around the upper floors presented an almost carnival atmosphere. Mary Jo remembered arriving not long after Christmas, only to discover that Indonesia's entire Moslem community totaling more than one hundred and seventy-five million were preparing for the month of *Ramadan*, the ninth month in the Islamic calendar, during which fasting is undertaken during daylight hours. The *Hari Raya Idulfitri* celebrations following *Ramadan* would fall almost simultaneously with Chinese New Year. To Mary Jo, it seemed that the economies of the entire region would grind to a halt when this occurred, as more than one and a half billion people from China through Malaysia, Singapore and Indonesia, closed their businesses to join family and friends for the celebrations.

Their driver followed Jalan Gunung Sahari until reaching Ancol, then right into Martadinata. Ten minutes later, as their vehicle turned and twisted through Tanjung Priok's narrow back-streets, both Hamish and Mary Jo felt uneasy with their surrounds. The harbor was not even considered a safe place during the day, let alone this far into the evening and, although the nature of her work often resulted in her being placed in dangerous situations, there was just something sinister about harbors which had always made her uncomfortable. She was about to suggest that perhaps they were lost, when Harold Goldstein called out.

'Here we are,' he announced, almost proudly, patting the driver on his shoulder. He peeled off a number of bills and passed these to the man.

'Terima kasih,' the driver thanked his fare. Mary Jo could not believe that Goldstein was about to send the taxi away, aware it would be impossible to find another when they were ready.

'I wait here?' Mary Jo was relieved to hear the driver ask, and was amazed that her co-passengers were even considering the question.

'Yes, you wait here, *terima kasih,*' she intervened, flashing a handful of Rupiah notes. The taxi driver nodded, beamed at the three foreigners, then killed his engine. He would sleep there outside the restaurant until they returned. The small group climbed out, and to Mary Jo's dismay, stepped directly into a shallow, muddy puddle, causing her to leap for the broken pavement, barely visible under the dimly lit doorway. She heard both the men curse loudly as they too scrambled to avoid slipping and, reaching safety, examined their shoes to see what it was they had stepped in.

'Come on,' Harry encouraged, advancing carefully into the single-story structure. The Cahaya Laut restaurant's muddy entrance was, to say the least, disconcerting, and in no way reflected the fine cuisine found inside the noisy establishment. As they made their way further into the packed restaurant Mary Jo could not believe her eyes at the spectacle before her.

There were more than two hundred determined diners crammed claustrophobically into an area suitable for half that number, all attacking the various servings covering their round tables with a gusto reminiscent of scenes she had encountered in the alleys of Shanghai. The three forged ahead through a steady stream of departing guests, stopping near the cashier's post to wait for a table. Harry called out something but this was lost in the incredible surrounds of overwhelming chatter.

'Sorry?' the others called back, leaning closer to hear.

'I said, it's great, isn't it?' Goldstein shouted proudly, his face beaming with anticipation as he stepped back to permit several waiters to struggle through, carrying dishes of steamed eel and barbecued turtle. A Chinese cook clad in a filthy singlet suddenly appeared, yelled at one of the waiters while brandishing a large kitchen knife threateningly, then retreated to his domain still cursing the intelligence of the other man's ancestors. The manager appeared and directed two of his staff to clean a table vacated only moments before, as he assisted the three foreigners into their cramped space.

'My god, it's bedlam!' Hamish McLoughlin complained, leaning back to permit another waiter access to their table. Chopsticks and small soup bowls added to the clatter as these were placed noisily on their table, while tired waiters rushed to comply with their employer's and guests' demands. Sticky, plastic-covered menus were then dropped onto their table, along with an assortment of small dishes containing a variety of pickles and sauces. Someone appeared and splashed lukewarm tea into hurriedly-washed, miniature porcelain cups, while a more senior waiter succeeded in pushing his way to where they were seated, to take their orders.

Harry pointed to the drinks list, ordering beers all around. Wine was not available; just cognacs, whiskies, soft drinks and beer.

'I'll order?' he suggested, to the relief of the others. The experienced vistor pointed to a number of dishes he believed he understood, and accompanied by confused gesticulation between the pair, the waiter finally managed to understand what it was the foreigner wished to order, and scribbled impatiently on his pad. To Hamish's surprise, the Bintang beer arrived cold, and he grinned at the others as they touched glasses in toast.

Mary Jo was a little disappointed that their venue made it impossible to communicate. She had hoped for an opportunity to discuss the IMF's position regarding current negotiations with the Indonesian Government. Now, she realized, Harold Goldstein had cleverly removed that opportunity with his selection of dinner locations. She looked across the table wondering if Hamish McLoughlin's presence had been orchestrated, to prevent an in-depth interview.

Crab and asparagus soup was served, by which time all three had given up any further attempts at talking. Soon, other dishes arrived, and Mary Jo's resentment at the evening's outcome all but disappeared as the first tantalizing aroma of suckling pig reminded her that she had missed taking lunch in Bandung. Having never mastered the art during her many visits to China, she struggled with the chopsticks until an observant waiter provided forks and spoons. Mary Jo watched, as both men expertly separated pieces of deep-fried, sweet-and-sour *kakap* then shared the fish with her. By the time they had eaten the tender squid, steamed prawns, Cantonese rice and *kai-lan* leaf which had been soaked in oyster sauce, surprisingly, the restaurant had all but emptied.

'Where have they gone?' Hamish asked, his watch showing it was ten o'clock.

'Same thing happened the last time I was here,' Harry replied, accepting a warm, wet towel from the waiter. He wiped his face slowly, releasing an audible sigh of satisfaction with the moment. 'I was brought here last visit by the Finance Minister. A couple of Chinese businessmen tagged along, probably to pay for the evening and, before I could do anything about it, I found myself drinking XO cognac as if there was no tomorrow.' The IMF official then shook his head, remembering what followed.

'With my experience, I should have realized that the Chinese element wouldn't have settled for just a few social sips. Anyway, once I discovered that the government officials had surreptitiously slipped away and gone home, I decided that I'd had enough and insisted that I be taken back to the Hyatt.' Both Mary Jo and Hamish listened attentively, somewhat bemused that someone as well-traveled, and as senior as Harry had found himself in such a predicament.

'Anyway, the Chinese hosts were reluctant to let me go and short of causing an incident, I agreed to finish another bottle with them. There's not much more to tell except one of them fell over that railing over there,'

Harry explained, his expression serious, 'and we had one hell of a job pulling him back up and inside. Needless to say,' he added, his face breaking into a smile, 'he was covered in mud and whatever unmentionables lurk in these filthy harbor's waters.

Mary Jo noticed that the last guests were settling their bill. She decided to delay their own departure, taking advantage of the changed ambiance. As Goldstein concluded his anecdote, she waved to the waiter and requested coffee.

'Why don't we finish up at the hotel instead?' Hamish suggested, spoiling her plan. She decided to be blunt and plunged in hoping for at least some time to probe Goldstein for information regarding the current crisis.

'How about ten minutes, here?' she asked, smiling sweetly. Hamish McLoughlin shrugged.

'Okay by me, but I don't think I could stomach their coffee. Harry?'

Goldstein's eyes flicked unnoticeably. 'Okay, Jo. But I'm not sure there's a great deal to tell you yet,' he fenced. He knew that by agreeing to meet with Mary Jo, she would aggressively pursue her questions. He had hoped that Hamish's presence would provide sufficient distraction.

'I don't want to put you on the spot, Harry, but New York expects an in depth submission from me, and I thought the information would be far more reliable coming from you, than those bastards over at the Indonesian Ministry of Information. God, Harry, it's incredibly frustrating trying to extract real facts from these people,' she pleaded.

'All I can suggest, Jo, is that the IMF is hoping that something more concrete will eventuate out of next month's meetings. For now, there really is nothing much I can say. I'll tell you what, though. I'll give you whatever I can after the next round of talks. How's that?' he suggested, hoping that this would suffice. He really could not divulge that, as they spoke, Washington was in the process of preparing new guidelines for the Indonesians which, he expected, would result in the most severe ramifications should these not be adhered to by the Indonesian government.

Realizing that she had hit a brick wall, Mary Jo retreated graciously, smiling at the rebuff.

'Exclusive?' she asked hopefully, knowing that this would be unlikely.

'Sure, sure,' Goldstein laughed, pleased that she had reacted this well. He raised his hand and called for their check. 'Anyway, you could always pick Hamish's brains for your story,' he teased, grinning widely now.

'Now that's a possibility,' McLoughlin joined in, pleasantly surprised with Jo's behavior. She seemed to lack the aggression he associated with media types. 'Why don't we go back to the Hyatt and talk over coffee there?' he suggested again.

They agreed, and Harry paid the bill, leading the way outside where their driver remained, sound asleep. Within minutes they were speeding back towards the city, the traffic around the *Selamat Datang* statue noticeably lighter as they arrived at the Grand Hyatt.

'I'm afraid I'll have to leave you two to it,' Goldstein said, stifling a yawn.

'Not even a nightcap?' Hamish offered, surprised as it was only eleven o'clock.

'Sorry,' he apologized, reaching over to squeeze Mary Jo's hand. 'We'll catch up next month,' he promised, and winked at McLoughlin. 'See you at breakfast, Hamish. Goodnight,' with which, he walked away towards reception. They watched as Goldstein collected his room keys and messages, and waved as he stepped into the lavishly decorated lift.

'Still want that coffee?' Hamish McLoughlin asked, hoping she would not stay.

'Perhaps something a little stronger. It's been a long day,' she replied, placing her arm through his. They returned to O'Reiley's and found a table hidden in a softly-lit corner of the bar. They selected their drinks, then settled back to talk, enjoying each other's company. The atmosphere was more subdued, the number of guests reduced to a few.

Sitting across the dark onyx table, Mary Jo decided that she approved of the Scot, wondering how, as a banker, he managed to maintain the deep suntanned features which complimented the man's obvious athletic form. He was certain to work out, she guessed correctly, at ease with Hamish's warm and convincing smile.

'Do you know why Harry was so reluctant to reveal what's happening?' Jo asked. Hamish looked past Mary Jo, distracted by the flickers of light at the other end of the bar as a couple there lit their cigarettes. Suddenly, something triggered a distant memory and he could taste the warm, comforting tobacco smoke as it entered his lungs. He returned his gaze to the attractive woman sitting opposite, pleased that he had given up smoking more than fifteen years before. He addressed her question.

'Jo, this country's in one hell of a mess. The surprising thing is, no one here seems to care. Corruption has permeated all levels of society, and the First Family, along with their cronies and relatives, continue to rip the guts out of the country. My guess is, they're bankrupt; or at least, on the verge of financial collapse.'

'Why doesn't the World Bank or the IMF just bail them out?' she asked, not displeased with the opportunity to hold some discussion which might, in some way, contribute to her overdue story.

'Their case is different to that, say, of Mexico, Jo.' He looked around for the waiter and, having gained his attention, indicated that they would have another round. 'How much do you understand about the workings of the IMF?' he inquired.

'Not as much as I should, considering my profession,' she admitted. Hamish instantly admired her for her honesty. He had struck few journalists who would have suggested anything but the contrary.

'A quick lesson, then?' he asked, not patronizingly.

'Providing you promise not to bore me to death,' she smiled, and for a moment Hamish acknowledged that Mary Jo certainly had a refreshing directness about her manner.

'Okay, here goes,' he started, pausing only to sip the remaining whisky. 'Firstly, the IMF is charged with the responsibility for safeguarding the stability of the international monetary system.' He moved slightly, making himself more comfortable before continuing.

'I have found that, with the exception of a small circle of financiers and economists, the IMF's activities are considered to be shrouded in mystery. More often than not, it is confused with the World Bank but, in fact, it is something of a cooperative institution with almost two hundred members. These are countries which have joined voluntarily, believing that the IMF is perhaps the best forum for buying and selling their currencies, thereby stabilizing the flow of capital around the world. The IMF maintains, although some would argue that this is not the case, that it has no effective authority over the domestic policies of its member nations.' Mary Jo raised an eyebrow at this.

'I'll explain a little later,' he said, accepting the fresh whisky and taking a quick mouthful. 'The IMF offers its members rational advice to assist whenever this is believed beneficial. For instance, some nations splurge a considerable proportion of their foreign exchange on military purchases. When the IMF identifies such problems or activities, it offers friendly advice, and rational argument to dissuade the nation in question from continuing on this course. The IMF can't force any of its members to adopt any specific policy except, of course, the requirement that contributing nations disclose information relating to their monetary and fiscal policies. The members agree that the IMF should maintain some authority over their payment policies as history has proven time and time again, that without a global monitoring body, today's system of payments in foreign exchange would fail.'

Hamish rested momentarily, observing Mary Jo to determine if she followed. Satisfied that she understood, he continued.

'Each currency has a value in terms of other currencies, whether this be the Baht, the Franc or even the crumbling Rupiah. Whether it's a government or a multinational company, business depends on the effective flow of capital which is controlled through the exchange of each countries currency. The genesis for the need for an organization such as the IMF can be found back in the events of the Great Depression of the 1930's, when banks failed by the thousands and world trade virtually collapsed. Those who could still afford to do so changed whatever money they had into gold. This later created another problem when national treasuries, as was the case in the United Kingdom, failed to meet the demand for gold. This eventuated in the U.K. leading the way for the abandonment of the gold standard. Confusion reigned.

Some countries, mainly gold producers, maintained their currencies tied to gold, while others could not, creating uncertainty in the value of their money. This, in turn, caused complex problems whenever these nations attempted to exchange their currencies with those still tied to the precious metal. The old-fashioned method of payment was reintroduced by some nations, using the barter system instead of money. World commerce became very confused as it was almost impossible to determine the value of one currency, in relation to another.'

'There were a number of unsuccessful conferences called to resolve the problems associated with currency exchange but these failed to address the real issues. It was not until a joint British-American proposal resulted in the formation of the IMF in 1944, that the world had some semblance of order applied to the international exchange systems.'

'I thought Indonesia once withdrew from the IMF?' she interrupted.

'Yes, that's true,' he agreed, 'as did Cuba and a number of Eastern Bloc countries at that time. But,' he added, 'all of these rejoined with the exception of Fidel.'

'And the IMF does not have the power to just lay down the law, say, to Indonesia and direct them to toe the line or they won't receive any assistance?' she asked, uncertain that she had heard correctly before.

'That's what they claim, sure,' he answered. 'Each member country deposits whatever funds they consider appropriate. The more they subscribe, the greater the say they have in IMF affairs, and the more they may borrow in times of need. The largest depositor is the United States, giving it some twenty percent control over all votes. Obviously, this then gives the American Government the strongest voice in determining policies.'

'The members may borrow up to three times their own deposits with the IMF, which has its own line of credit of twenty-five billion dollars for such emergencies. This, together with its cash reserves, would normally cover any of its members immediate needs. However, Indonesia requires considerably more than it is really entitled to receive, and certainly well in excess of earlier bail-out packages such as that provided to Mexico.' He looked to see if she still followed his explanation.

'It's okay, I'm keeping up,' Mary Jo advised.

'Good. It's important to understand that IMF members are expected to follow a basic set of economic guidelines, pursuing policies that will benefit the country, and the IMF as a whole. Although the IMF has no means of coercing delinquent members, it can apply considerable moral pressure to ensure that they abide by the rules.' Hamish could see from her look of disdain that she correctly interpreted the situation.

'In other words, toe the line or you won't receive any funds?' she suggested.

'Or worse,' he replied. 'The offending nation could have its membership terminated.'

'And where does that leave Indonesia?' she asked, confident that she knew already what his reply would be.

'In the proverbial,' he answered. 'Unless the Indonesian Government accepts that they must initiate radical reform, it's my guess the IMF will refuse to provide any further funding. One would have to agree, Jo, that under the current circumstances it would be futile to give these people more money when it's obvious that so much is just siphoned off by those in power.' Mary Jo nodded in agreement. She intended writing more about the corruption she had already evidenced during her brief stay.

'Just how bad is it here?' she persisted.

'My guess is that we might see a major meltdown if the IMF and World Bank dig their toes in and insist on the reforms necessary for Indonesia's long-term survival. Let's just say, I'm not recommending further investments here for the time being. Hell, it's less than a month since I last visited and the rapid deterioration evident over those few weeks is, to say the least, startling.' Mary Jo guessed that his current visit was not going too well. Curious, she steered the conversation towards his own activities.

'How is Perentie Limited faring here?' she asked, taking Hamish by surprise. He collected his thoughts, lifted his whiskey and swallowed the remaining Chivas before responding. He knew he must be circumspect, more so as this attractive woman survived off information she extracted from casual conversations such as theirs.

'I'm now merely a consultant,' he answered, smilingly. 'My visit is purely to determine how Perentie's investments here are stacking up under the current conditions.'

'How do you think they will stack up?' she insisted, observing his reaction closely.

'Oh, I guess they are probably going to experience some tough times until the economy recovers from its slump,' he replied, not at all happy with the change in the conversation's direction. 'I have a few meetings in the morning before returning to Hong Kong. How about I check with Perentie first to see if they would be happy with an interview?' Mary Jo understood the rebuff and accepted this, wishing to leave the door open for a later opportunity.

'Wow,' she said, light-heartedly, 'brushed off twice in the same evening!' With this, they both laughed, and she could see that he was relieved to be off the hook. She made a mental note to do some digging into the Perentie group's activities in Indonesia. Mary Jo looked around the bar, and the staff took this as a signal that they required service. By now, O'Reiley's was all but deserted, the band had packed up and disappeared, the bartender struggling to contain a yawn as he went about cleaning his station.

A waiter approached to refill their glasses but Hamish raised his hands and politely refused.

'Enough for now,' he said, recognizing that he was tired.

'Perhaps we can get together again sometime,' Jo suggested sincerely, having enjoyed their brief encounter.

'You can count on it, Jo,' he promised, pleased that they had met.

It was getting late, and they agreed to part company. Hamish escorted Mary Jo out through the lobby, waiting until she climbed into her taxi before he too retired, in preparation for what he anticipated would be a most difficult day.

As he lay in bed, tiredness gently flowing from his body, it was not matters relating to Perentie's exposure in Indonesia which occupied his thoughts. Instead, images of Mary Jo flowed through his mind and, as his breathing slowed with the promise of sleep, he imagined that he could smell the delicate perfume he had detected earlier in the evening, and his lips curved slightly as he smiled.

The following morning Hamish McLoughlin rose, refreshed, and in high spirits. But his demeanor soon changed as the day wore on, once he discovered Cendrawasih Taxis' true financial situation and the resulting effect this would most surely have on the Hong Kong financiers.

At first, he refused to believe the incredible change in fortunes his former company would undoubtedly undergo as a result of this one failed investment in Indonesia, until one of the Taxi company's directors alluded to where the money had gone. Only then did he accept for certain that the situation would be unrecoverable.

The Indonesian President's daughter had issued the instructions, and the directors had obeyed, leaving their company short by almost two hundred million American dollars.

Chapter Six

East Java - Surabaya

Haji Abdul Muis & General Praboyo

'*Asalamalaikum, Mas Praboyo,*' Haji Abdul Muis intoned, holding both hands clasped as if in prayer, welcoming his guest in traditional manner.

'*Terima kasih, Pak Haji,*' the *Kopassus* Commander rejoined, respectfully. The two men then sat in the opulent, almost garish lounge chairs, the setting a gift from one of the Haji's followers. Praboyo looked around the room, surprised. He had expected something more in keeping with Muis' position as leader of the *Mufti Muharam* millions, and not the ostentatious display of wealth with which he had surrounded himself.

Gone were the traditional hand-carved ornate Javanese teak tables and chairs which would be found in similar households. Gone too, were signs that the occupant was a respected *Ulama*, a religious councilor; one of *Allah's* chosen. Instead, these had been replaced with a state-of-the-art thin line television receiver, linked to a bank of video recorders which, in turn, were connected to a remote-controlled parabolic dish Praboyo guessed would be sitting outside, pointing at any one of the numerous satellites overhead. There was a library of compact discs positioned alongside a bank of stereo equipment, and General Praboyo eyed this enviously, reminding himself to have a similar set purchased and sent over by the Military Attache in Singapore.

The imported chrome and smoked-glass cabinet clashed not only with the settee, but with the colorful wall carpet. Set between two unframed paintings, the likes of which Praboyo had never laid eyes on before, the carpet's colors screamed volumes of the decorator's miserable attempts at the *avant-garde*.

'*Ah, I see you like my carpet?*' Muis asked, proudly. He had selected this himself during a visit to London. General Praboyo smiled, nodded, searching for words of praise.

'*It is very beautiful,*' he lied, '*Tuti would love the colors.*' At the mention of Suhapto's daughter, Muis' face became serious, almost stern.

'*You have never discussed our association, I trust?*' he asked, watching the younger man's eyes to detect the truthfulness of his answer.

'*No, never,*' he replied. This was just one of the many secrets he had kept from his wife. Praboyo was relieved that his mother had agreed to play such an important liaison role between the two parties. It had been imperative that information concerning his relationship with Abdul Muis be contained. Meetings such as these were risky, he knew, and Praboyo endeavored to restrict the frequency of such, in the interests of security. When secret negotiations had first been initiated at his mother's suggestion, she had warned that her own religious bias might represent a stumbling block to her son's aspirations. She had offered to convert to Islam against his objections, and had done so, to facilitate the union of both camps.

Praboyo understood the extent of her sacrifice, but was relieved that she had surrendered to the mullah's demands. He adored his mother, and was deeply grateful for her love, constant vigilance, and sound advice. It had been she who had orchestrated for Praboyo to meet the homely President's daughter, Tuti, urging Praboyo to make the necessary sacrifice in the interests of family and career. He had followed his mother's advice and proposed to Tuti Suhapto, the affair resulting in a fruitful, although sexually dissatisfying union. Anxious to steer the conversation towards the *Ulamas* recent visit, Praboyo asked if his tour had been successful.

'*You should visit the Middle East some time,*' Abdul Muis responded, not evasively. His eyes sparkled, his memory fresh with the success he had achieved. '*It is expected that you would visit Mecca for the holy pilgrimage, 'Boyo,*' he advised, dropping the first syllable to Praboyo's name as intimate friends might.

The general recognized the gesture, pleased that this conversation would remain informal. He sat quietly, permitting the Haji to describe his most recent goodwill tour through the Arab states, orchestrated to promote the *Mufti Muharam* Party. Praboyo was impressed with the list of well known names which rolled off Muis' tongue, fascinated also that his ally had cemented such relationships with these powerful Moslem figures. Praboyo had never questioned the purpose of Abdul Muis' journey. In his capacity as leader of the *Mufti Muharam* Party, it seemed only natural to the general that Muis visit other leading Moslems, in no way suspecting this man's hidden agenda. Finally, having exhausted the subject of his visit, Muis permitted his guest to lead their conversation towards the real purpose of their meeting.

'Muis,' Praboyo started, also informally, *'you have witnessed how quickly the situation in our country has changed.'* He looked directly at his host, Muis's face reflecting his own thoughts. *'We might be obliged to move earlier than expected. There are rumblings amongst the officer corps. I am very concerned that if we don't move quickly, we could lose the opportunity to others.'* Praboyo waited for a reaction and, detecting none, continued.

'The Bapak is very tired,' he said, truthfully. The President had appeared on television with members of the IMF, having signed an amended agreement for the billions the country so urgently needed. The people had been shocked to see the change in his demeanor; it was almost as if he had lost the will to continue as their leader. His speech seemed slow, even slurred, his face puffed from loss of sleep. They had never seen their President in such a vulnerable state before.

'I need your agreement, Muis, if we are to move now. The President may not survive much longer, particularly with the pressure he's under to resign. If I were to speak to him, and tell him that the Mufti Muharam will stand behind me, he could be swayed into agreeing that I become his interim President for the remainder of his term. You know how the Bapak feels about you and your Party. He is very supportive. But the military is most unlikely to agree to my assuming leadership, unless we continue with our original strategy.'

Muis firmly believed that had the President seen it in his heart to appoint his son-in-law, Praboyo, as army chief-of-staff, then this conversation may not have taken place. Muis had no doubt that Praboyo would have then used his new powers to remove any who threatened his ascent to the Presidency, including outspoken Muslim leaders. Still, he listened. Praboyo offered a unique opportunity and Muis knew he would be foolish not to accommodate the young general, at least, for now.

'Towards the end of the President's original term we will call an election, only this will be won not by the ruling Perkarya Party. Instead, as we have agreed, Perkarya will be abolished. As President, I will issue this decree. In its place, Mufti Muharam will become the vehicle to maintain our control. Those amongst the military who have openly voiced their opposition against me will be replaced, commencing with the Christian generals. As Vice President and leader of more than thirty million faithful followers, the results of any future election would be a forgone conclusion. How could we not win?'

Praboyo was convinced that this result could be achieved. His concerns with openly identifying with the Moslem parties would, he knew, cause the Americans to distance themselves, perhaps even withdraw their support. Once he had assumed the Presidential mantle, the general was confident that the United States would reconsider their position. After all, he would be the leader of the world's largest, if not most powerful, Moslem nation. They would have to deal with him.

Muis listened attentively, his real feelings towards the President's son-in-law masked by his expressionless features. The Moslem leader needed this man. He would use him, building his own power base until the arrogant General Praboyo's services were no longer required. Muis accepted that it would be almost impossible, at this time in the country's development, for any Moslem party to consider contesting an election without the full support of the military. And that was most unlikely, considering the stranglehold senior officers held over both Houses. The one thousand seat Parliament was controlled by the President, his family, cronies and all of the military factions. The ruling party, the *Perkumpulan Karya* or, as it had more commonly referred to, *Perkarya,* was in fact a functional group consisting of factions from all levels of society, and controlled both the Lower and Upper Houses of Parliament. Even the President's children occupied seats in government. Muis pragmatically accepted that without Praboyo's assistance, it would be nigh impossible for him to achieve his own dreams; an Islamic state, with Haji Abdul Muis as its leader.

Then there was the question of Haji Muhammed Malik and his *Ulama Akbar Party.* Muis had been only too willing to identify with the other Moslem group which could boast more than twice his own following. That they had covertly agreed to throw their support behind the President's son-in-law had really been the catalyst for Muis' own commitment. Although Malik's strength lay in the number of followers he could call upon, it was Abdul Muis' party which had taken the more aggressive and openly critical position in relation to the current economic crisis, providing leadership to the entire Moslem community.

Muis considered the man before him to be the ultimate opportunist, but he would use the powerful general as Praboyo was guaranteed the Presidency by virtue of his marriage into the Suhapto family. Muis acknowledged that there were others far more suitable to lead the country. However, these were all senior officers in the military, and unlikely to be willing to share power with another. Muis realized, as did Praboyo, that his ascent to the Presidency would be met with considerable resistance, not only from within the military, but also from Indonesia's near-destitute people. The *rakyat* had watched as the First Family had used their positions to accumulate wealth at the expense of the people, and would not be amenable to any of the Suhapto clan assuming the nation's helm. Their legacy of graft, corruption, and intimidation had deeply scarred the country, leaving the people bitter towards those in power. But if Praboyo were to be openly supported by the *Mufti Muharam,* this would provide him with a Moslem mandate and a sense of legitimacy to his position. It would be a comfortable relationship; at least for the first few years. For now, they both needed each other. The Haji smiled.

'Of course you have my trust and support,' Muis answered, outwardly pleased. *'The Mufti Muharam will stand with you 'Boyo. I have spoken to the other ulamas. They will continue to support us on the basis that we do change the Constitution; Indonesia will become an Islamic state. Secondly, I have assured them that in my role as Vice President, I will continue to maintain my leadership position with the Mufti Muharam.'*

General Praboyo was ecstatic. This was the answer he had hoped to hear. Armed with this information he was confident of securing support from the remaining senior officers who, until then, had been reluctant to commit. His face broke into a wide, relieved grin.

'Then it seems that we both have a great deal of work ahead.'

Their alliance sealed, the two powerful men rose to their feet and smiled warmly, their faces in no way reflecting the real content of their hearts with respect to their ultimate designs for the other. The conspirators parted, the historical moment passing unrecorded as General Praboyo hurried back to Jakarta, while Haji Abdul Muis remained behind, preparing for his own great leap into the Indonesian political arena.

* * * *

HONG KONG - JANUARY & FEBRUARY, 1998

'...and in line with the company's articles of association, the directors, with the deepest regret, now advise its shareholders, staff and government bodies that Perentie Limited is insolvent, and has been placed in immediate liquidation.'

Reporters pushed and shouted as the announcement was made, each screaming for more information as the amazing revelations were disclosed by the company's Chairman. Within minutes the shock waves were felt thoughout Asia sending stock markets to new lows on all exchanges. With amazing speed, staff and records were removed from the investment house's offices, leaving stunned thousands wondering how this could have happened to what had been previously considered the darling of the fund management industry.

Fighting erupted as staff, both local and foreign, exited the company premises, disbelieving that their blue-chip organization had, indeed, collapsed taking hundreds of millions of dollars with it. Across the South China Sea, the following morning witnessed sixteen Indonesian banks close their doors in Jakarta, leaving desperate depositors lining the footpaths outside, shocked and bewildered by the closures. Two of these were directly controlled by Nuri Suhapto who, upon hearing that her banks had been forced to close by the Central Bank, immediately demanded that the Governor rescind his instructions, and permit her to trade. But Governor Sutedjo remained adamant, citing IMF demands to justify his actions.

An atmosphere of gloom enveloped the region as the Rupiah continued its plunge, and the public transport system collapsed leaving tens of thousands of Moslems stranded throughout the country, unable to visit their families for the traditional religious holidays. Within days, the mood turned violent and, for the first time in more than three decades, the voice of the people shook the very foundations of the Suhapto dynasty, with major riots erupting throughout most major cities, resulting in looting and damage on a scale not seen since the anti-Japanese demonstrations of 1974.

* * * *

INDONESIA - MARCH, 1998

The President's Daughter

Tuti Suhapto threw the porcelain lamp across the room in anger before realizing that this had been a gift from Nuri, her older sister. Quickly, she examined the damage and decided to blame her servants for her tantrum, once Nuri discovered the missing piece. Tuti knew that this would surely happen, as nothing ever escaped her sister's persistent, prying manner.

The cause of this behavior, a note from an unknown party claiming to be her friend, remained crumpled on the floor. She stamped her foot, then angrily retrieved the *surat-kaleng* poison-pen letter, deciding that this time she would confront him with the evidence.

The President's daughter then stormed from the room, leaving broken, colorful porcelain pieces scattered across her private lounge. Her temper unabated, she then proceeded to her husband's study and, without knocking, opened the door and flung this open as if expecting to catch Praboyo *corpus indelecti* with one of the staff.

'Boyo....,' she screamed, her voice carrying through the magnificent mansion, sending fear through the servants' quarters. Without exception, they had all fallen victim at one time or another to their lady's scathing verbal attacks, and violent tantrums. Her voice cut off in midair when Tuti realized that Praboyo was indeed not alone, and she moved quickly to recover her situation.

'Oh, Boyo,' she cried, the trembling in her voice not altogether fabricated, *'one of the servants has broken my favorite lamp!'* She then bit her lip, placed her hands together in front, and addressed her father. *'I'm sorry, Bapak, I didn't know you were here,'* she apologized, knowing that her submissive behavior would do the trick. The President smiled knowingly, and permitted his daughter to move closer, kissing him affectionately on the cheek.

'Don't be so upset,' he admonished in a fatherly tone. Tuti seized the opportunity.

'But Bapak, it was a gift from Nuri!' she protested, feigning disappointment at the tragic loss of the unwanted item. Her father merely smiled, then patted her hand lovingly.

'I'm sure your sister will be able to find a replacement,' he said, and for a moment her temper threatened to flare, recognizing in her husband's eyes how close she had come to revealing the true state of their domestic situation.

'I'm sorry to interrupt you, Bapak,' she offered, retreating from the room. *'I'll come over to the house later if that's all right.'*

'Bring the children,' the President suggested, pleased with his large family. With this, Tuti excused herself and then went in search of something else to occupy her time until her father departed, and she could confront Praboyo alone.

She need not have waited, for immediately after the President stepped outside to walk with his personal security the short distance to his own home, Praboyo had climbed into his Mercedes and was half-way out the gate before Tuti realized what was happening. She wanted to run outside after her husband but decided against this, returning instead to her bedroom where she changed, then called her own driver, instructing him to take her to an address in suburban Tebet.

There, parked not fifty meters from the woman's house, the Indonesian President's daughter waited, her anger growing with each passing minute she believed her husband to be inside. An hour passed, then another, and still Praboyo did not appear. Finally, accepting that they might have met elsewhere, she burst into tears, sobbing instructions to her terrified driver to take her home.

* * * *

General Praboyo lay back naked, watching the exquisite Menadonese girl undress slowly, his excitement growing, his impatience to be inside her burning him deep inside. The young starlet, already well rehearsed in the required routine let her dress slip slowly to the floor, anxious that her partner be ready. The memory of their first encounter still fresh in her mind, she deliberately dallied, moving provocatively, but out of his reach, waiting until he was completely aroused. Even her soft, light-brown skin could not hide the faded bruises; her reward for his earlier impatience, and bruised ego.

She removed her bra slowly, then placed one hand against the dresser for balance, using her free hand to complete the undressing performance. Advancing on tiptoe, she moved around the double bed, feigning shyness, and lay alongside her man with one hand across her small, firm breasts, the other placed over the tiny suggestions of pubic hair dotting her womanhood.

She was ready.

Praboyo's hands touched her breasts then groped impatiently as he rolled over, forcing himself roughly upon her, her smell the only aphrodisiac he needed. She felt her muscles tense as he penetrated, but willed her body to accept his, lifting her hips to avoid the pain she had experienced during earlier couplings. As his breathing grew stronger, louder, his thrusts filled her completely when, with a loud groan, she felt him suddenly shudder as the warm flow signaled he had climaxed.

For a few, brief, moments her lover lay atop her then, with a grunt of what she interpreted as satisfaction, he rolled to one side and out of bed, without so much as one word to the beautiful, promising actress. She watched as Praboyo strutted to the bathroom, relieved that she had pleased him, and confident that he would continue to call. Her small, delicate hands touched her breasts, where tiny nipples remained erect, revealing their secret. Although relatively inexperienced, she knew that her lover's rushed attempt at love-making was responsible for the emptiness which remained with her, inside, but she also knew that this would never be mentioned between them.

The memory of the humiliating beating he had administered just weeks before had not discouraged her from accepting further invitations, as the rewards for these casual interludes with General Praboyo were more than even she could have imagined. She had been ensconced in an exquisite, well-guarded villa in Tebet, provided with servants, an almost limitless wardrobe and a new car. She had not hesitated in accepting her demanding role, even though this meant severing all ties with friends and, for the time being, her family back in Menado.

As she lay, listening, she could hear Praboyo completing his ablutions and uttered a silent prayer that he would not discard her as quickly as the others she had learned of, although she did accept that this would be inevitable. Barely seventeen, the not so naïve young actress believed that her beauty and youth would keep him interested long enough for her future to be financially secured.

The girl entered the bathroom after Praboyo had finished, knowing that he would be long gone before she too had completed bathing, although this in no way offended her. He would leave another gift on the dresser, she knew, and this comforting thought occupied her mind as she lay in the discreet hotel's spa, not concerned that their future rendezvous must also be held away from her own precious accommodations. Praboyo had explained; his wife had grown suspicious. They had to be more careful. Her role as mistress in no way bothered the talented young girl, as she was indeed grateful for the opportunity, even with the knowledge that discovery by the President's daughter would undoubtedly guarantee her harm.

Undaunted by this possibility, she lay back in the tub permitting the spa's gentle spray to massage her body, unashamedly contented with the warm sensation which suddenly flowed through her body, as her thoughts drifted back to the young man she had left behind in Menado, and how he had always pleased her.

An hour later, secure in the belief that life just could not be much better than it was, the young actress returned to Tebet, delighted also with the magnificent present Praboyo had left on the dresser for her. She turned into the quiet *cul de sac* and smiled at being back in the safety of her own villa, totally unaware that barely minutes before, a dark blue Mercedes had departed the scene, carrying with it the promise of a scorned, vengeful woman.

* * * *

That evening, and before Praboyo had returned from his tryst, Tuti telephoned her *dukun* who, having listened patiently to the demanding woman's tirade, arranged an appointment for the following morning, instructing the President's daughter to prepare a number of items he would need.

Upon her arrival, the unlicensed practitioner prepared a potion containing ground, white rhinoceros' horn powder and traditional herbs, and mixed these with minutely chopped strands of Praboyo's pubic hair which Tuti had retrieved from her husband during the night, at the *dukun's* request.

He closed his eyes and chanted incoherently, casting the desired spell. Tuti paid the herbalist handsomely and returned home, confident that the potion could be easily disguised in Praboyo's food. She hoped her husband would soon lose interest in his Menadonese mistress. And if he did not, Tuti was determined to find another solution.

* * * *

Chapter Seven

Hong Kong - March

Hamish

Hamish McLoughlin had been pleasantly surprised when Harold Goldstein had opened the conversation with an offer for him to consult to the Geneva based organization. He knew of the merchant bank, having learned of its involvement in Indonesia as a result of his own position in regional financial circles.

'They are very conservative, Hamish,' Goldstein had advised.

'The address says it all, Harold,' he had responded, 'no need to preach to the converted.' He accepted the coffee and winced as the steamy liquid burnt his lips.

'You can sort out the finer details with them, later,' the IMF representative suggested, 'but I must make it quite clear that I am acting only as a messenger.'

'That's clear, don't worry.' McLoughlin understood that the introduction had come via his friend, and should not be misconstrued as Goldstein acting in any way for the Swiss-based group. It was not uncommon for bankers to seek outside employment recommendations from independent bodies. Harold Goldstein had explained that information regarding the position had come to his attention while attending a recent cocktail party. There, quite by accident, he had been involved in discussion with a group when one of the Geneva bankers inquired if those present could recommend a senior financial consultant to advise them regarding their Indonesian investment portfolio.

'I suggested your name, Hamish, and they have asked for an introduction,' Goldstein had explained. 'I made it quite clear to them as well that what happens after that, is entirely between you and their board of governors.' McLoughlin understood. Harry had to consider his own position with the IMF. 'That means I don't want my name brought into any future conversations at all,' he insisted, seriously. Hamish looked at his friend and nodded in concurrence.

'I understand, Harry. And thanks,' he said, sincerely.

The following week Hamish McLoughlin flew from Hong Kong to Geneva, where his credentials were well received and his generous contract to act as a consultant to the merchant bankers consummated with exceptional Swiss speed. His instructions required that he maintain a watching brief over the bank's investments in Indonesia. Armed with a suitcase bearing letters of appointment and limited powers of attorney, Hamish McLoughlin found himself heading back for Indonesia where he would request, on behalf of his principals, direct access into the financial machinations of those companies which had borrowed from the merchant bankers. Amongst these he had not been surprised to discover, were a large number of companies associated with the President's family.

Within a week of his arrival, Hamish admitted to himself that the task he had undertaken was, indeed, a most formidable one. The more he delved into the intricate corporate dealings of each of his client's Indonesian borrowers, the more he became convinced that the entire structure supporting the country's economy was in imminent danger of collapse. Then, as he pieced together the fragile jig-saw which constituted this immense financial empire, Hamish McLoughlin was stunned to discover why his investigations always led him back up the same corporate path. Out of fifteen hundred companies listed as being either wholly owned subsidiaries or controlled joint ventures, more than twelve hundred of these were either directly or indirectly owned by members of the Presidential family, or his cronies. And the total indebtedness of this group exceeded fifty billion dollars.

And the question on everyone's lips was, *Where had all the money gone?*

* * * *

Harold Goldstein

Following Hamish's appointment, Goldstein returned to Washington where he received confirmation that his friend had arrived in Jakarta, and commenced his investigations for the merchant bank. In the future, whatever Hamish reported would flow through to Switzerland, from where the information would be forwarded in regular dispatches, to Tel Aviv.

Harold Goldstein had served Mossad's Directorate of Economic Intelligence Affairs for most of his banking career, having been recruited before entering the IMF. He had studied in London, then moved to Geneva where his masters lobbied to have their operative accepted into the Fund, and transferred to Washington where he remained, his appointment to executive management providing Tel Aviv with direct access to all information relating to the Fund's activities and, in many instances, confidential economic data not normally divulged by member countries. Goldstein had been successful in placing other Israeli operatives into target areas such as Malaysia, Singapore and Thailand, but it had been Mossad's deep concerns over Indonesia that had placed ever increasing demands on his time.

Finally, when it had become obvious that funds were being siphoned away under the guise of investments in aviation and other state-run technology interests, Goldstein had orchestrated for one of his finest financial analysts to be placed in Jakarta, where the IMF was meant to be given access to Ministerial records relating to these out-of-budget expenditures. The agent had maintained a watching brief over the Indonesian government's disbursement of funds, which in turn alerted Mossad to any discrepancies discovered as a result of ongoing due diligence procedures.

At first the investigator made some headway, tracing more than twenty million dollars which had been allocated for the purchase of equipment for the state-owned aircraft assembly plant. An audit revealed that these funds had moved overseas, the Israeli-controlled merchant bank in Geneva finally tracing the funds to an account, identified as one of the many operated by Osama bin Ladam to launder capital used for the acquisition of sophisticated weapons technology. When it was discovered that the Indonesian Minister responsible for this massive donation to the terrorist organization was none other than L.B. Hababli, Tel Aviv decided that he would have to go.

A year later, when Mossad intelligence sources operating through their Jakarta-based embassy confirmed rumors that Hababli would be appointed Vice President, Israel was stunned, and moved quickly to remedy the problem. Indonesia's currency had already collapsed from two to seven thousand against the dollar, and when President Suhapto announced that Hababli would be his deputy, the Rupiah was driven through the floor, reaching seventeen thousand against the dollar before the day was out. The resounding response was meant to send the embattled President a message to reconsider Hababli's appointment. Instead, the aging Javanese leader dismissed these attempts to thwart his own strategies, convinced that it was the Americans who were conspiring to have him removed.

The IMF teams were dismissed by the Indonesian Finance Ministry, leaving Goldstein, therefore Mossad, without any access. Of the available candidates known to Goldstein, only Hamish McLoughlin had the necessary analytical credentials, the Asian regional exposure to high-level finance and, at the same time, fitted the profile of a merchant banker. Harold Goldstein had made the appropriate calls, approached Hamish, and within the fortnight, Mossad's flow of information recommenced.

At no time did Goldstein give Hamish McLoughlin any reason to suspect that his employers were anything but bona fide merchant bankers. Their investments in Indonesia had been substantial and, prior to the recent collapse, these had been profitable. Now, with an ailing President and the reality of L.B. Hababli as his legal successor waiting in the wings, Israel's concerns grew, for it was Hababli who had arranged legislation passed the year before, paving the way for Indonesia to develop nuclear power plants, and its own supply of plutonium.

* * * *

WASHINGTON

National Security Agency

The communications intelligence analyst first recognized the increase in activity from photography obtained during the satellite's eighth crossing for that day. The Imagery Requirements Subcommittee, the interagency intelligence group which controls the movements of United States spy satellites, had been focusing on India's missile sites, concerned that they might take retaliatory measures in response to Pakistan's recent launch.

There was no doubt that the level of activity and the increase in equipment and personnel at this location warranted further investigation. The COMINT officer had searched all NSA records and remained mystified as to the purpose behind the new facilities. Following revised directives, implemented as a result of CIA and DIA reports from American posts in India, the satellite's targeting was reconfigured, placing this new site under constant surveillance.

The analyst checked the site for any detail he might have overlooked, but found nothing, confident that if the Indian Government *was* up to something there, this COMINT section would be the first to know. He removed his glasses and rubbed tired eyes, then returned to the photographs for one final examination. The captured imagery indicated nothing suspicious, and the analyst annotated these findings in his hourly log, confirming that nothing had been detected which might suggest anything alarming was taking place on the Indian subcontinent.

* * * *

Indonesia

The President

President Suhapto remained silent as he listened to each of his advisers offer their opinions in relation to the International Monetary Fund's demands. He appeared confused as to how his country could have possibly arrived at this juncture, destabilized by the growing Asian financial crisis. He had dedicated the greater part of his life to the Republic, first as a soldier fighting for its independence, and later as its President, guiding its growth, while nurturing his people.

Suhapto had little difficulty recalling the state of the nation when he took control during the bloody years of civil war. Then, the country was officially bankrupt. Inflation ran at ten percent per week, there were few imports, and foreign investment was practically non-existent. Even his military could not function. There were no spare-parts for the Soviet armaments, and little money to purchase uniforms and food for the troops. He remembered that, at the time he assumed office, his people's life expectancy was less than fifty years, and the literacy rate not much above forty percent. Now, sitting quietly listening to his advisers, Suhapto felt extremely weary, almost too tired to fight yet another battle, particularly one against an enemy he did not understand. *What had suddenly happened to his country's wealth? What had triggered these events which now threatened to destroy everything he had achieved?*

However, the country's financial crisis was not what now occupied his mind. He had become gravely concerned with his son-in-law's insistence that elements within the military were considering aborting the forthcoming session of Parliament to prevent his reappointment as President. Suhapto always knew that it would come to this; after all, there had never been a change of leadership in his country for more than a thousand years which had not been effected by violence. And now, if what young General

Praboyo had to say could be believed, then he should pre-empt those responsible, and before their initiative gained any significant support.

Praboyo had requested the audience at which time he had relayed his suspicions that the current Armed Forces Chief, Lieutenant General Fahmi Tjahadi was in complicity with several other senior ranking officers intent on thwarting the forthcoming elections. Praboyo acknowledged that he had no hard evidence, only that of rumor, but he did insist that the current Strategic Army Forces Commander had been spending an unusual amount of time with Tjahadi, the Chief of Staff. President Suhapto was aware of existing animosities; that there had been little love lost between the two men, particularly as Praboyo enjoyed a special relationship with his President. The thought had also crossed his mind as to how much trust he could really place in his ambitious son-in-law. The uncertainty could not have come at a worse time, he thought, his mind returning to the purpose for the morning session. He attempted to concentrate, but his head was still clouded with his most senior general's imminent treachery.

'*..and the IMF now confirms that, unless we adhere to the guidelines as stipulated in the draft agreement, they will be unable to provide the funds we have requested.*' The Minister finished his report, looked directly into his President's eyes, and was surprised with the initial lack of response. The *Bapak* appeared tired, he thought, wondering if the rumors relating to his health had any substance. He dismissed this thought, realizing that Indonesia seems to thrive off rumors relating to their aging President, and his family.

'*Why do you think the IMF wishes to penalize us with these cruel demands?*' Suhapto asked, amazed that an organization such as this could expect overnight solutions to his country's dilemma.

'*They have given us two weeks to commence removing these subsidies, Bapak, otherwise the first installment will not be made. Perhaps we should consider what they have asked,*' the Finance Minister suggested anxiously. The first payment of four billion dollars would not, he realized sadly, be sufficient to cover their immediate needs. The country's coffers were in desperate need of a major injection. Deep down the Minister was exasperated with his President, conscious that responsibility for the current financial crisis effectively lay with the First Family, and their excesses.

'*If we were to agree to just some of their demands?*' Suhapto asked. Those who had studied this man would agree that the former general was, indeed, a most Machiavellian creature. Although many believed that his decisions were often simplistic and lacked substance, he had managed to rule his country with an iron hand, successfully removing any resistance or opposition to his leadership.

'Then, at least, we should be able to continue our dialogue with them, Bapak. The most important issues are their demands for banking reform, and cancellation of a number of cooperative agreements.' The adviser was reluctant to be more forthright regarding the IMF demands, and their call to have the many monopolies controlled by the First Family, abolished. To suggest such action to the President would be sheer folly. He glanced around the conference room wondering how many of those present had managed to transfer their funds overseas before the most recent debacle involving the Rupiah.

His eyes came to rest on the man whose nomination as the next Vice President was responsible for that calamitous day the week before, when the exchange rate plummeted from eight thousand to the American dollar, to seventeen thousand on international markets. At that moment, the focus of his attention, Dr L.B. Hababli caught his eye and smiled, and the adviser responded, while inwardly despising the President's choice. *What on earth had swayed their leader to propose this man as his Vice President?* he postulated, knowing, as did those closest to the country's leadership, that Hababli had little experience, and was openly criticized by the military. He had no service background, and was not even Javanese.

Born in a small village near Gorontalo in Northern Sulawesi, the adviser believed it would be most unlikely that the Javanese Moslem Generals would ever permit this man to succeed as President. But then, of course, he knew that Hababli had the President's ear, and more importantly, his support. His thoughts returned to the problems at hand as Suhapto spoke.

'We should implement the order to remove subsidies on cooking oil, kerosene, and pesticides,' the President announced, surprising all present. Immediately, they all looked at each other, stunned with the decision. There was not one present who did not clearly understand the ramifications of removing subsidies on these basic commodities. *'Tell the IMF that we agree to do this. Tell the IMF also that we will consider their other requests once they have finalized their undertakings as discussed.'*

'But Bapak,' the Minister for Home Affairs appealed, *'that will send the prices of those items soaring! There's certain to be unrest if we do this.'*

'The Armed Forces must then be more alert, and take control of the situation,' was the President's response. He had made his decision, and there would be no further debate. *'We must do what is asked of us,'* he declared, rising slowly to his feet, indicating that the session was finished. He nodded, then turned and walked slowly from the room, accompanied by his adjutant, and personal assistant, leaving Cabinet Ministers and other advisers to watch his departure in silence.

Alone, resting from the demanding meeting, President Suhapto considered his decisions of the past days and nodded silently to himself, believing that his actions would circumvent any possible threat to his power and his family's wealth. He recognized that, in selecting Hababli as his choice for Vice President he had offended some within the military but in doing so, believed that he had also strengthened his own position. It would be unlikely that his opponents would have him removed as long as Hababli remained Vice President. As for the subsidies, once the IMF had completed the final installment of the forty billion dollar package, he intended reinstating the subsidies anyway.

In the interim, he accepted that there would be considerable unrest as a result of his decisions. This would keep *ABRI*, his military occupied which, in turn, would provide him with the opportunity to rethink the armed forces leadership. He knew there were rumblings amongst the senior officers; his son-in-law, Praboyo, continued to keep him informed.

As his thoughts drifted, he was reminded of an earlier era, when he too had grabbed the golden ring, and became the nation's leader. It had not been too difficult, he remembered, moving to undermine the former President's position until finally taking control on behalf of the people, knowing that he had the support of the American Government. His position as the *Kostrad* Army Strategic Forces Commander had given him the necessary strength to defeat and remove all other opposition; that, and the fact that many of his superiors had all been murdered, clearing the way for his rapid ascent. With this thought in mind, President Suhapto made his final decision for the day, deciding to reward his son-in-law for his loyalty, while further shoring up his own position in respect to the military.

The following morning the Palace announced the appointment of General Winarko as the new Chief of the Armed Forces, and the promotion of General Praboyo from the *Kopassus* Special Forces to become Commander of *Kostrad.* Foreign military observers scrambled to determine what might evolve as a result of this most recent power play, considering the ramifications of Praboyo's appointment to the powerful Strategic Forces as its commander.

When the new line-up was announced, the President's tactics became clear. He had promoted his outgoing Chief of Staff to a more senior, political post, one which distanced the suspect officer from any direct control over troops. Foreign military attaches were caught off-guard, having little information regarding the new Chief of Staff, Lieutenant General Winarko. Within hours, the handsome Javanese General's photograph was flashed around the world and, before evening fell, details of his service records were already well known to most foreign governments. The surprise announcements prompted rumors within political circles that the President was strengthening the First Family's support base in preparation for his reappointment, and in so doing, had again demonstrated his gift as a masterful tactician.

Chapter Eight

JAKARTA - APRIL 1998

Hani Purwadira

Hani showed mock distaste when her girlfriend pointed to a group of male students and pulled playfully on her arm, encouraging Hani to follow.

'Don't be childish!' Hani pouted, her resistance obviously feigned.

'Come on Hani, let's see who they're talking about,' Wanti pleaded, recognizing one of the young undergraduates gathered nearby, laughing at some anecdote. As the girls approached, the boys turned and welcomed them. Wanti moved directly to the side of a tall Sumatran lad who smiled awkwardly, obviously embarrassed by her attention. Although the students were all of a similar age, the girls' advanced maturity placed them well ahead of their counterparts.

'What's the gossip?' Wanti asked, in her typical forward manner. Hani remained silent, clutching several textbooks to her chest. Realizing that she stood so momentarily annoyed the smaller student, recognizing that she had developed this habit whenever alongside Wanti and her well-formed breasts.

'No gossip, just organizing next week's rally,' an older boy responded. He eyed Hani closely, pleased with what he saw.

'What will you be demonstrating for this time?' Wanti asked, not really all that interested, but pleased to be amongst the boys.

'We are going to express our dissatisfaction with the government's removal of subsidies,' said another. *'Will you support our demonstration?'*

Hani remembered her father's instructions and immediately regretted having joined the group. He had been quite explicit, warning her not to become involved in campus political activities. The most recent outbreak of riots had been efficiently, and brutally suppressed within days. As helicopters maintained their vigilance in the capital's sky overhead reminding the students that the Minister for Education's warning prohibited students from demonstrating off-campus, rumors claiming that some of their number had disappeared, spread quickly.

Hani knew many of the student activists and accepted that it was important that she not become involved, remembering her father's insistence that she avoid any such participation. Hani was tempted to join with her friends, but obeyed, albeit reluctantly. The general's suggestion that the penalty for non-compliance would result in her returning to Sukabumi, prompted Hani to swear that she would obey his command.

Prior to *Kolonel Purwadira* relocating his family from the provincial mountain city of Sukabumi to the capital where he would assume his new post as the Jakarta Garrison Police Commander, the West Javanese-born officer discussed the city's political environment at length with his wife and three children, extracting undertakings from all that they were to adhere strictly to the code of behavior expected of those associated with the senior position he had accepted. Upon their arrival, Hani's father was promoted to Brigadier General in line with others holding similar positions throughout the Police and Armed Forces. As members of the military elite, opportunities previously considered unachievable suddenly became a reality, to the delight of all.

It was considered mandatory for their mother, *Ibu* Purwadira to participate in activities directed under the auspices of the Police Women's Foundation. There, she learned, the bulk of all finances which flowed from non-taxable collections and generated by the Foundation's commercial activities were directed to the senior officers and their families, to supplement the relatively meager salaries provided by the government. The family easily settled in to their new life style, and the children were placed in the best schools. When Hani learned that she would be attending the *Uber Sakti University*, she was ecstatic, fulfilling her dream to attend such a respected institution. Before her father's promotion, such a possibility would never have entered her mind.

Her thoughts were interrupted by Wanti, returning her to the moment.

'What do you say, Hani, are you game?'

'When will this take place?' she asked, knowing full well when it would be. She had to find a way out, without appearing to be non-supportive.

'Next week,' the Sumatran student jumped in. *'Come on, Hani, why don't you join in for once?'* Sensing she was trapped, Hani elected to leave before saying something she could not later retract.

'If I can find time then,' she promised.

'Hani, are you sure?' Wanti shrieked.

'Catch you later, Wanti,' was all she said, smiling at her closest friend while strolling away, nonchalantly.

Although conscious of her father's instructions regarding such student political assemblies, Hani was, nevertheless, tempted. It seemed that she was the only one in her group who had not participated at least once, in the on-campus demonstrations. She regretted having raised the matter with her mother, whose resulting tirade had continued for days. Since then, *Ibu* Purwadira had warned her again and again, not to be so foolish, such reminders now dreary and tiresome.

Hani was annoyed with her mother's treatment, and her bossy behavior. *Didn't she recognize that her daughter was no longer a child? Of course she would not jeopardize her father's career!* Hani frowned, thoughtfully, recalling her most recent scolding. Her mother's demeanor had changed since their move from Sukabumi, and Hani felt that she had borne the brunt of her transformation from an unknown district policeman's wife, to darling of the Indonesian police hierarchy's social set.

Her father had warned Hani of the secret military intelligence presence on campus, whose agents had been tasked to monitor student activities. And the General was certainly in a position to know. As Garrison Commander, it was his responsibility to coordinate many of these covert activities. As she walked casually away from the boys the thought crossed her mind that even a group such as this could easily have been infiltrated by such elements. Uneasy with this possibility, Hani hurried off to prepare for her next lecture, knowing that Wanti would catch up before returning home that day.

* * * *

Lily

Lily Suryajaya listened attentively as the lecture came to a close. Satisfied that she had managed to make notes of the more salient points mentioned, Lily gently closed her book and looked around the small hall, wondering just how many of those present would be able to find employment, once they had graduated. She expected that those of Chinese extraction would be employed by family associated businesses. Lily believed this to be only fair; the families carried the burden of financing their children's education, and would expect to benefit in some material way, in return.

Lily wished she had been closer to her uncle. She knew that the value of a local degree would not be considered on a par with those obtained by studying overseas. She was aware that many of the students present would not have been accepted had the college staff not been coerced, either by direct pressure, or the customary envelope containing some thousands of dollars. She knew that without her father's influence, Hani Purwadira would not be in attendance.

Childish giggling from one corner momentarily distracted Lily, and she observed a number of girls engrossed in conversation with the Police Chief's popular daughter. She caught Hani's eye and smiled, but the general's daughter looked straight through her. Lily knew that she was deliberately being ignored and, although this stung, she understood why. Over the past few months the social and political climate had changed.

Racial discrimination was not all that evident on campus, as there was a modicum of social integration between the students. It would have been difficult for this not to have been so, with more than thirty, quite separate ethnic groups represented within the student body. Lily had never really understood why, in a country as diverse as Indonesia, the collective indigenous feeling was to stigmatize the Chinese for what came naturally to them as a race.

Lily accepted that her goals may be different to those of Hani, Wanti, and her other *pribumi* friends. She knew that, unlike their Chinese counterparts, only a few of their number would go on to enter the workforce, most marrying before completing their studies and starting families while she, on the other hand, would be building her career, and searching for ways to contribute to her family's welfare. She knew that her physical needs were no less different than Hani or her friends, it was just that Lily had decided to be more responsible in addressing these feelings. She recalled how the boys back in her home town would often quip, suggesting within earshot, that Chinese girls were different sexually. Lily could not understand why they acted so, and why young men would wish to perpetuate such myths.

Lily accepted that her relationship with Hani had been instigated at the request of her uncle, and Hani's influential father, the Brigadier General, but she was saddened that their friendship did not extend to her being included amongst Hani's campus friends. As a young, determined, Chinese woman, she had learned to accommodate disappointment. Nevertheless Lily still enjoyed the attractive West Javanese girl's vibrant company, and looked forward to her next visit, during which, Lily would teach the other girl how to swim.

Their association had evolved as a result of her uncle's suggestion that Lily encourage the General's daughter to visit their apartment, and take advantage of the condominium's excellent facilities. Unbeknown to Lily, Hani had only accepted these invitations to visit the Chinese student in her uncle's luxurious surrounds, under pressure from her father. It seemed that the two men's mutual interests could be served by strengthening these ties socially. Hani, however, had never invited Lily to visit the Purwadira home.

Hani's visits began to have meaning for Lily, even though she quietly acknowledged that their relationship had been built on their families' needs, and might not be all that permanent. For Lily's uncle was a *cukong*, a Chinese middle-man and broker to those influential in government and the military.

Even as a child, Lily was raised to understand the value Chinese placed on such relationships for, without these, their safety would remain under threat by those who envied their race's pragmatic determination, and economic success. She had been taught to remain subservient to the greater number and nurture friendships should these be offered. In her home town of Situbondo, Lily had spent most of her spare hours assisting her parents in their store, as was the norm with others of her ethnic background. She worked, and when not gainfully occupied helping her family, Lily studied. There just never seemed to be any spare time to play.

When the opportunity arose for her to study in Jakarta, she had gratefully accepted her uncle's kind offer, and now repaid his gesture by studying hard and behaving well, to show that she was worthy. Lily respected her aunt and uncle, as if they were her own parents.

Lily often overheard snippets of conversations referring to the old Chinatown office where her uncle still maintained his core activities of money-lending and influence peddling. Her uncle, *Oom Setio*, was in no way rich by Jakarta Chinese standards, although in Western terms, he could be considered so.

His wealth had been slowly accumulated over three decades, his first opportunity arising from his association with an earlier Metropolitan Chief of Police. The general's appetites far exceeded his salary, placing him at the head of a long list of corrupt government officials and officers who made their way to *Oom Setio's* unimpressive shop in Kota, the capital's Chinatown. There, they would find the tallish, almost obese Buddha-shaped man sitting behind an undersized desk, the *cukong* dressed in pajama trousers, his upper torso covered only with a singlet.

It was in these deceivingly austere surroundings that *Oom Setio* had dispensed considerable amounts of money in exchange for favors, contracts, and the occasional falsified document to permit one of his more recently arrived colleagues to legally remain. His was a respectable profession amongst the Chinese, and as such, the *cukongs* never once questioned the ethics of effecting bribes, as these helped relieve the moral responsibility of doing business in a corrupt environment. Setio maintained this facade of near poverty until changing times required that he at least dress to conform with his peers who, as was the practice amongst the emerging *cukong* class, preferred to travel to Singapore or even Hong Kong to display their wealth in more receptive environments.

Before President Suhapto's presidency had entered its third term *Oom Setio*, and many of his race and class, had achieved considerable wealth, and in so doing, established strong lines of communication with those in power, whose own fortunes were derived from this comfortable association. Lily, as did most Indonesian Chinese, clearly understood the necessity for these arrangements to remain intact as, apart from the enormous riches generated, there was an unspoken undertaking that as long as the *status quo* remained, the Chinese would not have to fear for their safety.

Lily had learned, that subsequent to the horrors of the Sixties' *Years of Living Dangerously* when all Chinese had been irrationally targeted by indigenous Indonesians, subsequent generations had enjoyed a radically changed political and social climate, one which even witnessed the country's First Family develop close commercial and social ties with Indonesians of Chinese extraction.

Lily admitted that as each generation had broken new ground, so too, it seemed, that many of the younger Chinese developed an air of superiority and quiet arrogance towards their less fortunate fellow-countrymen. Over the past months, racial tensions had re-ignited as the gap between wealthy and poor widened dramatically. Even the language changed. New, and even more derogatory racial terms evolved as the seeds of envy grew, threatening another harvest not dissimilar to the devastating race-related riots of earlier years. Incredibly, neither indigenous nor the Indonesians of Chinese extraction were conscious of the growing similarities between current trends, and those which had precipitated earlier racial confrontations.

As Indonesia exploded into a *Nirvana* of commercial opportunities, the bonds between the forever-patient Chinese and influential officials strengthened, removing any suggestion that all was not well. When the Year of the Tiger entered, dragging the world through the first quarter of

1998, Indonesia boasted tens of thousands of millionaires, most of whom were Jakarta residents of Chinese extraction. Lily often listened quietly, as *Oom Setio* quite openly discussed his affairs with members of his family. She had never asked but was reasonably confident, that her uncle's wealth would be in excess of ten million dollars, if not more. Lily calculated that given the value of the properties she knew he owned, if they were to be sold, *Oom Setio* would have a handsome sum of money indeed, to disperse amongst his family and relatives.

Lily knew that it would be most unlikely that she would ever become a beneficiary of her uncle's wealth. She was just grateful for the food and shelter he had afforded her, and the opportunity to attend the Uber Sakti University which, she also knew, had required *Oom Setio's* direct intervention to ensure her acceptance. All but one of his children had been sent overseas to complete their schooling. The remaining child, Layla, had recently turned twelve and attended the Ora Et Labora school in Kebayoran. She would be expected to follow her brothers and sisters to Australia, or America to attend university, when the time arrived.

Lily's thoughts returned to her friend Hani, who had finally agreed to join her for a swim in the condominium pool. At first, Lily had assumed that Hani's reluctance to take advantage of the luxurious setting was due to her not wishing to be seen in public together. She had wanted to say that this would not represent a problem as the entire apartment block was owned, and occupied, by Chinese. Later, Lily was to learn that Hani had mainly been deterred because she was not an experienced swimmer, and did not wish to appear foolish in front of the others. Also, Hani had complained, the sun was far too hot and she really did not wish her fine, light-brown skin to darken like some peasant girl. Lily had suggested an early evening swim and, after some deliberation, Hani had accepted.

* * * *

Hani's Father

Hani's father, Brigadier General Purwadira had not found it necessary to trek down to any *cukong's* lair for, in this day and age, the *Oom Setios* of the world had moved into a new era, one in which they now dressed in expensively tailored suits, and were driven directly to the senior military officers' headquarters in highly polished Mercedes without any fear of recrimination. In his position as Jakarta Garrison Commander, the General most certainly would never have considered it a requirement of his post, that he resort to asking any of the Chinese directly for favors. To the contrary, it was *he* who expected that these brokers and middlemen approach him, as had been the accepted behavior over more recent years.

The General's thoughts moved to his family and, for a brief moment, he became troubled recalling the warning he had given his daughter, Hani. He was tempted to send her back to Sukabumi where she could remain with her aunt until the current troubles were resolved. She would be safe there, as student activity had been easily contained by the resident military forces and, he knew, the local students just did not have the same fire in their hearts as was evident on Jakarta campuses.

General Purwadira opened the top drawer to his oversized, highly polished teak desk and extracted a *kretek* cigarette from its packet. He lit the clove-scented cigarette and drew heavily filling his tarred lungs, enjoying the warming sensation as the smoke relaxed his mind, removing some of the mounting tension which had threatened to ruin his day.

His eyes fell back to the disturbing reports which lay scattered across his desk. Annoyed that the responsibility for investigating the kidnappings had fallen upon his shoulders when he knew that those responsible were shielded by the President's own son-in-law, he cursed the former Javanese *Kopassus* Commander, convinced that the missing students had been Praboyo's handiwork.

Eleven more families had filed missing-person's reports at police stations within his jurisdiction. Purwadira counted silently, placing the number of students who had suddenly disappeared from their universities over the past six weeks, at around thirty-five. *Where in the hell was Praboyo's Special team hiding these youngsters?* he worried, concerned also with the possibility that they could be dead, their bodies buried somewhere within the heavily-wooded areas behind the Special Forces Command Headquarters.

The growing number of missing students had not gone unnoticed by the Press, and although the police general had few concerns as what the domestic press might print, he was particularly worried with what might appear in the international papers. Reminded that he had agreed to an interview, General Purwadira called his personal assistant and instructed the officer to postpone the meeting until the following day, apologizing to the foreign journalist that he had been summoned to the Palace, and would not be able to meet that day, as earlier agreed.

Satisfied that this was a sensible decision to make, the Jakarta Garrison Commander then ordered his aide to contact his golfing partner, *Oom Setio*, and inform him that he would tee off at two o'clock at the

Kuningan Golf Club. He then left his headquarters, his spirits lifted with the thought of beating the Chinese yet again at his favorite game. Within minutes of the general's vehicle leaving the garrison compound, he had all but dismissed the startling information contained in that morning's daily report, accepting that it would be foolish of any career officer to even consider taking the matter any further for fear of revealing those behind the student kidnappings.

Pleased to have put the problem behind him, General Purwadira later settled down to play eighteen holes of golf. His handicap was in no way impaired by the knowledge that, somewhere, and in all likelihood in a place not too far away from where he played that day, the bodies of those missing students whose names had been brought to his attention would be gone forever, buried in unmarked graves.

* * * *

Mary Jo & Hamish

Mary Jo received the news with indifference, having half-expected her interview with the police general to be postponed. It had happened before, and the American journalist had soon learned to accept that either Indonesian 'rubber-time', or some fabricated excuse would result in most of her appointments being derailed. At first, she found it extremely irritating. Now, after several months, Jo had assimilated somewhat to local practices, never really confident of achieving those interviews she so desperately needed until actually sitting face-to-face with her subject. General Purwadira's typical last-minute cancellation had left her with a hole in her day, and when she received the phone call, the afternoon suddenly brightened.

'Feel like a few drinks, perhaps a swim around the pool?' Hamish McLoughlin's now familiar voice invited. He had phoned regularly since returning to Hong Kong, promising to provide her with details relating to the Perentie collapse. She was flattered by his frequent calls, and although they had met only once, Mary Jo was delighted that he had returned to Jakarta.

'As it so happens, I'm available,' she accepted. Mary Jo's response had little to do with her professional activities. Life in Jakarta, even with its socially active expatriate community, had its downside for single foreign women. Particularly if that person was associated with the Western Press, for business circles avoided mixing with members of the Fourth Estate, concerned that their companies' activities might be jeopardized should they be at any time mentioned in the foreign media. All accepted that the Indonesian Government was most uncompromising in its attitude towards journalists, particularly those associated with Australian newspapers.

'Great, Jo, I'll wait for you pool-side. We can have a late lunch.'

'Be there in less than an hour,' she promised, with some alacrity, quickly changing into her white, two-piece bikini, before wrapping a brightly colored rayon sarong around her waist. Mary Jo checked her makeup, placed her sunglasses inside her handbag and left a note for her assistant with the servants. She located a pair of open-leather casuals buried deep inside the walk-in robes and slipped these on, standing before her bedroom dressing mirror for one final inspection. Then she hurried outside to the waiting taxi her guard had hailed, and instructed the driver to take her downtown to the Grand Hyatt Hotel where Hamish McLoughlin waited.

As they drove through Kemang and into Kebayoran Baru, Mary Jo's trained eye identified the increased presence of troops around these two suburbs. Armed Personnel Carriers were positioned at strategic intersections, and they passed numerous truckloads of soldiers dressed in full battle-dress as the taxi continued towards the city, where further evidence of the military build-up became evident.

Commencing from where the statue expatriates irreverently named Hot Plate Harry threatened to leap from the roundabout, Mary Jo witnessed a growing number of people gathering as she continued towards the city's centre. She searched for signs of student participation but saw none. Mary Jo could see from their solemn faces and raised, angry fists, that the crowd had become belligerent, and she became concerned as the traffic slowed to a crawl, the road ahead partially blocked by the mass of people. Her driver turned, his face covered with concern.

'It will be all right, miss,' he attempted to assure her, unconvincingly. Suddenly someone banged the side of the taxi, scaring the hell out of her as she turned, fighting the growing panic when she discovered that the road behind had been smothered with pedestrians. Another loud hammering towards the rear of the vehicle alarmed her even further, and she could see from the driver's wide eyes that they were in extreme danger, caught in the centre of an evolving demonstration.

An angry fist hit the window closest to her face threatening to shatter the safety glass, the force of the blow sufficient to send fear through their hearts as others joined in the attack. Brought to a standstill, vehicles ahead and those caught in adjacent lanes were not spared, as the mob grabbed whatever they could for leverage and rocked the cars from side to side, the passengers too terrified to leave the relative safety of their sedans.

Suddenly, Mary Jo heard the crowd cheer, and she caught a brief glimpse of a Toyota's tires as the demonstrators successfully turned the Japanese vehicle on its side. In that moment, fear drove her to open the door and run, but she could not, completely at a loss as to why her door would not open. Fortunately, it was locked. She had unconsciously engaged the lock when entering the taxi earlier, a habit she had developed while living in New York. As her panic grew and she yelled at the driver to assist, the air cracked loudly, and Mary Jo instinctively threw herself across the seat, recognizing the sounds of automatic weapon-fire.

The crowd roared and turned to flee in panic. Police armed with riot gear appeared, swinging batons indiscriminately as another round of shots was fired above the retreating crowd. Amazingly, within seconds the road ahead appeared devoid of troublemakers, the remaining undamaged vehicles taking advantage of the lull to flee before the opportunity was lost. Mary Jo's driver did not hesitate, driving his own gas pedal to the floor, sending their taxi sliding into the wrecked Toyota ahead. Even the wailing screams of metal tearing against metal could not discourage the man to slow down, his passenger now just as terrified as before.

'For god's sake!' she yelled, still attempting to recover her balance as the car slid dangerously. 'I said, slow down!' she screamed, this time with some effect, as the driver eased his foot from the accelerator a fraction. Mary Jo cried out again, relieved when the terrified man obeyed and only just in time to negotiate the entrance to the Grand Hyatt hotel. Incredibly, the taxi then stalled inside the driveway.

Shaking from her ordeal, Mary Jo leaped from the damaged car and stood, fumbling inside here purse for the fare. The driver lowered his eyes when she offered payment, gratefully pocketing the money as she entered the hotel and disappeared from view.

Inside the magnificently appointed hotel, Mary Jo slowly climbed the stairs leading up to the Fountain Lounge on the mezzanine level. There, unnoticed by the other guests, she dropped into a chair and examined her unsteady hands, immediately wishing she hadn't given up smoking. Although this was not the first time Mary Jo had been exposed to danger, accepting that her profession would require some risk, the events of the past minutes had badly shaken her. A waiter fussed, but she merely smiled and shook her head when he offered her refreshments.

The view to the street was partially blocked by a number of excited guests and, having regained her composure, Mary Jo moved to a more commanding position. She stood there amidst the others, observing rows of anti-riot police marching in close formation towards a number of demonstrators who had foolishly failed to flee. Armed only with rocks, they were no match for the well-trained police. Reinforced by a number of armed personnel carriers, she watched in silence as the Jakarta Garrison troops appeared, running past the lines of police, their protective shields, helmets and uniforms reminiscent of costumes from some science fiction epic.

Mary Jo remained standing there watching as the violence continued, annoyed at having left her cameras at home. In one final bloody clash, it was all over, the remaining demonstrators easily subdued by the troops. These consolidated their position, kicking and punching civilians who had fallen injured to the street. As the troops continued to deal with these citizens directly in view of the astonished hotel guests, another detail of soldiers appeared and dragged the unconscious victims away. An air of disbelief hung heavily amongst the guests, shocked by the brutal display. Slowly, they moved back to their tables as light, classical music accompanied their chatter, the guests too excited to even consider the dessert buffet and *a la carte* snacks for which this well frequented lounge was so renowned.

Mary Jo decided that as the troops had secured the area within view, there was little point remaining in the lounge although, in the distance, she could still see evidence of the unrest as isolated columns of smoke appeared to the north. Still disappointed at having missed an excellent photo opportunity, she left the lounge and made her way outside, to the lagoon-styled swimming pool. There, she found Hamish McLoughlin sitting amongst the lush tropical garden setting, enjoying a drink at the swim-up bar, as if oblivious to the sporadic gunfire and sirens on the streets below. She waved, removed her wrap-around skirt, and placed this over her handbag. Then she casually entered the pool and swam over to where he was sitting.

'Thought you might have changed your mind,' he greeted her. Mary Jo detected surprise in his voice.

'Did you miss the excitement?' she asked, astonished that he seemed not at all disturbed by the riots. Hamish grinned, his eyes shielded by sunglasses.

'No, not entirely,' he replied, 'the view from up there is quite something.' He pointed to the hotel's upper levels. 'Once it started, I tried to phone but you had already left. In truth, I expected you'd turn around once you realized what was happening.' Mary Jo could see that he was not being critical.

'It was ugly,' was all she could muster, alerting her companion to her distress. She forced a smile, then ordered a Bloody Mary, pleased that he hadn't pressed. 'Tell you about it later,' she promised, beginning to relax in the warm, tropical setting. She accepted the cocktail, removed the straw from her glass and finished the vodka and tomato juice in one attempt. Hamish nodded to the bartender and placed his hand on Mary Jo's lightly tanned shoulder.

'Hungry?' he asked, realizing that she was upset. He removed his sunglasses and placed these on the tiled bar.

'I wasn't but too many of these on an empty stomach might not be such a good idea,' she said, grateful for his company. 'Are we eating here?' she looked around the delightful setting, content to remain in the relaxed atmosphere.

'Why don't we grab something light now, and save ourselves for dinner?' he suggested, assuming Jo would want to stay. 'Your choice. Tonight you may have Japanese, Cantonese, seafood, or whatever you like.' She looked at Hamish and raised one eyebrow, the alcohol's soothing effects beginning to flow through her body.

'Sure, why not,' she smiled, not overly anxious to return to her villa. Not, at least, until she had recovered from her journey into the city. The bartender offered them menus and they ordered sandwiches, requesting that these be served under one of the thatched-roofed structures set back from the pool, out of the sun's punishing rays. After they had finished eating, the afternoon became unusually quiet and they lay back and relaxed, the absence of further violence on the streets below, reassuring.

'What really brings you back to Jakarta, Hamish?' Mary Jo asked. The last time they had spoken it seemed that he was still preoccupied with the mess created by the Perentie collapse.

'Well, I decided to escape Hong Kong for awhile. Although I was not really associated with the group apart from the occasional consulting exercise, I found it impossible to conduct any business while the stigma of Perentie's collapse remained. Most of Asia is suffering right now and I just thought I'd come down here for a few months and see what opportunities might come along.'

'Opportunities? Here?' she challenged. Hamish McLoughlin nodded, sitting upright to stretch. He did not want to be evasive. It was just more convenient for him not to divulge his association with the Geneva merchant bankers. Besides, the confidentiality clause had precluded his discussing his work with those not directly associated with their investments. He had to be discreet. There were huge amounts of capital at risk and he was determined not to test Mary Jo's integrity, nor place her in a position where she might be influenced by his activities.

'The Indonesian stock market has fallen to incredible lows, Jo,' he started to explain, 'and this, in reality, means that the stock of those companies whose operations are still viable are undervalued. When the Rupiah collapsed, shares in all of the companies listed on the Jakarta Exchange were being traded for as little as twenty-five cents in the dollar. God,' he continued, 'theoretically, the market here is bankrupt. It's shed more than seventy-five billion dollars over the past six months!'

'But won't most of these companies now collapse without capital, and the huge foreign currency debts they have on their books?' she asked.

'No, I don't believe so, Jo. Some of these have sound dollar incomes. Their shares have been dragged down with all the others, and this just might be the time to buy.' She wasn't convinced, and he could see this from her expression.

'But the political climate.....' she argued, leaving the statement hanging.

'Sure, I agree. That's one of the reasons I'm here. There's no rush,' he said, 'I'm not jumping in until I see how the government handles their current problems. And I mean the social unrest, not just the financial difficulties they have on their hands.' He lay back on the sponge-filled mattress, adjusting his sunglasses as he did so.

'So, you're going to be around for awhile, then,' Mary Jo stated, not unhappy with this prospect. She admitted that she was attracted to him, and was relaxed about seeing where this would lead. These few hours together had been remedial for her, conscious of just how long it had been since she had really felt this comfortable with a man.

'Well, at least until I wear out my welcome,' he joked.

'Good,' she said, releasing her skirt, revealing the bikini again. 'Then you can invite me down here anytime,' with which, she hurried across the hot surface and lunged into the blue water, her attractive figure followed by appreciative glances from a number of onlookers. She swam around the oddly-shaped pool for several minutes then stood on her toes and waved. Hamish strolled over to the water's edge, and dived in.

'Macho man!' she teased, referring to the hot tiled surface.

'Didn't feel a thing,' he laughed, swimming up to her. 'Hey, you're quite a swimmer.' He had observed her strokes and decided that she'd had coaching sometime in her past. They stood together, savoring the moment.

'I really enjoy the water,' Mary Jo replied, 'but I couldn't swim a stroke until I was nineteen. It was far too cold most of the time.' Hamish suddenly realized just how little he knew about this woman, and reached out for her hand under the sparkling water. She accepted the gesture, squeezing his hand in response. Droplets of water ran down her forehead and Hamish wiped these gently away before they reached her eyes.

They stood facing each other, and he eased closer, waiting for her to respond. Mary Jo hesitated, raised herself on tiptoe and kissed him softly, then pushed away playfully as she dived under the water to escape. Hamish followed, easily catching up with his powerful strokes. They swam together for a few more minutes, then climbed out of the pool, neither speaking as they toweled themselves down. Mary Jo ran a comb briefly through her wet hair, after which she wrapped the sarong around her waist, covering the wet bikini. She slipped into her casuals and stood waiting for Hamish to sign the check, offering her arm as he led her away from the pool, and upstairs to his suite via the dedicated lift.

They entered the room, greeted by the noiseless flow of chilled air and, as he closed the door, Mary Jo moved immediately to the bathroom to remove her wet costume. She reappeared moments later, and walked softly towards where Hamish prepared their drinks. She reached up, slowly, pulling at the thick, towel-cloth gown covering his shoulders and he turned, momentarily catching his breath as the sight of her naked body came into view. He permitted her hands to roam, finding, then releasing the loosely tied cord around his waist. Her cold hands moved inside the gown, and slowly around his warm body, stroking the curvature of his back sensuously before slipping down to release his wet swimmers. Already aroused, he tugged impatiently to assist, and as these fell to the floor Hamish wrapped his arms firmly around her, pulling Mary Jo hungrily towards him.

Their mouths met, the warmth of her tongue sending urgent, pulsating messages through his body and he groaned as her hand found the under side of his erection and stroked gently.

Mary Jo pulled back slightly, permitting his hands to find her breasts and, when he bent down to kiss her soft, pink, erect nipples she took his hand, then guided his fingers down, over her firm stomach, continuing on their path until he found the soft, moist mound and she involuntarily shuddered.

They kneeled, still locked together in embrace, and Hamish leaned forward, holding Mary Jo as he lowered her gently to the carpet, her hands guiding as he entered the warmth of her eager body. She groaned, loudly, as he thrust forward filling her completely, his senses afire as blood rushed through his groin, driving him faster and faster. As their bodies slapped together, their excitement achieving almost unsustainable levels Hamish held her tightly, and rolled onto his back, knowing this would heighten her pleasure.

Immediately, the tempo changed with Mary Jo accepting the dominating position. She pushed forward, fiercely, then gasped, rocking away only to thrust forward again, her partner's hardness driving her uncontrollably. He raised his hips in concert to meet hers, their momentum growing, the warm swell inside rising, spreading through their entire bodies until Mary Jo suddenly cried out, loudly, as muscular spasms inside erupted, driving rolling, orgasmic waves in their path. She cried out, again, her moment of ecstasy prolonged by her partner's climax exploding deep inside, and Mary Jo felt him shudder, then groan, as the warm release flowed into her.

Moments passed, then she leaned forward, her legs clasped together inside his. She raised her head, and they kissed, tenderly, their bodies still floating, captured by the moment. They remained locked together, exhausted but complete, finally surrendering their bodies to sleep. In the hour that followed, night descended. The chill of the air-conditioned room brought them alive, sending both shivering to the king-size bed. They climbed in between the sheets and held each other tenderly, finding warmth, their body scent still tantalizingly fresh in each other's minds. Their hands roamed, softly, touching, and they kissed, their bodies reacting to the sensual messages until they coupled, their love making this time less frenzied than before. Then they slept.

When Mary Joe finally awoke, it was still dark outside. She looked across at the man beside her and decided that she had desperately needed this interlude. She lay contentedly, looking out through the plate-glass window across the Jakarta skyline wondering what the future would bring. Then, recognizing that this would be an ideal opportunity to return to her villa, she dressed, then quietly slipped away, returning home by taxi through the capital's unusually deserted, early morning streets.

Chapter Nine

WASHINGTON - MAY

Early morning showers had cleared, the soft, summer's day welcomed by the capital's residents as they prepared for the weekend. But there would be no respite for the Administration's senior officers as they monitored events on the other side of the globe, events which now carried the promise of a bloodless transition of power to their nominated successor.

'General Winarko is handling the situation well, Admiral,' the less senior officer advised. 'We talked at some length. I have passed the Joint Chiefs' assurances to him, and we have agreed to meet for a few hours during my visit to Singapore this week.'

'What about President Suhapto?' Admiral Brown asked.

'Winarko feels that the old man is desperate to hold on, looking for alternate solutions to remain in power. It's going to come to a head within days, he said. I explained that we are all hoping for a bloodless transition and he gave me his undertaking that it would be so.'

'When?' the Chairman of the Joint Chiefs of Staff asked, impatiently.

'Tomorrow, perhaps the day after,' the senior naval officer replied, then added, 'but no later than Friday.' Both U.S. officers then briefly discussed the deployment of the Seventh Fleet and the ships which had been sent to Indonesia to standby in the event American citizens were to be repatriated.

Admiral Colin Brown replaced the receiver and considered the import of his discussion with Admiral Barnett, CINCPAC. It was most fortunate, indeed, that the Commander in Chief of the U.S. Pacific forces had been on a first name basis with General Winarko for some years. The quietly spoken Javanese officer had given his word and the Admiral was inclined to accept the man's assurances that there would be no military coup, that the transition would be effected on a constitutional basis. Brown reflected on the CINCPAC's almost cynical comment. It seemed more than a little ironic that the man whose nomination as Vice President precipitated the single worst trading day on Asian markets in recent history, was now to become Indonesia's interim President. But how long will he be able to hold on?

Admiral Brown then instructed his assistant to patch him through to John W. Peterson, Director of the CIA. Several minutes passed and they were connected, the Admiral first relaying details of General Winarko's conversation before waiting for the CIA Director's response.

He listened, the intelligence chief's voice devoid of emotion as he disagreed with Admiral Barnett's assessment of the Indonesian situation, intimating that another initiative had already commenced, one which was supported by the CIA. Admiral Brown's white knuckles gripped the handset firmly, the only evidence of his disguised anger. Their conversation over, the Chairman of the Joint Chiefs of Staff sat ruminating, then suddenly slammed his fist down hard on his desk, causing his personal assistant to rush into his office.

Admiral Brown glared at the officer. Then, observing the young woman's surprised expression, attempted a weak smile and waved her away. Then he returned to the confusing situation at hand, his anger with the CIA's involvement in no way diminished as he considered the ramifications of the United States Government backing an Indonesian Palace coup, led by the abrasive, and arrogant General Praboyo.

* * * *

INDIA

The Western Desert

Bandopadhaya checked his watch, then hurried back to his four-wheel drive anxious to return to the village before the eastern sky filled with the sun's first rays. But it was not the threat of the dry, debilitating heat which prompted this haste, but fear of discovery.

'It's clear,' he reassured the man sitting in the back, then jumped into the vehicle and barked at his driver, 'Go!'

The soldier did not hesitate, slamming his foot down hard, throwing a trail of sand behind as the wheels finally took hold, carrying the Israeli scientist and his security officer away from the nuclear site, and the scrutiny of the incredibly powerful American spy satellite's lens as these passed by regularly, overhead.

'I can't believe that they still don't know,' Bandopadhaya shouted above the engine's whining noise. The Israeli remained silent, not wishing to be jinxed by stating the obvious. He knew that they had been extremely lucky. His team's suggestion to create the diversion might have been successful, he thought, but every spy satellite roaming the heavens would soon be directed to these dry, arid plains, searching for their secrets. He hoped that he and the other Israelis would be long gone before detection could occur.

They approached the village and were stopped by heavily armed soldiers. Satisfied with their identification they were permitted to pass and enter the temporary shelters erected and dismantled with each new day. There, under the waning cover of darkness they gathered the remainder of their equipment, then climbed aboard the helicopters which would take them back to their main station.

Bandopadhaya clung to the overhead grip as the heavy Sikorsky 58-T lifted slowly, wallowing above the ground as its slow-whirling blades chopped through the early morning air sandblasting everything in their wake. He caught a brief glimpse of the jeep's headlights as the driver accelerated away, leaving nothing behind which might attract unwanted interest from the prying eyes above.

Two hours later the team landed and the scientist hurried into the briefing room, where a gathering of senior Indian officials waited nervously.

'Good morning, Mr. Prime Minister,' he said, wincing as he smiled. The dry desert conditions had sucked the moisture from his skin, leaving his lips cracked and swollen.

'Good morning,' the Hindu leader responded. 'Are we ready?' The Israeli scientist's blue, cutting eyes looked directly at the powerful figure and nodded.

'They're ready,' he said, and those gathered broke into a thunderous cheer.

* * * *

Jakarta

Mary Jo & Hamish

Mary Jo had been alerted to the city's deteriorating situation when, just before three in the morning, she had taken a call from New York. Cursing her office for not having allocated sufficient funding for her own car and driver, she found herself at the mercy of the unreliable taxi service once again. Unable to coax any to her villa, she had finally resorted to waking Hamish McLoughlin at his hotel and asked his assistance. He had accompanied the nervous hotel driver to the outer suburb and waited while Mary Jo and Anne loaded additional gear to avoid having to return. They then left for the hotel with Hamish, driving past truckloads of soldiers who poured into the burning city to reinforce the Jakarta garrison.

The two women waited for daylight, by which time they were able to persuade one of the hotel staff to rent them his Honda, Mary Jo not caring how ridiculous she may have appeared as the smaller Anne steered the motorcycle away from the luxurious hotel. They followed the billowing clouds of dark, ominous smoke, visiting the sites of more than a dozen buildings guttered by fire, twice falling from their motorbike as rioting mobs and looters filled the streets.

By late-afternoon, exhausted and emotionally drained, Mary Jo and Anne dragged their tired limbs back the three kilometers from their last site to where the military had barricaded the road, forcing them to cover the remaining distance on foot. They returned to the hotel where Mary Jo paid the unhappy Honda's owner an additional fifty dollars for the minor damage incurred as a result of their falls. She deposited Anne in the coffee shop and, ignoring stares from the other guests, made her way up to the Regency levels, and to Hamish's suite. He poured her a vodka, and they sat together, Mary Jo finding the opportunity somewhat therapeutic as she described the horrors still fresh in her mind.

'My god, Hamish,' her voice trembled, 'there were more than two hundred bodies inside.'

Hamish took her hands and held them comfortingly. 'Who were they?' he asked, obviously shocked by the story Mary Jo had just related.

'Anne asked the police present, but no one seemed to have any idea at all. She said they claimed that these were the bodies of looters caught inside the inferno,' her tired voice explained, 'but there are suggestions that these might have been itinerants caught in the complex, unaware that the building had caught fire.'

Hamish looked at her sympathetically, unable to visualize the charred corpses. He could see that she was exhausted. Her slacks were torn, and there was an ugly, reddish abrasion to her right elbow where she had apparently hit the pavement as a result of their spill.

'Do you want to stay here tonight?' he offered, 'you could have a distracting massage and sauna if you feel up to it.' Mary Jo shook her head.

'Then you should have that seen to, Jo,' he said, pointing to the damaged skin.

'I have to get back to download and file all of this,' she said, indicating the large leather case containing her equipment. 'Why don't we meet up later, after I've finished?' She rose wearily, managing a smile. 'If I can convince the hotel taxi service to take me home and wait, I'll come back in. Okay?' the tiredness in her voice evident.

'Are you certain you're up to it? he asked, walking her to the door

'Sure,' she replied, kissing him lightly. 'Where will you be?'

'If it's after seven, I'll wait for you in O'Reiley's. Okay?'

'Great,' she said, waving as she headed for the lifts.

Hamish waited until she disappeared then returned to his papers, read through these one more time, then phoned downstairs to the hotel's secretarial service. He arranged for the documents to be picked up and typed, then Hamish changed and spent an hour working out in the gymnasium before hitting the sauna. By the time he had returned to his room, the report had been completed, and placed on the desk alongside his electronic notepad.

Hamish then showered and dressed, poured a generous serving of whisky and settled down to examine the document before him. Thirty minutes later, satisfied with his evaluation of the situation, Hamish McLoughlin took the report back down to the business centre and waited until it had been faxed to his associates in Switzerland.

He watched as the machine hummed, sending the detailed report halfway across the world, wondering how its contents would be received. He glanced up at the row of clocks, each set to a different international time zone, noting that his clients in Geneva would already have arrived at their bleak banker's offices. He retrieved the document and slipped this into an envelope, instructing the secretary to have it sent to his room, then headed directly for the bar to wait for Mary Jo.

* * * *

While Hamish McLoughlin sat alone, sipping his second whisky, the contents of his financial analyses were being carefully examined, on the other side of the globe. There, having completed his evaluation of Hamish's submission, a concerned financier used his private phone to dial an off-directory number in Tel Aviv. He relayed a brief synopsis of the report, along with his own recommendations, replaced the receiver, and waited. In less than an hour he received instructions. The merchant banker then moved swiftly, his organization successfully disposing of more than two hundred million pounds in stock associated with the Indonesian President's family holdings, citing liquidity concerns as the reason for the heavily discounted transactions.

As a consequence of rumors sparked by this sell-off, a further fifty percent was shaved off the value of the Indonesian currency, as word spread quickly through international financial centers from London to New York and back across the Atlantic, suggesting that the Indonesian President's family holdings were on the brink of collapse. The following morning the World Bank would freeze a pre-arranged bridging loan of one billion dollars and the IMF representative, Harold Goldstein, would inform the Indonesian Government that due to the country's continuing political instability the International Monetary Fund would be unable to consider further financial assistance at that time.

In Tel Aviv there would be smiles all around as those present at the Mossad briefing agreed that Indonesia's attempts to move the world's largest Moslem population towards achieving its own nuclear defence capability would now be delayed, hopefully indefinitely. In Washington, the American President would nod solemnly when his meeting with the nation's senior military and security advisers concluded, the question of replacing the Indonesian leadership, now the remaining issue.

In China, the Chairman would brood over the information at hand, then decide to delay devaluing the nation's currency until at least after the American President's visit. Events in Indonesia would in no way derail his long-term strategies to acquire control over the archipelago's rich and extensive natural resources. His main concerns were how long China could protect itself from the Soros-styled raiders, the Chairman conscious that the special territory of Hong Kong certain to be targeted.

But in Islamabad, where Chinese-assisted Pakistani scientists worked through yet another long and demanding night, the mood there would be quite different to that of its neighbors. Instead, the realization that their most secret project neared completion and would be tested within days would only heighten their general feeling of euphoria.

Chapter Ten

Washington

The President listened, his Chief of Staff's lament still fresh in his mind.

'The media is hunting hard on this one, and we'll have to give them something soon. General Praboyo's already spoken to the Press in Jakarta, and we should expect some flak from that interview,' Dean Scott had advised, minutes before leaving the Oval Office meeting to continue in his absence.

'How much information do we have regarding these so called death squads?' the President asked, directing this to the Defense Intelligence Agency Director.

'Firstly, Mr. President, it should be made quite clear that Praboyo is no longer the *Kopassus* Special Forces commander. Sure, they will continue to point the finger at him, but this is because of his relationship to Suhapto.' The Director glanced at the others. Peterson, the CIA Director, and Admiral Brown had entered together, their heated verbal exchange prior to the meeting indicative of the uneasy relationship these two powerful men shared. 'As for reports suggesting that there are death squads running around kidnapping students and political activists, well,' he raised his hands as if in surrender, 'the DIA Attache in Jakarta has nothing which would suggest that these have any substance.' He appeared calm but inside his stomach burned, the beginnings of an ulcer.

'Are we still training these units?'

'No sir, we're not,' the Director replied. 'We discontinued all operational contact with *Kopassus* when the current crisis hit.' The President nodded, pleased with this information. His Chief of Staff could emphasize this point during the next media conference. The President was buoyed that his public approval ratings had recovered, and wished that the Indonesian situation would just disappear, particularly since media attention had begun to focus on his imminent China visit.

The Washington Post had reported that U.S.-trained military units in Indonesia had been involved in kidnapping and torturing students and dissidents, and that these incidents had commenced well before General Praboyo was promoted from the Special Forces to become the *Kostrad* Strategic Forces commander. The Post had been relentless in its investigations, revealing that reliable Indonesian sources claimed ties between the United States Defense Intelligence Agency, General Praboyo and his former command, *Kopassus*, were still strong.

The possible involvement of Praboyo's former troops was, potentially, of considerable embarrassment for the Pentagon, as the U.S. military had maintained strong ties with the *Kopassus* units, having participated in training exercises involving America's highly skilled guerrilla teams. General Praboyo, it was revealed, had attended both Advanced and Army Special Forces Training in the United States. Over the past seven years, U.S. Special Forces troops had conducted more than thirty counter- terrorism, sniper skills and rapid infiltration training exercises with *Kopassus*.

The President was cognizant of his country's ongoing need to maintain its military sales to countries such as Indonesia. His Administration was still keen to finalize the sale of nine F-16's to Jakarta but the current political climate prevented further dialogue. That, and the fact that the country was most unlikely now to be in a position to pay for such purchases. In order to satisfy the clamorous human rights' lobbyists, he had sanctioned a ban against the sale of small arms, helicopter armaments and armored personnel carriers several years before, but this decision had been merely to distract attention from his military's more disguised activities there. Now, these covert activities had come to haunt him and the President knew he had no choice but to distance himself, and his Administration, from those involved.

'Does the CIA still support General Praboyo? he asked, catching Peterson by surprise. Admiral Brown turned to stare directly at the Director, anticipating his response.

'Yes, we do,' Peterson answered.

'Why?' his Chief asked, annoyance in his voice.

'Because we believe that he is the only one capable of taking Suhapto's place. Yes, we agree that General Winarko appears spotless and obviously pro-American. But that won't automatically give him the Presidency. It's far more complicated than that.'

'Mr. President, we've been over this all before,' Admiral Brown interrupted, shooting a warning look at Peterson, but the President raised his hand; he wished to hear the Director finish.

'What about the Vice President, what's his name … Hababli?'

'For anyone to succeed President Suhapto, he would need to have *ABRI*, the Indonesian military on side. L.B. Hababli does not have such support, and international monetary circles have clearly indicated their positions in respect to his recent appointment. He suffers from megalomania, everything he touches turns to shit. An Indonesia under Hababli could only end with another coup. Having him at the nation's helm would be unthinkable. On the other hand, we acknowledge that Praboyo does have some problems as well. Petty rivalries and jealousies in relation to his family ties to the Presidency have prevented him acquiring the necessary *ABRI* backing. But, there again Winarko has a similar problem. He has not placed his stamp on the Armed Forces as yet, having only held the Chief of Staff's position for less than three months. Also, he is still viewed by some as being far too close to Suhapto.

Our intelligence confirms that there are serious rumblings with the Indonesian forces; quite frankly, there is every likelihood of a major split occurring, and not just between the Praboyo-Winarko camps. There are other pretenders waiting in the wings, any one of which are capable of challenging Winarko. But it is our position that they would not contest Praboyo's anointment as President, providing his father-in-law supports the move.'

The Director turned to the Admiral. 'We should not lose sight of the fact that Praboyo has always been committed to maintaining a close relationship with our forces. Concerns about his father-in-law's push for a Moslem state would not be an issue, once he takes control. Of this we're reasonably confident. Also, there is the question of the Suhapto financial empire. The country could not recover if the First Family's assets, along with its substantial Chinese associated interests, were not to be repatriated. It is most unlikely that President Suhapto's children would ever consider bringing back their billions should one of their number not still maintain control over the Presidency.'

It was Admiral Brown's turn to nod in agreement. Peterson made sense, although the Joint Chiefs' Chairman would not alter his own opinion regarding General Praboyo. He believed the man to be a dangerous cowboy, brutal to the extreme, and most certainly arrogant in approach to others. Brown did not believe that Praboyo would act in the manner Peterson had suggested. The United States would be buying itself a great deal of trouble in the future, if they supported Praboyo's claim on the Presidency.

'Mr. President,' he started, 'the Joint Chiefs believe that General Winarko should be given our full support. Besides, Praboyo's former association with *Kopassus* will not disappear even if he should become Indonesia's next leader. The Western Press will never let us forget that he came to power through the excesses of these death squads, and that would put paid to any further defence aid or military sales to the country. Congress would never let it pass.' Admiral Brown's comments went straight to the heart of the matter. He knew he had scored, his President's face had twitched measurably with the mention of Capital Hill. 'Once calm and stability has been restored under a Winarko Presidency, the Chinese will return. They always have in the past.'

The American President believed this to be true. That, coupled with the sensitive human rights abuses placed accusingly at General Praboyo's feet, influenced his decision.

'I am inclined to agree with Colin,' he said, supporting the Admiral, while looking directly at Peterson. 'The Chinese will wait, then when things have returned to normal they will return. As for the Suhapto billions, perhaps we can ask Treasury and State to have a look at having their assets seized should it come to that.' It was clear to the CIA Director that the President's decision had been influenced by the prospect of excessive media attention concerning Praboyo's U.S. ties. He remained quietly considering his options, realizing that they were running out of time.

'We'll go with Winarko,' his Chief announced, 'Just make sure he fully understands that we won't support a blood-bath. When Suhapto goes, that should be the end of it,' he insisted, and both men nodded solemnly in concurrence.

An hour later, Wall Street commenced trading in New York. The exchange reacted to the data which had flowed from Geneva, via London, plunging Indonesia into financial darkness, while sending the Japanese Yen into an unprecedented tailspin. The panic driven markets crashed, then rose, and fueled by rumor, plummeted again, finding some semblance of stability towards mid-afternoon as blue chip stocks recovered in value. But it was not the economic collapse of the world's fourth most populous country which triggered the greatest losses of the day.

Just when they thought the worst had passed, hoarse-voiced traders looked up in dismay as the announcement flashed across the overhead screen. In that moment, Indonesia's woes paled in significance as the

Indian Government proudly announced the successful detonation of a fifty-five kiloton nuclear device close to its neighbor's border. The world held its breath, anxiously, awaiting Pakistan's response to this provocative act, and for the Moslem nations to respond.

It was the eleventh day of May

* * * *

Jakarta

General Praboyo

Lieutenant General Praboyo grinned widely as his old friend entered and, unobserved by their subordinates, childishly threw mock salutes at each other.

'How are you finding Kopassus?' Praboyo inquired.

'Much the same as when you left it,' the brigadier answered, grateful that his friendship over the years with this man had delivered the Special Forces Command to him. Between the two of them they now controlled two of the most powerful military forces. Praboyo knew he could depend on the man before him, especially should he require someone to watch his back, as he expected he would, in the not too distant future.

'Any problems with the Americans?' Praboyo had managed to convince the Defense Intelligence Attache that *Kopassus* had not been involved in the student kidnappings in any way whatsoever. Several students had been released, due to their family connections, after interrogation. They were warned of the consequences should they reveal anything of their detention to the press, family or friends. The others had been too badly beaten to risk returning to their families. They had been executed, their bodies hastily thrown into unmarked graves behind the rifle range.

'Have you selected the teams I asked for?'

'The men are ready. We have enough uniforms to confuse the situation.'

'Then all we have to do is wait,' Praboyo declared, encouraged by this news. He had initiated the formation of a number of Special squads to prepare for off-campus student demonstrations, which he expected to take place at any time. Praboyo was determined to use these covert tactics, believing that the standing orders issued by the Jakarta Garrison commander not to use live bullets, would only delay the inevitable.

The men from his former command had been trained to infiltrate other military units whenever the Special Forces believed this necessary.

The teams under discussion had been provided with police uniforms and would be deployed to shoot to kill, whenever the students' demonstrations finally spilled over and onto the streets. These men both firmly believed that the students would then retreat to their campuses as they had in the past, where the ringleaders would be arrested and later tried for their subversive activities.

A month had passed since the President had been re-appointed by Parliament, and his mascot, Hababli, had been elected as Vice President. Praboyo had hoped that he might have been considered for the position but was satisfied, for the time being, to remain where he was until a more appropriate time arrived. Considering the current political situation, he believed that might be sooner than even he had anticipated. The *Bapak* President had become most concerned with security, ordering his military to increase its presence within the capital. The generals had complied, and twenty-five thousand crack troops were trucked in from other parts of Java.

Civil unrest continued to plague the country, the students becoming bolder after President Suhapto announced his new Cabinet, taking advantage of the public's awareness that the IMF had postponed all payments due to the blatant, ongoing nepotism. Tuti Suhapto and other members of the First Family's clique had been given prominent Cabinet positions, and would now govern the country.

Food had escalated dramatically in cost, and the country's finances were in total chaos. Suspected of hoarding rice and other essential commodities, Chinese everywhere were targeted by angry mobs, reports identifying attacks in even the most remote towns and villages, throughout the country. Suddenly, for the first time in more than thirty years, there was a justifiable fear amongst the Chinese that the crisis would not be contained, and that to remain in the country would be suicidal.

Those who could afford to do so had already transferred their funds offshore, following their money once seats became available. This additional currency drain further exacerbated the financial crisis, and the Rupiah went into an uncontrollable spin, generating even greater hardship for those already struggling below the poverty line. The students, acting as self-appointed representatives of the people challenged the military's authority, no longer disguising their contempt for those in power, placing placards with the most derogatory caricatures and slogans around the university campuses. Praboyo knew that it would not be long before student activities spilled out onto the capital's streets, providing the catalyst his Moslem associates desired. Haji Abdul Muis would call upon his thirty million followers, and there would be a changing of the guard.

And when this happened, he would be ready.

* * * *

Lily

The new wave of rioting rekindled fears of further unrest as the economic crisis continued to bite, sharpening divisions between the poor and the ethnic Chinese minority which controlled Indonesia's commerce, viewed by many as the real culprits for the country's economic plight. Rice shortages had become even more acute, now rationed in the cities whilst in the countryside, many villagers had resorted to eating leaves to survive. Suspected of hoarding, many Chinese were dragged from their homes and murdered.

Lily's apprehension grew as she listened to her uncle *Oom Setio* discuss the latest attacks on Chinese shopkeepers with members of their community. They were confused, as it was obvious that the growing ground-swell of anti-Chinese sentiment was being either ignored by their once friendly President or, as some of their number suggested, even encouraged.

'*... but you heard what the military had to say on television last night!*' the textile merchant argued, '*the army is asking for an investigation into Chinese business affairs!*'

'*Yes,*' others joined in, agreeing. The broadcast was seen by most Jakarta residents, or at least, those who spoke the local language.

'*I can't believe that they will actually investigate the Low family!*' This, from one of the major cement distributors whose entire fortune had been derived from the Low relationship. '*What's going on over at the Palace?*' he asked, not really expecting that any of their number knew.

'*I've heard that Chinese owned shops are going to be burned out in Bogor,*' an agitated property owner moaned. *Oom Setio* was considered to be one of the leading members of this community and most looked to him for guidance and advice.

'*It seems that you might be right,*' the textile king agreed. '*I have personally seen signs painted on houses and shops belonging to indigenous traders stating they are not Chinese; but what concerns me more, many have also painted signs across their gates that they are Moslems.*'

'*What are you going to do with your family?*' Setio was asked. He didn't hesitate, anticipating their families' safety to be foremost on their minds.

'*They'll be safe in Jakarta,*' he answered, reassuringly. '*The ethnic violence is mainly concentrated in the smaller, country towns in Java. This city can't afford to turn on us. The military knows that not to protect us would result in more than half of Jakarta closing down. I believe that last night's announcement was made to accommodate the President's family. They have attracted a great deal of attention over the past months, and the Bapak has been very clever, deflecting much of the growing animosity towards his children and friends by permitting anti-Chinese sentiment to be expressed through these violent attacks.'* He paused, and they all waited for him to continue.

'I don't think this will continue much longer. Once the IMF has permitted the funds they have committed to flow into the Treasury, then I expect we will see the military cracking down hard on the students, and everything should soon return to normal after that.'

'I agree,' one of the major shareholders in the country's largest car assembly plant offered. *'We have seen this all before. Remember the anti-Japanese riots of '74?'* he asked, knowing that none amongst them would have forgotten those frightening days when anti-Tokyo feeling spilled over onto the streets, resulting in an entire shopping centre, *Pasar Senen*, being razed to the ground. Chinese shops had been looted, the gold-shops first to come under attack. *'Well,'* he continued, *'this is similar in many ways.'* He looked over at *Oom Setio's* serious face. *'We should just be careful about our movements until the situation settles, keep off the streets at night, and avoid any confrontation with the pribumi people.'* The suggestion that they should avoid contact with their indigenous countrymen brought solemn nods.

'Are you keeping your children out of school?' another asked. Some had already done so, while others had sent theirs overseas to Singapore and Australia immediately after the ethnic violence had erupted.

'No,' *Oom Setio* replied, shaking his head, *'my children will remain at school. But, for the time being, I have instructed them to return home once their lessons are finished and keep off the streets.'* Several of those present nodded in agreement.

'How long do you really think this will continue?' someone asked, not addressing any one in particular.

'Not long,' Setio promised, wishing that this could be true, *'probably a few more weeks then things should return to normal.'* This response was met with meditative silence whilst in the adjacent room, Lily Suryajaya listened, then immediately offered a silent prayer that her wise, and prosperous uncle's predictions would indeed come to pass.

In the week that followed, Lily continued with her studies at the Uber Sakti University amidst signs that the mood between *pribumi* students, and those of Chinese extraction would continue to deteriorate.

But it was on the Friday, as Moslem students prepared for their late-morning prayers, that Lily experienced what it really meant to be a foreigner in her own country. Without warning, her friend Hani Purwadira had looked in her direction, and then raised the issue concerning the number of Chinese students occupying university places which, she emphasized, was unfairly disproportional. Lily was stunned by the outburst, bewildered that Hani could turn on her so.

The ensuing discussion had been vitriolic, with cutting exchanges wounding both ethnic groups present. In minutes, well-established relationships and friendships were in tatters, ruined forever as students took sides, many screaming insults at each other, their adolescent venom erupting as previously concealed hatreds spewed forth. Although security had prevented the clash from becoming physical, when it was all over, students glared at one another, their eyes and hearts filled with hate and Lily knew then, beyond doubt, that it would never be the same for her again, at least, not in this country.

Fighting back tears, Lily had cut classes, returning home early, feigning illness when her surprised aunt noticed her enter their apartment. Even as she lay awake that night, her soaked pillow evidence of the torment which had ripped her heart, Lily felt little animosity, only extreme sadness towards her former friend, Hani. The explosive confrontation of just hours before continued to pervade her thoughts, preventing sleep and she cried, again, smothering her choking sobs with the pillow. Finally, in the early morning hours sheer exhaustion thankfully carried her away, her convoluted dreams even more distressing than the reality of the day before.

She overslept and, when woken by her aunt who immediately became concerned with Lily's red, swollen eyes, Lily complained that she had been awake most of the night, suffering from stomach cramps. Her understanding aunt had placed her arms lovingly around her niece, and insisted that she remain home for the day. At first, Lily had protested, then finally acquiesced as flashes of the frightening confrontation came flooding back. She clung to her aunt tightly, comforted by her presence. Secure in the knowledge that she was safe, she lay back in her bed and rested, oblivious to events unfolding as she slept, events, which would not only adversely affect Lily's future and those of her race, but would also dramatically change the course of Indonesia's history.

It was the Twelfth day in May.

Ten Days in May

"The greatest happiness is to vanquish your enemies, to chase them before you, to rob them of their wealth, to see those dear to them bathed in tears, to clasp to your bosom their wives, and daughters."

Genghis Khan

Chapter Eleven

Jakarta

Uber Sakti University

Army Corporal Suparman climbed the last flight of stairs then stepped out onto the concrete deck overlooking the entrance to the University. Crouching low, he selected a position which would provide not only adequate cover, but also a clear view of the street and the buildings across the way, and waited.

The Special Forces *Kopassus* sharpshooter knew that the others from his team would be similarly situated along the roof tops, their weapons identical to the one which he now held, wrapped in gray cloth, the color of the Police uniform he now wore. Suparman removed the sacking and inspected the Steyr. It was not his first choice for the job at hand, but as his targets would be relatively close, he was satisfied that the weapon would do the job. He checked the 1.5x optic sights out of habit, then settled back to wait for the streets to fill with demonstrators, as he knew they would.

* * * *

Hani

At first, Hani Purwadira had resisted calls to join the student action group, fearing discovery by her father. She was aware that many of the other generals' children had been secretly encouraged to participate in the demonstrations by their fathers, and she was tired of the whispers, accepting that she would never really have any close friends unless she joined with the others in voicing their opinions.

Hani had required little persuasion to take a position against those considered responsible for corrupting the Indonesian leadership. Naïve to the core, she fell in behind her friends calling for an end to Chinese dominance of the Indonesian economy, accusing them of promoting corrupt practices which kept the Suhapto government in power. Hani was not ashamed to admit that she had always harbored such feelings towards the Chinese, recalling how, as a young child when her father was still quite junior in rank, the Purwadira family was poor, and depended on handouts from the local shopkeepers and traders, for their survival. As she had grown older, Hani had become resentful of their control, their wealth, and their academic achievements. It had taken little to unleash her suppressed, racial sentiments, pleased for the opportunity to demonstrate her true feelings.

Of course, she dared not reveal her new role as a student activist to her parents. Her mother would have been horrified, and the thought of her father's reaction, should someone tell, tempted her to reconsider. It had been Wanti's constant sniping which had finally won her over, and as it seemed harmless enough, she abandoned her former position of non-involvement, throwing herself energetically into campus political activities.

Hani had admitted privately that she was pleased with the changing political mood in her country, although her relatively immature mind had yet to consider the consequences of this. It had not entered Hani's head that her own family might also suffer from such drastic change, particularly in the event the nation's military leadership implemented reform.

Unaware that growing and divisive cracks within the armed forces had prompted many of the country's high-ranking officers to urge their own children to join their fellow students on the streets, students of Hani's ilk rushed in blindly, in some instances becoming even more aggressive than their peers.

That morning, Hani had eagerly joined the many thousands of students, gathered in preparation for their march to demonstrate against the Suhapto Government. The air was filled with an almost carnival atmosphere as the students laughed at each others' placards, exercising a freedom of speech hitherto unknown in the Republic.

'Here, Hani,' one of the third year students called, taking her by the arm, *'you can help hold this banner.'* Happy to be now included as one of their number, Hani stood beside several other female students and took hold of one end of a banner painted with the slogan, *Who elected Suhapto?* Somebody pushed from behind, then giggled, causing Hani to turn.

'Hello there!' Wanti called, surprised to see her friend participating. *'What will your father say?'* she teased. Hani merely laughed, the mood lifting her spirits even more than before. There was a sense of growing

euphoria as they all started to chant, proudly holding their banners and placards high for the people lining the streets to see.

* * * *

Mary Jo

At first, to her untrained foreign ears, the garbled cries made little sense.

'Down with Suhapto! Down with KKN!' Mary Jo heard them call, in unison.

'Down with Nepotism, Collusion and Corruption!' She heard them chant, learning from Anne, her assistant, what it all meant.

'What are they saying?' she shouted, caught up in the excitement as banners and placards carried high above the student lines bravely declared their opposition to the government.

'*KKN* means *Kolusi*, *Korupsi* and *Nepotisme*,' she heard Anne explain, forced to yell, her eyes misty as she made little effort to reflect her own opinion and support for the massive wave of humanity sweeping down the street.

'Keep up, Anne!' she shouted, re-loading and passing the cartridge to her assistant. Anne did so, becoming the American journalist's shadow as she darted around, crossing through the student lines, crouching, then holding her camera high for angle opportunity as the waves of young men and women washed past, determined to be heard.

'Over here!' Mary Jo urged, forcing her way through the spectators lining the streets as tens of thousands of students swarmed off the campus demanding the resignation of their President. She kept shooting, each frame recording the historical event, as students carried their message to the people. Mary Jo ignored the presence of other foreign media faces as they too dashed around with their cumbersome equipment, catching the historic scene for CNN and other leading television broadcasters. She reloaded, moving with the main body of demonstrators, conscious of the growing presence of uniforms along the way.

The chanting grew in intensity, fueled by the appearance of the military. Mary Jo's concern that a confrontation was inevitable caused her to move away from the advancing column. As she searched for a more advantageous position to continue filming, it became increasingly difficult to maintain her footing as spectators crowded the footpaths to view the spectacle. Their calls of encouragement added to the cacophonous assembly, their combined chants becoming a roar.

'Down with corruption! Down with manipulators!' they cried out in unison, the demonstrators' numbers swelling to uncontrollable proportions as the spectators joined the column of students. Towards the center, Hani's group held their banner high, chanting as they marched, reveling in the mass excitement.

'Bring back justice! Bring back our rights!' their voices called, rising to an incredible level as they left the university's perimeter and entered the busy street. There they were confronted by the police, and for a moment the demonstration faltered. Mary Jo, her height an added advantage, captured the moment as she held her camera over the heads of those blocking her path. A student leader called out loudly, and immediately the chanting recommenced.

'Down with corruption! Bring back our rights!' they screamed, surging forward to push their way though the barricade of intimidating anti-riot troops.

'Go back to your campus!' the officer ordered, standing in the middle of the street, directly in the demonstrators' path. Behind and to both sides, rows of anti-riot police stood ready, their see-through shields held in anticipation of the inevitable hail of rocks they knew the students carried, and would throw without the slightest encouragement. Tear gas canisters appeared, and Mary Jo knew then that the police were determined to end the demonstration right there.

'Turn back!' the police captain screamed again, his voice drowned amidst the chorus of anti-government voices descending upon him and his baton-carrying troops. The wave of protesters threatened to engulf the officer, and he panicked.

'Fire!' he screamed, pointing with his pistol. The squad directly to his left raised their weapons and fired, aiming low so that their rubber bullets would hit the students below the waist. The first volley shattered the air, the shock stunning the students in their tracks.

* * * *

Above, and hidden behind the concrete wall overlooking the sudden confusion, the *Kopassus* Special Forces sniper selected a target and gently squeezed the trigger, releasing his deadly missile at a speed of some eight hundred meters per second. He hadn't even required the scope; he could see the student's head clearly, even without the sights. Somewhere down amongst the terrified demonstrators a young second year student turned, his face covered in grotesque surprise as the air around suddenly exploded with a distinctive pop, and he spun, then collapsed to the ground.

* * * *

'My god, they're shooting!' someone cried out loudly.

'They're shooting! They're shooting!' others joined in as the students attempted to disperse, their escape blocked by the sheer mass of their own numbers.

'I'm hit!' one student screamed, the impact throwing him to the ground where others tripped over his body, attempting to flee.

'They're using real bullets!' one of the third year students cried, dragging a wounded boy out of harm's way. He too, fell, struck viciously in the head by an over-zealous, baton-waving policeman. Panic swept through their columns as the students realized that their comrades were not falling just to rubber bullets. Within a few, brief moments, the street exploded into a battle-ground as the more militant students hurled missiles in response to the attack. Five policemen fell under the first hail of rocks, only to be replaced by others who advanced, shooting blindly at the sea of white shirts before them. The air filled with screams as gunfire continued to cut through the young bodies, struggling to escape the deadly bullets.

'Help me! Help me!' Hani cried out, terrified as she scrambled back to her feet after being knocked viciously to the street. As she rose, a soldier swung at the girl next to her, bludgeoning the young student repeatedly with his baton.

'Stop it! Please stop it!' she cried, horrified as the attack continued, even as the bloodied girl lay unconscious on the ground. Someone pushed, and Hani fell heavily, her knees hitting the tarred ground as she reached out to protect herself from the fall.

'Hani! Hani!' she heard someone cry, and before she could scramble back to her feet, she was hit cruelly from behind, and collapsed in pain. As she lay there, stunned, the dust rising from the dirty street choking her nostrils, she stared, horrified, at the almost surreal picture before her. From her angled perspective, thousands of legs scurried through her blurred line of vision, their owners' panicked screams a thunderous roll as they pounded the ground in their endeavors to escape the savage onslaught. She thought she could hear more gunfire but, at that moment, Hani lost consciousness as she was brutally kicked by one of the advancing troops.

* * * *

Corporal Suparman aimed again, this time deep into the University grounds. The 5.65 mm round ball found its target, tumbling as designed, tearing the soft tissue as it ripped through the student's body, the wound at the point of exit the size of a man's fist. Satisfied with the result, the sniper then covered his weapon and retreated back down the concrete stairwell to the ground floor. As he exited from the rear of the building, screaming spectators fleeing in terror provided sufficient distraction for the soldier to escape, unnoticed, arriving at the prearranged point where he regrouped with the others in his team.

* * * *

Back on the street, the real police continued to fire rubber bullets into the student rally, while others advanced swinging their truncheons indiscriminately.

Mary Jo had sensibly retreated a short distance from the bloody scene, continuing to film as the fighting continued. Across the road, two young women had taken refuge in a roadside telephone booth. Their screams were ignored as two soldiers smashed their way through the glass door, viciously clubbing their victims until they fell amongst the broken glass, unconscious. As Mary Jo turned her attention to a number of police gathered around one of their victims, repeatedly kicking the man's head, another volley of shots rang out, and she ducked, instinctively.

Water cannon forced the remaining rock-throwing demonstrators to retreat, creating a clear path for the advancing soldiers, called in to support the anti-riot squads. Mary Jo watched, continuing to document the events as the heavily-armed militia swept through the street, leaving no doubt as to who was in charge. She moved back across the street, taking care not to impede the soldiers as they continued in pursuit of the fleeing students. There, alongside the footpath, Mary Jo knelt to examine one of the victims. She checked for a pulse and discovered that the girl was still alive. Rising to her feet, Mary Jo scanned the area anxiously, relieved to discover Anne standing beside one of the foreign cameramen across the street. She knew that it was dangerous for her Indonesian assistant to be present and waved, indicating for her to remain where she was, concerned that she could easily be mistaken for one of the demonstrators should she attempt to cross the street at that moment.

Mary Jo remained standing beside the unconscious body as soldiers continued to fill the area. Finally, when first aid teams arrived, she left the girl in their care, confident that she would survive her ordeal, and went in search of her assistant.

Inconspicuous amidst the confusion, the *Kopassus* Special Forces team, still dressed in their borrowed police uniforms, slipped away undetected, leaving behind four dead Uber Sakti University students and a street littered with injured. They had achieved what they had set out to do; the killings would enrage the students, and they would now have their martyrs. But that would be the end of their destabilizing activities. Realizing that the military's patience had come to an end, the students were now expected to return to their classrooms and cease their off-campus demonstrations, knowing that their refusal to do so, would only result in many more of their number being executed on the streets.

* * * *

Mary Jo & Anne

'Are you all right?' Mary Jo asked again. She could see that her assistant was suffering from shock.

'Yes, thanks Jo,' Anne answered, grateful that she'd had the sense to remain with the foreign cameraman when the shooting commenced. 'Did you get what you wanted?' she asked, but somehow it just didn't come out the way she meant.

'Plenty,' was all Mary Jo said. She understood; she'd been there herself. The shock of being trapped amongst the panicked crowd as bullets flew overhead was not something she would easily forget. 'Let's get back to the villa.'

They drove in silence, each captured by their own thoughts and fears. Mary Jo knew that she would remember that day for the rest of her days: the terrified young faces; the mayhem as the first shots rang out; and the body of a student lying dead with his head half-blown away. She had no idea how many had been killed and injured. It was impossible to know as many would have been dragged to safety by their comrades. As for the bodies of those killed, Mary Jo knew that the police and military often disposed of these to avoid public outcry at the real numbers killed during such confrontations.

'Take Miss Anne home,' Mary Jo instructed the driver as she climbed out of the car. There was nothing more that Anne could do; it was obvious that she was still suffering from shock. Her assistant's face suddenly changed, her eyes opening wide.

'No, please Jo,' she pleaded, 'may I stay?'

'It's okay, Anne,' Mary Jo replied, misunderstanding the young woman's intentions, 'I can finish up by myself.' This was greeted by Anne's shaking her head.

'Please, Jo,' she asked again, 'I don't want to go back out on the streets just yet. The police will surely stop and check incoming city traffic. I would be alone, Jo, and they would know that I work for the media. It's on my identification pass.'

Mary Jo immediately understood, annoyed that she had not recognized the obvious. It would not be safe for Indonesian journalists to travel alone. She knew that this country had an extremely poor record in relation to its Press. Many had died; many more had just disappeared. The police involvement in the shooting of students would guarantee that there would be a cover-up. They would move quickly and efficiently, removing whatever evidence there might be, and this would surely include detaining local journalists.

'Stay here for the night,' she said, forcing a smile. Anne climbed out of the vehicle and placed her arms around the American woman, squeezing her affectionately.

'Terima kasih, Jo,' she said, gratefully. They moved inside, met at the door by an anxious team of servants whose knowledge of the shootings had somehow preceded their *nyonya's* return. Mary Jo had never ceased to be surprised by the servants' communication network. With their masters absent, the telephones would have rung continuously, passing news and gossip through their amazing network.

'Madame has a message,' her housekeeper explained. This had not been written down, having never learned how to do so. *'Mister telephoned from his hotel,'* she relayed, and Mary Jo knew that this would have been Hamish, and went to return his call in the privacy of her bedroom.

'Are you okay?' she detected his concern. 'It's already on CNN,' he informed her, 'and I was worried.'

'I'm okay, thanks Hamish. In fact, we've only just returned to the villa. Anne is still with me, and she's pretty well shaken by what happened.'

'CNN says that there were something like six killed, but it looked like many more than that from the coverage.' He left the statement hanging, hoping she could add more.

'It's hard to tell, Hamish. There were thousands running in all directions. Once the shooting started, we all went for cover. No one expected the police to open fire, at least not with live rounds!' Scenes flashed across her mind as she visualized the chaos she'd witnessed.

'Are you coming in?' he asked, 'the place is abuzz here at the moment.'

'Give me a couple of hours to file, then I'll phone. I might try and get some other coverage on the way, if I come down.'

'Jesus, what a job!' he complained, immediately regretting the statement.

'Yes,' she retaliated, her nerves still shot, 'but it's my job,' with which, she hung up and went to complete her outstanding tasks, wishing she had not been as brusque as she had. Mary Jo set about writing her story while Anne downloaded the photographs in between answering the many calls they received concerning the Uber Sakti incident. They checked these together, the colored still-frame scenes coming alive on her computer monitor for them to relive those dangerous moments of just hours before. Satisfied with her coverage of the student shootings, she connected to New York and sent the material to her editor via the Internet connection.

Mary Jo then returned her calls, agreeing to meet with other journalists who were to gather for drinks downtown. She looked up at her Seiko wall-clock hanging over the printer, and was pleased that she would have plenty of time to shower and change without the usual rush. It was just after five, and Mary Jo asked her staff to call a taxi for six o'clock.

At seven she was still sitting, waiting impatiently for a driver to come; at eight she flung the book she was reading angrily across the room and undressed. At nine o'clock, a faint glow over Jakarta could be seen by air-crews more than one hundred kilometers out over the Java Sea and, by midnight, the blazing sky surrounding the Indonesian capital signaled the world, that the once stable archipelago had now commenced its slide, into the darkness of anarchy.

* * * *

JAKARTA

The First Family

Tuti tried to recall when the family had last gathered in crisis, deciding that she could not remember, only because this had never happened to them before.

'We should all leave,' Timmy Suhapto declared. He, more so than the others, had borne the brunt of the latest accusations to appear on placards which, to their dismay, had been televised, worldwide.

'We must wait for Bapak to return from Egypt before taking any decisions,' Nuri announced. She stared accusingly at her youngest brother, Timmy,

as if he had been entirely responsible for their dilemma. The students and foreign media had again targeted her brother's car import activities, citing the favorable conditions relating to duties and other government charges as an excessive display of nepotism. Timmy's fully imported cars were permitted into the country in direct opposition to his elder brother's assembled models, and those built by other organizations which had invested hundreds of millions of dollars to create local employment, and save the country's foreign exchange. Timmy had called his car the 'East Wind', and these were sold at a price considerably below that of similar models assembled locally. Thousands of his fully-imported vehicles now stood idle in warehouses around the city as the economy collapsed. He simply permitted the company to collapse, leaving huge debts owing to the Korean suppliers. Even though the 'East Wind's' floor price had plummeted to less than one third of their cost, nobody would purchase the cars, fearing that these would soon be targeted by roving rioters. Insurance companies had refused to provide civil unrest cover due to the breakdown of order, and apart from military jeeps, tanks, armed personnel carriers and fire engines, the streets were now all but devoid of most vehicular traffic.

'You want us to wait another week?' another brother asked, fearful of the growing disdain for their family. Two weeks ago what was taking place now would have been considered unthinkable; impossible. For more than thirty years they had all enjoyed a most privileged life-style as members of the First Family. He looked around the rather austere setting of his father's home, wondering how this could have happened, now that they were virtually prisoners in the President's castle. He observed his older brother sitting almost aloof besides Nuri, and felt a twinge of envy as he was reminded of the number of occasions they had taken sides against him. Their joint holdings were at least five times that of the other children. Most of these assets, he knew, had been cleverly hidden from the people through a myriad of off-shore shelf-companies, nominees, and tax-havens such as the Channel Islands, and would easily exceed twenty billion dollars. But it was the sizable amounts of cash on deposit in Switzerland and Singapore numbered accounts, which played with his mind, as he had estimated that the older children must have gathered more than another thirty million dollars, all of it untaxable, and untouchable.

'Why did Bapak have to leave when the situation was this bad?' Tuti asked, addressing none in particular.

'You know why!' Nuri snapped, *'and he should never have left considering his health.'*

'Do you think the Arabs will help?' Timmy asked, hopefully. He understood that his father had flown to Cairo to attend a conference which might result in its members pressuring the IMF not to dally any further.

'The Foreign Minister is now with Bapak. I think he is going to ask him to return to Jakarta before the conference ends,' the only non-family member present advised. They all turned to look at the newly appointed Vice President, looking ridiculous, as usual, his chair appearing oversized under the man's small frame.

'Pak Hababli,' Nuri asked, *'what is happening with the military? Why hasn't General Winarko moved against the students and put an end to this disgraceful display against the Bapak?'* L.B. Hababli beamed at this opportunity to demonstrate that he was, in fact, a member of this elitist group. Sitting there amongst the six Suhapto children, he was not an unfamiliar face. Nuri had never really understood how Fortune had continued to smile on this little man, although he had repeated the story so many times over the years, she accepted that truth or fiction, most now believed the fable relating to how he came to enjoy his favored position with the President.

Nuri was not convinced with Hababli's favorite tale; that his father and the then young General Suhapto were close friends; that at the time of his father's death Suhapto had visited and paid his last respects, then taken Hababli under his wing. Nuri preferred to believe that her father had most probably entered into some commercial relationship with the Hababli family as, at that time, General Suhapto was the regional commander for the province in North Sulawesi where L.B.'s family lived. Nuri recalled that, during the Soekarno years, the military commanders had often been obliged to search for their own funding, to feed and clothe their troops.

She was also aware, that it was those very conditions which had also thrown the now powerful Salima group together, a relationship which had evolved from the time her father had been commander of the Central Java *Diponegoro* divisions. With this recollection, the President's eldest daughter's face tightened, and she frowned. Her father had been dismissed from his command, his career in tatters. Had it not been for his bravery in Sulawesi and later, in Irian, Nuri had no doubts that they would not be sitting where they were, today.

She preferred to believe that L.B. Hababli's position had been more a result of her father's confidence in his technical expertise, than that of an adopted younger brother as he so annoyingly claimed. Nuri snorted softly at L.B.'s meteoric rise, recalling also the number of damaging decisions her father had made to support the self-proclaimed technocrat. Nuri looked at the man her father had selected as his Vice President, still curious as to why he had done so. L.B. had continued to embarrass the family, the government, and the country. *Why then*, she asked herself silently, *had Bapak chosen this man?*

L.B. Hababli's nomination had caused the currency to implode; this much was evident to her. In her mind she counted the number of occasions when L.B. had unwisely chosen projects to enhance the nation's image, only to preside over the eventual collapse of these, at the expense of those around him. Nuri was uncomfortable with the knowledge that he did not even have the support of the military, something she considered a prerequisite to holding the position he now enjoyed. She remembered how he had lost their support, casting her mind back to when her father had foolishly agreed to L.B.'s acquisition of the entire former East German fleet.

Nuri remembered how, at the time, Hababli had promised the military that the ships would all be refurbished in Indonesian shipyards. It was when he had orchestrated for the refitting to be completed in India, that the then Minister for Research and Technology had come unstuck, losing his limited support base within the military hierarchy. Nuri watched L.B. fidget like some oversized child, while waiting for his response to her question.

'The general has assured me that he will contain the students,' he answered, unconvincingly. *'General Winarko does not wish to use measures which might be construed by the international media as excessive. With the death of the students..'*

'What?' the President's eldest son shouted, angrily, *'Excessive? Half the country's towns and cities are under siege by students. Why doesn't he act?'* The Vice President lowered his head, reluctant to engage in this conversation any further.

****

Vice President Hababli sympathized with them all. He too had become very concerned with the current situation, the recent currency debacle, and the angry mobs outside in the streets. His own financial empire had suffered dramatically since the outset of the current crisis. He wanted to explain to those present that they were not the only ones who were in danger of losing hundreds of millions of dollars should the IMF not move quickly to salvage the nation's economy.

Since he had first been recalled from Europe by the President some twenty years before, L.B. had worked quietly building his own financial empire. Today, through his family holdings, he enjoyed considerable wealth, most of which being derived from the control he had exerted over the Batam Island industrial park, across the straits from Singapore. There, he and his associates had built an empire consisting of hotels, golf courses, steel-rolling mills and tourist projects, ostensibly to compete with the small island nation across the water. He had appointed one son to the holding company's helm, and the other to oversee his pet project, an aircraft manufacturing plant in Bandung. L.B.'s aviation engineering skills were put to the test, and to his chagrin, the IMF had now insisted that the government close the plant due to its loss-making history.

Hababli gripped the arm rests and pulled himself forward, placing his feet firmly on the carpet. He accepted that his role in this household would always be tenuous, at the best of times. He also understood that he should never, never be seen to be in opposition to those present, having witnessed them vent their spleen on others. L.B. had been as surprised as any other when the President had informed him privately that he would be the new Vice President, but realized that this would not, at any time, place him above any in the First Family. He knew his place; and this often meant that he had to forgo projects to the Suhapto children, or risk appearing to be a threat, to their growing greed. He accepted that the Suhapto children expected their dynasty to last, in perpetuity.

'I trust General Winarko will do as the Bapak has ordered,' he offered, hoping that the mention of their father's name would remind them that the President still had the military's support. *'We should wait to see what are his wishes once he returns. In the meantime, you should all remain close to home, as Winarko has requested. He has placed additional troops around your residences, and Praboyo's Kostrad security has also deployed soldiers to guard our homes and families.'* L.B. was pleased that he had in no way appeared to suggest that he was in charge during the *Bapak's* absence. Having mentioned the Army Chief of Staff and General Praboyo's names they appeared placated, remaining silent, as they considered their options.

Several awkward minutes passed before L.B. coughed, and informed the group that he was required elsewhere.

* * * *

Hababli departed, leaving behind an atmosphere of ominous gloom. For the first time in their lives, the Suhaptos were concerned for their safety, particularly as their father was not there to protect them. Tuti looked at her brothers and sisters, identifying something she had never seen in this household before. Their faces were covered with fear. Suddenly, she broke into tears, and ran sobbing from the room calling for her mother, coming to an abrupt halt in the empty room where, whilst still alive, she could always be found ready to offer comfort, whenever needed.

The realization that her mother could no longer protect them frightened her even further, and Tuti ran sobbing to her own house down the street, watched by the surprised, and heavily armed troops guarding the street outside.

Chapter Twelve

Egypt & Indonesia

The Indonesian President

President Suhapto was assisted into his seat while his entourage waited patiently outside, on the tarmac. The hot, moist, equatorial evening added to their general appearance of fatigue, their expressions reflecting their disappointment in failing to secure the support Indonesia so desperately needed, at that time. The Cairo summit had, in that respect, been a dismal failure for the Republic, and members of the Indonesian contingent were apprehensive as to what they might expect upon their return, knowing that they would arrive amidst mounting civil unrest, as seen on television throughout the day.

President Suhapto had reluctantly canceled his remaining discussions following his Foreign Minister's recommendations to return home. The country was in disarray, the threat of a total collapse imminent. His concern had grown with news of the students' deaths, understanding what grave consequences these might have as his trusted military moved to restore order. His thoughts turned to his family; his children, and grandchildren. General Winarko had assured him that they were safe. He had spoken at length with his son-in-law, General Praboyo, and as a result of their discussion, Suhapto had made his decision to return. He had read something in Praboyo's voice which greatly disturbed him; an echo from the past. The stewardess observed her VIP shiver and moved swiftly to cover the President with a blanket.

Suhapto now understood that there were forces working against him, and that these were not just those of *El Nino* or international currency speculators. The cool response he had received from what were normally receptive allies had alerted the President to his predicament.

Once considered as the leader of the world's non-aligned nations, Suhapto had been deeply disturbed by the air of indifference encountered amongst the many who had been his friends. He no longer had the support of those who had sworn their loyalty to serve him as their unchallenged leader.

Suhapto knew that even his most trenchant critics would be silenced if he could manage his way out of this crisis. His position was being seriously undermined by elements within his own power-base and Suhapto recognized that he had no choice but to return immediately and deal with the treachery, swiftly. And this, he was determined to do.

As the aircraft carried its precious passenger through the night, he refused to sleep. Instead, he revisited those events in his life which he believed had been instrumental in bringing him to power, and the faces of those whose paths had crossed his. He recalled his childhood, his mother and the difficult days of Dutch colonization, and closed his heavy eyelids, resting his white-haired head comfortably into the padded rest.

* * * *

Had it not been for his mother he would never have made it into civil service. She had remained his strength through the years, and only now did Suhapto recognize that he had, in fact, transferred much of his love from his mother to his late wife. In many ways, they had been so alike, he thought, and yet at the time he had not been conscious of these similarities.

He had entered service against the Allies, joining the Japanese sponsored militia. It was during their occupation of his native Java that he had acquired many of his skills, which he later utilized during the prolonged war for independence. His promotion to senior rank could not have come at a more appropriate time, and Suhapto's heavily-lined face in no way revealed the emotional tide which swept through his heart as the memory of his first child's birth flashed through his mind. He adored his daughter, Nuri, amazed how easily she had accepted those responsibilities his wife had carried until her recent death.

Suhapto still missed the woman, terribly, saddened also that her advice at this perilous time would not be forthcoming. He honored her memory, and how she had played such a major role in their lives and those of others, including his enemies. *Ah, yes, his enemies,* he mused, acknowledging that these had been numerous over the years, the early contenders mostly gone, only to be replaced by others who coveted the helm. He dismissed these ghosts which threatened his meditation, caring not for the millions who had lost their lives in campaigns he had waged in order that he might remain king.

His mind filled with childhood experiences and the captivating shadow-plays depicting the *Ramayana* epic as these danced behind their *dalang's* screens, and he was reminded of the similarities between this art-form and his own journey through life. Suhapto believed that he had become the greatest puppeteer of them all and, as master *dalang*, would continue to manipulate those beneath him, their movements controlled just as surely as the characters which danced in the shadow-world of the Javanese *wayang kulit* plays. Overcome by fatigue, the President drifted into a fitful sleep.

Forty-five minutes out of Jakarta's Halim Perdanakusumah Air Force Base where the country's military leadership had been tortured to death by communists decades before, the Indonesian President was woken by his aides and prepared for their imminent arrival. They landed without incident, the aircraft coming to rest directly outside the military terminal, the more than five hundred Special Forces troops inconspicuous in the shadows.

Suhapto stepped down from the aircraft and appeared to be immediately whisked away to the relative safety of his home. Two black limousines swung into view, providing the state-owned television cameras a full view of the leader's arrival, and apparent departure. The broadcast returned to the station's studios, with millions of viewers none the wiser that the former general had, in fact, been secretly ushered away from the scene to a waiting helicopter.

Unaware that many of his closest allies had gathered earlier that evening and decided to end their President's rule, Suhapto's confidence was restored as the capital's lights came into view. The irony that history had again repeated itself was lost on the exhausted leader as his helicopter delivered him safely to the palace. There, minutes later, he stepped down onto the pad and followed the very same footsteps his predecessor had taken, under identical circumstances when he too had been desperately clinging to power.

* * * *

The First Family

When news of the indiscriminate shootings spread across the Republic, the effects were not as General Praboyo had anticipated. Although similar incidents had occurred before, never in the country's history had the media been permitted such access and, in consequence, international satellite coverage of live sequences filmed by foreign journalists shocked viewers around the world. Across the country, from Sabang to Merauke students refused to be further intimidated, streaming onto the streets demanding the immediate resignation of their President, and for those responsible for the students' deaths to be punished.

The following days witnessed widespread demonstrations throughout Jakarta, effectively bringing the capital to a standstill. Rioting and looting became the order of the day, as tens of thousands vented their anger at those associated with the influential First Family. Shops and offices were closed. Chinese unable to flee overseas barricaded themselves inside their dwellings as the city braced itself against further onslaught.

'Don't go out!' Praboyo had ordered, but it really was not necessary. Alarmed by the growing number of demonstrations calling for her father to resign, Tuti and others in the family clearly understood that it would be foolish to leave the security of their well-guarded homes. She watched her husband's vehicle leave, then went to the phone to call her elder sister.

'Nuri,' she asked, anxious to hear what the rest of her family planned, *'why don't we go to Singapore?'*

'No, Bapak insists that we all stay here where he can protect us,' came her reply.

'It's not safe in Singapore?' she asked, incredulous at the suggestion.

'Of course it is!' Nuri snapped. Tension was running high in all their households. She had just returned from a lengthy discussion with the President, more confident now that the current situation would soon be resolved.

'Then why shouldn't we just leave and return when everything returns to normal?' she whined, wishing then that she had just departed without alerting any of her intentions. She listened to her older sister explain that they must remain in the country to demonstrate that they were not concerned with the civil unrest, nor the undisciplined student mobs' disrespectful behavior towards the First Family. Distressed by the pervasive influence Nuri had over their father and other members of their family, Tuti knew that it would not serve her purpose to phone the President directly and seek his permission to leave. Remaining was Nuri's idea, she thought angrily.

They finished their conversation and Tuti returned to the children's room only to find that they were still fighting, bored with having to remain indoors. She screamed at the servants to do something, anything, to occupy their time, then locked herself in her own bedroom, wishing she could escape. Alone, her mood darkened even more as the image of Praboyo in his mistress' arms filled her thoughts.

* * * *

Hani

Hani had never known such pain before. When she awoke, some minutes passed before she could identify her surroundings. The splitting headache reminded her to take the medication the doctor had prescribed, her efforts to reach for the tablets were accompanied by severe pain. It seemed that there was not one bone in her body which did not ache.

Her shocked and disapproving mother had fetched Hani from the hospital where she had remained, unconscious, for an entire day. Once she could identify herself, the authorities realized the delicacy of their predicament, moving quickly to contact General Purwadira's office. Shocked to discover that his daughter had participated in the demonstrations, and angered that she had been injured by his own forces, General Purwadira went hunting for the police officers responsible for the shootings.

His instructions had been specific; the troops were to use rubber bullets. When investigations suggested that live rounds could have been issued in error, he was devastated.

Now having rested well into the third day since her traumatic experience, Hani discovered that her father had been relieved of his command in disgrace. At first she blamed herself, believing that her participation might have resulted in the decision to remove him as Garrison Commander. But then, as her head cleared, her mother explained that the General had become the government's scapegoat for the student shootings. His career in ruins, Hani's father was urged to leave the capital, a pariah amongst his own officers. When he departed, he did so as a broken man, wrongfully accused, his pension all that remained to reflect his many years of loyal, and diligent service.

Bewildered by their sudden change in fortunes, Hani left Jakarta, and followed her family back to their home town of Sukabumi.

* * * *

Mary Jo & Hamish

Although the level of conversation had risen to a point where communication could only be achieved by shouting, the atmosphere was electric, the bar inundated by members of the foreign press.

'Over here!' Mary Jo called, waving to Hamish as he made his way to her group. Introductions were made, the bonhomie apparent as the journalists laughed and joked with each other, relating incidents of other times and places. She knew most of those present, having crossed paths in such unenviable locations as Bosnia and Ethiopia, and other countries where man had set upon man, intent on destroying the other.

'What's happening?' Hamish leaned closer and spoke loudly. He had seen little of Jo over the past thirty-six hours. Jakarta's hotels had become swamped with expatriates and their families, now too frightened to remain in their splendid mansions. Buildings continued to burn throughout the city, looters continued to run amok, and the death toll now exceeded one thousand.

The international airport had been besieged by tens of thousands wishing to escape the country, its racial violence and the threat of civil war. Foreign governments acted quickly, arranging the evacuation of their citizens with unscheduled mercy-mission flights. There was a genuine fear that it would soon be impossible to leave the country by air as roads to the Sukarno-Hatta Airport became partially blocked by demonstrations and soldiers barricading the main arterial roads. Hamish tried to communicate with Mary Jo again, but she shook her head.

'Later!' she yelled, indicating with her free hand that she had no intention of competing with the band, and Hamish nodded in agreement. He raised his hand and attracted the barman's attention. He would know what to serve; Hamish McLoughlin had been in residence long enough for most of the staff to know his name and habits. He reached between a couple of inebriated souls and retrieved his whisky.

Thankfully, the music stopped, the band having finished its first set. Mary Jo completed the introductions, and Hamish could see that her face was flushed from the alcohol. He guessed that she had been there for sometime, most probably matching her friends round for round as they recounted anecdotes from their pasts.

'Are you all staying here?' he asked a tall, thin, ginger-haired type sporting a pencil mustache.

'Good lord, no!' the man laughed. 'We're bunked four to a room at a friend's house. Besides,' he added, 'all the bloody hotels are full.' The British journalist then spotted someone across the crowded bar and made his way over to another group.

'Have you been outside the hotel at all?' Mary Jo asked Hamish.

'No, you'd have to be crazy to go out there right now.' Mary Jo recalled Hamish did not approve of the risks she took.

'Maybe you should try it, sometime. Want to come with me tomorrow?' It was not a challenge. She knew that he worried about her.

'No, Jo,' he said, far from interested, 'I'll leave it to the professionals.'

'What will you do tomorrow?'

'Sit around and wait to see what's happening with the Swiss.'

When Hamish had finally revealed the precise nature of his association with the Swiss merchant bankers, it had been done so on the premise that Mary Jo would not take advantage of any information he might inadvertently or otherwise reveal to her. He had also extracted an undertaking that she would not pursue any leads relating to his clients' activities in Indonesia.

Recently, Hamish had inferred that the Geneva-based group might be considering winding up their activities in Indonesia, at least until the situation became more conducive to foreign investment. Hamish had mentioned that he was surprised that they had kept him engaged this long. Mary Jo wondered what would happen to their relationship should Hamish leave. They had grown closer over the months, and she felt comfortable with him around. Hamish was an intelligent, energetic man, and Mary Jo knew that she could not expect him to remain in Jakarta forever, especially living permanently out of suitcases the way he did. She gave him a motherly pat on the arm, and offered to take him with her again.

'I'm serious, Hamish. Anytime you would like to come along,....' Mary Jo was half-way through the sentence, when she heard someone call out, his voice louder than the rest.

'That's not how you make Black Russians!'

Mary Jo paused, mid-sentence, the familiar resonance of the voice behind catching her off-guard, as its owner castigated the barman over preparation of the unusual drink. When she turned and saw Eric Fieldmann's rugged, handsome features, she faltered, mesmerized by his presence.

'Jo?' the CNN cameraman in her group asked, touching her lightly with his hand to gain her attention. Her mind snapped back from some distant journey, and she laughed, a little too loudly, as she over-reacted to seeing him there.

'Well!' she said, her voice attracting the attention of others outside her group, 'if it isn't the famous Fieldmann!' with which, Mary Jo flicked her head before realizing that the long, fine, blonde strands which had adorned her head when they were lovers, had long since been abandoned for a style more practical to her work. She glanced across to see if he had heard, without realizing that almost everyone present in the bar had.

Mary Jo felt the hot, burning flush sweep across her face.

'Hello, Jo,' she heard the familiar voice call. She turned to face Eric Fieldmann, as he pushed his way towards her. 'My God, Jo! Is it really you?' he called, reaching out and taking her arm as someone swore, wiping some of the newcomer's spilt drink from a sleeve. At that moment, her feet turned to lead. Then she looked up at Eric eyebrows raised.

'Then it really *is* you?' she pretended, mock surprise lighting her face. She placed one hand on his wrist and turned to her group. 'For those of you who have not been blessed, this is the famous Eric Fieldmann,' she announced, attempting to deliver the comment facetiously, instead, her voice filled with admiration. It did not go unnoticed. Hamish extended his hand and introduced himself.

'Hi, there, Eric, I'm Hamish McLoughlin.' They shook hands, then the others who had yet to meet the well known foreign correspondent stepped forward, some almost subserviently, and introduced themselves.

'What are you drinking?' someone asked, competing with the busy crowd for the barman's attention.

'Seems that you're well known,' Hamish suggested, conscious of the attention the other man's presence had attracted. 'Are you covering the riots?'

'Yes, me and half the entire goddamn Western Press,' he answered, waving his hand to indicate he meant those in the bar.

'When did you get in?' Hamish accepted another whisky as he spoke.

'Just a few hours ago. Getting through that airport would make a story in itself,' Fieldmann said. 'Don't hold much hope for those expecting to leave. The soldiers were throwing barricades across the road as we came in.'

'Have you managed to get a room somewhere yet?' Hamish glanced at Mary Jo, her cheeks still flushed.

'Yes,' he replied. 'Our lot had already secured rooms before my arrival. Thought we'd drop over and catch up with some of the others,' he indicated, this time with his head. 'We're staying at the Mandarin across the road.'

Eric Fieldmann extracted a card from his pocket, and offered this to Hamish who squinted under the dim lighting as he read the words 'Foreign Correspondent' under the well known international daily's title. Hamish extracted his wallet with one hand and reciprocated. The other man smiled, observed closely by Mary Jo as memories came flooding back of the intimate moments they had enjoyed together.

'I hear you're based here now, Jo?' Fieldmann asked. He already knew the answer. He had checked when first advised he would be traveling to the area.

'Sure am,' she confirmed, still struggling with her inner feelings. They had parted on good terms but Mary Jo had never quite forgiven him, even though she recognized that it had been her own decision to leave and follow her career interests elsewhere.

As Mary Jo and her old acquaintance talked, the warmth in their voices was not missed by Hamish. He watched, becoming aware from Mary Jo's occasional touches, and Eric's response, that the two had a history, and this disturbed him in some way. Hamish listened to their banter, annoyed with the sudden twinge of jealously. He observed her eyes and, even with the amount of alcohol she had obviously consumed that session, Hamish could detect a warmth in her expression, rekindled by this chance meeting. With mixed emotions, Hamish turned to order another round when he caught the barman's signal and moved closer to the bar.

'Someone wishes to speak to you, *tuan*,' the hotel employee indicated, pointing outside politely with his fist closed. Hamish McLoughlin's eyes followed, identifying one of the business center's secretaries waving to attract his attention. He caught Mary Jo's eye.

'Geneva,' was all he said, and left, pushing through the now boisterous throng. The band had commenced playing as he cleared the bar and approached the efficient woman waiting outside.

'You have had several calls from overseas, Mr. McLoughlin. The last was urgent, so I brought these for you to read.' She handed a number of small, sealed envelopes containing his messages. He tore these open and read the contents while she waited. Hamish had made a habit when traveling of always informing the hotel telephone operators as to his whereabouts. He thanked the secretary, deciding to return the calls from the privacy of his own room. Hamish hurried upstairs and dialed the number which had appeared on all four messages, and spoke directly to his client in Geneva. When he had finished, Hamish glanced at his watch and was surprised to discover that he had been talking for more than half an hour. The merchant bankers had requested that he proceed to Switzerland as a matter of utmost urgency. He had little choice but to accept, undertaking to leave immediately.

Considering the status of the international airport Hamish knew it would be unwise to expect to secure a seat overseas from Jakarta. However, he believed that this would be possible from other exit points such as Bali, Surabaya and even Batam Island in the north. He phoned the business centre and asked them to arrange immediate seating to any of these destinations and, within the hour, Hamish's ticket had been confirmed to Surabaya, via Bandung. He would have to drive to the mountain city and board his flight from there, early the following day.

Cursing the civil unrest, Hamish McLoughlin packed hurriedly and informed the hotel reception that he would require a car and driver immediately. He knew it would take at least three, perhaps four hours considering the current circumstances, to reach Bandung. It would be senseless expecting to complete the journey in the morning, and he believed that his decision to fly to Surabaya and then onto Singapore from the port city to be the most practical solution.

Hamish phoned the concierge and requested that they send a porter to take his baggage down to his car, while he returned to the bar to inform Mary Jo of his departure. By this time, he had been absent for more than an hour.

* * * *

'You look great, Jo,' Fieldmann flattered, his hand gently holding her upper arm. Mary Jo smiled through the light alcoholic haze, warmed by his comment and the extended drinking session.

'You don't look too bad yourself,' she responded, admiringly, her face flushed not only from the alcohol. Eric was not as tall as Hamish, nor was he as good-looking, but there was something about his confident manner and encouraging smile which Mary Jo still found enticing. She felt something stir, deep down, the warmth flowing up through her insides. *How long had it been?*

'We're going back to the Mandarin to have a few drinks there. Want to join us?' he asked. Hamish had been gone for at least half an hour, and she had no idea how much longer he might be. Mary Jo lifted herself to tiptoe and peered across the crowded bar. She knew that once Hamish started talking banking on the phone, he would often lose all track of time. It had happened before. She could leave a message with the barman.

'Sure,' she said, 'why not?' Fieldmann informed the others in his group that he was ready to leave, taking Mary Jo by the hand as he led the way through the packed bar. She followed, willingly. Suddenly, it was just like old times, and she was swept by a feeling of elation.

They walked outside, Jakarta's muggy tropical air instantly assailing their bodies as they strolled across the near-deserted roundabout and over to the Mandarin Hotel. There they met up with another group of expatriate journalists who had congregated in the Captain's Bar and, before she was aware of how it might have happened, Mary Jo found herself alone with Eric Fieldmann in his room.

* * * *

Hamish rechecked O'Reiley's Pub and still could not find Mary Jo. He asked the familiar barman if she had left, and was informed that she had departed with the group she had been drinking with earlier. Hamish remembered Fieldmann saying where they were staying, and he went to the hotel phones and asked to be connected the Mandarin Hotel's main bar. Having stayed there he knew that it would be unlikely that the journalists would be anywhere else.

The barman there could not find anyone fitting her description and put the call back to the operator. Frustrated, and increasingly impatient to get on the road, he asked to be connected back to the Captains Bar once again, where he asked for *Tuan* Fieldmann. The barman passed the phone to the group of noisy journalists.

'Who do you want?' a near-drunk voice demanded.

'Is Eric Fieldmann there by any chance?' Hamish inquired, ready to give up and leave. He could call her from Bandung or Surabaya and explain.

'Just a moment,' the voice replied, and then, 'hold on,' he offered, 'I'll have the operator put you through,' with which, he handed the phone back to the barman and asked him to tell the operator to connect the caller to the correspondent's room. Hamish listened to the clicks as the hotel's telephone system found the correct number and connected.

* * * *

The phone rang several times and Mary Jo looked at the locked bathroom door wondering if Fieldmann was going to answer. When he didn't and the ringing continued, she sighed, and lifted the receiver.

'Hello,' she said, a thought passing through her mind, 'Eric is currently indisposed,' she giggled, listening for a response, greeted only by silence. 'Hello,' she tried again, but there was still nothing. Mary Jo shrugged, looked at the mouthpiece as if half-expecting to see the caller, then hung up. 'Goddamn phones,' she muttered, then banged on the bathroom door and told Fieldmann to hurry as she wished to use the bathroom herself. When he did not emerge immediately, Mary Jo decided to return to the Captains Bar and use the toilets there. As she hurried across the lobby, she stumbled into a team of journalists, rushing from the hotel.

'What's happening?' she called, not wishing to stop.

'The students have occupied the Parliament,' one of their number obliged, shifting the weight of his gear as he did so. 'Looks like the army is going to clash with the students again,' with which, he was gone, chasing after the others. Even in her inebriated state, Mary Jo sensed that history was in the making, and she should be present at the scene. She hurried to the bathroom, emerging minutes later to phone her villa.

Mary Jo spoke to her assistant, Anne, the alcoholic haze clearing as her brain clicked into gear.

'Get moving, Annie,' she ordered, having already advised her which equipment she needed.

'Where will we meet?' Anne asked.

Mary Jo thought for a few moments. 'Wait for me at the steps to the main building.'

'Are you sure you don't want me to pick you up?'

'No', she replied, glancing at her watch, 'I'll take a hotel taxi.' Arrangements in place, Mary Jo rushed outside only to discover that none of the drivers would risk the short journey. She wasted valuable minutes arguing with the staff, during which time she learned that the other journalists had been picked up by associates in their station vehicle. She knew that Anne would already have left the villa and, in a pique of anger, she set out on foot, finally flagging down a passing student on his way to join the demonstration.

* * * *

As Mary Jo's long strides took her along *Jalan Jenderal Sudirman* and away from the hotel, she was unseen by the occupants of the vehicle which had, only moments before, pulled out of the Grand Hyatt Hotel on its journey to Bandung. Inside, Hamish McLoughlin sat staring out through the heavily tinted windows, his anger at Mary Jo's behavior growing as images of her naked lying beneath another man filled his mind, tormenting him even further. Mary Jo's transgression remained clouding his thoughts as he continued on his way to Bandung, and even after he departed the country.

* * * *

Tel Aviv

In view of the deteriorating situation in Indonesia, General Saguy had issued instructions for McLoughlin to be recalled, his contract to be determined. Although Hamish's astute financial skills had provided Mossad with the knowledge it had required at the time, his services were now no longer of any real value. It was time to prepare for any sudden change in the country's leadership.

The Mossad director's concern revolved around who might assume the nation's helm as it was apparent that Suhapto would soon fall. The possibility that Vice President Hababli was next in line, sent a chill through his spine, for it was Hababli who had been responsible for orchestrating the flow of government funds into Moslem extremists' hands. That, and the man's penchant for elaborate military acquisitions, made the man even more dangerous than his mentor. General Saguy's position remained clear. Should Hababli manage against all odds to become the next President of Indonesia, then every effort would be made to ensure that he would not remain in that position of power long enough to pose any long-term threat, with his idiosyncratic ways.

When Hamish McLoughlin arrived in Geneva, he would be advised of his contract's termination.

Chapter Thirteen

Jakarta Houses of Parliament

Mary Jo

Mary Jo felt dreadfully weary. She rubbed reddened gritty eyes with the back of one hand, the dull thumping pain in her temples gaining tempo with every movement. Mary Jo had been there almost fifteen hours straight without a break. It had taken more than two hours to find Anne amongst the multitude of students and spectators now numbering, she guessed, in excess of fifty thousand. She looked down at her clothes and shook her head sadly, wishing she had worn something less spectacular into the hotel the night before. Her entire body ached. Severely hung over and desperate to remove the metallic taste in her mouth, Mary Jo had resorted to drinking the thick, suspiciously-dark sludge which passed for local coffee, made available with the sudden influx of roadside vendors.

She had spoken to many students at the scene, recording those who spoke English, photographing others as an almost carnival atmosphere prevailed. She was curious to observe the lack of response from the soldiers who walked amongst the students, apparently making no attempt whatsoever to dislodge the demonstrators from the green-domed Parliamentary buildings. By noon she was exhausted and Anne drove her back to the villa where she bathed and changed, then rested for an hour while the servants prepared a quick lunch.

Mary Jo took a few minutes to phone the Hyatt and was stunned to discover that Hamish had checked out.

'Did he leave any message?' she had asked.

'No, miss,' the operator advised.

'Are you sure?' she demanded, believing the girl had not even bothered to check.

'I will connect you to the front desk, miss,' the operator offered, and Mary Jo went through the procedure again, the reception staff confirming that *Tuan* Hamish McLoughlin had left late last night and had driven to Bandung.

She struggled to remember the sequence of events leading up to her departure from his hotel but her memory was clouded. Vaguely she recalled Hamish leaving not long after bumping into Eric Fieldmann. Mary Jo decided that Hamish had been delayed by one of his international calls. This had happened before. She frowned. Obviously he would have tried to contact her and had been unable to do so. *Why had he gone to Bandung?* she wondered.

Pressed for time, Mary Jo returned to the city, arriving on their motorbike, just as the crowd broke into an incredible roar. She waited impatiently while Anne parked the Suzuki, then pushed through to the centre of the throng gathered outside the main steps. Mary Jo raised her camera, activating the zoom lens to snap a student standing on the building's roof brandishing an oversized red and white flag. The chanting recommenced, the air electric as the youths taunted the soldiers bringing the confrontation to flash-point.

'Suhapto resign! Suhapto resign!'

'Hang Suhapto! Hang those who murder students!

'Reform, Reform, we want reform!' the students screamed, their voices filling the air as soldiers looked on, seemingly indifferent to the fact that the country's Houses of Parliament had been occupied by the demonstrators. They had their orders; they were to avoid any further student deaths.

* * * *

Listen to me!' Abdul Muis called, the prominent figure appealing to the demonstrators. *'Listen to me!'*

Those closest to the man turned to others behind and yelled loudly, *'It's Haji Abdul Muis. Be quiet! Listen, he wishes to address the demonstrators!'* Immediately a hush descended upon the thousands gathered there, many surging forward in order that they might hear the powerful Moslem leader's words.

Satisfied that he had control over the situation, Haji Abdul Muis raised his outstretched arms and called upon the students to pray for those who had died days before, cut down by police bullets. The students obeyed. Then Abdul Muis raised his arms again, addressing them with a fire none in this country had heard since the days of Soekarno's charismatic appeals to the people of Indonesia.

'Fellow citizens,' he commenced, *'the time has arrived for Suhapto to step down.'* This was met with thunderous applause, the main body of the demonstrators cheering wildly for never before had someone of the Haji's standing ever displayed such courage in defying the brutal Suhapto regime.

'I have made the call to the Mufti Muharam and can tell you now, that come this Saturday, one million of my followers will march down the streets of this city in support of your demands and those of the people of Indonesia for Suhapto to resign!'

Abdul Muis' statement was met with an incredible roar as the demonstrators cheered the religious leader, their response swelling his chest with pride. Now he was certain that he had made the correct decision. Earlier he had agonized whether he should take such a grave risk, and place his safety in jeopardy. Muis knew that Praboyo's men were prowling around somewhere out there in the dark. Although he had nothing to fear from the General, Muis was not overly confident that Praboyo's troops would not open fire on the students as they continued to occupy the government buildings.

He had phoned the Jakarta Garrison to inform them of his intentions to address the students, suggesting that his presence might have a pacifying effect. The new commander had insisted that he take military bodyguards, but wisely Muis had refused the offer. Standing before these tens of thousands of students he now believed that his timing could not have been more perfect and that the government was clearly on the verge of collapse.

Abdul Muis had considered waiting for the final curtain to come down on the Suhapto regime and then step in alongside General Praboyo, once he had assumed a caretaker's role over the Presidency. But he was concerned that Praboyo might not be able to succeed with his ambitious strategy.

Muis's move was motivated by his uneasy feeling that perhaps his ally, Praboyo, may have stronger enemies than first envisaged. Muis had publicly joined the growing anti-Suhapto movement in order that his future position and options remain flexible. The government could not, he knew, afford another martyr at this time, especially one of his standing within the Moslem community. He hoped that this would be clearly understood by those who may be tempted to have him removed, that the threat of his thirty million followers tearing the country apart in the event of his death was a very real possibility.

Muis firmly believed that he could easily muster one million Moslems to flood Jakarta's streets in opposition to Suhapto, but he would never have considered such bold action without Praboyo's support. Cleverly he had identified this opportunity to place his *Mufti Muharam* at the forefront of the political push to remove Suhapto, riding on the gathering momentum fueled by the students' anger over the recent shootings. Muis had been as stunned as any other that the military had arbitrarily opened fire, killing and wounding so many. It was apparent that whoever had issued the order to shoot on that day had brought an end to Suhapto's rule, just as surely as any assassin's bullet.

* * * *

'We must have new elections,' his voice cried out, *'and initiate reforms quickly to prevent further suffering! We must force those from power who are corrupt, and place those at the country's helm who are fit both morally and spiritually and eradicate the evil which has destroyed our country!'* The students greeted this also with a salvo of wild cheering, their chanting making it almost impossible for Muis to be heard.

'We must demand that the people are given the opportunity to embrace Allah freely, and receive their rightful representation through the Parliamentary process. If the people of Indonesia ask, I will offer myself to my country to participate in these changes.' Again the crowd roared.

'And we should hold to account all of those who have corrupted our people, becoming fat from the sweat and misery of others. We must not permit the Chinese to take control of our economy ever again!' The students swung into action, their chants picked up by others as their racist slogans carried through the evening air.

'Down with the Chinese! Down with the likes of Lim!'

'Down with the Chinese, ban corrupters such as him!'

'Hiduplah Abdul Muis! Long live Abdul Muis!

Although there was a considerable number of Chinese students who attended the university, few would have dared attend such demonstrations, remaining behind locked doors hoping, as did many in the community, that President Suhapto would soon take stern measures to restore peace to the country.

Abdul Muis continued to harangue the now devoted gathering, recognizing that as he spoke, foreign journalists were busy setting up lighting for their cameramen. He watched with pleasure as daylight arrived, revealing the swelling numbers of foreign journalists and, tired as he was, Muis smiled benevolently as his picture was captured for readers and audiences around the world.

He remained throughout the morning, strolling amongst the students offering them words of support and encouragement, posing whenever the opportunity arose, and speaking directly to those foreign journalists who wished to interview the man whose name, just days before, had been absolutely unknown to the Western media. Before mid-morning hundreds of thousands of words had been filed with editorial staff around the globe, and Abdul Muis's powerful Moslem party was reported in depth.

Amongst these would be Mary Jo Hunter's brilliant story on Haji Abdul Muis and the rise of militancy within his ranks. She would write of the growing evidence of Islamic extremists' influence over the powerful Moslem following, and highlighted the dangers of militant fundamentalism without realizing just how prophetic her words might be. For, in the years that followed, the *Mufti Muharam* would strike terror in the hearts of Christians throughout the Indonesian archipelago, and result in one of the greatest exoduses ever to be recorded in modern history.

* * * *

Lily

Due to the civil unrest *Oom Setio* had instructed members of his household to remain within the condominium, preferably inside their own apartment. Lily knew from their conversations that her uncle was alarmed at the increased levels of racial violence. Her uncle had little choice but to remain in Jakarta. The Chinese broker believed that his absence would only act as a catalyst for others to destroy what he had taken years to build. Satellite news only reinforced what they already suspected. The airports were impossibly inundated with fleeing residents, tourists, businessmen and even embassy staff. What chance would they have, even if they weren't too frightened to make a dash for the airport?

Lily sat beside her cousin, Layla, watching the CNN broadcasts. She turned to the national station, TVRI, the presenters carrying on as usual, unable to report the country's deteriorating situation due to strict censorship imposed by the Suhapto regime. Lily then switched over to the President's son's private channel, but this was the same. It was as if they were living in two separate worlds.

She slipped off the sofa and wandered into the kitchen where her aunt was busily preparing their midday meal.

'Are you ready to eat?' her doting aunt asked. It seemed that whenever a crisis arose, she would disappear into the kitchen and commence cooking. Lily knew that this generation believed that stuffing oneself with food often assisted to place one's problems in the correct perspective.

'No, not yet,' she replied, wondering why their servants had not appeared for work that day. Lily strolled back out to the lounge, observed Layla now watching cartoons, and made her way outside where she leant against the balcony railing. She peered down wistfully at the swimming pool twelve floors below. Despite her pleas she had not been permitted down to that level alone and thought her uncle a little extreme. Lily had never felt uneasy within the complex grounds. The well-paid security guards always smiled whenever she visited the pool for her daily workout, and not once had she experienced any animosity from the well-paid, blue-uniformed men who patrolled the huge building. Below Lily could just make out a number of foreigners swimming and felt resentful that she would miss another opportunity to train.

Across the city she could see evidence of the ongoing violence as clouds of smoke threatened to blanket the capital's skyline. She had watched with mounting concern when students had taken control over the Houses of Parliament and the Moslem leader Abdul Muis had addressed the huge rally in the most inflammatory way, accusing Chinese of being jointly responsible, with the President, for the country's economic collapse. It was then that her uncle had insisted that the three women remain inside where they would be safe. Although this building was predominantly Chinese occupied, *Oom Setio* had comforted them, denying that residential properties such as theirs had already come under attack. The billowing dark clouds evident from their windows were, he had assured them, from offices and shopping centers which had been identified by looters as belonging to the First Family.

Lily watched the small figures below as they swam around the setting where, one week before, she had spent the entire afternoon in the pool with Hani. The memory of her friend's sudden, vehement attack still saddened her. She wondered if she would ever be able to face Hani after what had taken place, accepting now that nothing would ever be the same again.

She expected that *Oom Setio* would stay to protect his interests but was unsure whether this would involve her remaining in Jakarta with her uncle as nothing had been discussed, at least not with her. Events had overtaken her family with such speed, she was confused as to what the future might hold.

A loud banging caught her attention and Lily turned to see her cousin

Layla running for the door. Immediately she was gripped by fear, knowing that her uncle always called to alert his family from the underground car-park, before catching the lift.

'Wait!' she yelled to the younger girl, leaping inside to prevent her from opening the door. *Oom Setio* had been adamant. They were not to open the door to anyone during his absence.

'Who..?' the twelve year old started to ask, having already released the security lock and opened the door. She was not tall enough to peek through the spy-hole. As she did so the door crashed inwards under the weight of intruders, smashing Layla to the floor.

'Ibu!' she screamed, her mother already running to see what was happening. *'Ibu!'* Layla screamed again, staring up at the young men who had invaded their apartment.

'Shut up!' one hissed. Lily was certain she recognized the face. *Was he one of the building's security guards?*

'What do you want?' her terrified aunt cried, bending down to protect her child.

'I said, shut up!' the first man yelled, then stepped forward and struck her fiercely with his fists knocking Layla's mother unconscious to the ground. Lily's first reaction was that they were after money. They would know that *Oom Setio* had gone out. She suspected that they would steal, then run, knowing that it would be most unlikely anyone would take chase once they had fled the building. Her mind raced. *What could she offer them so they would go, and leave them alone?*

'You!' another man barked, pointing at Lily. Her stomach filled with fear. He brandished a long, home-made carving knife, and advanced threateningly towards where she stood.

'Lie down!' he ordered, but Lily's mind locked, overcome with terror. *'I said, lie down, you filthy Chinese whore!'* the man screamed, lifting his knee suddenly, striking her savagely in the thigh. The excruciating pain ripped through her body, the shock so severe, her cry choked in her throat as she fell to the floor.

'Get this one first!' she heard someone say. As she lay there writhing, Lily could still see her cousin. Two of the men dragged her a few steps, then closed the apartment's front door behind.

'Please! Please don't hurt her!' she heard herself cry, Layla was now aware of what was happening, but too terrified to scream. *'Please!'* she sobbed, again, *'we have money. Please stop!'* she begged, *'I will find the money for you!'*

'Grab her arms,' the first man ordered, another then bending down onto his knees to hold Layla's tiny, outstretched limbs.

'No! Please!' Lily cried out loudly, *'don't do this to her!'* then felt the stinging pain as a third thug reached down and hit her with his rough open hand.

'Ibu! Ibu!' Layla cried out, but her mother was unable to assist, her unconscious body lying crumpled on the floor. *'Lily! Lily!'* she pleaded, *'please Lily, help me!'* The first man ripped her panties away, freeing these from her legs as he groped impatiently to release his own clothing.

'No! Don't! Please don't!' she whimpered, her choking sobs suddenly cut off in midair, a look of startled disbelief crossing her face as her attacker lunged brutally forward and entered her.

'I...b..u...!' the twelve year old screamed, then screamed again while Lily lay stunned, witnessing the savage rape. She closed her eyes, her feeble attempts to block out the horrific scene unsuccessful as the man grunted loudly, his excitement rising as he continued his abuse. Then suddenly a shrill cry pierced the air as the attacker cried out, leaving no doubt in his victims' minds what this was really all about.

'Allahu Akbar!' he screamed, *'Allahu Akbar!'* the Moslem chant sending another chill through Lily's heart.

Spent, the man jumped to his feet laughing, and nodded to the other who had held his prey's arms, to follow. One by one, the others gleefully took their turn raping Layla as Lily watched helplessly, noting that all shouted the same terrifying words as they climaxed. When they had finished her cousin's bloodied body lay twisted like some broken, discarded doll, Layla's glazed eyes wide open, her face frozen in an expression of continuing shock. Lily looked across to where her aunt had fallen, observing that she had regained consciousness, and now sat on the cold marble floor. Dazed, she turned and saw her daughter lying silently within reach, and bent forward to take Layla in her arms.

'Kill her!' Lily heard one of their attackers hiss from the other side of the sofa, and she tried to cry out but she choked on her fear. She heard steps then a cracking sound, followed by a sickening thud as her aunt's head smashed against the marble, killing her instantly.

'And her!' the voice ordered. Lily gasped, her body trembling uncontrollably as she felt the warm flow break loose and run down her legs, knowing that death was imminent.

'Wait, you fool!' their leader yelled, *'get the jewelry first!'* She felt strong hands grip her shoulders roughly, followed by tearing sounds as clothing was ripped from her body.

'Where is the money and gold?' the pack's leader demanded. Lily remained standing, naked, shaking, her hands crossed to cover her shame.

'In.. the.. bedroom,' she sobbed, her answer earning her a savage blow across her face. She lifted her hands instinctively and one of the men laughed, making a lewd gesture which Lily clearly understood.

'Show us!' the man snapped, grabbing her wrist and twisting it cruelly. Lily cried out, but her whimpers only attracted more laughter. She led the men into her uncle's bedroom where they set about searching for whatever *Oom Setio* had hidden there. They found her aunt's jewelry and discovered several thousand American dollars in one of the bedside drawers. Satisfied there was nothing else secreted away, undiscovered, they divided their spoils, Lily watching while silently praying that they would leave without killing her as they had the others. One of the men left, grumbling that he had expected more. Another cast her a glance, sending a chill through her spine.

'What about her?' he asked, nodding in her direction. She could see that the other man was considering her presence. When he smirked at his friend, her heart went dreadfully cold.

'I'm ready,' he said, placing his booty on the floor beside the bed. *'Get over here!'* he snarled, but Lily's legs were locked in fear.

'No, please!' she begged, choking back the bile in her throat, watching the men advance. One took her by the arm and led her to her uncle's double bed. She did not resist; she knew that would only make it worse. Naked, she was pulled down roughly by her assailants, their hands moving excitedly, forcing her legs wide. Lily cried out, the shock causing her to bite her lip as one of the men mounted her quickly, then, mercifully, she was struck, brutally, and fainted, remaining unconscious throughout both attacks.

When Lily awoke she screamed at the concerned figures standing over her, the unfamiliar faces of neighboring Chinese tenants gathered around where she lay naked, stunned at the callousness of her attackers. That she had been left alive, in itself, was a miracle. She was bundled along the hallway by a number of women, and taken into their apartment where she remained until her Uncle Setio returned home and learned of the deaths of his wife and youngest daughter.

In the course of that one day, one hundred and sixty-eight women of Chinese descent were raped in Indonesia, twenty with such brutality the victims died. Of the total number, one hundred and fifty two cases occurred in the capital, Jakarta. Reports continued to flow into police posts as the ethnic violence targeting young Chinese girls went unpunished, many still in their early teens; some dragged off buses and attacked in broad daylight, and in full view of others. Many attacks went unrecorded, the victims either too frightened or fearful of the disgrace their community would undoubtedly cast upon them. With the exception of a few, their reports all contained one thing in common; the attacks had been carried out by men who made no attempt to disguise that they were Moslems.

Lily's cousin and aunt were cremated, and during those few days of preparation her uncle spoke not once, his silence accusatory as were his grief-stricken eyes. She had survived and would now carry some of the blame. That week, Lily left what was once her city of dreams forever.

Overcome with shame, Lily sadly caught the train home to the East Javanese town of Situbondo where she was met by her mother, and taken back to her humble beginnings in awkward silence. There she would remain, the horrors of the attack revisiting as frequently as she dreamt, the chant of her Moslem assailants etched forever in her mind, so that she would never forget.

'Allahu Akbar! Allahu Akbar!'

* * * *

General Praboyo

The two powerful men remained in conference for less than half an hour, after which they parted. The *Kopassus* commander returned to his headquarters while Praboyo headed for his father-in-law's home to attend his own crisis meeting, called by the President's eldest daughter.

Praboyo's gambit in having the Chinese come under attack was a dangerous game he knew, accepting that his strategy would inevitably stir strong feelings both domestically and amongst Indonesia's neighbors. His close friend and ally who commanded *Kopassus* had not hesitated when asked to cut the Special teams loose, their instructions to specifically target young Chinese women apparently successful. Once he held power Praboyo would demonstrate that he would hold no truck with anti-Chinese sentiment, reversing the current trends, encouraging them to return with their vast capital.

When he arrived at the tastefully decorated residence and was ushered inside, General Praboyo was surprised to discover that Vice President Hababli was to be present during the private family discussions. Praboyo decided that he would be his customary, forceful, but charming self.

An hour later, his chest swelling with pride, Lieutenant General

Praboyo left the First Family's home in the company of his wife, convinced that he would be appointed as the Armed Forces Chief of Staff, his promotion a product of growing opposition towards President Suhapto from within the military.

The President had given his word; his son-in-law would be nominated as his successor before the end of the current Presidential term. Praboyo understood what went with the appointment. There would be considerable resistance to his usurping General Winarko's authority. He would have to be extremely careful and move quickly to quell all opposition by having those officers who were loyal, quickly and firmly ensconced in the more strategic commands.

Praboyo prepared himself mentally for what steps he would take once the President had made his announcement appointing his son-in-law to the country's most powerful military position. He would have his own man take over the *Kostrad* command, and issue orders to have *Kopassus* Special Forces guards placed in strategic positions.

He considered General Winarko and decided that he could be useful. How to secure the man's loyalty would be the problem. Praboyo expected some resistance from the man. After all, he already held the position Praboyo coveted and was unlikely not to resent the President's change of heart. Winarko's proud Javanese heritage would make it impossible for him not to feel bitter. Praboyo understood that a compromise might not be avoidable; he would need to examine his options in greater depth before the announcement.

A smile suddenly replaced the growing frown on Praboyo's face, reminded that he still had the one wild card which would unseat Winarko should this be necessary. Abdul Muis had already broken new ground siding with the students. Praboyo thought the move to be politically opportune, but was concerned that in light of recent developments he might be obliged to consider having Muis shunted off somewhere, before his influence grew to represent any real threat.

And then there were the Americans. General Praboyo would contact Colonel Carruthers and inform him of the President's announcement in advance. Praboyo smiled again, anticipating the American Defense Intelligence Agency Attaché's surprise when he learned that Praboyo, whose skills were developed under the watchful eyes of American instructors, would be elevated to the position of *ABRI's* Chief of Staff within twenty-four hours.

Still savoring these thoughts, General Praboyo, Butcher of East Timor and Indonesian Presidential aspirant, prepared himself for what he knew would be a most historic day.

* * * *

The First Family

'...and it is therefore not only my opinion, but also that of the Perkarya functional group's senior leadership, that President Suhapto must step down immediately.' The shock statement brought looks of total surprise as the House Speaker, one of President Suhapto's staunchest allies and closest friends since he took power, announced that he could no longer support the ailing President. Local reporters clamored for further detail, shouting to be heard as the Speaker waited for the noise to abate in order that he might continue.

'Who will replace the Bapak?' a reporter yelled, his question foremost on the mind of all present.

'A new President must be appointed according to the Constitution,' the politician replied.

'Will it be the Vice President?' another asked, glancing angrily as those who pushed from behind, *'or will General Winarko assume control until there are fresh elections?'*

'As I have just said,' the Speaker answered sharply, annoyed with the question, *'whatever takes place must be in accordance with the Constitution.'*

'Will you personally speak to the President?' someone called out, the room suddenly flooded with lights as the government television station cameras commenced rolling. Journalists shielded their eyes with notepads, surprised that the cameras were present.

'Yes, I am leaving for the Palace to discuss our decisions with Bapak Suhapto now,' he advised, rising as he fielded this question indicating that the press conference was over.

News of this incredible development was broadcast live across the nation, the ramifications of President Suhapto being asked to resign by his own political party signifying, to some, that the end was near. A thunderous cheer reverberated through the air as the students outside became aware of the announcement and they recommenced chanting, calling for the despised leader's head.

'Gantung Suhapto! Hang Suhapto!' their cry taken up by the many thousands who had joined the demonstrators in support of their cause. Soldiers remained cool to the student presence but permitted the occupation to

continue. Their response alerted the media to the obvious; that there were those amongst the military leadership opposed to their President who condoned the student activity. They had seen it all before as many of their number had participated in the demonstrations which had brought the former dictator to his knees. Then, as the cancer of corruption consumed the government from within, they had become disillusioned. When news broke regarding the House Speaker's announcement, smiles of satisfaction crossed the faces of many senior officers, while others remained stunned at the treachery.

Not fifteen minutes drive from where the students prematurely celebrated the President's downfall, General Praboyo lay with his mistress in her suburban retreat, oblivious to events unfolding during this interlude. Her familiar smell excited his senses, taking his mind on a journey far from the complicated machinations which at that moment threatened to destroy Praboyo and his dream to become President. As his body moved rhythmically, his mind filled with carnal pleasure, the Menadonese girl's warmth engulfed him and Praboyo surrendered, surprising his lover with the intensity of his climax.

Their tryst at an end Praboyo drove back to his headquarters, his spirits high as he entered the Merdeka Square compound, where he was greeted by an anxious adjutant.

'The Bapak has been calling for you repeatedly,' he was informed. Alarmed, General Praboyo instructed the officer to call ahead, advising the President that he would be there immediately. He covered the short distance through Menteng within minutes and was startled as he approached the barricades blocking this well-guarded street. The familiar red-colored berets were gone. In their place he was astonished to see that elements of the First Infantry Brigade had assumed control. Their colonel approached Praboyo's vehicle.

'Pak Praboyo?' he asked, peering through the now opened driver's window.

'What are your men doing here?' Praboyo demanded.

'General Winarko's instructions,' the brigade commander answered, and Praboyo detected a hint of insolence in the man's voice. The colonel then ordered the barricade removed, and saluted as the general angrily slammed his foot down hard causing the officer to leap sideways. Furious with Winarko's bold move, he drove the short distance to the President's home and stormed inside. There he discovered ashen-faced members of the First Family gathered outside their father's main guest room, waiting nervously as discussions continued inside. He ignored them all, including his wife,

Tuti, and marched forward intent on confronting those who were with the President. He flung the doors open angrily, and was startled by the familiar sound of weapons being cocked. Waves of anger engulfed Praboyo as he stood, speechless, staring at the two automatic weapons pointed directly at his chest. He looked at the President sitting across from a group of men he knew to be Parliamentary factional leaders. Behind these stood his rival, General Winarko.

'Bapak?' he asked, confused by the scene before him. The President looked up at his son-in-law, his face tired but expressionless.

'Leave us,' was all he said, then turned to face the man whom he had once considered amongst his closest friends. Stunned, General Praboyo turned slowly, his movements uncharacteristically stiff as he returned to the family room.

He went to his wife's side and gripped her arm, squeezing it tightly.

'What's happening?' he demanded harshly. Tuti winced, pulling away from her husband.

'They are trying to force the Bapak to resign,' she spat, her voice filled with venom. *'Where have you been? We have been trying to contact you for hours!'*

'Who's behind this?' he snapped, turning to examine their faces. *'Is it Winarko?'*

'Why don't you wait, 'Boyo,' the eldest daughter, Nuri, suggested. *'My father has asked that we remain calm, and wait until he has finished with those inside.'*

'Wait?' he retorted, *'wait for what?'*

'Our father will want to talk to all of us. He said we should wait and he will explain what is happening. Please show a little patience for once, 'Boyo!' Nuri answered testily, then turned as the two large teak doors leading to where her father was in conference swung open. They remained silent as those inside took their leave of the President, and departed in uncustomary haste.

General Winarko was last to leave. As he passed through the family room, he stopped, and smiled at Nuri before bidding her goodnight, deliberately ignoring Praboyo's presence. Then, he too slipped out into the night, leaving the Suhaptos to spend their last night together, as the country's First Family.

Chapter Fourteen

PRESIDENTIAL PALACE - 21ST MAY 1998

Mary Jo

Mary Jo waved her Press pass as she hurried into the crowded hall, already jammed to capacity with cameras and media representatives from all parts of the globe. Anne followed, having wheeled the motorbike, their now preferred mode of transport, into the designated parking area.

'Is it true?' she overheard one of the foreigners ask, 'will he really do it?'

'That's the rumor.'

'I wouldn't bet this month's cheque on it,' this, from the Asia Week journalist who had been stuck in the city for days. The mass exodus continued, fueled by food shortages as supermarket shelves remained bare. 'He has offered to step down before,' he added, 'at least twice that I can remember.' Mary Jo pushed closer to the front maneuvering around the congested scene as cameras blocked her advance.

Suddenly, there was a hush as President Suhapto appeared, accompanied by Vice President Hababli, senior *ABRI* officers, and others. Mary Jo did not bother with her recorder. She knew that Annie would be somewhere amongst the throng and would tape the announcement, and translate this later. Cameras flashed as the aging President moved towards the microphones, his stiff movements and puffed face mirroring his fatigue. He coughed, then extracted some notes from inside his modest, gray safari-jacket and commenced to read.

'To the people of Indonesia,' Suhapto said, his voice carrying an edge of sadness as millions around the world listened, an interpreter providing an instantaneous English translation softly in the background.

'You are all aware of the difficulties which have beset our nation. During these recent times I have carefully followed developments which have led to civil

unrest and understand the people's aspirations in seeking reform. Based on my conclusion that these initiatives must be addressed in an orderly, peaceful and constitutional manner, and in the interests of maintaining national unity and cohesion within the Republic, I formed a council to implement the desired changes to the Cabinet, and commence the reform processes that you have sought.

'As your President I have endeavored to resolve the crisis through the advisory reform council but, faced with the growing burden of resolving our many problems, some members of this body have resigned, rendering it impossible for me to continue.' He coughed, then paused, regaining his breath. *'Considering this development I am of the opinion that it would be difficult for me to implement in a good manner, my duties in governing the State.'*

'People of Indonesia. After careful deliberation and consultation with members of Parliament, I have decided to declare that I have ceased to be the President of the Republic of Indonesia as of the moment I have completed this statement. In line with Article Eight of the Constitution, I hand over the office of President to Dr. L.B. Hababli, the Vice President, to conclude the remainder of the Presidential term which will come to an end in the year two thousand and three.

'For the assistance and support given to me during the period I have been your President, I thank you all and trust that in your hearts, you will forgive me for my shortcomings and mistakes. May the Indonesian nation remain victorious, and may you continue to adhere to the principles of the Panca Sila and the Constitution.

'I express my thanks also to members of the outgoing Cabinet. In order that a leadership vacuum does not exist, I now ask the Vice President to take his oath here, today, before members of the Supreme Court of Indonesia.'

The assembly watched in silence as L.B. Hababli stepped forward and took the oath of office, while Suhapto looked on, his hands clasped subserviently in front, Hababli's unexpected appointment proof of Indonesia's eternal, political deceptiveness. *Was there a smile on the outgoing President's lips?*

Mary Jo continued shooting, acknowledging that she was witnessing perhaps one of the most historic events this country would record, her lens capturing the serious expressions of those standing on the dais.

A murmur passed through the media as the handsome General Winarko then stepped forward to address the people of Indonesia.

'It is my duty, as Chief of Staff of the Indonesian Armed Forces to confirm that ABRI will continue to support the Constitution and our new President. I call upon all factions to follow, and work together to overcome the problems with which we are faced as a nation. I wish also to state here, that former President Suhapto and

his family will remain under the protection of the Armed Forces. Terima kasih.' Having thanked those present, the four-star army general then stepped back out of the limelight before he could be quizzed by the press.

Mary Jo's Nikon F90 worked overtime, catching the historic moments as her lens moved from Suhapto to Winarko, across to the new President and those who waited in the wings. There, she spotted a familiar figure, and checked the monitor before snapping Haji Abdul Muis's profile as he turned away.

Around the world millions sat transfixed to their television sets as they witnessed what they believed would be the final chapter in the Suhapto saga, whilst those who understood the Javanese mind clicked their tongues, wondering what the former President's game plan would now be, believing that the master tactician would continue to manipulate, preserving his powerful kingdom with the aid of his former adjutant, General Winarko.

* * * *

Exhausted, Mary Jo returned to her villa early. She was asleep when Winarko's troops stormed the Parliament and removed the students. Apart from bruised pride, the youngsters evacuated the buildings without any casualties being recorded. As the soldiers swarmed through the buildings wielding lengths of rattan cane, resistance crumbled, and the weary youngsters went peacefully, many bussed back to their universities under army supervision.

'Sorry, Mary Jo, but it was all over before I even knew.' Anne had broken the news to Mary Jo the following morning.

'It's incredible that no one was hurt,' Mary Jo commented. 'If it had been that easy, why hadn't the military removed the students before this?' Anne shrugged her shoulders.

'Perhaps they were content just to have Suhapto out,' she replied, 'don't forget that they are to face term exams in three days.' Mary Jo considered this and came to the conclusion that the students had just run out of steam. They prepared their equipment, then climbed aboard their Suzuki and headed into the city.

When the two journalists drove downtown they discovered that the military had been active through the night, preparing for the one million *Mufti Muharam* followers to descend upon the city. The roads leading to Merdeka Square had all been barricaded, as were other protocol streets around the capital. Armored personnel carriers and tanks stood ominously at most major intersections, while twenty-five thousand crack troops prepared for the onslaught. Windows and doors were locked, traffic was near non-existent, hotel guests remained inside and, as Mary Jo clung to the motorbike speeding along the deserted streets, she had difficulty believing that this was a city of more than ten million inhabitants. *Where had they all gone?*

Anne steered the bike into the Hotel Indonesia grounds and parked in a 'keep clear' zone. Ignoring the security guard's glare, they entered the hotel and went directly to the top floor of the southern wing, the aerial view confirming their suspicions that the demonstration had been called off. Abdul Muis had let the students down and, in so doing, had squandered his own credibility. *Had he done a deal with the new President?*

The women returned to the villa. Mary Jo filed her story with New York highlighting the morning's surprising non-attendance by the *Mufti Muharam* millions. Her article provided an overview of the week's incredible events, depicting a nation slipping dangerously towards total anarchy. As families continued to search through smoldering buildings for missing relatives, others waited tearfully for their children to return, unaware that many of these had been kidnapped and murdered by the *Kopassus*, Special forces, their bodies buried where they would never be detected.

Her story would reveal, that in the nine days following the student shootings, more than twelve hundred people had been killed, with several thousands more seriously injured. Mary Jo expected the number to grow as reports from outlying provinces continued to flow into the capital. The damage to property had yet to be calculated, but she knew that more than a thousand shops and major centers had been destroyed, including many of the McDonald's and other high-profile food chain stores. Eight hundred movie theaters had closed, more than a quarter of these having been damaged in fires which had been lit during matinee sessions when those inside had been predominantly children. The number of churches severely damaged or destroyed reached three hundred, the minority Christian population now refusing to gather for prayers outside the relative safety of their homes.

Life, for the city's inhabitants was one of angst and fear, with most of the expatriate population having already fled, or camped at the airport, waiting, hopefully, to be repatriated. The airport remained impossibly crowded as ethnic Chinese fought for seats, fearful of the continuing racial violence which had already accounted for many of their number. Commerce had ground to a halt; banks remained closed as the Rupiah danced through previously considered impossible levels, and government utilities failed, sending the cities sliding further into darkness.

Hababli's fledgling government appeared not to have the people's confidence, and the list of major international firms announcing their withdrawal from Indonesia, grew by the hour. Calm had not been restored to many provincial capitals as separatists took advantage of the country's politically confused state, pushing the archipelago dangerously close to full civil war. Food prices spiraled, placing basic commodities out of reach for millions living in rural areas, further exacerbating the volatile conditions.

Mary Jo had mentioned Haji Abdul Muis in her submission, attaching the photograph she had taken during Suhapto's hand-over ceremony. She inferred that the Moslem leader's failure to support the students suggested a changing agenda, and perhaps even a developing alliance between those who perceived themselves heirs to the nation's leadership. Mary Jo implied also that now the way had been paved for new elections to be held, elections which would provide the opportunity for previously prohibited parties to re-emerge, the world could expect to see Indonesia's Moslem parties consolidate their positions in any future government.

Having filed her story and received acknowledgment from New York, Mary Jo discovered that her larder was empty, concerned that there would not be any food left on supermarket shelves for them to buy, she phoned around, but most of her acquaintances had deserted the capital and, as news was breaking elsewhere, it appeared that many of her media friends had taken to the road in search of new material. Deeply disappointed that she still had not heard anything from Hamish McLoughlin, she asked Anne to take her down to the Sahid Jaya Hotel where they ate in silence, together.

That night, as she lay awake alone with her thoughts, Mary Jo experienced a wave of loneliness she had not felt since her affair with Eric Fieldmann had ended. She accepted that her professional choices had often prevented her casual relationships from developing into anything really meaningful, but she admitted that Hamish's sudden, and unexplained departure had, in fact, cut her to the core.

* * * *

Lieutenant General Praboyo

A short distance from where his President *cum* father-in-law had stunned the nation with his resignation less than thirty-six hours before, General Praboyo stood arrogantly in front of the television sneering as the Armed Forces Chief of Staff, Lieutenant General Winarko, again warned the nation that the military had assumed the role of guardian to the outgoing President and his family. Praboyo, Commander of the Strategic Army Forces, realized that this would not apply to him, and that he had but hours to consolidate his precarious position. Changing into battle-dress, he checked his sidearm and hastened outside to where his *Kostrad* troops waited in silence.

Launching himself cockily into the armored Jeep, Praboyo crossed his arms and nodded at the driver to proceed to the Palace, where he would demand that L.B. Hababli place him at the head of the country's armed forces, a promotion he believed he not only deserved, but one which had been guaranteed by the former President. Convinced, that with the backing of *Kopassus* and his *Kostrad* infantry divisions and airborne brigade, the thirty-thousand-strong force could easily assume control over the capital, and would do so should the new President renege on his appointment. He was deeply troubled that the *Mufti Muharam* might now reconsider their agreement and distance themselves from him. His intelligence had informed Praboyo that Abdul Muis had been observed in discussions with both Winarko and the new President. He knew he had to move quickly and shore up his power-base before this happened.

Driven by his deep resentment towards Winarko, Praboyo's hand remained close to the weapon at his side as he ordered his troops to follow, determined to use whatever force was necessary to reclaim what he believed to be his rightful place.

* * * *

The New President

President L.B. Hababli's head was still swimming at the speed of events which had placed him at the helm of the strife-torn republic. The transition from scorned Cabinet minister to Vice President, and then to the exalted position he now enjoyed, had transpired in less than ten weeks.

Never in his wildest dreams had the former engineer ever imagined that he would be elevated to this position, recognizing that he was greatly indebted to the *Bapak*, and General Winarko, for their faith, and trust. Being of non Javanese extraction, and having no military background whatsoever, he had beaten the pundits; he would be the third of five kings, fulfilling the twelfth-century prophecies of *Joyoboyo.*

Hababli realized that his tenure might be brief if he failed to win the immediate support of students, *ABRI,* and the international monetary authorities. Should he succeed, he could claim the Presidency in his own right, and retain the leadership well into the new millennium. The conundrum was how to strike a balance between the vested interest groups he now represented, and those which waited impatiently for their share of the spoils.

He would need to display leadership skills expected of a President, while accommodating those responsible for keeping him in power. Contemplating his dilemma, Hababli removed the black, over-sized *pici* from his head and nervously scratched the balding scalp underneath, wishing he could phone his mentor, the *Bapak*, and seek his advice. But he knew this would be dangerous, and must endeavor to be seen as his own man.

The ugly mood which had brought him to power continued to threaten national security and he was painfully aware that his real relationship with the former President must remain concealed, or become subject to the peoples' wrath. He must appear to distance himself from Suhapto and his avaricious children, and accept that his own house required attention as well if he was to succeed.

His own family controlled close to one hundred companies. He thought he'd been clever in the past, disguising ownership of the shipping yards, hotels, factories and other investments through nominees. Yes, he had acquired considerable wealth, but believed his significant contribution to the economy over the past twenty years justified this accumulation of assets. Hababli estimated that the value of his extensive holdings was in excess of two hundred million dollars, and expected this to grow rapidly once the Indonesian economy recovered.

His thoughts turned to the more serious of his immediate problems, and how he might convince Abdul Muis to mobilize his followers in support of his Presidency. The chilling prospect of more than a million *Mufti Muharam* Moslems turning against him was of grave concern. Hababli feared any such demonstration would provide the catalyst his opponents desired, that the military would be capable of controlling such large numbers.

He had been disappointed with the students' reaction to his appointment. Subsequent to their initial jubilation upon hearing of Suhapto's resignation, the youngsters had turned their attention towards him. Placards and effigies depicting him as the former leader's stooge appeared, and he was livid that these had been screened on national television.

Deep in thought, the newly appointed President did not hear the heated exchange taking place outside, and was startled when an aide burst into his office, dragging him back from his deliberations.

'What is it?' he asked, his concern rising when he noticed the flurry of activity through the open doorway. Soldiers were running across the highly-polished, white marble floors with their weapons raised.

'It's General Praboyo!' the white-faced colonel answered, his voice reflecting his own surprise.

'Praboyo? Here?' Hababli's concern turning to fear. *Had he already heard?*

'Yes, sir. He insists on meeting you.' The colonel waited for a response, but Hababli appeared deathly still, his mind racing as he worried what the unpredictable Praboyo might do. The President knew that the general would be furious with him, his eyes darted around the room wondering if he could escape.

In the early hours of the morning, before the first call to prayers heralded the new day, Hababli had, with considerable reservations, agreed to General Winarko's requests. The brash Praboyo would be immediately removed from his position as commander of *Kostrad* and transferred to Bandung, out of harm's way. Winarko would reshuffle the *ABRI* leadership, preventing those who might be tempted to overthrow the fledgling government, from effecting their *coup*.

Outside, in the main foyer, he could hear General Praboyo shouting at the Palace guard commander.

'Let me pass!' he ordered, but the other officer stood his ground.

'Get rid of the weapon, then we'll talk,' the colonel argued.

'I am giving you an order!' Praboyo's voice rose, his anger evident.

'You can not pass carrying a weapon!' he was told.

'Get Hababli out here, then!' he shouted, his voice carrying clearly through the building. Outside, elements of *Kostrad* forces waited, dressed in full combat dress and heavily armed. Three Saracen armored personnel carriers stood, threateningly, guns pointed towards the Palace entrance, while two Scorpion light tanks blocked the main gates, preventing both escape and access to the grounds. As the officers argued, Hababli was ushered away through an adjoining room into an area which could be better defended.

'The President is not here,' the guard officer lied. His ruse appeared successful as he observed a flicker of doubt cross the other man's face. *'Look, General,'* he continued, taking the advantage, *'why not leave your weapon here with your men? I'll leave mine as well.'* Praboyo seemed confused by the suggestion. He hesitated, turned to his men, barked an order for them to remain alert, then unbuckled his belt and passed the holstered gun to an aide. By this time, Hababli had been hurried through the upper levels and had reached the flat, concrete roof.

'Let's go,' he insisted, marching towards the President's office. *'I'll just satisfy myself that he's not here.'* His heavy army boots struck the marble loudly sending their ominous message that he was coming. He reached the room where he suspected Hababli would be, and stormed in unannounced. His eyes darted around searching for the man who had betrayed him and, at that moment, he heard the familiar sound as a helicopter lifted away from the roof-top pad, his anger spilling over with the discovery that the President had escaped.

Praboyo's plans to take him hostage and declare martial law, had been narrowly frustrated. Now, empty handed, the cold realization that he had missed the one opportunity which might have brought him to power, only added to his rage.

'Get me Winarko!' he bellowed, and the guard officer nodded, deciding that this would be best for all. He phoned the Chief of Staff's personal assistant and within minutes located the General. The officer then briefed Winarko, and handed the telephone to Praboyo.

'You are very foolish,' Winarko said, in a controlled voice.

'I still have the support of Kostrad,' Praboyo responded, arrogantly.

'That won't be for long,' the more senior officer declared, calmly. Praboyo detected a smugness in the other man's tone, and clenched his fists.

'I can also count on Kopassus,' he claimed. He had not spoken to the Special Forces commander that day; now he understood why his friend had been unavailable.

'No you can't,' Winarko replied. *'He was replaced two hours ago.'* Praboyo's face tightened.

'There are others who will support me,' he tried, but unconvincingly.

'Forget it, 'Boyo,' Winarko said, *'you're finished. The Americans will not support you. I have already spoken to their Embassy. Carruthers has been recalled.'*

Praboyo pulled the phone away from his ear, tempted to smash it to the ground but, instead, swore at the other man. For a brief moment there was silence, then Winarko spoke to him again. He listened, intently, the armed forces chief outlining the steps he had taken to prevent Praboyo from effecting his coup.

As the other man rattled off the list of officers who had either been relieved of their commands, or promoted away from direct control over any troops, Praboyo knew he had lost. In pragmatic fashion he accepted defeat, agreeing to abandon his attempt to seize power, and in typical Javanese style his superior offered a compromise which he knew he must accept.

With forced smile he returned to his waiting troops and dismissed them all, then instructed his driver to take him home to his wife. When he informed Tuti of his posting to the *ABRI* Staff College, in Bandung, the irony of this appointment was lost on them both, for her father had also been relegated to this lesser position by his chief of staff, in another time, when he too had challenged those in power, and lost.

But had Praboyo known this story, it might have lessened the burden of his heavy heart, as his father-in-law had used his own exile to re-group, waiting patiently to fulfill his destiny as President of the Republic of Indonesia.

* * * *

In the days following Suhapto's shock resignation, General Winarko reshuffled his *ABRI* leadership. At first, there was surprise, then confusion as Praboyo's sidelining became known, and his successor also replaced less than eighteen hours after being appointed commander of the powerful *Kostrad* Strategic Forces group. Christian generals were quietly shuffled out of harm's way, the *Mufti Muharam's* powerful influence suddenly becoming apparent as the new Indonesian leadership bowed to their demands. Although assured of American support, Winarko decided to postpone his own claims on the Presidency. The country was teetering on bankruptcy; this was not the time to take control. He would wait.

For a brief time tensions eased as the new government set about restoring stability and international confidence, desperate for the IMF and the World Bank to restore the flow of funds to the ailing economy. Then, precisely seven days to the hour when *Bapak Suhapto's* reign had finally come to an end, the world shuddered again.

From Libya to Cairo, across to Baghdad, Teheran, Kabul and Islamabad, and down the Malay-Indonesian archipelago, hundreds of millions of faithful followers swarmed into the streets, rejoicing, when Pakistan's Moslem leaders announced that their scientists had detonated a twenty-kiloton device in response to the Indian tests. A frightening, new era had arrived and with it, the first Islamic nuclear bomb.

Refugees in Crisis

Bangkok
Vietnam
Malaysia
Sarawak
Singapore
Kalimantan
Indian (Indonesian) Ocean
Sumatra
INDONESIAN
WARSHIPS FLEET
Jakarta
Java
Bali
PELABUHAN RATU
SAMUDERA
BEACH SLAUGHTER
Christmas Island
EAST JAVA
REFUGEE FLEET
BALI DISASTER

Samudera Beach - Pelabuhan Ratu Refugee Route
East Java - "LIly's" Fleet
US - Seventh Fleet
Indonesian Warships
Tomahawk Missile Path

Chapter Fifteen

Mary Jo

The melancholic strains of Idris Sardi's golden violin filled the empty room, adding to her feeling of depression. Mary Jo sat slumped in the cane chair, observing the once lush surroundings of the deserted hotel's beer garden, wishing she had not returned to the now neglected resort. Gone were the prized and well-cared for orchids and shrubs; gone too were magnificent tapestries and paintings which greeted guests as they entered the well-appointed lobby. She knew that the hot, humid, equatorial climate was not entirely to blame for the hotel's rapid deterioration; the country's failed economy had contributed to that. The colonial-styled resort had become one of the Republic's many idle monuments, reflecting the nation's dramatic decline as it continued to slip towards anarchy.

Mary Jo looked up at the overhead ceiling fans, the cutting edges blackened with neglect and spotted a *gecko* lizard, upside down, waiting for passing prey. Above, and to the centre of the atrium, splinters of light touched a broken porcelain lamp, hanging idly in lost splendor. Across the terrazzo-tiled courtyard, a fountain fed water into a lily-covered fish pond. Mary Jo guessed that the golden carp which had so fascinated tourists in the past, would have been amongst the first to disappear from this scene, no doubt to grace the barren table of some staff's hungry family. She sighed, more so from exasperation than from weariness. *Who would have thought that the country would slip this far in less than one year?*

With one hand, Mary Jo extracted one of the filtered *kretek* cigarettes from the plastic packet and, with practiced mechanical motion placed one between her lips and lit this with the throw-away, plastic lighter. Her lungs immediately identified the taste of clove as she inhaled deeply, the warm, soothing sensation calming her frayed nerves. She remained still, permitting the cigarette to carry her thoughts away, inhaling from time to time as she sat alone, unconcerned that to others she might appear untidy, although she was in desperate need of a bath. Relaxed as the nicotine entered her blood, Mary Jo stretched, recalling the long, tiring drive back into the cool hills, away from the filthy, scorched Surabaya sidewalks, and the monotonous, steaming, muggy climate, that perpetually clung to the Java coast.

More than a year had passed since she had last visited Tretes, the hillside mountain resort area south of the Javanese port-city of Surabaya. Here, the air was noticeably cooler, and the thought of sleeping without an air-conditioner appealed to her. Electricity had become unreliable. Deprived of sleep, the erratic, mechanical thumping of compressors starting, then failing, often drove her to despair and, in desperation, she had decided to flee to the mountains, to rest. Now, observing the deteriorated surroundings, she was uncertain if her escape had been such a great idea. Lazily flicking the ash from her *kretek* onto the unswept floor, she considered returning to the city, then decided that there wasn't much in the choice. Even her accommodations in Surabaya had become neglected, and now, claustrophobic.

Mary Jo was unsure if the country would ever recover from the malaise which had stifled the nation's economic recovery. And, as events continued to unfold with the inevitability of a Greek tragedy, the destabilizing, decolonization process had begun. Indonesia was slowly, but surely, ripping itself apart as separatists in many of the twenty-seven provinces agitated for independence from the Javanese.

She had just returned from the eastern string of islands which led from Java and Bali, across to Timor and New Guinea, as world attention again focused on the bloody uprisings. Within months of Hababli becoming President, the inhabitants of Timor, Ambon and Irian Jaya, the western half of New Guinea, grew confident that the centralist Indonesians would establish a dialogue which would lead, ultimately, to independence. Their timing was perfect; the Javanese dominated archipelago was suddenly confronted with uprisings in North Sumatra as hard-line Moslems declared their region autonomous, refusing to acknowledge the Indonesian imposed Constitution. When fighting had again erupted, Javanese troops had been deployed to deal with the Aceh separatists, inflicting a bloody and devastating defeat upon the fundamentalists, as they had done in the past. Buoyed by their success, these battalions had then been airlifted to North Sulawesi where, to *ABRI's* chagrin, the Menadonese rebels proved more resilient, taking as many lives as they lost during the first of two major battles.

Convinced that the central government would be too preoccupied with further outbreaks in East and West Kalimantan, the Timorese challenged the reduced troop presence, resulting in the systematic slaughter of tens of thousands of East Timorese by the feared *Kopassus* groups.

Fighting had broken out, simultaneously, throughout the thinly populated mountain regions of West Irian. There, the still primitive tribes went to battle against greatly superior forces, their archaic spears no match for the Indonesian soldiers' automatic weapons, helicopter gunships, and OV-10's which randomly strafed isolated villages across the highlands.

Within six weeks, the disastrous uprisings had been brutally, but successfully, put down. In the months that followed, the first waves of refugees boarded their flimsy vessels and fled their traditional lands, driven by the fear of retribution and empty stomachs. As thousands of children died, the first flood of East Timorese heading towards Northern Australia were turned back by Australian Navy coastal patrols, resulting in these displaced people changing course, towards the less-hostile, and many, smaller islands, across to Bali.

The United Nations High Commissioner for Refugees estimated that approximately one hundred thousand East Timorese had escaped the brutal Indonesian soldiers by boat, only to be subjected to further atrocities as their numbers threatened to inundate the sparsely populated, and lesser islands. The refugees met with fierce resistance wherever they landed. Unwelcome, starving and bewildered as to how the world could permit this genocide to continue, they were finally captured and herded into camps, where many of their number died of malnutrition and disease, even before Hababli could celebrate his first anniversary as President of Indonesia.

Mary Jo had temporarily moved her base of operations to Surabaya, placing her almost a thousand kilometers closer to the eastern trouble spots. She had retained the Jakarta villa, and along with her assistant, Anne, they had become regular passengers on the revamped feeder airline service which now operated throughout the island. Garuda Airlines had all but collapsed, unable to repay three hundred million dollars in foreign currency debts.

The four Garuda subsidiary and affiliated companies which, until the year before controlled the domestic skies, had either sold or returned their remaining aircraft, to repay part of their massive debts before going into receivership. It appeared that the former First Family also had substantial interests in the airline industry, but when the crunch arrived, they simply bailed out, leaving the industry to follow the same path so many of their other investments had taken. Many of these aircraft now flew as unscheduled charters, tourism having never recovered to a level which could make airline services economically viable. As she sat contemplating the events which had brought her this far, Mary Jo revisited the months following Suhapto's fall, and the uncertainty which prevailed.

By the time the International Monetary Fund, the World Bank and the Asian Development Bank had commenced effecting payments to stave off a total collapse, one which threatened to spark a further round of currency failures, the country had passed the point of no return. Confidence in the new Indonesian leadership continued to wane as, one by one, familiar faces belonging to the former President's clique reappeared, their renewed cloaks of respectability unable to disguise the country's failure to reform. Then too, as swift retribution came to selected scapegoats held responsible for the nation's demise, many *ABRI* officers vanished altogether, while others slunk away quietly, to lick their wounded prides in anonymity, angered by the injustice that those really responsible, would go unpunished.

It was a time when new alliances were forged, when deals were struck and loyalties sworn. But it was also a time of deceit and empty promises, as the ambitious jockeyed for power, their eyes fixed on the forthcoming elections. And when these finally arrived, the will of the people was again ignored, the seeds of discontent finding fertile ground when it became obvious to all, that nothing had really changed.

Then, the country erupted.

At first it appeared that the students' previous occupation of Parliament had been merely a rehearsal, for when the election results became known, both Houses were all but destroyed in the ensuing attack. This time the students came prepared. When a phalanx of government troops attempted to remove students for the second time in eighteen months, the soldiers met with armed resistance and retaliated. The first volley fired accounted for more than thirty students, all shot dead inside the Parliament's chambers.

Inflamed by this action, the youngsters reacted unexpectedly.

Refusing to be intimidated by the superior fire-power, they hurled home-made petrol bombs at the troops, determined to remain where they were. The air cracked again with another barrage of bullets, then the soldiers charged with thrusting bayonets, cutting and stabbing into the throng. In less than fifteen minutes, more than two hundred students lay dead, inflaming their tens of thousands into suicidal attack, their numbers so great, the soldiers broke ranks and were overrun. Armed with their enemies' weapons, the students retained possession of the buildings, their hate fueled by the number of dead comrades. Unable to control the contagious violence, the military's assault had released a powerful frustration, and the students completely destroyed both Houses of Parliament.

Flames licked the city's late-evening skies carrying their promise of events to come while the city exploded with hate, the fragile layer separating the wealthy from the underprivileged suddenly shattered, exposed to the fierce and relentless heat.

The following days witnessed the bloodiest street rioting in the country's history as troops and students clashed repeatedly, the military crushing the demonstrators in one final pitched battle at the University of Indonesia, leaving more than two thousand killed in that one horrific week. President Hababli declared a state of emergency, unwisely imposing a nation-wide curfew as he suspended Parliament and imposed direct military rule citing not only the continuing violence, but also the destruction of the national Parliament as justification for these measures.

This further incensed the people, more so those who lived in isolated areas far from the civil unrest as their very existence depended on their freedom to farm and distribute their harvest to markets. Road blocks appeared in the most unlikely places, manned by well-armed soldiers demanding tolls. Many peasants were shot out of hand, their deaths never reported as the military moved through the villages, raping and pillaging their own.

During this period of rapid destabilization, Mary Jo had practiced caution when traveling through the provinces. Once, she had been threatened at gun-point and, on that occasion, genuinely believed she would be shot. Another time, her vehicle had skidded off the road into a tree, knocking both Mary Jo and her driver unconscious. A thin, red scar above her temple remained as a reminder of how close she had been to death.

And then, whilst covering the Free Aceh Movement's mobilization of cadres in North Sumatra, her assistant Anne had been badly beaten and hospitalized for days when freedom fighters mistook her for a Javanese informer. They had flown into the area immediately after reports arrived concerning the separatists' most recent uprising. Mary Jo had anticipated that fighting would erupt again when Aceh attempted to break away from the Republic. The minority group of four million had fought against Javanese domination for decades, dating back to the Eighth Century when Islam had been first introduced into Indonesia through the vibrant ports and culture of North Sumatra.

As a major foreign exchange earner, conflict between the Acehnese and their militant colonizers had boiled over into bloody, full-scale war when Jakarta had refused to consider the North Sumatran people's case. Mobil Oil's gas production and the gas-fed petrochemical industry continued to cause extensive environmental damage in the area.

Activists had continued attacks against the Arun Gas Fields, demanding that at least some of the fifteen billion dollars generated each year by this operation be reinvested in local development. Villagers, who had been forced into resettlement programs as their native lands had been appropriated, appealed to their absentee landlords for compensation. But the Javanese ignored these pleas, sending the callous *Kopassus* troops in to deal with the subversives. Mary Jo and Anne had documented the brutal clashes which had come perilously close to costing Anne her life.

Memories of the prematurely aged woman came flooding back as she remembered the interview, just hours after she had been released from the infamous Rancong detention centre. When Mary Jo first sighted the emaciated small-framed woman, she was reminded of scenes reminiscent of another era and asked Anne to postpone the interview. But, the woman had insisted, only too pleased to be given the opportunity to reveal the inhuman treatment detainees suffered inside their prison.

'Ibu,' Mary Jo had offered, unsure if the interview should continue, *'we can do this tomorrow, if you wish?'*

'No,' she replied, her face reflecting the strength of character which had kept her alive during the brutal incarceration. *'Please do it now. Tomorrow will be another challenge. And who knows, they might come and take me away again.'*

'Did they hurt you, Ibu?' Anne had asked, holding the woman's hand.

'No,' she lied, leaning painfully to one side. Her back had been beaten so many times, she could not remember. She pulled at the new cloth Anne had given her, running the material between her fingers. Suddenly, the realization that she was free and alive, caused heavy fearful tears to spill down her cheeks. Fifty-five year old Jumilah had been detained for four weeks inside the prison, never expecting to survive the ordeal.

Mary Jo had done her homework before visiting Aceh. She had learned that Free Aceh Movement was founded by Hasan di Tiro, a descendant of one of Aceh's leading noble families. He unilaterally declared independence in 1976, the year Indonesia officially annexed East Timor, and initiated an armed struggle against the central government. Although, at first, there were some successes, after several years the separatists' struggle was effectively quelled, breaking out thirteen years later, in 1989. With far wider support from the local population, the separatists had forced *ABRI* onto the defensive. Concerned that the educated elite had openly sided with the insurgents, many academics were put on trial and given harsh sentences. Aceh was declared a war zone by Jakarta, and the following year General Praboyo's *Kopassus* Special Forces were sent to the area to hunt down Free Aceh Forces, with orders to kill anyone even suspected of being a Free Aceh supporter. In the ensuing melee, *Kopassus* troops slaughtered thousands without trial, summarily executing North Sumatrans where they stood.

In one incident two members of a local football team had been hanged from the goal posts while parents were forced to witness the execution. Then, they too were murdered, their bodies decapitated, their heads taken back to the village and placed on poles for all to see.

Upon hearing these stories, Mary Jo had insisted that Anne arrange for them to visit the notorious Rancong detention centre in the town of Lhokseumawe. With President Suhapto gone and General Praboyo's *Kopassus* finally recalled, bereaved women started to come forward, recounting the horrors of the Javanese occupation. Vivid stories of husbands and children disappearing or being brutally beaten to death, tales of public humiliation, of women being publicly raped by the soldiers; accounts of prisoners being held in barbed-wire cells while dogs were unleashed to kill; these and a host of other incidents, were all recorded by Mary Jo and revealed to her international readers.

She reached out, and touched the strong-willed woman before her.

'Ibu Jumilah, please tell us about conditions inside,' Anne asked, surreptitiously bringing the tape recorder closer to the broken-spirited woman's mouth. For a moment, her eyes glazed over as recollections flooded her brain. Then, in the presence of freedom, the air sweetened by the knowledge that she had survived, Jumilah spoke.

'I was threatened before they released me,' she said, slowly at first, then the words spilled out in a torrent, Mary Jo's reassuring presence sufficient to trigger the truth. *'They didn't beat me today. But they beat me every other day,'* she said, not at all embarrassed to lift her *sarong*, revealing the deep, purple and black bruising which extended from her shins, high above her kneeline. *'They said that if I told anyone anything bad, I would be re-arrested.'* She looked up into Mary Jo's eyes. *'You are a foreigner; they would be scared of you and what you might say. Will you promise to watch after me if I tell you what really happened inside?'* she pleaded, turning her head to look back over her shoulder in the general direction of her recent prison.

'Yes, we'll take care of you,' Anne had promised, prepared to do so even if Mary Jo could not. *'Ibu,'* she then asked, her voice filled with obvious admiration for the woman, *'please tell us about what it was like inside.'* Jumilah did not hesitate, comforted by the guarantee she had solicited.

'Every waking hour, when we were not being punished by the soldiers, we could hear the screams of others out the back of the detention center. At any time during the day, our guards would strut past, selecting the women they would use, then drag these from the filth we lived in, forced those they had chosen to bathe, then service all the soldiers. One girl, I think she was eleven, was only there for two weeks. She was raped five, sometimes ten times each day. Finally, the Kopassus guards strangled her. They left her body for us to see. We were terrified after that.'

Mary Jo learned that Jumilah's story was not unusual. The Javanese soldiers often moved around the streets at night, arresting wives and daughters at random, throwing these women into prison for the benefit of the visiting soldiers. In Jumilah's case, Mary Jo learned that she had been arrested simply because the *Kopassus* troops had decided that the area in which she lived might have housed Free Aceh Separatists. In the one night, more than one hundred women were arrested and detained in the filthy conditions. Some were old, others barely into their teens.

'They used electricity here,' Jumilah said, placing her hands on her breasts and ears, *'and here,'* she trembled, her hand falling to her lap. *'All the young women were raped. Others, because they were too old or too frightened, were beaten. Some, until they died.'*

Mary Jo had offered Jumilah money; had it not been for Anne's insistence, she would have refused. As the proud Acehnese grandmother was taken away, there were tears in the eyes of all present, and for Mary Jo, her memory of the strong-willed uneducated but gracious woman, evidence that the North Sumatrans resilience was perhaps more than the Javanese had reckoned with.

Following this incident, Mary Jo had flown to Indonesian Borneo and covered the mounting unrest across Kalimantan's provinces. There the traditional land owners waged war against the Javanese settlers who had been transported under a government programme called *transmigrasi,* a scheme to populate the vast, underdeveloped island. The Dayak's propensity to slaughtering strangers had not waned over the centuries, their long-houses' interiors decorated with the heads of those who had strayed too far inland. These indigenous people considered the Javanese migrants as interlopers, and part of the central government's long-term plan to displace the original inhabitants as they had in other provinces such as Bali.

Fighting first broke out near the western city of Pontianak, and then spread to Banjarmasin in the south. Everywhere, the story seemed the same. Small diamond concession holders had been murdered near their diggings; imported labor working the open-cut coal concessions had mysteriously disappeared, and the homes of Javanese officials had been razed.

Mary Jo had visited both these isolated provincial towns, the scenes reminiscent of what she had witnessed elsewhere. Buildings had been gutted, schools destroyed, farmers murdered and, not surprisingly, a mass exodus by sea had occurred wherever violence had threatened. Further inland, where the former President's cronies had stripped the great forests, fires continued to burn, fueled by huge coal outcrops previously hidden by the thick, jungle growth. Even endangered species were not spared as the fires raced through the thick, dry timbers, destroying their natural habitat. Smoke spewed into the skies, covering the once-dense tropical forests, blanketing an area twice that of Texas, and for the third year in a row, both Singapore and Kuala Lumpur's inhabitants were obliged to wear masks across their faces to reduce health risks.

Mary Jo then flew up to the western port of Balikpapan where even the army's substantial presence failed to prevent the city's destruction. And so the story continued. Further to the north where Pertamina, the state owned oil and gas company, had invested billions of dollars, the fields were threatened as subversive elements attempted to destroy facilities along the rich coastal concession areas and foreign expertise vacated their essential posts, leaving the less-experienced engineers to fend for themselves. With its substantial oil and gas reserves then under threat, the Indonesian Government was obliged to send ships and amphibious forces to the area. At last it would appear the Hababli's acquisition of the former East German fleet would bear fruit.

As Mary Jo flew from Samarinda in the north, she flew over the small armada, noting that the navy had sent two of its Yugoslav *Fatahillah* class frigates. She remembered reading that these were armed with Exocet surface-to-surface missiles. Mary Jo also managed an aerial photograph of the former East German *Parchim* class corvettes moving slowly through the Makasar Straits, and wondered immediately if the Indonesian Navy had drawn upon its Eastern Fleet at a time when these warships were essential to controlling the Timor exodus.

Here in Kalimantan, Mary Jo noted that the Chinese had again suffered the brunt of the violence. Their shops and homes had been destroyed first, only then were these followed by those belonging to the Javanese.

And, as Borneo burned, nations which shared the northern part of this great island prepared for the worst. In the towns of Kuching and Kota Kinabalu Chinese locked their doors, fearing an outbreak of racial unrest similar to that which had struck the country twenty years before. And in Brunei one of the world's wealthiest men prepared to leave for Europe as his people considered their own racial mix, with half of the small nation's three hundred thousand of Chinese descent, and unable to obtain passports or a higher education. As Mary Jo continued to document the archipelago's decolonization in process, the rest of Asia waited, apprehensively, anticipating the worst.

Then, when it appeared that conditions could not possibly deteriorate further due to the refugee crisis, Thailand threatened to withdraw from the Association of South-East Asian Nations, throwing regional politics into another tailspin. Neither Thailand nor Malaysia's coastal patrols could stem the flood of illegal immigrants flowing across the narrow Malacca Straits, and both nations appealed to the United Nations High Commissioner for Refugees for assistance. Mary Jo had climbed aboard a charter flight, and headed for Kuala Lumpur to cover the discussions.

Memories of those few days brought her back to the present, and Mary Jo looked critically at the freshly-lit cigarette she held between nicotine-stained fingers, wondering why she had elected to remain in this godforsaken place called Indonesia.

* * * *

Lily

Lily waited until the unruly mob had passed before dashing across the road to the small general store. Inside, her heart still pumping excessively, she nodded at the shopkeeper then went about filling her mother's order as quickly as possible, not wishing to remain away from her own building longer than was necessary.

Her eyes ran down the short shopping-list, bitter that her family's meager possessions were all but gone, sold to pay for food, sold to buy protection from the marauding gangs and their increasingly frequent attacks. Their harvest of hate, raised in the shadows, continued unabated, even in the light of day. Without money, their lives would be worthless.

'*This one?*' the woman asked, indicating the poorer quality rice with the scoop in her hand. Lily nodded affirmatively, no longer embarrassed that her family purchased the lower-graded beras. There was a time, she remembered, when the shopkeeper would hurry out to greet Lily's mother should she enter this store. Now, everything had changed; and for the Chinese the effects had been calamitous.

'Sugar?' the woman inquired, her tone more than insolent. Lily watched as a kilo of the sweet, unrefined crystals was weighed out and poured into a brown, paper bag.

'What else?' the voice was insincere, its owner pleased how the table had turned for the once wealthier family from across the street. Lily checked the list again, gently chewing at the inside of her lip. Her mother had asked for flour, but Lily could see from the open jute bag against the wall that weevils had taken up residence inside.

'Do you want flour today?' the shopkeeper asked impatiently. She moved towards the open bag expecting this would be so. Lily's order rarely varied. She bent to scoop the flour into another bag while her customer remained silent, deciding that it would be more sensible to separate the weevils later than enter into a war of words with the Javanese woman. Their role reversals over the past year had been most humiliating. Lily carefully placed her purchases in the string bag she carried and waited for her change. She did not complete her mother's order as she hadn't sufficient funds. Even the poorest quality rice had risen by more than twenty percent that week and, she noted, the weevil-infested flour was now selling for double that of a month before.

'Terima kasih,' Lily thanked the shopkeeper, politely, almost subserviently, moving to the store's doorway to check the street. She could feel the woman's eyes burning into the back of her neck as she left, and ran back across the road to where her mother waited, peering through the concertina-styled sliding steel security gate she had partly opened in preparation for her daughter's return. As she raced across the pot-holed narrow street, Lily glanced nervously in both directions, praying that she not be seen by any who might wish to do them harm. Safely across, she squeezed through the steel gate quickly, catching her dress on one of the protruding rusty screws which held the mechanism together. Ignoring the scratch Lily placed her shopping down, then dragged the heavy gate together, locking the two sides with practiced hands. Then, she lifted the string bag and followed her mother as she shuffled towards the rear of their two-story concrete dwelling, the home which had become their jail.

Although they had not actually been incarcerated by the authorities, Lily and her mother literally felt imprisoned in these surrounds. Since her father had passed away within months of her return from Jakarta, Lily's mother's own health had deteriorated and, unaided, she could no longer climb the stairs to the bedrooms. Now, with only the two of them to consider, Lily had taken charge of their lives while waiting for some ray of hope to deliver them from their ethnic hell. At night, they slept downstairs, huddled together on the kitchen floor where Lily had placed a mattress for them both. Their electricity had been cut off months before and, had it not been for their well with its tiresome hand-pump, they would have abandoned these accommodations and sought refuge with others.

Lily knew that they could no longer turn to their church for comfort. Rumor had it that even the missionaries had abandoned many parts of rural Java, and very few churches had escaped the torches of the angry Moslem mobs. Like so many others she was confused by the racial and sectarian violence. It mattered not that many Chinese were practicing Buddhists; either way she felt that they were doomed.

Lily's gaze moved slowly around the narrow room, coming to rest on the well-worn family bible. On the wall above, and between fading photographs of her father and grandparents, there was a wooden cross. They prayed each evening, but it made little difference apart from some temporary solace her mother derived from the ritual. None came to save them from their plight and Lily worried what they had done to deserve this fate, wishing she could put a real face on her god.

Evenings were spent talking, sometimes reading under the bright kerosene light, but as her mother's will to live grew weaker by the day, Lily now spent most of her time watching over the prematurely aging woman, sensing that she had very little time. At night, when sleep finally came, Lily's mind was repeatedly subjected to the torture she had suffered during the savage attack in her uncle's home. Lily's nightmares were so vivid, her screams would often waken their neighbors. She would thrash around, her arms flailing wildly in the dark whenever her mother moved to comfort her stricken daughter.

It had taken months before Lily had been able to discuss what had happened with her parents. By then, she learned that her uncle had left the country, undertaking never to return. He had sent some money, but this had not been enough to provide for their escape. When her father died, her mother's jewelry became their only means of survival. Each week Lily would venture out in search of someone who might wish to purchase the small golden trinkets her father had bought over the many years of marriage. In years past, it would not have been so dangerous to trade such items as all of thc gold shops had belonged to fellow Chinese. With their shops in ruins and their wealth looted by rioting mobs, these traders had either vanished or fled, leaving empty dwellings as evidence of the racial unrest. Now, Lily was obliged to trade mostly with the pribumi, the indigenous and mainly Javanese people who had so despised her race. And it was extremely hazardous for her to be seen on the streets of Situbondo, the scene of some of the worst racial riots the country had witnessed during the past months.

There was growing evidence that the two major Muslim political groups, although at loggerheads with each other since the elections, were collectively inciting their followers against the Christians and Buddhists. Either way, the Chinese were being specifically targeted by marauding gangs which roamed the greater part of Java, burning property belonging to these groups and the homes of Moslems who dared oppose this racial and religious cleansing.

Lily had remained in Situbondo only to care for her ailing mother. When the time arrived, she would flee aboard one of the small coastal fishing-boats which offered safe passage to other islands, where the Chinese could live without fear. Bali, she knew, was one such destination, as the two cultures had assimilated well over the centuries. After her father's death, Lily's mother, continuously depressed by the absence of her life-partner, had stubbornly refused to leave when the opportunity arose. Lily believed that her mother had now lost the will to live. Now even if she relented, their remaining reserves would barely cover the passage for one. Their greatest fear now was not that they might starve, but their safety as they could no longer afford to pay for the protection without which, they would remain in danger.

As each day passed, Lily waited with growing apprehension for her mother to die, while one by one, others of their ethnic minority within this small East Javanese community managed to flee, before they too were found lying butchered in their own beds.

* * * *

Hani

'Get out!' Hani screamed. Her seventeen-year old brother had entered her room without warning, while she was dressing. She threw the hair-brush at the door, but he had already escaped her wrath.

The atmosphere in the Purwadira household had remained tense, since the family returned from Jakarta in disgrace. Her father's inadequate pension was insufficient to support his family. Inflation had taken care of that.

In less than a year, their savings had all but disappeared and, as they no longer enjoyed the benefits accorded senior officers and their dependents, the former general had been reduced to seeking assistance from those he once commanded. Unable to understand the calamity that had befallen them, this dramatic, and sudden turnaround in their fortunes had affected her mother most. These days Ibu Purwadira would rarely leave the confines of their small home. The embarrassment of their abrupt change in lifestyle had struck her hard, and she had never forgiven her husband's fellow officers for their betrayal.

Hani had been unable to continue her studies in Sukabumi. Her younger brother was expected to complete high school within the next months and Hani thought about this, shrugging as she sat facing the oval-shaped mirror, not really concerned about her brother's future. She believed that he would most likely join the ranks of the unemployed just as the others in this family had done.

'*Hani!*' she heard her father's voice and sighed. She knew he would want her to do some chore or other; he always did. Her mother would pretend not to hear, or even feign sleep. If ignored, her father would become angry and lash out, his tongue sharper than any she had heard. Hani slammed the partly-opened drawer shut, wishing she could move in with her sister, at least for awhile.

'*Hani!*' her father roared, and she responded, rising slowly to see what he wanted. She was wearing a faded light-blue tank-top, which hung loosely over her breasts and half-way to her jeans. She checked her hair one more time, retrieved her hair-brush from the floor then strolled out to where she knew her father would be.

Outside on the porch, the retired general sat with a colleague discussing the mounting security problems which now plagued the rural communities. When Hani appeared, the men halted their conversation, her father covering documents with some loose papers she noticed lying on the deeply-scratched coffee-table. He looked up, then smiled, but his eyes conveyed no mirth.

'*Hani, I want you to press my uniform,*' he said, frowning as his eyes fell on his daughter's bare midriff.

'*Which one, father?*' she asked, surprised at his request. In earlier times this task would have fallen to one of their servants. Now, without their presence, the responsibility for the laundry and other household chores had fallen upon Hani. In months gone by, when she had suggested that her mother might wish to iron her husband's clothes, the woman had suffered an apoplectic rage then locked herself away in the bedroom for days.

'Ask your mother to give you my battle-dress,' he ordered, *'she will know which ones I mean.'* Hani did as instructed, finishing this task while her mother remained in her room resting. She informed her father that his uniform was ready, then slipped out of the house quietly and hurried down the street before the General became aware of his daughter's absence. He had been overly strict with the girls, unwittingly driving his youngest daughter into an early marriage.

Hani walked quickly, ignoring the irritating *becak* driver who followed, his wiry muscular legs pumping the iron three-wheeled pedicab closely behind as he hustled for the fare. Hani had no money to squander on the ride. Besides, it was not that far to her sister's home which lay three blocks down the street, behind the central markets. As she walked along the dusty broken street, Hani tied a handkerchief around the lower part of her face, then opened her umbrella to protect her skin from the sun's savage rays.

She heard the harsh blaring sound behind, and stepped off the road onto the cluttered footpath to avoid being run over by the bus. The over-laden monster rumbled past, followed by clouds of dust and thick, brownish, suffocating diesel smoke which sent pedestrians scurrying away in panic. A wave of motorcycles drove noisily by, their riders and passengers choking in the wake of the bus ahead.

Hani waited for some minutes before continuing down the road. Where possible, she kept to the footpath but, as roadside-peddlers had already staked their claims over most of the uneven pathway, Hani found herself competing with the undisciplined traffic flow once again.

'Hey, Hani!' she heard someone call. Glancing back, she squinted, unable to identify the face hiding behind the motorbike helmet. Her eyes fell on the jacket's insignia and hesitated. Then as recognition came, she pulled her handkerchief loose and stepped forward and pinched the rider's arm, causing him to wince with the playful gesture.

'Hi Budi,' Hani greeted her childhood friend. *'Where are you going?'*

He disengaged gear and killed the small engine. Fuel was expensive and becoming scarce. He lifted the visor covering his face then removed his helmet. Budi extracted a rumpled, soiled cloth from his pocket and wiped his face before responding.

'I'm leaving for Samudera Beach. Want to come?' he answered, teasingly. It was a familiar game they once played as teenagers. The fishing harbor was a favorite destination for young couples seeking some privacy from their own over-crowded homes. Hani had been down to the seaside several times, but never with Budi.

'Okay, then,' she laughed, *'but you'll have to get me back before dinner!'* Budi's smile widened, enjoying the light banter. The round trip would require at least four hours, and as it was already late afternoon, neither took the other seriously. Hani noticed the young man's eyes roam briefly, his gaze returning to hers, embarrassed that she might have read his thoughts. Her petite frame filled the jeans perfectly, her tiny, almost child-like, bare waist giving her the appearance of some half-dressed doll. Hani removed the golfer's cap and, with a practiced wave casually flicked her head, releasing her black, shining, shoulder-length hair.

'Where were you going, just now?' he asked, still sitting astride his prized possession. His father had given him the money for the Honda just months before the market had collapsed.

'I was going to visit Reni,' Hani answered, *'just to get out of the house.'*

She knew that Budi would be aware of the circumstances surrounding the Purwadira family's return to the mountain city. His own family had moved from their former home into a larger house. Budi's father had prospered where others had failed. He now headed the state-run, local electricity authority which provided many opportunities to supplement his government income.

Power failures had become endemic as the country's infrastructure continued its rapid decline. Poor maintenance, due to insufficient funds, contributed to the system's erratic supply, but it was primarily graft which prevented the power company from operating efficiently. Hani understood from conversations she had overheard that townspeople who enjoyed almost continuous power supply, paid dearly for this privilege. She flashed a smile at the young man, then looked up the street in the direction of the markets.

'I'll give you a lift,' Budi offered. Hani appeared reluctant, taking some seconds to decide.

'Terima kasih Budi,' she said, thanking him as she slid onto the pillion seat and, sitting sideways, placed her right arm around his waist while holding her open umbrella with the other. Budi fitted his helmet, restarted his Honda and, following his passenger's directions, they soon arrived at their destination.

Hani slid off the motorbike and stood straightening her clothes as Budi looked on admiringly.

'Want me to pick you up later?' he asked, hopefully. He had not seen her for some time, and was surprised at how she had matured.

'Would you?' she replied, demurely, placing her hand on his arm. *'I'll only*

be here for a few minutes, Budi. Come in and say hello to Reni,' she suggested. Budi considered this, then shook his head.

'I have a few messages to run for my father. How about I come back in an hour?' Hani thought about this, then smiled.

'Terima kasih, Budi, you are very kind.'

'Okay then, it's settled. I'll pick you up at four o'clock,' with which he gunned the Honda's engine and drove away, waving with his free hand. Hani watched him disappear as he wove through the disorderly traffic, almost hitting an oncoming truck head on. She checked her clothing again, then entered her sister's cramped accommodations to wait for Budi's return.

At four o'clock, and true to his promise, he arrived and drove Hani a short distance out of town, further into the hills. There, alongside the highway leading down to the southern coast, they found a Padang-styled roadside restaurant which served traditional Sumatran food. Hani was delighted that Budi had chosen this place. She had not been out with anyone for more than a year, and the pleasure of being there lifted her spirits immeasurably.

'Tell me about Jakarta,' Budi asked, selecting the dish of curried brains to start. They could eat whatever they wished from the amazing selection, paying only for those dishes they touched.

'Let's eat first, Budi, I'm starved,' Hani pleaded, not particularly keen to discuss the past. Budi laughed, scraping the remains of the otak onto his rice.

'Okay, but you've got to promise not to eat then run.' Hani smiled at his response, pleased that she had put him off this easily.

'It's a promise,' she agreed, not at all anxious to return home too soon.

Waiters dashed around the busy restaurant, obviously a favorite of the coach drivers. The smell of cooking oil hung heavily in the air, and Hani guessed that the oil would have been recycled more than once, because of the current shortages. Hani had counted more than a dozen buses parked outside, their passengers now busily gorging themselves on the hot, spicy food.

Hani spooned the steamed rice into a larger bowl, then passed this to Budi. Together they attacked the selection of curried and fried offal dishes. As they ate, they talked, demolishing more than one serving of *paru-paru* and *hati goreng,* the fried lung and liver dishes whetting their appetites even further. Within minutes of eating the *babat pedas,* both gulped their sweet, iced-tea as the chili-laden tripe burned its way to their stomachs. With tears in their eyes, and brows covered with perspiration, they continued to fill themselves with the highly spiced food as one busload of travelers departed, while another poured inside to take their places.

Finally they both had enough. Budi raised a small dish, offering it to Hani who shook her head, pulling a childish face as she did so.

'Enough!' she moaned, patting her still flat stomach. Budi agreed, then paid the bill. They remained awhile longer at the restaurant, sipping iced tea and as it would soon be time for the evening prayer period, they decided to return to Sukabumi, and their homes.

'You still haven't told me about Jakarta, Hani,' he complained, as she slipped off his bike not far from her house. Hani had asked Budi to drop her at the corner, fearing her father might see.

'Well, if you're really interested, you might invite me out again,' she suggested, crossing the fingers on one hand behind her back. She had enjoyed the afternoon, and wanted Budi to ask her out again.

'Tomorrow, then?'

'Yes, Budi, for sure,' Hani responded, happily. She squeezed his arm gently, then turned to walk the short distance home. *'I'll wait for you here. Okay?'*

'What time?'

Hani thought for a moment. *'You don't have anything to do for your father?'*

'Sure,' he replied, *'but I'll tell him that I have something important to do. I'll pick you up at ten in the morning, Hani, then we could take a ride down to the coast if you wish.'* He was not at all certain that she would agree.

'You want to take me to Pelabuhan Ratu?' she asked, surprised but pleased. Pelabuhan Ratu was the harbor village area adjacent to Samudera Beach.

'If your parents will let you go.'

'They won't,' she said, her heart sinking at the very thought of asking.

'Then why tell them?' Budi suggested encouragingly. He could see that Hani was considering this and pressed on. *'We could be back early in the afternoon.'*

'Are you sure, Budi?' she wondered, not really needing any encouragement. *'It would be very bad for me if I didn't return before dark.'* He understood, and nodded affirmatively.

'I promise to get you back in time, Hani.' She bit her lip, deep in thought. It would be wonderful to escape for the day.

'Okay,' she agreed, not entirely confident of her decision. Hani feared her father and clearly understood the consequences of being caught out. *'I'll be here then,'* she agreed, then added, *'but please don't leave me standing here alone.'*

'Don't worry,' he said, *'I'll get here a little early so you won't have to wait.'*

With this, Hani smiled widely and waved goodbye with her fingers, then strolled slowly home, turning her head and smiling in acknowledgment as Budi streaked past. She watched him turn at the corner, and disappear from view. Then, with a sigh, she went inside to prepare for the *Magrib* prayers, noting from the cheap Taiwanese wall-clock that she had only just made it back in time. She looked into the small room her brother occupied and was surprised to find this empty. She washed, and changed into more appropriate house-clothes, then knocked on her mother's door to join her in prayer. Her father would have left for the mosque for this purpose, leaving the women to fulfill their religious duties at home. There was no answer, and so Hani knocked again then opened the door to enter.

Inside, she could see her mother asleep on the bed. Hani smiled, moving closer on tip-toe so as not to awaken her, knowing that she would not be indisposed to missing the prayers. Fading light cast a faint glow between partly-closed curtains, touching her mother's face as she lay peacefully on the bed. Hani advanced further, curious that she had not undressed before retiring as her mother would never sleep in this attire. Her eyes darted around taking inventory, noticing the torn envelope on the bedside table and the paper lying crumpled on the floor. She bent down and retrieved the letter, but was unable to read this in the poor light. Hani leaned over her mother, concerned as the room was uncomfortably hot, assuming that she had fallen asleep with the windows shut tight.

Her hand brushed her mother's arm, shock registering immediately on the young woman's face as the cold, lifeless limb alerted Hani that something was dreadfully wrong.

'Ibu?' she cried out, her concern turning to fear as she pulled her mother's body up into a sitting position, and shook her, but there was no response.

"Ibu?' this time louder, anxiety sweeping through her body. Her next cry caught in her throat, unable to escape as realization of her mother's demise took control. Hani choked, and grabbed her mother fiercely, holding her tightly to her small bosom as the room was suddenly filled with her long painful wail, the chilling cry immediately raising the alarm.

Concerned neighbors rushed into the house. They knew that Hani was alone, as it was no secret that the general had left earlier, dressed in uniform, and accompanied by his son. They had observed the jeep full of soldiers arrive and take them both away. Several women comforted Hani, whilst another hurried away to inform the deceased's other daughter, Reni.

Within the hour, the two young women sat together, their tears already exhausted, bitter that their mother had taken her life. The empty bottle of sleeping tablets had been discovered under her bed. The enigmatic letter Ibu Purwadira had found upon waking earlier, had said it all. Her husband had left and taken their son with him. The general's intentions were very vague. He had not indicated whether he would return, nor where he had taken their son and this implied to the desperate, heart-broken woman, that he had deserted her.

Earlier, Ibu Purwadira had read the brief note, but she did not weep. Instead, unable to face the further shame of having been abandoned, the once elegant woman believed there remained only one course of action available to her. She bathed, dressed in her finest clothes and carefully applied her makeup, then swallowed the half-bottle of prescription tablets, and lay down in her fine clothes to die.

It would be days before news of his wife's death would reach General Purwadira. He had left his home to join with General Praboyo, a chance to redeem himself, and recover his shattered career. In the following weeks, he would assume command control of the Bandung metropolitan police, once Praboyo had seized power. By then, his son would have enlisted, and commenced basic training in the newly-created military forces which would, when ready, challenge General Winarko for control of the country.

Chapter Sixteen

Geneva

Hamish

Hamish McLoughlin loosened his safety-belt, then adjusted his seat to allow for a better view of the landscape below. As the Boeing 767 climbed into the midday sky, he could see clear across three nations, their borders dominated by the majestic Alps, still blanketed with mantles of snow. He would be in Kuala Lumpur by morning. There he would board the Fokker F-28 which had been chartered to the United Nations Commissioner for Refugees and travel the length and breadth of riot-torn Indonesia, conducting on-site investigations into the refugee camps which had suddenly mushroomed throughout the archipelago.

Although he had revisited other parts of Asia during the past eighteen months, Hamish had not returned to Indonesia since the night of his hurried and confused departure from Jakarta and the events which had thrown the nation into turmoil. He had watched President Suhapto's resignation via satellite in his hotel room in Geneva.

The following week, when he had parted company with his Swiss-based employers, Hamish was tempted to return to Jakarta and confront Mary Jo in person, finally deciding against this course of action. He had phoned a number of times and left messages, but she had not responded, suggesting to Hamish that their relationship had come to an end. He considered his options and, recognizing that he desperately needed a break away from Asia's demanding cultures, Hamish had grabbed his unpacked bags and flown to New York, where he spent several months feeling miserable with himself before re-establishing his network within the financial community. A year had dragged by before Hamish had admitted how much he missed the Orient, and he left New York as suddenly as he had arrived, and flew to Hong Kong. To his dismay, the city with its teeming millions had changed under its new masters, much of the old character gone, forever.

The new airport had opened and most of his old acquaintances had left the former colony in the wake of the Asian meltdown. In discussions with the few who remained he detected an air of fatalism which soon convinced him that he should leave. He spent but a few weeks wandering his old haunts, crossing to Macao by ferry and trying his luck at the tables, absorbing what remained of the old familiar ambiance, the pungent cooking smells and noisy pedestrian traffic, tourist faces filled with anticipation and the contradictions of wealth and poverty which still screamed their presence at every turn.

It was not long before Hamish acknowledged that he was no longer suited to the changes which had occurred in his absence. Appalled by what was happening throughout Asia, he decided to reposition himself in Europe where the markets were more vibrant and opportunities for his expertise would be more lucrative. He boarded a Cathay Pacific flight to Geneva where, by chance, he met the United Nations High Commissioner for Refugees socially, the event changing the course of his life immediately.

Hamish McLoughlin accepted the position with the UNHCR to provide financial evaluations with respect to Asia's looming refugee crisis and did so, not out of any mercenary considerations, but because he believed this role could offer a genuine sense of purpose and satisfaction. He realized that he had neglected to enrich his personal life, pleased now that he had undertaken to dedicate his skills towards more humanitarian pursuits than those of his past. It was only when he joined the six thousand strong organization did Hamish discover the enormous difficulties with which so many nations were faced when dealing with the socially and politically sensitive issues of refugees. The Geneva-based body engaged his services on a contractual basis and, although the UNHCR operated in more than one hundred countries, he specifically requested South East Asia as his territory and this was granted in view of his previous experience in the region.

Hamish's first official task had been to attend the mini-summit requested by Malaysia and Thailand as both countries faced new challenges with both illegal immigrants and refugees spilling into these countries. The breakdown of civil order in Aceh had seen thousands board small fishing boats and sail the short distance from Sumatra to Malaysia. The majority managed to bypass coastal patrols only to be caught during immigration sweeps and incarcerated in the already overcrowded detention centers. It seemed that the winds of reform had done little to change Indonesia and had now become but a flutter as the country moved towards the end of its second consecutive year in peril.

As his plane reached its cruising altitude high above the Alps, Hamish accepted the tray of hors d'oeuvres, smiling as the stewardess finished refilling his glass with Moet Chandon. He opened the International Herald Tribune lying on the empty seat alongside, immediately reminded of Mary Jo Hunter as he searched through the pages for anything which might relate to his brief. His mind returned to the recent Kuala Lumpur meetings, and his surprise when he had spotted her standing amongst a group of journalists covering the conference.

Mary Jo was dressed in sage-green slacks and matching safari jacket. Her appearance was almost masculine, the military-styled outfit out of place in the setting. At first he had hesitated, awkward with the moment. Then, as their eyes locked, he knew that it would be impossible to avoid talking to her, and walked towards the woman who had once enjoyed a very special place in his heart.

'Hello, Mister McLoughlin,' she said, her voice devoid of sarcasm, but nevertheless cool, as she extended her hand to accompany the forced smile.

'Hello, Jo,' was all he could find, hoping his embarrassment was not obvious.

'I didn't realize that you had changed careers until the handouts were passed around,' she said, referring to the information sheets the local United Nations office had circulated to the Press prior to his arrival. Her first words reminded Hamish of more pleasant memories and he smiled warmly with the recollection of their first meeting not long after she had first arrived in Jakarta.

'How long are you staying, Jo?' he asked, not knowing how to respond to her statement.

'Just long enough to cover what's happening here, then back to Surabaya,' she said. Hamish detected a sadness in her eyes, wondering what might have contributed to this.

'Will you have time to grab a bite together?' he asked, wishing the other journalists would give them some space.

'Sure, Hamish,' Mary Jo agreed, placing a cigarette between her lips and lighting this as he looked on with raised eyebrows. 'Fell back into the habit I'm afraid,' she said, observing his expression.

'I'll be finished about eight tonight, will that be okay for you?' Mary Jo shrugged, blowing a cloud of spent smoke through the air.

'Fine,' she replied, 'let's meet in the lobby bar.' Hamish nodded, pleased. That night, following the conference's first round of talks, they had met and, in order to avoid the constant stream of noisy journalists through the popular bar, Hamish had taken Mary Jo across the road for dinner, hoping that the Chinese restaurant recommended by the concierge would put them both at ease. There, they were escorted directly to a quiet, intimate setting, the atmosphere unusually subdued for that style of cuisine. Settled, each with a drink in their hand, it was Mary Jo who broke the ice first.

'Where do we start?' she asked, cutting directly to the chase. Hamish raised his glass, and touched hers gently, hoping they could put whatever had happened behind them quickly in as mature a fashion as former lovers might.

'I tried to phone you for days, and even left messages for you at the villa,' he explained. 'I tried again from Geneva for the best part of a week. I left messages but when you didn't return these, Jo, I thought you might have lost interest.' Mary Jo remembered the chaotic days and nights which had followed the students' occupation of Parliament. She had spent most of that week camped there, and could not recall having been given any messages by her servants.

'Why didn't you write?' she demanded, a little too loudly.

'I did,' he replied, 'I wrote to you from New York but you never answered that letter either.' He was telling the truth. Hamish had written to her, wishing her success and happiness, and was surprised that she had not received his mail.

'Bullshit,' she said, without any signs of rancor in her voice. Hamish breathed heavily, then played with his drink as he sat there observing Mary Jo.

'It's true,' was all he offered. She could take it or leave it he decided, not at all sure that his decision to meet with her, a sensible one. The wound had since healed; he bore her no malice, and yet he found himself on the defensive.

'Let's just put it down to the poor postal service then, okay?' she suggested, this time with a hint of sarcasm creeping into her voice. Hamish nodded slowly, and waved to the waiter. He ordered and when their four course meal was served they ate in silence. Hamish encouraged her to talk but her responses were short, almost bitter. Confused, he had given up any further attempts to lift the cloud which had descended upon them both, and an hour later they had parted company, their relationship even more strained than earlier in the evening.

Although he saw Mary Jo from a distance a number of times during press conferences neither made any attempt to speak. At the end of the week they had gone their own ways, both convinced that the other bore responsibility for their breakup.

Now, as his flight crossed the wide expanse to the north and west of the Mediterranean Sea, Hamish McLoughlin's thoughts addressed what lay ahead, and the possibility that their paths might cross again. Should this happen, he decided, it might be appropriate if he challenged Mary Jo to tell the truth regarding what had really transpired the night he had left Jakarta, when he had phoned, and discovered her in Eric Fieldmann's room.

* * * *

The Former First Family

Nuri paced the room restlessly like some caged untamed cat. The entire Suhapto family's movements had been severely restricted by the government. They were now virtually prisoners in their own castles. The interim President, Hababli, had needed to convince the Indonesian people that he was indeed serious about recovering assets from the former First Family. Nuri looked out through the flimsy curtains to where the presence of military guards clearly indicated that her family would remain in so-called protective custody for as long as Hababli had General Winarko's support.

Nuri was angry that the family had not fled when they had the opportunity to do so. Now they lived with the fear that not only would they be stripped of their wealth, but the possibility that some, or even all of their number might face trial, charged under the laws of the recently revised Constitution.

Accusations concerning her father's role in the kidnap and murder of his superiors back in 1965 had surprised them all. Nuri wondered why her father had not taken preventative steps years before to remove the political prisoner responsible for the damming revelations.

In the months following her father's resignation, Nuri and the other five children had wanted to leave Indonesia but their father had forbidden them to do so. At that time, Suhapto still believed that he would be restored to the nation's helm once the people discovered just how incompetent the interim President really could be. Now the entire family had been confined to their houses as prisoners, while President Hababli's shaky regime moved precariously closer to the brink of its own political abyss. Nuri despised Hababli. The thoughts of the pretender sitting in power, lauding it over his former benefactors, remained with her constantly, and she prayed that he too, would receive his just retribution.

Nuri's anger burned deeply when she was reminded that her family had become the source of Hababli's wealth. She had watched, her heart heavy with resentment, as the new President had slowly, but surely, stripped the Suhaptos of power in the most insidious manner. At first they believed that he was merely playing to the international monetary agencies. That had been the original arrangement between her father and Hababli made during the hours leading up to the transfer of power.

Hababli had then betrayed them all. Within days of being appointed to the Presidency he arbitrarily announced that existing contracts between government agencies and companies associated with the Suhapto family would be terminated. The Suhaptos watched as, one by one, the lucrative arrangements were unwound. Tanker contracts were canceled, power-plant operators were changed, monopolies were abolished and this madness continued until their empire had been slashed, through flesh and nerve, depriving the Suhaptos of all income. Then the asset-stripping commenced as Hababli's own cronies moved to plunder and dismantle the Suhapto family's conglomerate. Nuri estimated that assets valued at more than two billion dollars had been transferred to the new President's own family, these blatant acts of treachery encouraged by those who were once loyal to her father. Without their cash-flow her family had been unable to prevent the collapse of their domestic operations. Then there was the question of her family's numbered accounts.

As a further gesture of contempt, and paralyzed by his own dysfunctional leadership, Hababli had promised the Indonesian people that he would ask the Singapore Government to freeze all secret accounts associated with the former President's family. Although she knew that he had been unsuccessful, his actions had been sufficient for the banks to demand the presence of any of the signatories to these Asian Currency Unit accounts before any funds would be released. In effect, this permitted the bankers to hold what amounted to many billions of dollars in cash reserves belonging to her family, until such times as they were permitted to travel to Singapore in person.

Nuri's family had been informed that the Swiss bankers would require that at least one of her brothers or sisters appear before any of their deposits could be accessed. She expected that, in time, Hababli and his associates would come to some compromise regarding her family's hidden assets. The knowledge that their accumulated wealth, which she knew to exceed thirty billion dollars, would remain out of reach to those who headed the new Indonesian Government provided Nuri with some semblance of comfort, believing that she could always use these funds to negotiate their position.

Her thoughts turned to the others in her family, understanding their frustration with the drastic changes they had been subjected to since their Bapak surrendered power. Nuri accepted that not all in her family had fared well. Her younger sister, Tuti, had written asking that she seek General Winarko's intervention when her husband, Praboyo, had been placed on trial for the Uber Sakti University student slayings.

For Nuri, it mattered not, one way or the other should the arrogant and irresponsible General Praboyo land in military prison. The Suhapto family were of the same opinion; their demise was directly related to the student killings, the catalyst for the destruction of the Suhapto dynasty. General Winarko had interceded. The final compromise had been banishment to Bandung.

But the stigma remained, for Praboyo had never been cleared of his involvement in those shootings, his appointment as Commandant of the Staff College rescinded when the *ABRI* leadership dismissed him as a result of an officers' code-of-conduct hearing. Praboyo was discharged from the Army with his secrets intact. Diplomats and their military analysts conceded that the lieutenant-general's dismissal was a way of containing damaging evidence, which would most certainly have emerged in an open court, military tribunal.

Banished to Bandung, his name was rarely mentioned in any of the other Suhapto households, and Nuri felt saddened that Tuti had followed her unfaithful husband to the mountain city.

All telephone links into their homes were monitored, and Nuri now spent her days communicating with the outside world by letter. She expected that much of her correspondence would be subject to censorship. She expected that Hababli's rapacious greed would continue to drive the President's incessant intrusions into her family's affairs until he accessed what they had hidden overseas. Nuri was careful in what she wrote, determined to make Hababli's path a difficult one. On occasion she had deliberately written misleading information, hoping that this would add to the confusion in the search for her family's well-buried fortunes.

Nuri stopped pacing when one of the female assistants entered the lavishly-appointed drawing room, and handed her a bundle of letters. The woman remained waiting for instructions as Nuri Suhapto sorted through the mail, and was then waved away, without so much as one word.

Alone with her thoughts again, Nuri retrieved one of the letters she had set aside briefly reading its contents. She wondered why her censors permitted such hate mail to be delivered. She knew that there would have been many hundreds of other communications destroyed in the censorship process, and was annoyed with herself for reacting to the letter's content. Nuri rolled the accusatory letter into a ball, and threw this across the room, then sat down to read the remainder of her mail. She opened the letter from her sister in Bandung and read this slowly, saddened by the news Tuti's letter conveyed.

When Nuri Suhapto finished reading Tuti's note she became concerned that the contents had been read by others. Exasperated by her sibling's naiveté, Nuri sat pondering the consequences of what her sister had written regarding Praboyo, now less than confident that her ambitious brother-in-law's covert activities would not again endanger them all.

* * * *

Tuti had tried pleading to her husband but this had only resulted in a sharp slap from the back of his hand. She sat facing the vanity mirror examining evidence of his response. Praboyo's ring had left a small red welt, just below her right ear, and Tuti placed her finger gingerly on the wound, wincing as she did so. There would surely be a bruise and this, coupled with her husband's irrepressible behavior, sent another flood of huge weeping tears cascading down her cheeks.

Tuti was deeply taunted by the gossip that Praboyo had ensconced his mistress in the air force guest house not far from where he lived with his family. Consumed with anger, she wished she could muster the courage to confront the woman whose presence caused so much pain. Praboyo had been severely critical of her lately, their relationship rocky since her father had fallen from grace. She knew that their joint assets would ensure that their marital bonds remained intact. Although she was certain that he no longer loved her, Tuti was gambling that her cavalier husband would never abandon the considerable fortunes they had secreted away, safely hidden in Swiss and Singapore vaults. Tuti was relieved that she had followed her father's advice; Praboyo would not benefit financially from her death, and would still be unable to access the joint assets without her sisters' and brothers' approval.

Flashes of her father holding her lovingly on his lap brought tears to her eyes.

The late President Suhapto had slipped away in his sleep, his passing cheered by many, his memory cherished now by few. The children had wished to take his remains to be buried alongside their mother, but any foray into *Mufti Muharam* held territory could not be considered. Instead, in this land of eternal compromise, General Winarko had suggested to President Hababli that Suhapto be buried at Kalibata in the Heroes' Cemetery. He had agreed, providing the service was kept to immediate family and selected government officials.

On that day more than five thousand troops had been mustered as an honor guard, detailed to accompany President Suhapto's mortal remains to the designated resting place. Tuti had attended. Political differences had been placed aside, and she was grateful for the opportunity to farewell her father. Then, heavy with grief, she had returned to Bandung with her children, bitter that her husband, always immune from criticism, had refused to respect the occasion and attend the funeral.

Tuti suffered terribly from the loneliness imposed by her husband's banishment to Bandung, and the knowledge that she was effectively under house-arrest. She had no complaints with respect to their accommodations. Although the stately government mansion was well staffed, it remained a prison for Tuti and her children.

In a conciliatory move, General Winarko had agreed that her children could visit their family in Jakarta, although their movements were closely monitored during such outings. Nowadays even General Praboyo required written authority before being permitted to leave Bandung's greater metropolitan area.

Tuti had been surprised with Praboyo's docile acceptance of his banishment, as this was totally out of character. She had expected that he would rebel, jeopardizing the only chance he would be granted to redeem himself forever. Then, to her dismay, she learned that it had all been a cleverly disguised feint to conceal his true agenda, to overthrow the country's leadership.

Alarmed by the conversations she had overheard, Tuti confronted Praboyo and demanded a denial that he was, in fact, supporting another coup. His response had been to smile arrogantly, and turn away, the cold, cruel, and determined grin, the answer she had feared.

She lived with the constant threat of discovery, deeply concerned that the flow of seditious officers into her home where they often remained huddled in secret deep into the night, would be observed by others. The possibility that her husband could end up incarcerated in the Cipinang Prison filled her mind with each waking hour. Tuti appealed to her husband to consider their children but was ignored. In desperation she wrote to her sister, Nuri, in Jakarta, requesting that she take her children into safe custody until Praboyo came to his senses.

Tuti's letter passed through the censor's hands, its ambiguous contents phrased in such a manner as to deliberately confuse. A reply arrived within the week, and she became even more depressed.

Although Nuri had understood the nuances of her appeal it seemed that even she was now powerless to prevent Praboyo from embarking on his precarious journey.

Chapter Seventeen

Haji Abdul Muis & Mary Jo

'*We must advance across this valley of fear, and climb the mountain on the other side until we reach its summit. We must not wait any longer. The time is now. We must reassert our principles and pave the way for an Islamic nation, one which will overcome the adversity which continues to threaten our country, and its people. It is time for pure motives. It is also time that we cleansed our country of those forces which have fed the evil that has beset us all.*' There was hush as Abdul Muis ceased speaking. He raised his outstretched hands as the silence continued, then screamed, '*Allahu Akbar*' as loudly as his lungs would permit.

The crowd roared their approval, filling the air with the cry, '*Allahu Akbar! Allahu Akbar!*' '*God is Great!*', the stadium breaking into pandemonium as the white-clad *Mufti Muharam* followers continued their chants, the air reverberating with the sheer force of their collective voices. '*Hiduplah Abdul Muis! Hiduplah Abdul Muis!*' they called, '*Long live Abdul Muis!*' As their voices reached those outside, the echoing effect continued until the thunderous sound of two million voices enveloped the city.

The Moslem leader had commenced his crusade to turn Indonesia into a sectarian, Islamic state. He had become a most potent force for Moslem unification over the past eighteen months, claiming power at the recent elections. Although this was thwarted by the military, Abdul Muis continued on his mission of reunification throughout the archipelago, speaking to rallies, whipping his audiences into frenzies of racial and sectarian hate wherever he visited.

In a multi-faceted society long scarred by racial discrimination, he believed that his attacks against the Christians would be ignored by a military dominated by Moslem generals. But he needed the support of the powerful union movement which now threatened to attract membership from within his own ranks.

Having considered his own motives in depth, he proceeded, accepting that his actions would initially create even greater suffering for his people. Abdul Muis joined with the Union movement, the massive, and crippling strikes which ensued had further deepened the economic and political crisis. It had not been too difficult to persuade the unionists to follow. Massive reforms demanded by the IMF had only exacerbated the problems of hunger and poverty now experienced by hungry millions. Haji Abdul Muis had become a beacon, not just a spiritual leader. To the mass of thirty million unemployed he represented a promise, a way out of their economic dilemma.

Following the collapse of the Suhapto regime Abdul Muis had remained silent, as President Hababli moved to ensconce himself as the nation's leader in much the same manner as his predecessor. During his first months in office the interim President had paid lip service to the IMF and World Bank, cleverly disguising his own motives and vested interests until substantial sums of capital were advanced by these organizations. Abdul Muis watched, with continued annoyance, as Hababli moved quickly to shore up his own power-base both internationally and domestically. But, somehow, Hababli just did not have the qualities or the charisma demanded of the Presidency.

Within months of his appointment he awarded honors to his own brother and wife during a lavish nation-wide television ceremony. Abdul Muis sniggered to friends when Hababli appealed publicly for the Chinese community to return, pleased when they refused. Then, when the President tempted the foreign investment community with empty promises of reform, Abdul Muis believed that the interim leader's time was coming to an end. The foreigners were reticent to return with their capital, citing the re-emergence of cronyism and nepotism amongst the Indonesian leadership. Token gestures such as General Praboyo's show trial had done little to convince the West that things had changed. When Praboyo had fallen from grace Abdul Muis wasted little time in disassociating himself from the once powerful general, unaware that Praboyo's ambitious nature would bring the former allies into deadly confrontation.

Haji Abdul Muis watched with growing impatience as Hababli fell victim to his own ego, convincing himself in the most self-delusory manner that he was loved and admired by all. But it was when Hababli took a most dangerous path, siding with the United States and Great Britain against the world Moslem community, did Muis decide on the mechanics of how he might achieve his dreams. At a time when unity was all important to movements such as the *Mufti Muharam*, the President had openly agreed with the American attacks on Sudan and Afghanistan, raising the ire of the world Moslem communities.

When he learned of the *USS Valley Forge's* deadly Tomahawk missiles striking Bahri on the outskirts of Khartoum, reducing the al-Shifaa pharmaceutical plant to a smoldering heap, Abdul Muis was on the phone immediately, talking to Osama bin Ladam's deputy, seeking assurances that the wealthy philanthropist had not been killed or injured. Incensed by reports of the *USS Abraham Lincoln's* unprecedented attack on targets in Pakistan's mountainous region, Abdul Muis had immediately demanded that the President condemn the attack, but Hababli refused. Instead, appointing himself as spokesman for the world's Moslem community, President Hababli had condemned bin Ladam, unwittingly undermining Moslem unity. Muis had been livid. His relationship with the terrorist organization jeopardized by Hababli's need to be praised by the West.

Within weeks, the *Mufti Muharam* coffers started to suffer, a direct result of the President's untimely statement. Until placated, Osama bin Ladam had threatened to withdraw his support for the Indonesian movement, resulting in Haji Abdul Muis reconsidering his own strategies. He used the labor movement to further consolidate his position, then crippled the country's economy through prolonged strikes. The labor movement demanded representation and, supported by Abdul Muis' massive following, the world listened.

Under pressure from the international monetary bodies the government had finally bowed to their many requests to hold a full election for both Houses of Parliament which resulted in a stalemate between the *Mufti Muharam* Moslem Party and the Indonesian Armed Forces. When counting had been completed it was evident that the Moslem factions had performed even better than predicted by international analysts and had clearly won government. Rules governing the electoral processes were hurriedly amended. All of the minority parties were abolished, the justification being that their presence would only contribute to further instability. The two major parties, *Mufti Muharam*, and the reformed *Perkumpulan Karyawan* or *Perkarya Party* as it was known, each received an allocation of those votes previously awarded to the minority parties.

The threat of the world's fourth largest population being governed by hard-line extremists was unacceptable to the West, and General Winarko was given the nod to initiate whatever action was necessary to prevent Haji Abdul Muis from becoming the nation's fourth President. Before the two

Houses could meet to elect the country's new President, the ABRI leadership cried foul insisting that the results were not consistent with the will of the people, and accused the Moslem politicians of vote-tampering.

The situation had become tense. General Winarko acknowledged that his troops would be reluctant to shoot upon those who shared common religious beliefs, and a compromise was reached which promised but a brief respite, from what would ultimately be a Moslem challenge to assume government control. Abdul Muis recognized the stalemate, accepting that he would need more time to arm if he were to succeed. He knew that serving members of the military who shared his faith would be unlikely to break ranks and follow his lead. Although Moslem, he realized that the soldiers were more likely to remain loyal to the military, as all of the ABRI leadership was now Moslem.

L.B. Hababli, indecisive at best, became confused as to which faction he should support. At first it appeared that the military would object to his remaining at the nation's helm as its titular head, but then General Winarko acquiesced, his reasons based on sound financial considerations.

Although Hababli had managed to keep his sticky fingers in the till, extracting desperately needed dollars from the nation's treasury, Indonesia was, nevertheless, still theoretically bankrupt. The external flow of capital had all but ceased, and there had been no significant foreign investment enter the country since Suhapto stepped down. The Chinese still refused to return, tagging the recently-issued anti-discriminatory decrees as ineffective, and incapable of guaranteeing their safety.

The bulk of the Suhapto and Hababli fortunes remained untouched, in international vaults. The Indonesian Government had been unsuccessful in its attempts to access the billions these two Presidents and their families had ripped out of the economy. General Winarko had insisted that travel restrictions remain on the late President's family hoping that they would soon tire and negotiate some form of settlement. There was very little left to milk from the economy and, with both the World Bank and IMF watching closely, opportunities to manipulate government funding and contracts had become rare.

Abdul Muis had accepted the Vice Presidency to avoid any further acrimony between the military and his powerful following. But he did so knowing that Winarko's American allies would not have hesitated in having him killed had he refused. But he was not satisfied with the status quo, deciding to generate a Moslem ground-swell which even ABRI could not ignore, and in so doing totally eradicate all signs of Christianity throughout the country.

Abdul Muis decided that he would lead his people, if not as their President, then as their spiritual and religious leader, believing that he would only achieve his dreams by avoiding, at least for the time being, any direct confrontation with Jakarta's generals. His ground-swell would commence in the east of the densely populated island of one hundred million, and continue to grow as its massive wave flooded across Java to Jakarta sweeping all in its path. Resistance in the capital would crumble and he would fulfill his destiny to lead Indonesia, proclaiming the nation as an Islamic state.

In the weeks that followed his appointment as Vice President a further eighty-five churches were burned to the ground throughout Java and the island's twenty million Christians and Buddhists feared for their lives. There were many deaths associated with the sectarian violence but none were reported in the domestic press. It was then that the Jakarta-based student revolt had resulted in the destruction of the national Parliament. Hababli's imposed curfew and declaration of military rule had endeared him to none, and Abdul Muis had seized this opportunity to make his move.

As Abdul Muis traveled through Java his popularity grew even more, reaching its zenith when he addressed his home-town crowd of two million in the island's eastern capital of Surabaya. Now, as he stood facing his followers, he knew that the time had arrived to commit publicly to the path which would lead to the realization of his dreams. He cleared his voice and leaned closer to the microphone.

'Years ago, when I first assumed the leadership of the Mufti Muharam there were those who scoffed at our dreams. Some even suggested that it would be madness to consider that Indonesia could ever become an Islamic state.' The crowd responded, sections of the large gathering demonstrating their displeasure with those who had disbelieved.

'Today, in your presence,' he continued, his voice louder than before, *'I declare Surabaya as the seat of government for the Islamic State of Indonesia!'* The multitude greeted this news with another roar, the historic moment captured live by the international media. A group of Western observers who had been invited from the local consulate corps glanced at each other with surprise written clearly across their faces as Abdul Muis' speech was interpreted for them.

'Today, also, I officially announce that I have resigned as the so-called Vice President of the illegal government, recently formed and controlled by an American-sponsored military, in Jakarta.' Again, the crowd cheered with

pleasure. Because of deep-rooted cultural differences, the East Javanese despised those who lived at the Western end of their small island. Chanting Abdul Muis' name, a group towards the center of the crowd started to sway, then shuffle in a clockwise direction.

'Abdul Muis, Abdul Muis,' they sang, momentum building as the swirling mass moved together, the scene reminiscent of the huge numbers which gathered in Mecca during the holy pilgrimage month.

'Abdul Muis, Abdul Muis,' the thunderous chanting continued, as voices became hoarse, and dust rose to cover the amazing spectacle. As the sea of white moved before him his eyes filled with tears and Abdul Muis realized the first step in his dream of an Islamic state with Surabaya as its capital.

Down below, struggling to escape being trampled, Mary Jo Hunter dragged her assistant Anne towards the closest exit. They pushed and shoved against the over-excited, now uncontrollable mass, finally breaking through and making their way outside where the spectacle was not much different. The possibility that they could easily be trampled to death, should they linger, spurred them on. Although Mary Jo's long strides made it more difficult for the shorter woman to keep pace, Anne hurried to keep up, driven by the fear that the crowd's mood could easily turn ugly, and her American friend targeted by extremists present.

As they continued through the packed fields surrounding the stadium it seemed that the human mass would never end. Exhausted, their hearts beating rapidly, with saturated stained clothes clinging to their backs, the two women managed to find their way back to the hotel. Mary Jo filed her story with New York, alerting the world to Haji Abdul Muis' declaration, and the creation of the world's largest Islamic state. The next day she was granted an interview with the powerful religious leader.

* * * *

Anne had reminded Mary Jo how she should behave when first introduced to the mullah. Word had been sent that she was to come unaccompanied, as the Haji was fluent in many languages the assistance of an interpreter would therefore not be required. Abdul Muis' aide ushered Mary Jo into his presence, then left to conduct her interview alone in the magnificently decorated room.

Golden, hand-woven strands worked into the delicately embroidered wall-hanging glittered under natural light, falling through the mosque-shaped dome directly overhead. The Birds of Paradise depicted in the intricate work glistened, coming alive as Mary Jo moved her head mesmerized by the handicraft's beauty. She could hear children's voices somewhere nearby, their soft, melancholic chants drifting through the garden, as they continued to pray. The heavy, wooded-scent of sandalwood hung in the air, the atmosphere reminiscent of another world, one filled with tranquillity and order.

Mary Jo smiled, but did not extend her hand. Instead, she clasped both together as if in prayer, then bowed her head politely, waiting for Haji Abdul Muis' response. Delighted with the supplication, he returned her smile, graciously directing her to sit with a wave of his hand.

Mary Jo observed how he was dressed, inwardly smiling at the costume he wore. Gone were the Western clothes he had worn in the past, now replaced with long flowing robes, reminiscent, she thought, of paintings of historic figures such as General Diponegoro she had seen hanging in the national museum. His feet were clad in sandals; expensive, leather, hand-made sandals, partly covered by a long black and golden robe. A lightweight matching scarf hung casually around his neck, and the *Ulama* wore the traditional white rolled turban, as a sign of his position.

'You have lived in Indonesia for two years?' Muis asked, already aware of the answer to his question. The *Mufti Muharam* had an efficient intelligence service, most of the information regarding the American had been gleaned from her documents while registering at the hotel.

'Yes, *Pak Haji,'* she replied respectfully.

'And you enjoy my country?' he asked, and Mary Jo was certain she detected a twinkle in his eye.

'Of course,' she replied, suspecting he would know this to be untrue.

'But when your work is finished here, you will leave?'

'Yes,' she answered, recognizing Muis' attempt to deliberately place her on the defensive. 'but with a heavy heart.'

'Ah, yes,' he rejoined, pleased that she knew how to play the game, 'one must always follow one's heart.' Mary Jo smiled again, totally at ease with Muis leading the conversation. 'Are you married?'

'No, not yet,' she said, remembering that Indonesians rarely responded with the definitive 'no'.

'Then perhaps you will find someone while you're here,' he suggested. 'Now, should we commence?' Mary Jo placed her recorder between them, and went directly into the interview, starting with his family and schooling for background, surprised with his candor when recalling the bitter period surrounding the loss of his family. Muis required no prompting, obviously comfortable with the opportunity to provide the Western press with an accurate account of his childhood, and the events which had shaped his thinking. When he finished, Mary Jo changed tapes and, concerned that they would run out of time, asked the questions which were foremost on the international community's mind.

'Pak Haji, is the *Mufti Muharam* related in any way with Osama bin Ladam's terrorist organization?' Indonesia's Muis cocked his head, and answered.

'Yes, but they are not terrorists.'

'In what way do the two parties cooperate,' Mary Jo ignored his objection.

'We are both determined to prevent further injustices by the Americans and their allies against Moslem nations.'

'Injustices?

'Yes. Acts of aggression, such as we have seen over the past twenty years. The Americans think they rule the world. They are mistaken. Do you know how many world citizens now follow the teachings of the Prophet Mohammed? No? I will tell you. There are more than one billion people who have embraced Islam. We are a formidable power, and the United States and her allies would do well to remember that.' Mary Jo noted that with the rhetoric, Muis remained calm, his voice modulated, and calm.

'In what form does this cooperation take place?' she tried again, resisting the temptation to sit back and cross her legs in front of this man.

'We work together for the common good of Islam,' he said.

'When the *Mufti Muharam* attacks churches, Christians and Chinese, do they do this with your blessing?' Mary Jo asked, aware that the question was provocative. She watched Muis' eyes closely, searching for the truth in his answer.

'Islam is a tolerant faith. We are not responsible for the ethnic violence.'

'And the religious violence?'

'There are extremists in every organization. I cannot control them all.'

'Then you agree that there are those within your own following who are responsible for the destruction of churches and temples?'

'No. Those were the actions of marauding gangs, not religious zealots.'

'Then how do you account for the eye-witness reports that *Mufti Muharam* have systematically burned churches and homes belonging to the Christians?' she persisted. Muis' eyes narrowed, and Mary Jo felt a chill of fear, wondering if she had gone too far.

'These are unfounded lies. The *Mufti Muharam* has never encouraged its followers to engage in such activities. Who told you this?' he demanded, his voice still under control. He had expected a more enlightened approach from the foreign journalist. Muis wanted his face on Time and News Week covers, but not as a leader accused of harboring religious fanatics, even if this were true.

'I have seen the reports, Pak Haji,' she challenged, 'and photographs evidencing the racial violence.'

'Do you have them with you?' he asked, knowing that she would not.

'No,' she said, wishing she had thought to bring them.

'Then how can I comment on something I have never seen?'

'Are you saying that the *Mufti Muharam* is a non-violent organization?'

'Yes, of course. Islam does not encourage those things you have suggested.'

'But they still happen, Pak Haji, just the same.'

'Not here,' he argued, 'not in East Java.' Mary Jo could not believe her ears, recognizing that this line of questioning was going nowhere, fast.

'Sources in Jakarta state that it is your intention to declare a Jihad against all things not Moslem in Indonesia.' Now Mary Jo had crossed into the territory he had hoped she would visit. Foreign journalists were considered more credible than their local counterparts. His sources confirmed that this woman's credentials were such, any interview conducted by her would be given fair treatment. He had hoped she would want to know more about him, his life, his character, and his beliefs. Now, he feared, the interview might turn out to be detrimental to his cause.

'Sources in Jakarta?' he laughed, but she could tell it was forced. 'What would sources in Jakarta know about what we, in the *Mufti Muharam* plan for our people?'

'But you have already stated publicly that Indonesia must become a Moslem state. If this is so, what will happen to the thirty million who are not amongst your followers?'

'They can convert,' he said, simply.

'And if they don't?' she pushed, and a cynical smile formed on Muis' lips.

'Then they can leave,' he said, his voice devoid of any emotion.

'Thirty million people?' Mary Jo could see that he was serious. 'What will you do if they refuse?' Abdul Muis' face hardened, his eyes blinked, and he clasped his hands together.

'They will leave,' he said, his voice now barely audible, sending another cold chill along her spine. Suddenly, an aide appeared out of nowhere and went to his side, whispering in the mullah's ear.

'I am sorry, but I have been called away,' he announced, rising to his feet. Disappointed, Mary Jo also rose, wondering if her line of questioning had resulted in the interview's termination. *How had he signaled his aide?*

Mary Jo departed, cursing herself for being overly aggressive. She climbed into the waiting vehicle and snapped at the driver to take her back to the hotel, reflecting on her meeting with the *Ulama*. As the driver wove his way through Surabaya's congested streets, Mary Jo could not rid herself of the uneasy feeling that Haji Abdul Muis was indeed seriously considering how to remove thirty million people from Indonesia's shores.

* * * *

Mary Jo's suspicion that the interview had been terminated deliberately, was indeed correct. But not for the reason she had assumed. Within minutes of her departure Abdul Muis was on his way to Surabaya's harbor, where he waited patiently for the Panamanian registered freighter's crew to finish tying up alongside.

'Asalamalaikum,' each of the men replied as Muis welcomed each of the men, once they had been assembled away from the gangway.

'We are very proud to have you here,' he praised the men. 'the *Mufti Muharam* will sing your praises in time to come.'

Muis then watched as the men climbed into the back of a waiting truck, and then driven away to the specially prepared camp built on his land, deep in the East Java countryside.

Satisfied that the presence of the foreign contingent went unobserved, Abdul Muis then returned to his Surabaya home, and composed a brief coded message for Osama bin Ladam, informing him that his recruits had arrived.

Chapter Eighteen

The Indonesian Presidency

The Armed Forces Chief of Staff glared across the room at his lackluster President Hababli, annoyed with the man's propensity for attracting criticism. Hababli had been described by both the international and domestic press in the most unflattering way, his credentials to lead questioned repeatedly. His attempts to seal his legitimacy by soliciting a formal invitation to visit the United States had borne no fruit. Politically, the capricious President was naïve, his support base erased by his ineffective style. Winarko was also furious with Hababli for his off-the-cuff remarks and whimsical style of leadership.

In a country which prided itself on discussion and consensus, disunity now prevailed. The President's reaction to Haji Abdul Muis' startling declaration had been to lift the nation-wide evening curfew, a move which severely provoked his generals. Winarko had moved quickly to heal the rift but the damage had already been done. The chief of staff realized that he had lost some credibility amongst his staunchest supporters for permitting both Abdul Muis and Hababli to achieve the prominence they had.

'He certainly enjoys the role,' Admiral Sujono commented, following Winarko's gaze. The General turned his head slightly, dropping his voice to a whisper.

'Hope he doesn't become too accustomed to it.' The Navy chief grinned in a conspiratorial manner, hiding this behind a heavily-starched white napkin.

'Sometimes I wonder if the Rupiah would recover if we were just to remove him completely,' Winarko commented rhetorically. He was reminded of the time when Hababli's name was mooted as a potential Vice Presidential candidate under Suhapto. The currency had plummeted with the news. Then, in his first weeks as the interim President, Winarko was speechless

when Hababli announced his cure for the nation's food shortage problems. At a gathering of more than one million faithful, gathered for prayers, Hababli called upon the nation's Moslems to fast on Mondays and Thursdays, in an attempt to cut rice imports.

'It couldn't get much worse,' the other man suggested, *'perhaps it's worth giving it a try?'* Winarko realized that the Admiral was only echoing the thoughts of many within the *ABRI* leadership. They had urged him to take the Presidency for himself. Even the Americans had recommended that he do so but the General resisted making such a move. He needed to unlock the vast treasures the Hababli and Suhapto families had concealed offshore. Then he could also rid himself of the upstart he'd banished to Bandung.

A scowl appeared on the Chief of Staff's face as an image of the cocky, young Praboyo flashed through his mind. For a brief moment, the risk of losing any future access to the Suhapto fortune appeared tempting. Winarko believed he could happily dispose of this thorn in his side without loss of conscience, or sleep, and was confident that the day would arrive when General Praboyo would wish he had never crossed the line.

Winarko was painfully aware that the former *Kostrad* commander still enjoyed considerable support within the officer ranks and that any further move against Praboyo would most likely encounter formidable resistance. This had been evident when attempts to bring him to trial over the student shootings had clearly identified growing and substantial support for the sidelined, and now disgraced officer. He glanced back at the man sitting alongside.

'All in good time, Admiral. All in good time.' General Winarko cast his eyes around the formal reception, wondering if the IMF would be pleased with the extravagant scene. Ice sculptures set along the center of the dining area dominated the room, the delicately carved forms depicting a number of dolphins frolicking together. Red linen tablecloths covered long, narrow tables around which a skirt of white cloth had been hung, the colors representing the nation's flag. Silver filigree figures adorned each table, while the most brilliant orchids stood majestically in crystal vases completing the elegant setting. Winarko could see that no expense had been spared by the President's household, and considered the extravagant display a clear indictment of Hababli's inability to understand the national mood.

As his eyes roamed, he identified several of the more senior ambassadors amongst the guests, and the General became increasingly uncomfortable, conscious of what they might be thinking. His nation had become bogged in a quagmire of desperation, the result of Haji Abdul Muis' declaration. Winarko realized that the international community was anxious to see how he would react to Abdul Muis' most recent challenge but it would have to wait. There were more important issues he would have to address before taking up the sword against his fellow Javanese. Somewhere across the vast room someone rang a bell, bringing the guests to silence.

'Ladies and gentlemen,' the voice announced, *'I give you the President of the Republic of Indonesia.'* There was a distinct scraping of chairs as Hababli rose to his feet and smiled benevolently at the assembly. He stood, hands clasped close to his chest, his eyes locked on the slowly-melting ice sculptures which blocked most of his view.

'Firstly, I wish to thank my honored guests for attending this function at such short notice.' Winarko heard the Admiral alongside mutter audibly and ignored the uncomplimentary remark. Hababli opened with the customary pleasantries, talking of friendships and alliances, before arriving at the crux of his speech.

'As you can see, with the lifting of the curfew previously imposed as a result of student unrest, conditions are returning to normal.' Many of those present looked at each other, skepticism written clearly across their faces. The city's streets were still ringed with barbed-wire, and the military's strong presence still evident with tanks, armored vehicles and barriers positioned strategically round the capital.

'At a time when our great nation continues to count the cost of the disastrous climatic effects brought by El Nino and La Nina, we found it necessary to ask the world donor countries to assist us, once again. As you know, the IMF and World Bank packages which provided funding to Indonesia over the past year were not sufficient for our country to rebuild its economy and meet the targets outlined in those agreements. We have applied for further assistance but have been advised that due to the needs of others such as Russia, Japan and Korea, further funds will not be forthcoming.' The guests remained silent as they were painfully aware of the problems. Indonesia had received close to seventy billion dollars over the past eighteen months, most of which disappeared down some man-made black hole. International agencies such as the IMF would not advance any further funds, even if these had been available. The constant drain on resources over the past year had left the Fund coffers nigh on empty, with the American Government refusing to inject further capital until real reform took place, as had been promised previously.

'Tonight, I wish to take the opportunity to make two announcements.' This was greeted with an audible sigh somewhere close to where General

Winarko was sitting. The Chief of Staff covered his face with one hand, his head moving ever so slightly from side to side as he waited for what might follow.

'The first of these relates to our country's ongoing financial crisis. And, as a result of in-depth discussions with my Ministers for Finance and Trade, I have decided to implement radical reforms in relation to Indonesia's natural resources.' He cleared his throat, nervously, his eyes searching the room for support.

'Commencing immediately, all profit sharing and production sharing contracts which relate to the exploration, extraction or processing of natural resources are temporarily suspended. I expect that this announcement will not be received kindly but Indonesia is a nation in crisis, and these decisions are essential to the country's survival. In the future, when our economy has recovered, I would welcome the foreign companies involved to return and re-negotiate their contracts.' President Hababli paused, perspiration evident across his forehead. Ignoring the shocked expressions before him, he continued.

'The second announcement concerns the position of Vice President which, as you are all aware, has become vacant due to Haji Abdul Muis' resignation. According to our revised Constitution, this position should now be occupied by the senior House Speaker but, as there is none, I have asked Madame Megatante to fill this position.'

General Winarko looked up sharply, his face covered with dismay. He glanced at the other senior officers present, and it was obvious from their expressions that none had any advance warning of Hababli's intentions. His mind raced quickly. Hababli had either been very clever or extremely stupid again. The woman whose name had been mentioned headed one of the democratic movements which had been annihilated at the recent elections. Her late father was still considered by some to have been the greatest hero of the Indonesian Revolution. Winarko knew that by announcing her appointment in this manner, Hababli had cleverly circumvented the need to seek *ABRI's* consent which, undoubtedly, would not have been forthcoming. The shock of the first announcement had been lessened by the second amongst the foreign representatives present. Madame Megatante was held in high esteem amongst Western nations, which were hopeful that she would challenge the nation's leadership and bring the country back on track.

As for revoking existing contracts which, for years, had provided foreign oil and gas companies with their fair share of Indonesia's riches, it had happened before and Winarko supported the wisdom of this move.

The surplus billions which had previously benefited the foreign contractors should be redirected and used to feed Indonesia's starving population. There was really no other choice. The IMF and World Bank funds had shrunk to impossible levels. His country needed the currency generated from the massive deposits of gas and oil found throughout the resource rich archipelago.

President Hababli thanked his guests, then signaled his aides that he wished to depart. He bowed stiffly, then hurried away before Winarko had the opportunity to speak with him. Upon his departure, many of the stunned guests followed, some anxious to contact their own foreign ministries regarding the surprise announcements, whilst others raced away to phone their stockbrokers in faraway capitals, with orders to dump the relevant resource stocks.

Within hours of the announcements, Western governments condemned Hababli's seizing of oil, gas, and other resource-joint ventures. In Malaysia, Thailand, Vietnam and Cambodia, lights remained bright in cabinet ministers' offices as they too investigated the possibility of following Indonesia's bold precedent, eager for the bonus billions which might flow through their hands. In Melbourne, an indignant chairman of Australia's largest oil-producer swore at the Prime Minister when he was told that the navy would not be sent into the Timor Shelf joint production zone to protect Australian interests, as he feared a confrontation with the giant, Moslem neighbor.

And, as lights in those nations which had vested interests in Indonesia's lucrative oil and gas contracts continued to burn deep into the night, in the distant provincial capitals of Surabaya and Bandung, Abdul Muis and General Praboyo considered their options. In totally unrelated incidents, both men hurriedly revised their plans to seize power, advancing these as a direct result of Hababli's untimely announcements.

* * * *

A Nation in Turmoil

Haji Abdul Muis wasted little time consolidating his control over all of East Java, and had already penetrated well into the loosely-held central provinces as well. Moslem-inspired vigilante attacks raged throughout Java as the call for an Islamic state grew in intensity, whipped up by village zealots who seized this opportunity to settle old scores and ensconce themselves as religious leaders at the *kampung* level.

The military appeared powerless to prevent the radical and militant Moslem crusaders from not only destroying property across the island, but also the wholesale slaughter of non-Moslems as they fled for their lives.

In Central Java, where Christians, Buddhists and Moslems had lived in relative peace, side by side for centuries, neighbor suddenly set upon neighbor, brother upon brother the slaughter continued until the bloody scenes were reminiscent of General Sarwo Eddie's murderous campaign of 1965, when his soldiers slaughtered tens of thousands in their anti-Communist, cleansing campaign.

While Muis' butchers ran amok annihilating Javanese and Chinese Christians alike, a massive wave of refugees commenced to build and move *en masse* towards the small coastal ports where they hoped to escape, by ship. Many of the island's twenty million non-Moslems fled in terror, most carrying gold and heirlooms which they hoped to trade for safe passage. Fishing villages were suddenly inundated along the entire south Java coastline as the exodus continued.

They sailed to the closer islands first, their numbers swamping communities in Southern Sumatra, Madura, and into the western parts of Bali as the never-ending flow of refugees continued. Then, as those communities choked under the sudden influx of their traditional enemies, they reacted angrily to the Javanese presence, driving most back onto their vessels under threat of death.

Indonesia's small, coastal-fishing fleet owners were overwhelmed by the staggering fees they could charge for passage to Australia. The weather-beaten and under-powered wooden boats were dangerously overcrowded, many capsizing even before getting under way. One by one, fishing communities gathered their boats together to form floating villages to meet the incredible demand.

In most instances, the flotillas were guided by seamen who had previous experience sailing across the dangerous Indian Ocean to Australia. There, coastal patrols regularly seized Indonesian poachers and burned their ships before flying the illegal visitors back to their homeland.

Familiar with the dangerous seas which lay between the two countries, they would now become navigators, guiding the rickety ships to the southern continent. As these flotillas set out to sea with their precious human cargoes, hordes of refugees remained behind lining the shores, anxiously awaiting their turn to leave.

When the first waves landed along the northern Australian coastline, more than one hundred thousand illegal immigrants stepped ashore on the barren, hostile land. Alarmed that they were unable to prevent such numbers from flooding ashore, the Australian forces were immediately mobilized to prepare detention centers, stretching from Port Hedland, across to Darwin. Urgent requests for tents, bedding, food, generators and desalinization plants were slowly filled, many hundreds dying from existing conditions before the temporary accommodations could be erected.

Within six weeks there were fifteen such camps containing more than three hundred thousand hungry, desperate and greatly disillusioned refugees, horrified with Australia's stark and inhospitable Outback conditions.

Their hopes shattered, and faced with certain death should they return, the asylum-seekers simply settled down in the camps and waited obediently to be processed by the local immigration authorities. For some weeks, there was a lull. Then, as word spread that others had succeeded in entering Australia and had been permitted to remain, another wave of refugees arrived, swamping the Western Australian coastline from Broome to Carnarvon.

In that one fortnight, the State's population rose by more than fifteen percent, while the local inhabitants looked on in dismay, cursing the Federal Government for its archaic gun laws which had left them unarmed.

Canberra appealed to Jakarta to assist in preventing the massive migration, but these requests fell on deaf ears as the Indonesian military struggled to diffuse the threat of civil war. In consequence, the Australian Defence Forces went to full readiness, anticipating the worst. Orions were sent to assist monitor the country's two hundred miles limit. Two squadrons of F-111's and F/A-18's were repositioned to Scherger in Northern Queensland and Learmonth in North-Western Australia, whilst Darwin and Tindal Air Force Bases saw an immediate influx of Hercules transports ferrying personnel and equipment from southern bases.

In the Indonesian capital, the President refused to recognize that his country had ruptured; that the Republic was rapidly dismantling before his very eyes. All international carriers refused to land in Indonesia, the small number of tourists in destinations such as Bali were stranded, dependent on irregular charter flights for their repatriation. Anticipating the worst, Indonesia's neighbors went on full alert. The British Government sent its navy to East Malaysia and Brunei, while the American Seventh Fleet sailed through Indonesia's waters in full combat readiness.

Confused by his inaction and apparent support for Hababli, a number of senior *ABRI* officers called upon General Winarko, the Armed Forces Chief of Staff, to resign. When he refused, a major split occurred and this, coupled with Abdul Muis' unilateral declaration in Surabaya, threw Java into civil war. Spasmodic fighting broke out between rival army factions, causing most military commanders to review their own positions in relation to their country's desperate cry for help and their own vested interests.

In Jakarta, General Winarko's worst fears were realized when he discovered that the *Kopassus* Special Forces headquarters at Cijantung, just outside the city's limits, had been abandoned with intelligence sources reporting that the commander had moved 22 Battalion and the other detachments to Bandung.

He had no doubt that the other three battalions would fall in behind their commander and silently cursed himself for his error in promoting one of the *Kopassus* officers to command the Special Forces. The knowledge that he had lost the now ten thousand strong force weighed heavily, as these were highly skilled and experienced soldiers, veterans of the East Timor and West Irian campaigns.

He moved quickly to shore up his position, replacing the *Kostrad* Strategic Reserve's commander with his own adjutant just to be certain. Winarko believed that the key to success lay with his control over the capital. *Kostrad's* two well equipped divisions would, he expected, ensure this result. The Bogor-based 1st Infantry Division had moved back into the city and he was confident that he could count on their commander's loyalty. The airborne brigade he had positioned in Sulawesi would remain there, just in case. The other would remain on standby.

And so the cycle continued. By the end of the following week, the lines had been clearly drawn. Of the ten major commands, or *Kodams,* General Winarko had secured the loyalty of only four. Of the others, two of the commanders had lost control in Sumatra, and Bali, while his major concerns revolved around what was happening in the mountain city of Bandung, home to *Kodam III.*

He had been particularly saddened to learn that fighting had broken out within the command structure, his close friend Major General Sjamsudin reported killed in skirmishes between a quick-reaction battalion and two of the commander's cavalry support units.

General Winarko firmly believed that without the Bandung command, he could lose the capital. It was only when he discovered that the two infantry battalions stationed just south of the city had withdrawn, pulling back over the mountains to join up with the rest of their *Kodam* that he realized their strategy. But with the death of his friend, who would lead this most important command?

Winarko's answer came with news of an assault against the heavily-fortified Central Java Command in Semarang. He then knew he had erred in not having General Praboyo destroyed when the opportunity was at hand. Reports indicated that Praboyo had assumed control over most of Central Java, from Bandung down to the port city of Semarang and across the mountains to Jogyakarta, Solo and Surakarta. Winarko sent an emissary to Surabaya where Abdul Muis' powerful *Mufti Muharam* followers had joined forces with the East Java Command, but his officer had been executed the Haji's succinct response immediately understood by all.

Now, with three separate and very powerful entities, all vying for control over the densely populated island, he had no choice but to take control of the Presidency. Surrounded by conflict, President L.B. Hababli willingly stepped down, surrendering power to the Javanese General, Winarko.

* * * *

East Java

Haji Abdul Muis & Osama bin Ladam

The vessel had arrived hours before schedule, taking the Indonesians by surprise.

'You're early,' Muis stated, shaking the other man's hand warmly.

'We had fair winds,' Osama bin Ladam responded, metaphorically. He had survived a number of assassination attempts, due to the unpredictability of his itineraries. For bin Ladam, changing routes and timings, even at the last moment, was standard procedure. He refused to place his life entirely in the hands of others, deliberately altering his arrival in Surabaya as a precautionary measure against the possibility that word of his visit might have come to his enemies' attention. His eyes dropped to the mobile phone on the seat between them.

'I trust that is switched off?' he asked, aware that the phone's whereabouts could be easily tracked. Muis nodded but picked the instrument up just to make sure.

They drove in silence, covering the distance to Abdul Muis' rural retreat in under two hours. They passed through parched, arid countryside, crossing rivers and now neglected, dusty volcanic plains. The endless line of poverty-stricken Javanese tramped the worn, broken edges of the macadam a blur in their vision, as they continued, heedless of these conditions on their way.

Burnt-out villages, evidence of the two years of ethnic and religious violence, flashed past the car's smoked-glass windows unnoticed. Emaciated children, cast aside by desperate and starving families, lay alongside the once prosperous highway neglected their bellies filled only with hope and destined to die.

They continued their journey. A village school came into view and, with a cursory glance, Muis was satisfied that his edicts had been obeyed, for he could see the girls wore the mandatory white shawls. Veils would soon follow. Women and girls throughout the country would learn to fear the consequences of not complying with Islamic law.

The road narrowed, erosion having taken its toll, and slow-moving bullock carts groaned forward, cautiously, causing the Mercedes to slow to a crawl. Muis' driver immediately displayed his impatience, holding his hand on the horn until the road cleared. Ahead, the traffic had come to a grinding halt to permit oncoming vehicles to cross the now-single lane, bomb-damaged, concrete bridge. Trucks, buses, carts, and motorbikes poured off the remaining bridge, partially destroyed by Winarko's and Praboyo's air-strikes.

On their side of the river, Muis observed craters had been covered with thatched bamboo sheets and used as shelter by itinerants. Beggars, many with missing limbs appeared, their filthy, ragged bodies repugnant to those inside the air-conditioned car. For these scenes had become all too familiar to the powerful men, their vision of a greater Moslem world to be achieved for their own purposes, at any cost.

* * * *

Osama bin Ladam had been obliged to slink away from his Afghanistan mountain lair built, ironically, by American-sponsored anti-Soviet guerrillas, at a time when the mountain tribesmen were still considered U.S. allies.

With the collapse of Communism, alliances had changed and political terrorists such as Osama bin Ladam had suddenly found themselves out in the cold. He could no longer count on the support of the Iranians, nor the Afghanistan tribal groups who had once sworn loyalty to his cause.

The bloody confrontation between the Iranians and Taliban groups in Afghanistan had thrown bin Ladam's camp into confusion. The American strikes against his training facilities, and the constant satellite surveillance which had severely crippled his mobility, caused him to reconsider his place of domicile. Then, when Afghanistan's purist Taliban militia had insisted that he move his base of operations, the terrorist leader had contacted Haji Abdul Muis.

Bin Ladam had decided to test Indonesia's soil to determine whether he might move his operations to the fertile, untapped Moslem community. Tempted by the Saudi's commitment to place at least one nuclear warhead at his disposal, Abdul Muis had been most receptive to the idea, and eagerly assisted Osama bin Ladam to re-establish his base of operations in Java at the *Mufti Muharam* provincial retreat.

* * * *

Their vehicle gained speed as traffic thinned, bringing the powerful duo to their destination. To the untrained eye, the high-walled compound could have been the home of a wealthy, religious recluse. From a distance, the dome-shaped mosque's minaret provided a Taj Mahal quality to the setting, the tall spire in fact was an observation post and had never been used to call the faithful to prayer.

'You have done well,' bin Ladam complimented, as they drove through the second security gate manned by heavily-armed, dedicated troops, their weapons concealed under long, white, flowing robes.

'You will find that my retreat is totally secure,' Muis boasted but not without good cause. The complex had been constructed entirely by local labor, all sworn members of the *Mufti Muharam.* A three-meter high, cement-block perimeter fence had been erected around the ten hectare property, the top of the wall strung with razor-sharp, rolled barbed-wire to discourage even the most foolhardy from violating the camp's security.

Bin Ladam took note of the secondary observation posts discreetly disguised amongst coconut tree stands around the complex, pleased that Muis had taken his advice and further camouflaged the armed positions.

They drove directly to the main building, past the ten-man accommodation blocks and training facilities, where specialist courses in front-line terrorism were conducted for the few, select personnel recruited from Muslim minority groups in Malaysia, Thailand, the Philippines and other parts of Asia. Their driver eased the Mercedes into the underground garage where Muis and his guest were warmly welcomed by staff, and stone-faced security. A group of men stood in line, off to one side, and bin Ladam viewed them critically.

'Will they be ready in time?' he inquired, casting his eyes across the line of recruits who, within weeks, would be asked to give their lives for the cause.

'They'll be ready,' Muis promised, and ushered his guest inside.

* * * *

Bangkok & Kuala Lumpur

The delivery van turned off Wireless Road and propped, waiting for the Marine guard to wave him through. After a cursory inspection, the driver eased the vehicle forward slowly, following the route he had covered a hundred times before, down the side of the embassy to where he was expected. Bangkok's power supplies had never been reliable, the sensitive equipment housed inside the United States Embassy necessitating the constant electricity supply produced by the twin five hundred KVA machines installed to the rear.

The maintenance staff stepped out of the small building housing the powerful generators and waved to the familiar face delivering the drums of diesel fuel to the fuel store. The engineer walked to the rear of the van, just as the Thai Moslem driver whispered *'Allahu Akbar'* and died, his sweaty, trembling hands simultaneously activating the primary explosion required to ensure the effectiveness of the more powerful, and secondary detonation.

In Kuala Lumpur, a van similar to that used in Thailand for the attack crossed into Jalan Tun Razak, the traffic congestion delaying the deadly cargo's delivery by more than half an hour. When challenged at the U.S. Embassy's gates by Marine guards, the driver panicked, and attempted to charge the steel gates and, in so doing, failed. Shot twice, he was dragged from the vehicle, then taken into custody by local police.

The army bomb disposal squad was called, the soldiers successfully deactivating the two explosive devices within minutes of their arrival. The seriously wounded fanatic was kept under guard at the military hospital and interrogated by American officers the following day. Before he died, the young Malay confessed to being a member of the *Mufti Muharam* sect, admitting the existence of organized cells established to attack American interests throughout Malaysia.

He and his companions had all been trained in a pleasant rural setting, not two hour's drive from Surabaya, in East Java.

Chapter Nineteen

The Indonesian Outer Islands

Mary Jo

The two women walked back to their *Kijang* jeep in solemn silence, the horrific scene they had just witnessed further testament of the fierce cruelty which continued to pervade the country. The woman had been tied to a cross, then viciously assaulted by the *Kopassus'* interrogation team. Mary Jo had heard stories of the brutal tactics these soldiers employed but this had been the first time she had actually witnessed the results of such torture.

The villagers had taken them to the isolated clearing where another of the local women had been interrogated, then murdered by the Javanese soldiers. Evidence of their methods caused both Anne and Mary Jo to pale as their escort explained the use of their gruesome discovery. The bloody length of water-pipe remained where the soldiers had placed it, the snake they had inserted to further intimidate their prisoner, long gone.

'How can they be so cruel?' Anne asked, her face reflecting the agony she felt for the dead woman. She wiped tears with a sleeve, stifling a sob. Mary Jo could see that her assistant was still shaking from the experience. Anne placed her head in her hands and leaned forward in the seat. Then, without warning, she launched herself from the jeep and threw up. Mary Jo slipped out of the vehicle quickly and went to her side.

'It's okay Anne, it's okay.' She placed one arm around the shorter woman, and held her firmly. After a few minutes passed, she steered Anne back into the jeep and opened the cold thermos.

'Here, this will help,' she said, passing a plastic cup filled with sweet, iced tea.

'Thanks Mary Jo,' Anne smiled apologetically, embarrassed at having broken into tears. She drank, then passed the cup back. They spent some minutes composing themselves, then thanked the villagers. They gave their guides one of the small food parcels the women had become accustomed to carrying wherever they went.

'We'd better get going Anne. I don't think we should hang around here. The soldiers would be very angry if they found us here.' Mary Jo agreed. The driver swung into action, and they sped away from the grim scene as quickly as the narrow trail permitted. Three, back-breaking kilometers later, they rejoined the gravel road they had taken earlier and continued along this until reaching the broken asphalt road which would take them back into Dili.

Mary Jo had wanted to visit the police detention centers in the East Timor capital but had been refused permission by the local authorities. Although Jakarta had withdrawn the bulk of its *Kopassus* and other troops from the former Portuguese colony, these had been replaced with an equivalent number of hand-selected Javanese police. Locals she had spoken to days before had insisted that the Special Forces' torture chambers remained, urging her to visit Bairo Pite and Komoro for proof of their claims. The police commander had denied the existence of such centers. As Mary Jo prepared to return to Surabaya by plane empty handed, a member of Fatalin, the sole surviving East Timorese separatist movement offered to show them evidence of police brutality. Now, armed with proof that the terror campaign continued, Mary Jo wished only to get out of the dangerous town before the authorities discovered what they had seen and photographed. With four days left in their itinerary, the pair flew north to Menado, where they visited camps outside the city, then departed, flying across the Celebes Sea to Tarakan.

Three hundred miles west of Menado, and a similar distance southwest of the Philippines provincial city of General Santos, the pilot suddenly turned to the women and pointed, their aircraft now clear of cloud.

'We'll have to detour,' he said, tapping his headphones.

'What's happening, Anne?' Mary Jo wanted to know.

'Why are we changing course?' she asked the pilot. He tapped his phones again, raising his voice for her to hear.

'Can you see those ships over there?' he pointed again and this time Anne searched the sea to the horizon, locating a number of ships in the distance. 'I've just been warned not to approach those ships,' he announced.

'Whose are they?' Anne asked, having relayed this information to Mary Jo.

'American,' he answered, 'it's part of the Seventh Fleet.' When Mary Jo learned this she expressed surprise.

'I wonder what they're doing in Indonesian waters?' and grabbed for her binoculars. In the distance she saw a number of ships, amongst them a destroyer and cruiser but she was not sure.

'Perhaps we should give Tarakan a miss anyway, Anne,' Mary Jo suggested, 'and go straight to Balikpapan, then back to Surabaya.' Her assistant spoke to the pilot who nodded, made the necessary course corrections having checked his maps, and they continued on their way towards Borneo's western seaboard, Mary Jo preoccupied with the presence of U.S. warships sailing through Indonesian waters.

The following day, they returned to Surabaya. As their twin-engine Cessna flew low over the Madura Strait, Anne drew her attention to an unusually large number of fishing-boats gathered along the coast.

'Refugees?' she asked, guessing that this was probably so.

'Must be,' Anne replied, 'but I've never seen so many this far down the Strait before.' Mary Jo reached over and retrieved her camera bag, extracting her Nikon as she prepared to document the massive build-up on the flat, sparkling sea below.

'How many would you say there were?' she asked Anne.

'Many hundreds, perhaps even a thousand in those three groups,' she answered, pointing at the separate, floating communities anchored in the shallows.

'Ask the pilot if he would mind flying lower and around the fishing-boats,' Mary Jo requested, then changed batteries in her camera and reloaded. Moments later she braced herself with one arm strapped firmly around her seat as the Cessna banked abruptly, losing height as the pilot changed course. Mary Jo waited until he had positioned the vessels on the aircraft's port side, then she snapped what seemed to be a continuous line of wooden boats, all tied to each other to create a huge, floating, city. As they flew closer to the outer line, she could see terrified children scrambling for the safety of their mother's arms, whilst the more seasoned of the sailors stood motionless on deck, observing the small plane's interest as they flew past.

'Where do you think they're going?' Anne considered the question and slowly shook her head.

'These are Javanese boats. They wouldn't want to go too far to the east as that would take them towards the Timorese refugees' camps.' She thought awhile longer. 'Australia?' Anne asked, shrugging that she really had no idea as to their destination. A dry smile crossed Mary Jo's lips.

'How many people would you guess are down there?' she asked. Anne looked back at the congested fishing fleets and raised her eyebrows.

'I've seen those boats carry as many as a hundred on short journeys.' She glanced at Mary Jo. 'If they're only carrying say, fifty, and there's a thousand ships altogether, then,' she paused, calculating the number, 'there would be as many as fifty, possibly a hundred thousand refugees down there.'

'And you don't think the Australians might have had enough?' Mary Jo's forced, cynical laugh caused Anne to rethink the earlier question. She did so but came up with the same answer as before.

'That must be their plan. Others have done it. Where else could they possibly go?' she asked, but Mary Jo was still unconvinced. She was aware that the Australians had become increasingly hostile over past weeks, having towed more than two hundred fishing-boats back out to sea and fired over their heads. There were reports that a number of Indonesian boats had been sunk by coastal patrols, and Australian warships were becoming increasingly aggressive towards boats carrying the illegal migrants. Warnings that the navy had been instructed to sink offending vessels had been broadcast throughout the region, and Mary Jo believed the government to be serious in its threats to stem the massive flow.

'There's only one way to find out,' she said, pointing at the pilot. 'Ask him how far is the nearest airfield, and can he put down there.' The pilot partially removed his head-set again and listened as Anne leaned closer to make herself heard above the engine noise. They discussed Mary Jo's request, and she could see that the pilot was not too enthused with her idea.

'He says that he can put down here,' Anne said, pointing to the map the pilot had pulled from somewhere around his legs.

'Probolinggo?' Mary Jo asked, 'how far will we have to travel by road to get back here?' Anne placed her hand on the pilot's shoulder and asked.

'He says it's about a hundred kilometers.'

'We should be able to cover that in a couple of hours,' Mary Jo said, assuming they could hire a vehicle at the airport.

'Why don't we go onto Surabaya, Mary Jo,' Anne suggested. 'It's getting late and we could drive down tomorrow in three to four hours, taking our time.' Mary Jo glanced at her assistant, considering this option. It made sense, she thought, her concern being that the flotilla might leave before she had a chance to return. Traveling through East Java at night would be foolhardy, as the area was one of high risk, even to foreigners. The past weeks had seen Abdul Muis's position grow stronger, his followers swelling in numbers as the *Mufti Muharam* militants scoured the countryside, burning homes and shops belonging to Christians and even Buddhists. Mary Jo decided to follow Anne's advice.

'Okay, tell the pilot to take us back to Surabaya,' she ordered, a smile crossing her face when she observed the look of relief on Anne's. The pilot nodded, then he too turned to Mary Jo and raised his thumb in approval, not wishing to remain on the deck in Probolinggo overnight. He increased speed, then increased their altitude until the Cessna was back on its original course, leaving the floating mass of refugees behind.

* * * *

Lily

The soft ocean swells lifted the deck slowly, then lowered it again. Lily raised her body into a sitting position, hoping this might avoid the unpleasant, queasy sensation she felt as the ship's unfamiliar, and monotonous motion continued to concern her. She watched the other boats tied to hers bob around like huge corks as some distant ship's wake finally arrived, the small, almost undetectable surge passing through the floating village, spilling red, glowing charcoal from clay cookers.

Across from where she sat in her cramped space, Lily watched an elderly, toothless woman feed freshly cooked, barbecued grasshoppers to several very young children, dropping these into a porcelain bowl half-filled with steamed rice. Lily guessed, correctly, that this would be their only meal for the day. Usually, there would be sun-dried fish or even prawns to spare but as the fishing boats were all tied up here together, seafood had suddenly become as scarce as chicken, or even cat-meat, which local traders dressed and sold, disguised as fowl. Lily had no appetite. The suggestion of nausea had seen to that. She turned away from the children as they squabbled over the remaining grasshopper pieces, and raised her hand to shield her eyes from the hot, glaring sun.

* * * *

Lily had been aboard this twenty-meter wooden fishing-boat for less than two days, waiting as others continued to arrive and take their places amongst the thousands who had paid for their passage to Australia. Soon, they would leave Java's shores forever, risking their lives as they sailed to the south-east and freedom. The brokers who had demanded what was left of her mother's remaining gold trinkets had ordered Lily into their filthy, foul-smelling truck to hide under the canvas tarpaulin, along with thirty other Chinese who wished to flee Java. Under cover of darkness, they had then been taken from Situbondo the short distance to Asembagus and down to the coast some twenty kilometers north of Banjuwangi where their possessions were checked, before they were permitted to board the wooden vessels.

After paying for her mother's funeral, there had been little left of any real value that she could trade or sell, only the precious stash that had been set aside to pay for her escape. In the days leading up to her mother's final moments, more than half the houses and shops along their street had been burned by roaming Moslem gangs. She had waited in terror, fearful that their building would be next, her mother urging Lily to leave while she still had the chance. Then, the morning her mother died, Lily hurried down to the coffin-maker and paid the men there to take her mother to the cemetery. She dared not go herself; to do so would have only invited peril. Instead, when darkness fell, Lily slipped through the shadows, leaving her home of broken dreams to make her way to the broker's run-down garage. There, she paid for her passage to Australia and waited for her turn to climb into the filthy transport arranged for her and some others.

The truck had bounced along with its precious cargo until reaching the isolated departure point, across from Tanjung Island. When she discovered that thousands of her race had gathered for the ocean voyage, Lily had greeted this with mixed emotions, fearing that such numbers would surely attract the attention of the ubiquitous *Mufti Muharam* whose haunting message had been in evidence throughout all of East Java. She was shown which boat to board and had done so, not realizing that it might still be days before they would sail.

It had not taken long for Lily to become bored just sitting around in the debilitating heat. She had climbed across the closer boats, soon becoming familiar with others within this congested community, not at all surprised to discover that the majority of those present were of Chinese extraction. During her first night, she could not sleep as the boat rocked continuously, uncomfortable with her surrounds. With first light, Lily had gone ashore and wandered along the beach, impressed by the immense numbers who had gathered along the shore, hopeful of being granted passage to escape.

As Lily strolled amongst the thousands crowded together along the narrow beach, she was saddened by the number of abandoned children evident amongst the refugees, their empty eyes and expressionless faces tearing at her heart as they held their hands out to her, begging for food. She wished she could scoop them all up in her arms and take them away with her, away from the cruel fate with which they had been smitten, and the danger which lurked not far behind. But she knew that this was pure fantasy, and wandered back to her own group of fishing boats, miserable with what she had witnessed, pangs of guilt denying her any appetite for the rest of the day.

As she sat, protecting her head from the late-afternoon sun, she heard the aircraft and turned with the others, in time to observe the Cessna change course, then dip low over the ocean as it approached.

'It's the air force!' someone cried out loudly, sending panic through the fleet. Lily stared at the small, twin-engine aircraft, certain that their presence would now be made known to the roaming Moslem gangs, within hours. She watched the Cessna circle for a few minutes, then turn and fly away. As the small aircraft slowly disappeared from view, a shout went up, followed by a thunderous cheer as the lead fishing-vessel's diesel-engines coughed into life, signaling that the flotilla would soon be under way. The experienced captain assumed that the pilot would reveal their position to the navy. They would expect him to sail directly south through the Bali Strait, and this is where the military aircraft would strike to prevent their departure and appease the Australians. Without hesitation he changed course, deciding to go around the northern coastline of Bali, then turn south into the Lombok Straits where their transit was more likely to proceed undetected.

An hour later, when the sun settled behind Java's towering volcanoes, its fading rays turning distant, purpling thunderheads the color of mercurochrome, Lily had offered a silent prayer of thanks as her group, the last of two hundred boats, finally sailed past the Tanjung islands into the approaching darkness, turning south, towards the promise of a new life.

* * * *

BALI

The tall, handsome, titled Balinese accepted the binoculars, the distant scene confirming his worst fears.

'We can not permit them to land!' Anak Agung Ngurah Mudita announced angrily, turning to the group of elders. *'Once they're ashore, they'll remain forever.'* His statement was greeted with knowing nods. They had all seen it before.

Over the past months wave after wave of refugees had flooded across from Indonesia's eastern provinces. At first, their numbers had been but a trickle and the Balinese people, albeit reluctantly, provided sanctuary to the few thousands who had succeeded in fleeing East Timor. Although the *Udayana* Military Command was based in Bali, there were very few non-Javanese amongst the senior officers whose territory covered an area from Java across the thousand kilometers to Timor. To the locals' dismay, the military leadership had done nothing to stem the growing tide of refugees and, suspicious of their motives, the elders had decided to take matters into their own hands. It was one thing to accommodate the Timorese but a massive flood of Javanese into Bali would meet with the fiercest resistance.

Ever since the nation's first President had passed away, the Balinese had watched bitterly as their culture had been contaminated by the steady flow of Javanese Moslems. *Bapak Soekarno,* the nation's founding President, had been half-Balinese and would never have permitted the small, Hindu paradise to be subjected to such dilution. Now, as their people were transported to distant islands under guise of the national transmigration scheme, Jakarta encouraged the Javanese to occupy the over-populated province.

They had all witnessed the results of this Javanese colonization as large tracts of land were arbitrarily appropriated, the farmers poorly compensated, and Suhapto's family and friends slowly but surely, took control of the Island of the Gods. Religious and cultural customs were denied, cockfighting was banned, and sacred ground around Tanah Lot was desecrated to give way to condominiums owned by the First Family's cronies and relatives.

The normally soft-spoken man glanced at the others and felt saddened that it had come to this. Their ancestors had established their kingdoms here, more than a millennium before, bringing with them the culture of *Ramayana* and the architects who had built such wonders as Borobudur and Mendut in Java and, later, the city of Angkor Wat in Cambodia. They had sailed as far as Madagascar to the west, and fought against the Chinese in Nha Trang for control of the rich, delta lands to the south in Vietnam. Then, when the first fair-haired foreigners had appeared and threatened the Balinese, their ancestors had fought against these Dutch colonists. In the north, entire kingdoms had disappeared as wave upon wave of brave Balinese men were slaughtered as they fought to protect their land, refusing dominance by others over their spiritual domain. Now the time had come to fight again - this time against their distant cousins, the Javanese.

'Their boats must be destroyed before they have the opportunity to land!' All present turned to listen as Ida Bagus Ketut Alit spoke. They respected his opinion. He had acquired tactical experience serving under their unwelcome landlords.

'Do we have enough boats?' Mudita asked, determination written across his face. Time was running out. He knew they should move quickly.

'We have enough,' Ketut replied. They had but few weapons - the Javanese had seen to that. Any Balinese found in possession of a revolver or other firearm was now subject to the charge of subversion, and these men knew the offense carried the maximum penalty. They were counting on the intruders fleeing before they discovered just how poorly-armed the Balinese raiding party might be.

'Why do you think they have stopped?' Their coastal watch had tracked the three separate flotillas as they had sailed across the northern coastline, hugging the coast as if searching for a place to land. The Balinese believed that this suspicious behavior only confirmed the fleet captain's intentions to land in one of the lesser populated areas.

'Probably waiting for nightfall,' one of the other men answered. The others thought about this and agreed.

'How long will it take to get everything ready?'

'We can get out there within the hour. The vessels are all tied together, and they won't be expecting a hostile reception.' The men looked to their leader, anxious to get under way. He handed the binoculars to one of the younger men, then forced a smile.

'Well, let's get started,' Mudita ordered, leading the others down the track to where their mini-bus waited. The men followed silently, each deep in thought as they considered the risks they were about to take, ambivalent that their actions might attract the wrath of their Javanese landlords.

* * * *

Mary Jo

'They're gone?' she asked, her faced clouded with an incredulous look. They had departed from Surabaya well before sunrise, expecting to find the ships still anchored along the coast.

'He says they left late yesterday,' Anne relayed, inclining her head towards the roadside peddler.

'Which direction did they take?' Mary Jo demanded, her disappointment evident. Anne asked the question but the woman feigned ignorance, holding her palm open, knowing that the foreigner would pay for the information. Anne identified the gesture and, with an exasperated sigh, fished into her jeans for the equivalent of one dollar to give the woman.

'They went that way, to the east,' Anne said, nodding as the old peasant suddenly gushed with detail, now only too pleased to tell them all. Mary Jo squinted into the morning sun. She could just make out the volcano's silhouette in the distance, the customary haze yet to distort images as these familiar conditions would, when midday temperatures climbed towards their zenith.

'They went to the north of Bali?' she asked, confused by this path. 'Why would they sail that way?'

'They could have gone this way,' Anne said, pointing more or less south.

'The currents through here are very strong, Mary Jo,' she explained, 'and they might want to take advantage of the string of islands running towards the east before setting off for Australia.' Mary Jo looked at her assistant inquiringly, surprised that she was so conversant with the shipping routes. 'Indonesian fishing boats have been sailing down to the Australian coast for more years than any of us really know. I was with one of the Indonesian journalists who interviewed fishermen sent back from Darwin after their boats had been seized and burnt by the authorities.'

'So you believe that they are definitely heading for Australia?' Mary Jo asked, wishing she had a better understanding of the distances involved.

'For sure,' Anne answered, 'where else could they possibly go?' Mary Jo kicked at the dirt angrily and swore. She stared across the flat, shallow sea towards a small group of islands, her sunglasses enhancing the magnificent azure colors reflected by the warm, tropical waters. A flock of seagulls screamed nearby, clamoring over a small, torn piece of discarded silver paper carried by the outgoing tide. Mary Jo's eyes searched the horizon again, desperate for the story she believed waited out there - beyond her reach - but all she could see was a solitary, Bugis trader as it sailed past her line of sight.

Disheartened, they climbed back into the dilapidated, rusty Isuzu truck they'd hired, and instructed the driver to return to Surabaya. There was no point in remaining there. They had missed what Mary Jo believed would surely have been one of the great photo-opportunities of her career. She had not followed her instincts the afternoon before and insisted that the pilot land at Probolinggo, so she remained silent throughout the return journey.

That night Mary Jo received word that General Praboyo's tenuous grip on Bandung had further deteriorated, with General Winarko's forces consolidating their position at the provincial capital's gates. Abdul Muis' *Mufti Muharam* were reportedly approaching from the east, determined to take the city before Winarko. Mary Jo's Jakarta source predicted that Praboyo would have no choice but to retreat to Sukabumi. The tide was turning, and Mary Jo wanted to be there when Praboyo finally went down. She went together with Anne to discuss their mission with the charter pilot.

'Nobody in their right mind would fly you to Bandung.' He had flatly refused. *'Chances are, we would be shot down by Praboyo's air defence forces or even Winarko's.'* Mary Jo had attempted to sweeten her earlier offer, flashing her roll of dollars.

'Take us to Sukabumi, then,' Mary Jo had pressed. The pilot shook his head at the foreign woman's obvious stupidity.

'No, I'm not interested,' he answered her directly, in English. 'Have you any idea what would happen if we were hit by one of the many Rapier ground-to-air missiles ringing those cities?' the former AURI pilot asked.

'We need to get to Sukabumi,' she insisted. Mary Jo understood that ground fighting would preclude her flying back to Jakarta first, then crossing into the mountains. Her only way in was by air.

'I could fly you to Samudera Beach. You could then travel by road to Sukabumi,' he suggested. The pilot moved to the wall-map and pointed. 'We could fly due south from here, then follow the coast to Samudera Beach. There is a limited landing strip there.' He looked directly at Mary Jo, his face serious. 'But I can't wait for you, is that clear?' She did not hesitate. Mary Jo knew that she would be the only foreign journalist there - at the end.

'That's okay,' she said, smiling at her assistant, as Anne's face crumpled into a frown.

'Are you sure you want to do this?' Anne asked, in full agreement with the pilot. What Mary Jo proposed was extremely dangerous.

'I'll understand if you don't come this time, Anne,' she said, placing her hand on the other's shoulder. She could see that her assistant was tempted to decline but knew what her decision would be.

'You would not be able to get from Samudera Beach to Sukabumi without me,' Anne declared, knowing this to be fact. Besides, your *Bahasa* still needs some work.' After two years in the country, Mary Jo could converse reasonably well in the Indonesian language but still needed her assistant's presence during formal interviews and when traveling through the provinces. *Bahasa Indonesia* might very well be the national language but Mary Jo had found many pockets throughout the country where only local dialects were spoken, making her journeys even more difficult.

'Okay, then it's settled,' she said, smiling at her unhappy assistant, then left the Cessna pilot to make the necessary arrangements for their flight.

Chapter Twenty

President Winarko

The Acting President's thoughts went to the recent bombing in Thailand, still not convinced that this had been the handiwork of Indonesian Moslem extremists, as the Americans had claimed. Security had been beefed up around the U.S. and British Embassies in Jakarta but Winarko had ordered this more as a gesture of compliance than out of any real concern that the *Mufti Muharam* had been responsible for the attack. The usual number of fanatics had claimed responsibility for the bombing but Abdul Muis' following had not been amongst these.

The President's forces had reached an impasse with General Praboyo's well-fortified positions in the mountains. The solution to this problem, Winarko believed, lay with Abdul Muis whose grip over East and Central Java in itself posed a formidable threat. If he could come to some arrangement with the *Mufti Muharam,* troops presently engaged in blocking his advance along the northern corridor towards Jakarta could be redeployed, giving him superior numbers over Praboyo's.

Having spent some days contemplating this conundrum, President Winarko arrived at his decision to establish a dialogue with Haji Abdul Muis in Surabaya, in a bid for more time.

* * * *

Haji Abdul Muis

'Tell the driver I will leave for the country, immediately after prayers,' Muis instructed his aide.

'Will I accompany you?' his trusted lieutenant asked, but Muis shook his head.

'No, you should remain here. There is much to prepare before our guest returns to his own country.'

'You will accompany bin Ladam tomorrow?' his aide wished to know.

'Of course. We will return together.'

'I will make the necessary arrangements,' the loyal officer promised. Satisfied that all was in order, Abdul Muis went to his private chambers to bathe in preparation for Lohor prayers, while his aide warned the driver and immediate staff of their master's intentions. Muis had returned from Jogyakarta that morning, his hectic schedule interrupted by bin Ladam's summons. Muis had cut his visit short, driving back to accommodate the Arab who had elected to remain on at the training camp after the successful bombing of the U.S. embassy, as he was well aware that the Americans would be scouring the earth to locate the terrorist leader.

An hour later, at precisely two o'clock, Abdul Muis' Mercedes glided slowly through the heavily-guarded mansion's gates and joined the congested thoroughfare leading away from Surabaya City, before heading inland towards his rural retreat.

Before the *Mufti Muharam* leader's car had even left the city's outskirts, knowledge of his destination and itinerary had been relayed to a local number by one of his staff, who had undertaken to report Muis' movements to his friend at the Surabaya Post. Unaware that his actions might place his beloved leader's life in jeopardy, he had agreed to keep the reporter informed, promising to notify the man when Muis returned from Jogyakarta.

In turn, the well-paid informant contacted Jakarta and passed this information to the Defense Intelligence Attache at the U.S. Embassy, who had been waiting pensively, anticipating the call which his government hoped would put an end to the Muslim terror. Details of Abdul Muis' intentions were signaled to the DIA Chief in Washington, who was on the phone within minutes, arranging for the National Security Agency to have satellites increase surveillance over the rural target.

A directive was sent immediately, and COMINT officers attached to the Imagery Requirements Subcommittee section of the NSA went into action. They knew from intelligence data that Muis's journey would require two hours and programmed their satellites to focus on the country estate to determine any increase in activity which might signal their target's presence.

* * * *

Washington

Grim faced, the American President nodded in concurrence, the enlarged black and white photograph still in his hand.

'When?' he asked, addressing the Joint Chiefs' Chairman.

'We'd been waiting for confirmation of his arrival. With your order, launch could be effected immediately,' the senior officer replied, hoping the new President would not procrastinate. His predecessor had not hesitated during similar circumstances but the Chairman recalled that the other man had needed no urging to distract the public's attention from his not so private life and affairs.

'How is it that none of our intelligence services were aware of this facility until now?' the President repeated his earlier question.

'The complex is cleverly disguised. The small mosque set in the middle had us baffled, the reason we were satisfied that the compound was no more than a religious retreat for Abdul Muis. As for the accommodation barracks, it was not unreasonable to believe that these were there to house his own security guards and staff.'

'Does he have family with him?' the President asked, genuinely concerned.

'No. Muis never married.' The Admiral wished his Chief would get on with it, they were running out of time. It had been sheer luck catching Muis crossing the courtyard but, even without such solid evidence, Admiral Brown was confident of the intelligence analyst's assessments concluding that the terrorist leader had arrived from Surabaya. The subsequent satellite pass had confirmed his presence.

'If we're sure he's there, why target the Surabaya locations?'

'We could remove his entire leadership with simultaneous strikes. That would give President Winarko the advantage he needs.'

'Have you informed him of the strikes?' the American leader asked. Admiral Brown immediately glanced at the others present and hesitated.

'No,' he answered slowly, 'he would press us to include General Praboyo in the strike.' It was obvious that the President was uncomfortable with this situation but supported the Admiral's position.

'Okay. Now can you guarantee minimal civilian casualties?' he asked.

'The Surabaya targets are not in high density areas. The *Mufti Muharam* headquarters are located in a stand-alone building, surrounded by open areas. As for Muis' private residence, our intelligence suggests that the adjacent dwellings are all occupied by his counselors and other senior advisers.' The President sensed that the Chairman had avoided the question, both men recognizing that there would be some civilian deaths, acceptable under the circumstances.

'How do we know he won't leave his country hideaway before the strike?

'Muis' profile indicates that he would be most unlikely to miss the late-afternoon prayers. If it was his intention to return to Surabaya, he would have already done so. No, we're certain he will be there at least until the sunset prayers are over. That gives us ninety minutes. After that, we could lose him again. We don't have much time left, Mister President,' the Admiral urged.

The President searched the faces of those gathered in the Oval Office to see if they were all in accord. Their expressions said it all - America needed to extract revenge for the Bangkok embassy bombing which had taken so many American lives. Armed with evidence of *Mufti Muharam's* complicity extracted from the captured terrorist during the failed Kuala Lumpur attempt, as Commander-in-Chief he had no choice.

'Okay, let's do it,' he said, nodding to Admiral Brown who immediately left the room. The American President looked down at the satellite picture, the enhanced image of the turban and white flowing robes clearly that of Haji Abdul Muis crossing from his retreat, to the compound's mosque for the Lohor prayers.

* * * *

U.S. Seventh Fleet

The U.S. fleet officer had anticipated the call, alerted to the potential strike when targeting and routing information had been downloaded into the missile system - while the battle group had been put on standby hours before.

'Weapons release has been authorized by the Chairman of the Joint Chiefs of Staff and the President, John,' the familiar voice advised, setting into train the well-rehearsed routines required to ensure a successful launch. Minutes passed and the signal to launch the first cruise missiles was given by the cruiser's solemn-faced captain.

The Ticonderoga-class cruiser's crews remained silent, those who had never witnessed the spectacular event mesmerized as the first Tomahawk leapt from its vertical launcher, then climbed quickly into the sky, wings and air-scoops unfolding as the missiles own propulsion unit took over its guidance system leveling the deadly weapon at two hundred feet as it streaked towards its destination at nine hundred kilometers per hour. A second launch was initiated, then a third, the process continuing until no fewer than twenty missiles had been launched by surface ships within the battle group.

Their targets, twelve hundred kilometers south-south west, would be destroyed in just over an hour - the Tomahawks' two hundred kilo, titanium-encased warhead certain to achieve the desired results.

* * * *

Haji Abdul Muis

Earlier, the driver had slowed as they approached the damaged, single-span, reinforced concrete bridge, then pulled to the side of the road. A recalcitrant truck driver had jumped the line and others had followed, forming a second queue, parallel to the first, blocking the shaky bridge. Traffic in both directions had come to a standstill.

'Go and see what's happening,' Muis had ordered. The driver left the engine and air-conditioning running and obeyed, walking down the middle of the narrow bitumen road, where an angry mob had already gathered. Drivers and passengers had, by now, spilled from their overheated vehicles, joining in the developing altercation, shouting abuse and waving angry fists. Blows were exchanged, the crowd roaring their disapproval as the driver responsible for their predicament climbed back inside the truck's cabin and refused to budge.

Muis's driver assessed the situation quickly. It would take at least half an hour to clear. He withdrew his pistol and fired into the air once, sending the crowd scattering in all directions. Then he shouted at the line of drivers to listen to his instructions. He marched to the end of the double line of vehicles, waving his gun threateningly, forcing those arriving off the road. Then, one by one, he ordered the second line of traffic to reverse, some slipping off the road into deep ditches in panic, terrified that the fierce-looking, armed soldier might shoot.

Finally, the road on their side had been cleared, and the oncoming traffic slowly edged forward. By now, a similar situation had developed on the other side of the bridge with two rows of traffic bunched together, feeding onto the narrow bridge and creating yet another bottleneck. Then, amidst the angry shouting to hurry, a driver panicked, losing control, his truck plunging the articulated trailer behind, partly over the side. The vehicle hung precariously, the petrified driver unable to extricate the heavily-laden trailer from its predicament.

Aware of the accident, Muis' driver peered across the river, along the double line of oncoming traffic, then reported back to his master who checked his watch, annoyed that his journey had taken so long.

'Ring ahead,' Abdul Muis ordered, 'tell them to send another vehicle to meet us on the other side,' and he did so, security at the country facilities immediately dispatching a jeep to meet the Haji. More than an hour later, having walked across the bridge and through a kilometer of stagnated traffic blocking all movement on the other side, Abdul Muis climbed into the jeep, and was carried away, urging the driver to go faster as he wished to arrive in time to prepare for the *Magrib* prayers.

* * * *

Less than one hundred kilometers to the north, the first Tomahawks crossed the Java coast, cruising towards their targets. Each of the missiles had been fed with target and terrain information, taking position information from global positioning satellites for course direction and altitude. The first five missiles were directed to the rural setting, the remainder towards Muis' Surabaya home and the *Mufti Muharam* headquarters.

On-board terrain-following radar kept the Tomahawks from running into Java's mountainous terrain, using internal maps to determine precise location, distance to target, coordinates and any other relevant information. It could not have been easier if someone had put a red cross smack in the middle of Abdul Muis's forehead.

* * * *

Without warning, the first wave of missiles impacted six minutes later, Haji Abdul Muis' retreat disintegrating as all three Tomahawks struck the retreat, killing all who were there. Osama bin Ladam died as he had lived - violently - his body buried under tons of concrete rubble when the main building imploded under the explosive impact.

In Surabaya, the air ruptured as more than a dozen of the remaining Tomahawks found their targets, destroying the *Mufti Muharam* Headquarters and Abdul Muis' magnificent mansion. Many of the surrounding buildings were also destroyed, their occupants victims of the incredible blasts. In all, more than four hundred died in the Surabaya attacks. Of these, thirty had been children attending religious classes, held in an adjacent home.

Oblivious to the calamity, Muis continued on his way, surprised when his mobile phone activated, even more surprised when he heard the self-appointed President, General Winarko, on the other end of the line. They talked, Muis ecstatic that his enemy had requested a truce. Muis agreed to consider Winarko's proposal, promising to speak again before the day was out.

But this was not to be. A short time later, as he approached his place of birth Muis' jubilation froze on a stony face when, in the distance, he observed palls of billowing smoke climbing high into the fading sky, from where his personal mosque once stood, as guardian, overlooking his rural headquarters.

* * * *

WASHINGTON

The Oval Office

'Fellow Americans. I have decided to take this opportunity to address the American people to advise you of developments which are related to the security of our nation.' The President spoke, searching for the greatest effect, the timbre in his voice pitched as he had rehearsed so many times in the past, his face somber as he delivered his message.

'None of us will ever forget the horror of the cowardly attack on the United States Embassy in Thailand and the deaths of our fellow citizens at the hands of Moslem extremists.' He paused, waiting for the monitor to display his next lines.

'Based on reliable U.S. intelligence sources, I am now at liberty to disclose that our intelligence services have concrete evidence that the *Mufti Muharam* Moslem leadership was responsible for the suicide-bombing in Bangkok.

Today, my fellow Americans, on my orders, the United States Seventh Fleet launched a preemptive strike at sixteen thirty hours against the *Mufti Muharam* terrorists. I am pleased to inform you now, that the mission was successful. The targets being terrorist training camps and other facilities used for the preparation of explosive materials, such as those used in attacks against the American Embassy. I am informed that the *Mufti Muharam* leader, Haji Abdul Muis, was amongst those killed.

It is imperative that those nations which continue to harbor terrorists take note, that the American people will continue to take any measures deemed necessary to prevent the further spread of terrorism. Today, we have sent an unequivocal reminder of our determination to protect the property and lives, of all American people.

Thank you all and God bless you.'

Not until the following morning did the United States President learn of Abdul Muis' miraculous escape from death and, by this time, the entire Islamic world was in an uproar.

Chapter Twenty-One

An Islamic State

Waves of indignation spread through the world's Islamic community, with Moslem condemnation unanimous. The threat of an attack against Israel heightened tensions in the Middle East, the solidarity between formerly conflicting Islamic groups alarming, as shuttle-diplomacy was put to its greatest test in decades. The United States President refused to discount the possibility of further attacks against the Moslem terrorist leader, restraint finally imposed only when faced with the threat of a Chinese intervention in the region.

After the missile attacks, the Arab League protested strongly, passing a twenty-two member resolution urging the United States to avoid future action which would ensure public outrage in the Arab world. The Council condemned the American attack and the violation of Indonesia's sovereign territory. Libya's ambassador to the League, Mohammed bin Karim urged in his statement that the United States, as a permanent member of the United Nations Security Council and as a superpower, to respect the sovereign territorial rights of others and refrain from these aggressive actions. Arab nations all asked the Security Council to discuss the matter, requesting an investigation into the Surabaya strike which, they claimed, killed more than five hundred civilians.

Haji Abdul Muis' personal outrage was no less than that of his enormous following. He sensed that with bin Ladam's death, his hopes for the transfer of nuclear missile technology might now remain a dream and, in consequence, vented his wrath on all things American. The United States Embassy in Jakarta was attacked with petrol bombs, Marine Guards successfully holding their ground until President Winarko sent troops to disperse the angry demonstrators.

Throughout the Moslem camps, Abdul Muis' name became legend, his having survived the massive attack. His secret remained intact. Those who had known of Osama bin Ladam's frequent visits to Indonesia, had all died. Now, his followers believed he was invincible, achieving hero status even amongst those who had not previously supported the *Mufti Muharam.* Within days, President Winarko's tenure was threatened as many of his own forces transferred their loyalty to the man who many now considered their prophet, and their vessel of hope. Aided by this sudden surge in popularity amongst his enemies' ranks, Muis ordered his troops in a full frontal attack on his former ally, General Praboyo - his strategy to destroy the mountain stronghold, then sweep down across the plains to the capital, Jakarta.

Muis knew he was almost there. Once his forces were knocking at Praboyo's door in Bandung, and he went on to capture the provincial city, General Winarko's resistance would collapse. Muis was convinced that the President had requested the American strike which, ironically, had killed Osama bin Ladam by mistake. Muis would never come to understand that he owed his life to bin Ladam, incorrectly identified in the satellite photograph as Haji Abdul Muis.

That week, his head wrapped in the now-familiar white turban, his body draped in flowing robes Muis finally appeared on the cover of *Time Magazine*, the feature story titled, 'The Terror of Jihad' referring to the *Mufti Muharam* leader's recent declaration of Holy War against his opponents and the West.

* * * *

General Praboyo

The sounds of artillery-fire were coming closer. He knew he was running out of time. Abdul Muis' advancing forces had obliged the general to concentrate his forces on this front, weakening his position in the face of General Winarko's columns.

'Bangsat!' Praboyo swore, having read the message. His adjutant stood nervously waiting for further instructions, wishing at that very moment that he had not been so cavalier in following the General. *'Bastards!'* Praboyo cursed again, before turning to glare at the junior officer.

'What shall I tell them?' the adjutant asked, mindful of the accusatory look. Everyone, it seemed, was to be blamed for the General's tactical mistakes. The Catalyst of Confusion, Praboyo's irreverent nickname, was now on everyone's lips. His support had crumbled. The disgraced general no longer enjoyed their respect.

'Tell them to fight!' was the commander's unreasonable response.

'We're not going to withdraw?' the other man asked, shocked.

'Withdraw? If we abandon Bandung, we'll never recover the city once they seize it. We can't withdraw!' General Praboyo slammed his fist down emphatically, as two other officers entered. He glanced up, immediately fearing the worst as both men's grim faces reflected their tidings.

'What now?' he snapped, rising from behind his command desk.

'We can't hold them any longer,' the brigadier complained, *'they've broken through with the AMX's.'* Praboyo frowned at the mention of tanks. His cavalry battalions were equipped mainly with Saracens and Saladins, the obsolescent light-armored vehicles no match for the superior number of French tanks Winarko had managed to muster. The month before, Praboyo's tanks numbered more than seventy. He had fortified Bandung, controlling access to the city with Scorpions and PT-76s, and had placed the small number of French AMXs at his disposal, half-way down the mountain access roads. There, supported by two battalions of artillery, their Howitzers had managed to repulse both Abdul Muis and Winarko's attacks on the mountainous positions.

Control over the area from Bogor up to the mountains had changed hands more than a dozen times since the conflict had started. His inferior numbers had still managed to control the highways leading away from the capital, the tide changing when the Indonesian air force finally swung behind Winarko. His armored forces had been no match for AURI's F-16s and SU-30MKs, which had easily accounted for most of the rebel force's tanks. Although the air force generals had let him down by casting their lot with Winarko, Praboyo had still managed to secure the support of some of the younger AURI officers. When the confrontation first commenced, his air-support boasted seventeen of the aging A-4Es and eight OV-10Fs but more than half of the pilots had shifted loyalties, joining with Abdul Muis' forces, now advancing swiftly from the east. With the exception of two Puma helicopters, the rest had been destroyed on the ground.

When it had become obvious that Praboyo could not withstand a two-pronged attack many had deserted, preferring to throw their weight behind the *Mufti Muharam,* knowing that Winarko would be unlikely to show any mercy to those who had supported General Praboyo. Abdul Muis, however, had welcomed them with open arms. Now, he too was knocking on Praboyo's doors and, to the experienced officer, represented a far greater threat.

'And the Airborne?' he asked, expecting the worst. Before being removed as commander of the Kostrad Strategic Forces, he could count on the six

airborne infantry battalions based in Java. Although many had deserted Winarko to follow him, Praboyo had not expected that two of the three remaining battalions would be flown in from Sulawesi and used in this assault. His remaining forces were now greatly outnumbered.

'Dropping out of the sky as we speak.'

'Anything left of air-defence? Praboyo asked hopefully, but the brigadier had anticipated this question and was already shaking his head. Vintage eastern bloc anti-aircraft guns were no match for the OV-10s. He knew then, he had lost.

'We should retreat, Boyo,' his senior officer advised, the sense of doom descending quickly on those present.

'No!' Praboyo responded, stubbornly. *'If we vacate Bandung, then we've lost.'*

'Retreat to Sukabumi, Boyo,' the brigadier recommended, *'then negotiate with Abdul Muis from there.'*

'Muis!' Praboyo snorted, *'how could I possibly trust him now?'* The other officers did not respond. They knew it was most unlikely that the Moslem leader would want any part of Praboyo now General Winarko had the advantage. It was becoming increasingly apparent that the *Mufti Muharam* would control at least two-thirds, if not all, of Java by the time hostilities had ended. Praboyo shook his head in quiet despair. He had lost. If he was captured, there would be no forgiveness, of that he was certain. Neither Abdul Muis nor Winarko would be likely to show any compassion for their enemy. He would be paraded before the people in disgrace.

'Get Tuti and the children out first,' he demanded, and the room was immediately filled with an audible sigh of relief.

'We'll have them taken to Sukabumi by helicopter immediately,' the adjutant promised.

'Contact Winarko. Ask him to instruct his men not to fire on the aircraft. Tell him who's on board.' The adjutant nodded, moving quickly outside to make the necessary arrangements. *'Now let's see what we can salvage before Winarko blocks our retreat.'* Praboyo discussed their position with the brigadier and, satisfied that little else could be achieved by remaining there, he vacated the building leaving the other officer responsible for the withdrawal. Praboyo raced outside and jumped into a waiting staff car, ordering the driver to hurry.

As the vehicle sped through the streets congested with burnt-out armored-personnel carriers, trucks and battle-weary troops, he considered his options and decided that he had no other choice but to flee the country, taking Tuti and the children with him. Praboyo knew that it would be inconceivable that they could safely escape by air. All flights were monitored and any attempt to leave in this manner would, undoubtedly, result in their aircraft being destroyed. He knew that Winarko would grant Tuti and the children safe passage to Sukabumi but would never agree to any of the Suhaptos leaving the country, at least not while their tremendous wealth remained intact in Swiss and Singapore vaults.

Praboyo had not devised an escape plan. Until then, he had never considered the possibility that he might not win. His mind raced as the vehicle sped to its destination, coming to an abrupt halt in a cloud of swirling dust outside the grand old air force guest-house which housed his mistress.

* * * *

Half-packed suitcases and boxes were rushed outside to waiting vehicles as Tuti Suhapto conducted one final check. Jewelry, personal papers, a small collection of memorabilia, and a case filled with American dollars.

'Leave that!' she screamed at one of her children, her hand moving quickly through the air towards its target. The child cried out loudly, shocked that his mother had struck him. Tuti feared for her children, aware of what the *Mufti Muharam* vigilantes would do to them all should they be captured. This threat made her even more assertive, willing herself not to panic, her fear chilling the very marrow of her bones.

'Don't just stand there, pick him up!' she yelled at the two nurses responsible for the younger child. They grabbed the boy and hurried outside as instructed. Tuti turned, her eyes moving quickly, wondering what she had forgotten in their haste to leave. Unable to land in the densely-wooded area, their helicopter was positioned less than a kilometer from their home.

'Where's the General?' she demanded, glaring at her husband's adjutant.

'He's still at command headquarters, madam,' the colonel replied.

'Then take us there first,' Tuti ordered, deeply hurt that Praboyo had sent his aide, and not come in person.

'My instructions are to place you and the children safely aboard, and see that you are evacuated immediately, madam,' the officer argued, uncomfortable with his role. He disliked the General's wife immensely, particularly her cutting tongue.

'I'm not asking you, colonel, just do it!' she yelled, her voice edging towards hysteria. The adjutant knew he had little choice. There had been other confrontations in the past, the result always the same. Strong-willed, stubborn, and convinced that she had been born privileged, Tuti Suhapto

almost always had her own way. He acquiesced.

'Then we should leave immediately,' he pleaded, ushering the woman outside to where the others had already boarded the waiting vehicle. The colonel then gave their driver instructions to return to command headquarters. There they were greeted by a surprised group of soldiers who were in the process of evacuating the premises.

'Where is the General?' Tuti demanded, her face covered with anger.

'He left more than ten minutes ago, Ibu,' an NCO answered with deference.

'Where did he go?' she asked impatiently but none of the soldiers knew. Panic rising, Tuti knew that their lives were in danger. She could hear the fighting getting closer but was determined to find Praboyo and insist that he accompany them. Then suddenly, as the thought struck her, Tuti's face clouded and she leaned forward and screamed instructions at the driver.

'No! You can't!' the colonel argued hotly, *'we must leave before it's too late!'*

'Take me to the guest-house, now!' she yelled, frightening the driver. He gunned the engine and swung the vehicle around.

'This is foolish,' the adjutant appealed, *'Winarko's forces have already entered the city.'*

'Shut up, Colonel,' she snapped, anger welling up inside as they sped towards the guest-house. The driver pushed the vehicle to its limit, braking hard to negotiate a corner section covered with pot-holes. His passengers bounced around, one nurse shouting in pain as her head cracked hard against the overhead supports. They climbed a hill dotted with colonial-style homes, partly-hidden amongst stands of tall, elegant pines. As they crossed the summit, the driver turned into a driveway, waving as he drove past two white-helmeted military police guards stationed there.

There were two vehicles parked in front of the splendid structure. The first, a metallic-blue Mercedes sedan, and the other a military jeep. Tuti glanced at the stars affixed to the vehicle's registration plates. There were no other generals of Praboyo's rank in Bandung. She leapt out, tripping as she did so. She fell heavily, the pain shooting through her right arm as her elbow struck something hard. Before Tuti could climb to her feet, the driver had run to her aid and lifted her clumsily, holding her firmly as she struggled for balance. She looked down in dismay, the front of her dress covered with ugly smears from the fall. Tuti rolled her arm slightly, revealing a badly-skinned elbow.

Confused, for a moment Tuti teetered between tears of anger and humiliation before something inside snapped. The years of tolerating

Praboyo's indiscreet relationships, his blatant disregard for his family and his obvious contempt for the danger in which he had placed his wife and children exploded through her mind. Her eyes dropped to the driver's belt. Without warning, she grabbed for the open-holstered revolver and lunged forward, knocking the unsuspecting man off-balance. As he fell, Tuti retained her grip on the weapon, holding it close to her side as she limped determinedly towards the building. Before the colonel realized what had happened, Tuti had already entered the foyer and, ignoring the stabbing pain inflicted by the fall, she scrambled up the carpeted-stairway which led upstairs to the bedrooms.

'Tuti! Don't!' the colonel cried, formalities forgotten. He ran to the steps and called again. *'Don't do this, Tuti!'* She turned, her face smothered with anger, waving the gun threateningly.

'Get back!' she hissed, her finger wrapped dangerously around the gun's trigger. The colonel hesitated, then moved forward a step, encouraging her to hand the weapon to his extended hand. She fired to his left. The bullet screamed past his head, burying itself into the plaster before exiting, then crossing the foyer where it struck a marble column. The colonel paled, remaining deathly-still.

Tuti turned, then continued up the stairs until reaching the hallway which ran in both directions to a number of bedrooms and suites. She looked in both directions, as if uncertain as what to do next. Down the corridor to her right, Tuti could see where mud had been carried along the carpet. She looked down at her soiled dress and without hesitating further, marched down the hall, throwing the doors open as she went, then peering inside. Tuti stopped outside the second-last doorway and, gripping the handle firmly, she threw the door open wide and stormed inside.

Praboyo had heard the isolated shot when the weapon discharged. He thrust his lover to one side and leapt for his own weapon, lying hidden beneath an untidy mound of hurriedly-discarded, military clothing. He threw the clothes to one side, found his sidearm, and placed the automatic on the bed.

When the door was thrown open, revealing Praboyo standing, half-naked, attempting to climb into his trousers, Tuti stepped inside the room, facing the startled, Menadonese mistress. The girl's almond-shaped eyes opened wide in shock, her hands darting to cover soft, fair-skinned, youthful breasts.

Tuti stepped closer, stunned by the young girl's beauty, slowly lowering the gun's barrel as she approached. Tuti tilted her head inquiringly, the familiar fragrance of the girl's perfume triggering the response she had unconsciously tried to avoid. The barrel snapped up and Tuti waved the weapon menacingly, her hands shaking with rage.

'Tuti! Wait! I can explain!' Praboyo called, still struggling with only one leg in his trousers. She turned, the gun following so that it pointed directly at his chest, his nakedness blurring her vision.

'You bastard!' she cried, her heart breaking, faced with the reality of her husband's callous indiscretion. The room began to swim before her eyes, darkness threatening to swallow her whole.

'Tuti! Put the gun down! I still love you, Tuti!' Praboyo pleaded, still struggling to get dressed. She gripped the closest bedpost, steadying herself, the gun's barrel again falling away gently. Tuti felt the giddiness taking control. She glanced back towards her husband's mistress, now crouched on the bed with her arms wrapped around her bare, slender legs. As her eyes passed over the girl's beautiful body, they came to rest on a gold ankle-bracelet set with tiny, tear-shaped stones. As she stared at the fine piece of jewelry which had once been hers, slithers of light danced across the room's walls and ceiling, taunting Tuti even further. She turned her attention back to Praboyo. Her eyes filled with tears, her voice became but a whisper as she sadly shook her head.

'I loved you too, 'Boyo,' she said, softly, then squeezed the trigger.

Those downstairs heard the first shot and were still contemplating what to do when they heard the ominous report of a second bullet echo through the building. The colonel barked an order at the two military police guards who had rushed into the mansion with weapons drawn, ordering them to return to watch the children. Then, fearing the worst, he climbed the stairs slowly, his heart heavy with what surely waited for him inside the stately room.

* * * *

EAST JAVA REFUGEE FLEET

Lily

She coughed, grimacing as she rolled slowly onto her badly-bruised side. The uncomfortably-hard, timber deck had become unbearably hot under the midday-sun's scorching rays, her thirst reminding Lily that it was her turn to go ashore and fetch the water-filled plastic containers for those on her boat. She rose wearily, another coughing attack forcing her back to her knees as she struggled to breathe. Lily held her ribs as each racking cough sent piercing pain through her side, an injury she sustained during the fateful expedition into seas off Bali.

Only days had passed since they had attempted to sail around the northern reaches of the island. The moonless night had not afforded Lily the opportunity to observe anything but the occasional flicker of coastal lights, as they sailed past Singaraja, Tejakula and Kubu, before turning south into the Lombok Strait. It had been there that misfortune had struck. Ahead, the lead ships had fought to remain together as the notorious channel's swift currents challenged the diesel-driven fishing-boats. The seven knot current had forced the three flotillas closer to shore, where Lily's group became separated, contaminated fuel in the lead ship's lines causing their delay. By the time repairs had been completed the distance between the ships had grown considerably. She stood for awhile and could see the faint lights of Amlapura Harbor on the eastern coast blinking, as the swell played with the timber below her feet. Exhausted, she lay down on the deck, the monotonous diesel-engine hum gently coaxing her to sleep.

When the dark, evening sky had suddenly exploded into light, only moments passed before the refugees realized they were under attack. Panic swept through the unarmed fishing-fleets as the raiders continued their onslaught, firing wildly into the crowded vessels before torching the wooden ships. Molotov cocktails crashed against decks, spilling their deadly contents amongst the terrified refugees. Flames spread quickly, fanned by the late night breeze.

They could offer no resistance, their screams ignored as the Balinese raiders' small power-boats raced around the floating city, dousing decks with fuel and shooting indiscriminately. Many of the refugees threw themselves into the sea only to be crushed between the ships' hulls as these crashed together. Unable to swim, others cringed below decks, praying that their attackers would leave, finally succumbing to smoke and fumes as they lay down and perished.

Paralyzed with fear, Lily stood watching the fleet ahead burn, her eyes gauging the distance to see if she could swim to shore. It was then that the captain leading her group had wisely turned his vessel and taken advantage of the powerful currents. The others quickly followed his lead, distancing themselves from the savage scene which had already taken thousands of lives. Lily continued to peer back at the blazing ships, grateful that fate had placed her at the rear of the line.

Her heart filled with fear when she observed one of the powerful boats turn and take chase. She watched, transfixed at the oncoming sight as gunfire ripped through the night. Someone screamed and Lily threw herself to the deck, her heart thumping as the high-pitched whine of her attackers' twin outboard engines approached. Lily heard automatic fire as one of the men sprayed bullets arbitrarily in her direction the dull thudding noise of impact precariously close, as a companion fell dead alongside.

Lily's boat rocked from side to side, the sluggish diesel-engine threatening to die when one of the two crewmen collapsed under a hail of bullets. Spontaneously, she raised her head as something crashed against the wheel-house, then burst into flames. Lily knew that she would die unless she could get to one of the other vessels. As flames took hold, her fellow passengers' screams filled the air, panic gripping them all when those on the ship ahead severed the thick rope tying the boats together. Suddenly they were alone, their vessel on fire, the current taking them farther away from the others as the engine idled along ineffectively. She could see the distance growing between her vessel and the others, transfixed by the scene as another ship exploded into flames. Then, incredibly, the Balinese turned away, apparently satisfied with the results of their mission.

'Help me!' Lily heard someone scream and spotted the remaining crewman leaning over the side, buckets in his hands. She did not hesitate, going directly to his assistance.

'Start from up there!' he ordered, and she obeyed, throwing the sea-water hard against the wheel-house. The flames leaped back, threateningly.

'It's not making any difference!' she cried, rushing to fill the empty container.

'It's our only chance!' he yelled again, cursing the others for blocking his access. 'Get out of the way!' he screamed, kicking at two women huddled together in fear. More than half of the original complement had jumped overboard, five more lay dead, the rest too terrified to move.

'See if you can find some more buckets,' Lily ordered, dragging one of the women to her feet. *'You'll find them down there somewhere,'* she said, pointing to the open forward hatch. The woman scrambled down the hole, reappearing moments later with two more buckets. A young Chinese boy jumped to his feet and grabbed the two buckets, joining in the effort to save their small ship. They worked together, filling the containers from over the side, slipping and sliding along the rolling deck, throwing whatever was not spilt over the burning timbers.

Once the fire had been extinguished, they examined the damaged wheel-house, dragging the dead crewman's body away from the simple controls. The engine continued to chug along unaided but they knew from the sluggish noises emanating from below, that they needed more speed. The older man took charge, increasing the engine's revolutions and changing to a course which would enable them to rejoin other ships which had survived the attack. Later, they were to discover that these numbered fewer than one hundred. The final tally would show that more than twenty-thousand refugees had perished, many burned alive in their ships, while others were swept further out to sea when they attempted to swim to safety.

The remaining ships regrouped near Banjuwangi but fears of an aerial attack drove the ships down the Bali Strait, and around the Kucur Peninsula to Grajagan Bay and the safety of the sparsely-inhabited, south Java coastline. There, they remained, the fleet's captain reluctant to attempt the crossing in such small numbers. Radio communication had provided them with information suggesting that there was a major build-up of fishing-boats developing in both Cilacap and Pelabuhan Ratu, to the west. The captain had argued that the Australian authorities could deal with a fleet of their size but would be unable to prevent a group of six or seven hundred vessels arriving simultaneously. He suggested that they follow their original plan, which required that the huge number of vessels break into much smaller groups once within sight of the Australian coast. The captain had explained the dangers. A small fleet could easily be turned back by warships and coastal patrols. For most, this would be their only opportunity to flee their strife-torn country forever.

They had heard that the Australians treated refugees well. Lily's group was encouraged by the stories they heard about places such as Darwin, Port Hedland, and Dampier. She knew that none of those who had participated inearlier refugee migrations had been forced to return and that the success of their attempt depended heavily on landing on Australian soil. Once there, they could remain. As Lily listened to the unfamiliar destinations described by the experienced captain, she and the others had great difficulty believing that some of these Australian coastal towns such as Exmouth and Onslow, had even fewer inhabitants than the number gathered aboard their floating village.

Guided by their experienced captain, the refugees reluctantly agreed and settled down to wait for their next opportunity.

* * * *

SUKABUMI - WEST JAVA

Hani

She knew for certain that the distant rumbling was not thunder. The streets outside were filled with panicked citizens preparing to leave before the onslaught of Abdul Muis' murderous bands of thugs, news of their imminent arrival sending fear through their hearts.

'We must go, Hani, today,' Budi insisted, but she was unwilling to leave without word concerning her brother. Numbed by the news that her father had been killed when Bandung had been overrun, Hani had only Budi to turn to in her hour of need. She feared reprisals, and word that the *Mufti Muharam* forces were already marching towards Sukabumi had struck fear in her heart. Although Hani shared their faith, she believed that her father's association with the late General Praboyo virtually guaranteed that she would also be punished. Her sister had already fled Sukabumi without so much as a goodbye.

In the weeks which had followed her mother's death, Budi had become more than a friend. She had shifted her dependence to him, reciprocating Budi's feelings, grateful that he had been there during her difficult time. Then, when she had also lost her father, Budi had insisted that the young woman who had only recently become his lover flee with him.

'Are you sure your father has agreed?' she asked, for the umpteenth time.

'It's all fixed, Hani,' Budi replied, confidently, *'We will all leave together.'*

'But my brother…' she argued again, leaving the statement hanging.

'You can't wait any longer,' he said, angry that she did not seem to understand the risks in remaining. 'Besides, I must leave with my father this afternoon. It's our last chance and you know why.' His tone was not at all accusatory. They were both Moslems and neither supported Abdul Muis' *Mufti Muharam.* Hani wondered why Budi's father had delayed this long. Even his senior position as local head of the State Electricity Company had not prevented the ever-increasing attacks.

When their house had been burned to the ground just days before, Budi's father was finally convinced that none of them could ever be safe again. Abdul Muis' savages had spearheaded the attacks, obviously determined to destroy anything and everybody even remotely associated with religious beliefs other than their own.

Budi's father's sin had been to maintain power into the small orphanage run by Catholic sisters, sufficient it would seem to warrant attacks against his family and property. When the decision to flee was taken, Budi had pleaded on Hani's behalf, his father agreeing to meet the cost of all three berths aboard the ships leaving for Australia. They would depart from the Samudera Beach harbor and, as space was limited, everything they owned would be left behind. Everything, that is, except the thin, yellow, half-kilo gold bars Budi and his father would carry, strapped securely around their waists.

Hani looked around the empty house which had been her family's home.

'I'll come with you now,' she decided, sadly. *'I won't be long.'*

Budi waited while she completed packing the few items he had suggested she take for their voyage, her selection limited by the one small case each passenger was entitled to take on board. Satisfied that she could squeeze nothing more into the bulging airline bag, she changed into jeans with a matching denim jacket, laced up her white sneakers, removed her brother's baseball cap from the dresser and marched stoically out into the hall where Budi waited. Then, without another word, she followed him outside and climbed onto the back of his motorbike, tears blurring her vision as he drove them both swiftly away.

* * * *

Samudera Beach - Pelabuhan Ratu

Hamish

'Tell the pilot we won't need him until tomorrow morning,' Hamish McLoughlin shouted, now clear of the heli-pad where the drooping blades continued to rotate menacingly, even though the engines had stopped. The Indonesian nodded, bent unnecessarily and ran back to inform the pilot.

Hamish watched the interpreter, waiting for the man to return. The junior official had been seconded to him by the United Nations' office in Jakarta. Reluctantly, he had agreed to the daunting task of accompanying the three-man evaluation team, selected to inspect conditions amongst the refugees camped along that stretch of the south Java coast.

'Will you need me for the rest of the day?' he asked hopefully. Hamish McLoughlin looked at the others who both shook their heads.

'No, but don't go too far from the hotel,' he replied lightheartedly, knowing that the nervous official would not consider wandering outside alone. McLoughlin then turned to the others in his party.

'Seen enough?' he asked. They were all tired, their nerves frayed and tempers tested continuously by the frustrations they encountered.

'We should get back tomorrow,' the senior officer suggested. Hamish nodded. Although they officially traveled under the protection of the United Nations, there was no evidence of any such political umbrella here, only danger. Although joint coordinator for this survey, he bowed to his associate's greater knowledge and experience.

'Agreed,' he said, not unhappily. They had been fired upon earlier in the day, their interpreter then refusing to accompany the team any further. Hamish McLoughlin retired to his room to change out of the now filthy clothing, soiled during repeated attempts to maintain his balance amongst the slippery conditions encountered earlier.

He caught a lift to the seventh floor of the poorly-maintained hotel and immediately upon entering the room opened the French-doors overlooking the Indian Ocean. The smell of decay lingered, as listless air-conditioning struggled to combat humidity and years of neglect.

The dilapidated structure, built by the Japanese during the Sixties as a small token of their war reparation commitments, stood like some lone citadel, guarding the mythical ghosts and myths which thrived through local folklore. Hamish had smiled when their interpreter had asked the UNHCR team not to wear anything green whilst on or over the water, for Nyai Loro Kidul, the Queen of the great ocean which dominated this coast, was an unforgiving mistress.

He removed his damp shirt, then stood admiring the view from his balcony as a soft, fresh ocean breeze gently touched his suntanned-skin, the smell of salt heavy in the air.

In the distance, Hamish could see small fishing perahu making their way back to the main markets where they would sit and haggle for hours, negotiating a price for their catch. He had visited this scene earlier in the day, when the village had come alive, the evening catches off-loaded as he watched. Sharks, dolphins, swordfish, huge red sea bass, sting-rays and even turtles of incredible age and size were placed in rows for the traders to see. The overpowering stench of unused, rotting bait and unsold produce randomly discarded everywhere, with seafood scraps lodged decomposing in the cracked, and broken concrete floor, all tested his resolve. The others in his team had also paled when they entered the fish markets, their nostrils assailed by the smell of rotting flesh, sun-dried squid and waste from gutted catch.

'For chrissakes, Peter, do we have to do this?' he had asked the team leader, through gritted teeth.

'Won't take long,' was all he said, extracting a handkerchief to cover his mouth and nose. The others followed suit, stepping carefully between the rows of baskets filled with long-legged crabs, white-bait, fish heads and prawns. When they came to a trader squatting behind a basket covered with banana leaves, Hamish's curiosity got the better of him and he stopped. The fisherman looked up and grinned at the foreigners, his toothless features and gray stubble-face in no way betraying his true age.

'Does tuan wish to buy my catch?' Hamish waved for the interpreter to assist and, as he pushed his way to the front, the banana leaves were thrown back to reveal neatly carved hunks of dark red turtle meat, the dismembered body stacked carefully around the creature's severed head.

'Let's get the hell out of here,' he said, disgusted with the sight. The men had then made their way outside, leaving the congested markets behind as they strolled along the densely occupied beach, smothered with thousands upon thousands of refugees camped, waiting for their turn to board once the tide had changed. As far as the eye could see, fishing boats rested on their sides in the shallow waters, their sun-bleached timbers and gunnels painted with thick red and blue lines, and bows decorated with grotesque faces to warn the ocean's demons against trespass.

Further out to sea, in deeper water and beyond the breaking waves, the main body of the refugee fleets waited, their passengers already on board. When they had flown over the massive build-up, the team agreed that earlier estimates of five hundred vessels were totally unrealistic.

'What do you think?' Hamish had asked Peter, writing this on a pad nestled against his knee.

'Closer to a thousand, I'd say,' Peter shouted, his voice barely audible above the helicopter's screaming engine.

'How long will they wait?' he scribbled again. Peter raised his open hands and mouthed the words, 'who knows?' The pilot had then flown them along the coast in both directions where they spotted at least another two hundred boats steaming towards the main flotilla. Now, standing on the beach, Hamish understood how the earlier error in estimating the number of vessels moored together out at sea had occurred, as it was impossible to differentiate one ship from another within the floating mass, at least not from this elevation.

With each tide, another wave of smaller fishing-boats would ferry their precious cargoes from the beach to the waiting flotilla, then return to the camp where the brokers negotiated on the individual captains' behalf. Theirs was a most lucrative arrangement, for the brokers not only relieved the desperate refugees of most of their gold but also dictated who could go, and in what order. Armed soldiers, many of them army deserters from General Praboyo's forces, patrolled the beach to maintain order. They too demanded protection money for their services, extracting whatever they could from the easily intimidated refugees, including sexual favors.

With each new day thousands more arrived, streaming into the port town from across the mountains, placing incredible pressure on local infrastructure. There were no latrines. The mass of humanity had no choice but to complete their ablutions in public, and along the long stretch of shoreline not meters from where they cooked and slept.

As Hamish McLoughlin and the others commenced moving through the camp, many of those destined to leave rose to their feet, hopeful that the foreigners' presence might somehow facilitate their departure or at least offer safety from the growing threat of attack.

'*Give me money, mister,*' a snotty-nosed, ragged child begged, grabbing one of the men's trousers and holding on tightly with one hand. A filthy length of material had been slung around her neck, in which she cradled a toddler not much younger than herself. Peter, the team leader, turned and shook his head.

'Don't give them anything,' he ordered, sharply. 'You'll start a stampede if you do.' Within moments the small child was joined by others, who took up the cry.

'*Give us money, give us money,*' they chanted in unison, their mischievous faces enough to break one's heart. Several of their number moved closer, also taking hold of the man's trouser leg. He looked at the others helplessly, unable to proceed, a prisoner to the motley group of six year olds. At that moment their interpreter stepped forward and whacked one of the children hard enough to send them scampering for safety.

'How many did you say were camped here?' Hamish asked.

'Impossible to say,' his associate replied, 'but certainly enough to fill a small city.'

'Surely they don't all expect to get out of here?' he asked, understanding for the first time the enormity of the task the UNHCR teams faced. During this visit, he had spent most of three weeks accompanying representatives to remote camps situated thousands of kilometers to the east, and had returned filled with despair. Hamish's brief involved the preparation of an urgent submission for the High Commissioner in Geneva, in which he was required to provide definitive answers to financial needs in relation to the Indonesian camps. The United Nations resources had already been stretched beyond capacity and the High Commissioner intended seeking further, and more substantial funding from donor nations.

His journeys not only produced the information required, but also provided Hamish McLoughlin with a much greater insight into what was really taking place inside the barb-wire enclosures built by the Indonesian military to the east of Bali. These had been established to contain

Timorese and Irianese refugees more than a year before. He had been horrified to discover that, in many instances, Special Forces soldiers had turned these camps into their own exclusive brothels, forcing children of twelve and thirteen into becoming comfort women, some even before they had reached puberty.

In one such camp, Hamish had listened as his associates documented the distressing evidence given by sex slaves, victims of the brutal Javanese soldiers. In Dili, where many of the young victims had then become prostitutes operating in brothels near the Comoro Airport and in resorts and hotels such as Areia Branca, Mahkota and the New Resende Inn, the story had been the same. Once forced to serve as sex slaves to the Indonesian occupation forces, these children invariably found it impossible to escape their tragic fortunes.

'The real tragedy here is not so much the number of refugees,' Peter said, 'but what they represent.'

'I don't follow,' Hamish turned in time to discourage someone's hand from grabbing at his clothing.

'Look around. The majority of the people fleeing the country represents what remains of the entire Chinese community. Two years ago, they numbered something like eight or nine million. You were here towards the end of Suhapto's reign weren't you Hamish?' Peter asked, knowing this to be true. 'The really wealthy didn't hesitate, bailing out the moment sentiments changed, taking their wealth with them. What they left behind was a strata of Chinese who were not really wealthy but who suffered the brunt of the indigenous wrath. Those who didn't lose their lives certainly lost almost everything else.'

'What's your point, Peter?'

'Simply this. When you remove those responsible for ensuring the wheels of commerce keep turning, the country grinds to a halt. It would be fair to say that industry here survived only because of the Chinese presence. Without their commercial skills and money, this place will never get back onto its feet. You see Abdul Muis and his butchers are driving away the very people who could help rebuild the economy.'

'You don't think they'll come back once stability has been restored?'

'No way, not this time,' Peter retorted, sarcasm creeping into his voice. 'Who in their right mind would want to live here under a Muis-led Islamic regime?' He shook his head. 'No, I really think that the wound is too severe to heal. If I was in their shoes, I would be doing precisely this,' he said, waving his hand across the scene before them, 'and would never return here again, unless forced to.'

'But not all will escape. Surely the extremists will not see them all slaughtered just because they're Chinese?' Hamish postulated.

'I wouldn't want to find out, would you?'

'How many do you think remain?' he asked, not entirely convinced.

'We don't know. Again, my guess is that more than half of the ethnic Chinese population have already left over the past two years.'

'That still leaves some millions. How many of those would you say are in Java?' Hamish asked.

'Not that many. Probably less than half a million by now. Most have already fled to other islands, such as Bali. Many jumped ship in the year following Suhapto's resignation. Others have managed to slip into Australia, Malaysia, Singapore, even the Philippines. The refugee population still housed in camps in Australia is rapidly approaching a million. I know for a fact that the majority of these are Chinese.'

'Yes, and most will probably end up staying there as well. They won't be as much of a burden as mainstream Australia fears. These refugees have talent and the will to work. What little money they have will see them through. Besides, under Australian law they would be classified as political refugees, unlike the majority of Vietnamese who basically fled their country out of economic considerations.' Hamish recalled reading about the problems of multiculturalism which continued to haunt the Australian people, and wondered how they would cope with the massive influx of Asians.

'Let's get back to the hotel and document what we have here,' Peter suggested, cutting through the centre of the camp and heading towards the main road. They made their way to the narrow bitumen highway which led from Pelabuhan Ratu, back to their hotel, then along the coast to Cikotok where gold-fever had once driven workers hundreds of meters underground, mining the precious metal. The interpreter called their jeep on the mobile radio and they returned to Samudera Beach Hotel where Hamish now stood, observing the small fishing boats out to sea.

Something caught his eye and it was then he observed the plane approaching from the east, almost on the horizon, low over the ocean, as it flew over the refugee flotilla and camp before disappearing behind a copse of coconut trees blocking his view. He listened, half-expecting the twin-engine Cessna to reappear, concerned when the aircraft's engines faded into the distance, that the military might attempt drastic measures as they had done in the past to prevent the refugees from departing.

Chapter Twenty-two

Hani

'Here, I'll take that,' Budi's father removed Hani's airline bag from her shoulder, enabling her to climb into the small fishing boat unaided.

'Move forward!' the crewman ordered testily, pointing ahead as the last of his passengers boarded the overcrowded vessel. The tide was running out quickly and he had hoped to have made at least one more run before the sandbar blocked further access to the beach. As it was, this last group had to wade out more than fifty meters through the swirling, shallow water in order to board. Hani had slipped several times and, although the sea was not very deep, she was still terrified of being washed away.

Hani was no less superstitious because of her religious beliefs. If anything, her fears had become more exaggerated faced with the proposition of crossing this ocean, notorious for its violent storms and devastating seas. Then, of course, there was Nyai Loro Kidul to contend with. Budi had reminded her not to wear anything resembling the color green. She was surprised when he even checked the contents of her small bag, just to be sure. In a society bred on mysticism and fear, any symbolic gesture would be assumed to carry significant import. Along with thousands of others, they had prayed to their god prior to boarding, then cast flower petals as a token of their respect for the Sea Goddess into the treacherous and unpredictable ocean.

The crewman lowered the long-shank Johnson outboard engine into the water and they moved slowly forward. Hani looked at the small, incoming waves and was immediately gripped with fear. As their boat smashed through the first line of one meter breakers, Hani's fingernails dug deeply into Budi's arm, half-expecting to be spilled from the rocking boat at any moment. Their boat dipped and rose, then plunged forward into another wave, spray covering those closest to the bow, stinging their eyes with salt water. Clear of the breakers, the boat gained speed and within fifteen minutes Hani, Budi and his father were all safely aboard their designated vessel.

They went about familiarizing themselves with their temporary accommodations, Hani concerned with the number of passengers their ship carried and the condition of the wooden fishing-boat. She discovered that all the ships were devoid of any form of plumbing and was devastated when Budi explained the strange structure at the rear of the boat, the humiliation of attempting to balance on the stern platform during rough conditions, an experience she had yet to confront.

Budi could see that Hani was distressed and moved to allay her fears. He placed his arm around her waist, holding her comfortingly.

'It's going to be all right, Hani. Just wait and see,' he promised, but she was not so sure. The ship jerked in every direction under her unsteady legs, the long ocean swells passing through the fleet creating a Mexican wave effect added to her discomfort.

'When will we sail?' she asked again, still doubting her decision to leave.

'The brokers said that we should be leaving tomorrow. At latest, the day after,' Budi assured her. They had paid dearly to jump the queue ahead of others. Hani had learned during her short stay on the beach that many of those camped there had been waiting weeks for a berth.

* * * *

Their journey from Sukabumi had not been without incident. What would normally have been a two hour jaunt turned into a nightmarish expedition, ending after an entire day had been spent making their way through the congested traffic. Buses, trucks, cars, motorbikes and even farm-wagons blocked the flow in both directions, not that there were many returning from the coast. They were forced to turn back twice and, had it not been for their local knowledge of the surrounding mountain roads, Hani had little doubt that they would have failed to reach their destination. Heavily armed soldiers, many of whom having deserted their posts, blockaded the major roads and systematically stripped the refugees of their wealth.

Budi had spotted the checkpoint ahead and, with some difficulty, managed to turn their Honda around as Hani struggled for balance. Positioned uncomfortably between Budi and his father, who somehow managed to balance two of their three airline bags with the straps crisscrossed over his shoulders, Hani held on tightly as they maneuvered through the confused traffic, returning some distance to where Budi chose an alternate route. Each time they encountered roadblocks they doubled back, selecting alternative paths around the mercenaries, twice becoming lost amongst the thickly-forested mountain terrain. As night fell, traveling became increasingly difficult and, out of consideration for Hani, they rested for several hours in a small village, not fifty kilometers from the last pass which led down to the narrow coastal plain.

When they arrived in Pelabuhan Ratu, the harbor town which serviced Samudera Beach, Hani was astounded at the scene which greeted them. Teeming masses of refugees had inundated the coastal town, spilling over onto the beaches and surrounding fields, their numbers so great Hani's party were obliged to stop more than a kilometer from the port and continue on foot, pushing the motorbike before them. She could not help but stare as the incredible sight unfolded before them, the displaced people congregating hopefully together, arranging passage to leave before the *Mufti Muharam* arrived. When she realized that the main body of people were, in fact, ethnic Chinese, she was livid with rage and might not have continued had Budi not remained at her side.

They made their way slowly towards the fish markets where they knew the brokers congregated each morning, auctioning berths on those fishing-boats which had arrived overnight to join the massive fleet. There, amongst the cacophonous setting, they negotiated their passage directly with one of the brokers, Budi's plan to offer the Honda motorbike as a sweetener placing them at the front of the queue.

His father had extracted three of the small, gold bars from around his waist and these had sealed their arrangements. They had then taken their papers and waited on the beach at the place designated by their broker. He warned them to remain there until called, for there would not be a second opportunity should they wander away and miss their tender when it arrived. There, squashed amongst many others, they waited, watching the small fishing-boats arrive, then depart carrying the more fortunate ones away to the waiting fleet. As the day dragged on, the heat took its toll as some fainted, others collapsing from hunger or exhaustion, while a few amongst the elderly just gave up, surrendering themselves to oblivion, their bodies quickly carried to the rear lines and mysteriously disposed of without further ceremony.

Hani had remained with Budi's father while he went in search of food. While he was gone, Hani became concerned when she heard a loud murmur, the crowd's mood suddenly changing as the multitude rose to its feet. She stood, reaching on tiptoe to see what was happening and was surprised when a number of foreigners appeared, surrounded by hundreds of children. Hani protected her eyes from the glaring sun, squinting as the strange group approached.

Under different circumstances she might have been amused by the spectacle of three foreign men walking along the beach in the heat of the day, dressed as they were, their presence in contradiction to all around. But as they passed close enough for Hani to touch, she wondered what could possibly have brought these men to such a place and at that time. Within moments they all but disappeared from view, the sea of humanity swallowing the foreign men as they turned and made their way through the most densely occupied area, towards the main road.

Hani was still preoccupied with the foreigners, caught off guard when one of the men smiled kindly in her direction just as Budi returned with fried rice wrapped in banana leaves. They hungrily scooped the food into their mouths, washing this down with bottled tea. Then they settled down to wait for the tide to change again and their turn to board the tenders and leave. Finally, their numbers and names were called and Hani boarded with the others, her fear of the sea immeasurable.

Now, as ocean swells lifted her boat, dropping it gently then lifting it again, the mound of water passing soundlessly under the fleet in constant rhythm, Hani fought the uncomfortable, queasy sensation associated with motion sickness, wondering how she could possibly survive the final crossing.

* * * *

Mary Jo & Anne

'Oh, shit!' Mary Jo swore loudly as the Cessna yawed dangerously, the tires screaming as the aircraft hit the runway roughly and at an angle, before bouncing back into the air. Her stomach rose and she was thrown forward as the pilot dipped the plane's nose and landed the Cessna heavily on the emergency airstrip. She glanced at her assistant, Anne's silence testament of their rough arrival. The aircraft taxied along the runway towards a small group of buildings where the two women alighted, still trembling from their landing. The pilot assisted them with their gear, wished them luck, then hurriedly departed, anxious to return to the relative safety of Surabaya Field before his presence was detected by fighters. He had selected the coastal route believing that their flight would not be visible on radar this far south of Java's daunting volcanic range.

A group of children eyed them suspiciously and ran screaming inside the small buildings when Mary Jo and Anne approached. Moments later a woman appeared, pointing down the road to another group of houses when asked for directions. She snapped at her children, dragging one hurriedly inside, and slammed the door before Anne could ask her anything further. They walked several hundred meters before they were able to wave down a passing motorcyclist who, for a fee, agreed to call someone he knew with transport.

They strolled along the dusty road, Mary Jo's height and color attracting the attention of a number of village children standing together, under the shade of a mango tree just meters from a small stream. They stopped to rest, the heat of the day already too much, even for them. Mary Jo smiled at the bedraggled bunch. They had obviously been playing in the kali, probably swimming, she thought.

'*Give me money, miss?*' one of them asked. Anne turned and snapped but these village children were very persistent.

'*Give us money, nona bule,*' another shouted, using the derogatory word *bule* which, Mary Jo had already discovered, meant nothing less than 'whitey' with all of its racist connotations. Anne had explained that Indonesian people found nothing wrong in the use of such terms and expressions, believing it natural to have specific words which expressed their natural feelings towards each other. When Mary Jo suggested that Western people found the use of such terminology offensive, Anne had laughed. She pointed to many examples of Asian cultures which were most specific in their descriptions of others, such as the Chinese and Thai terms for any fair-skinned race, and tried to explain the varying cultural attitudes between how the Asians naturally accepted racial and religious differences, as opposed to peoples of Western thinking.

'You people are too thin-skinned,' Anne had wanted to say when Mary Jo had become a little irrational during their conversation. Instead, her Asian heritage insisted that she suggest to Mary Jo that she might wish to consider these things from an Asian perspective. After that, their relationship had become a little restrained, particularly as Anne believed that it was easy for her associate to take the high road during such discussions. Mary Jo had not been raised to Asian standards. It seemed that everything to her was either black or white.

'Give me the Nikon,' Mary Jo said, deciding to fill in time with some candid photographs of the village urchins in their natural habitat. Beyond the mango trees a number of elderly Sundanese villagers watched from the safety of their ijuk-palm-roofed dwellings, as their children played within reach of the foreigner. Someone cooked, the sharp, pungent smell of *belacang,* the shrimp paste drifting across the dirt courtyard to where they waited, whetting Anne's appetite, while causing her companion to pale.

Several of the older villagers ventured out to observe their strange visitor. One, her head wrapped in traditional style, wandered up to join the children, fascinated by the American woman's light-colored hair. Mary Jo watched the toothless woman approach, photographing the peasant's heavily-lined features as she smiled, and positioned herself amongst the children, her wide, callused feet broadened by years of toiling in the paddy-fields, anchors as she squatted on her haunches.

Mary Jo guessed her subject to be at least seventy years of age but this was not the case. Her lips and tongue, reddened by the addictive mixture of betel nut and tobacco, provided an almost grotesque picture when the woman smiled. A grandmother by the age of twenty-nine, Mary Jo's subject would have celebrated her fortieth birthday that year, had she known her own age. Years of toiling the fields under the fierce conditions had taken their toll. The shriveled-breasted old lady smiled, nodding her thanks when Mary Jo offered her last remaining Mars Bar, which the woman accepted as if this was some common day occurrence and slowly removed the wrapping. Mary Jo watched with interest as she carefully opened the chocolate bar, then folded the silver paper lining. Then, in typical village style, the village woman broke the chocolate into many pieces and passed these to the children, offering some back to Mary Jo and her assistant. Finally, she took the remaining crumbs and placed these in her mouth, then nodded her thanks for the gift.

By the time their transport had arrived, Mary Jo had finished the roll of film and some of the stress resulting from their flight had dissipated, leaving her in slightly better spirits.

* * * *

'We'll go and find accommodation, first,' Mary Jo suggested.

'That will be easier said, than done,' Anne replied. 'I'm not so sure we will find anything.' She was referring to the numbers sighted from the air as they flew over the port and surrounding beach areas. The multitudes below had occupied a stretch of sandy coastline covering several kilometers, their numbers spilling across the road into corn fields, trampling whatever harvest might have been underfoot.

'We'll get out of town and go down to the Samudera Beach Hotel,'

Mary Jo announced. She had never been there before but had often heard others refer to the popular destination. Anne shrugged her shoulders, uncertain that the hotel would even be operational. When their transport arrived, the women could not believe their eyes.

'Is it safe?' Mary Jo asked. She had seen some strange sights in her time but this home-made vehicle made her doubt the wisdom of risking their bodies and limbs. The village mechanics had taken a Honda diesel generator and affixed this to a simple chassis, the belt-drive system they had incorporated powering one forward wheel. Two long, extended handlebars steered the contraption, which was chained to a small, two-wheeled carriage.

'We don't have much choice,' Anne replied, placing their baggage on board. There were no seats. They sat with their legs dangling from the rear, their bottoms subjected to the hard timber flooring with each bump on the road. Once under way choking, thick, black diesel smoke added to their discomfort, Mary Jo swearing more than once as they made their way to the main intersection and stopped. There, they managed to flag down a passing mini-bus which took them the rest of the distance to the hotel, the women relieved to find that the resort was still functioning. They knew that it would be unlikely for the state operated electricity services to have survived in such a remote area.

Everywhere they had visited the story had been the same. Coastal villages managed to maintain their supplies of diesel fuel but regular petrol supplies had been depleted in isolated provinces within weeks of civil war first breaking out. As far back as 1968, when foreign investment had first returned to the country, diesel generators had been installed in all hotels throughout the country as a result of the erratic government power supply. Diesel had been heavily subsidized until the IMF fiasco of two years before but, even with the current prices, the precious fuel continued to find its way into the country, by ship. Kerosene and diesel - these were the two fuels that had kept Indonesia alive.

The hotel's staff apologized that their main restaurants and other facilities had all closed. There was no room service and they were advised that fuel supplies might not last the week. However, the staff had managed to keep the coffee-shop overlooking the pool open, where they prepared local dishes for themselves and the handful of guests currently in house. Mary Jo accepted her key, smiling when the self-appointed manager asked for American dollars. Anne negotiated transport for the duration of their stay, asking that a car be made available as quickly as possible. They then went to their rooms and deposited their baggage, agreeing to meet up again down in the lobby when the jeep they had requested arrived.

They drove to within a kilometer of the huge camp, continuing on foot as they made their way slowly through the congested scene, stopping to talk to some, photographing others. It was the children who saddened Mary Jo the most.

'Surely they can't all be orphans?' she had queried, looking down at a child whose forlorn look tugged at her heart.

'Many have been abandoned,' Anne explained, ashamed for those who had done so. 'That child over there told me that her parents have already boarded without her. She was playing with the others and became separated.' Mary Jo stared in the child's direction, anger rising with what she heard.

'Why didn't they go and look for her, or just wait?' Mary Jo asked, finding great difficulty accepting that parents were arbitrarily abandoning their children. This, she knew, was so out of character for Indonesians.

'I spoke to some of the others here Mary Jo. It seems that once they have paid for their passage, they only have one opportunity to leave. If they don't come forward when their names and designated numbers are called, then they miss their rides. Permanently.'

'Even so, Anne,' she said, without finishing what she really wished to say.

'Mary Jo,' Anne's tone was not critical, 'these people are mainly Chinese. When the *Mufti Muharam* arrive, which I'm certain will happen, those still here will most likely be slaughtered. Yes it's cruel, particularly for the children. But some might agree that it would be better for the parents to escape and start another family elsewhere, than remain and die.' Now there were tears in Anne's eyes, as more than a hundred children gathered around hopefully, hands extended as they begged for money and food.

'How much money did you bring?' Mary Jo asked, checking her own pockets.

'Don't do it, Mary Jo,' Anne pleaded, placing her hand immediately on the other's arm to prevent her from extracting anything from her pocket. 'We'd never get out of here if you do.' Mary Jo stopped, considering the wisdom in this, then sighed despondently.

'Let's get on with it then,' she said, pretending to ignore the screaming children who tugged and pulled at the women's clothes. Mary Jo continued snapping shots, while Anne assisted with reloading. They had been reduced to using the less sophisticated equipment, the Nikon F5 which had served Mary Jo faithfully over the years, still reliable in her capable hands.

As darkness fell, Mary Jo and Anne stood together atop a small spur overlooking the refugee camp, their elevation sufficient to see the distant fleet clearly. Thousands of tiny, flickering kerosene lights created the illusion of permanence and serenity. Mary Jo knew that there was little she could do here, particularly for those children abandoned as a result of the cruel decisions taken by their parents. But she sincerely believed that the world would be shocked into action once their story had been told and spread across the wire services.

'Tomorrow, we'll go out to the main fleet,' she announced, Anne casting her a look of disbelief in response.

'They won't take us,' she said, believing this to be so.

'We'll pay whatever it takes,' Mary Jo answered, determinedly. Anne became silent, considering the risks involved. Out there, anything could happen. Journalists were unpopular at the best of times, and she suddenly became concerned that her obstinate associate's life could be at risk should they proceed.

'It would be dangerous, Mary Jo,' she said.

'Then I want you to remain behind!' she ordered. Anne's initial reaction was relief. Then she realized that she was being tested again and became annoyed.

'You will need me out there to interpret,' she said, matter-of-factly.

'No, Anne,' Mary Jo insisted, 'I am serious. I want you to help me arrange a ride out there but I want you to remain behind.'

'Why?' she asked.

'Firstly, we most probably don't have enough dollars to pay for two. The charter from Surabaya took care of that. And secondly, if we are unable to communicate with Jakarta tonight, then I want you beside the phones until we get through.' Mary Jo had a share arrangement in place with one of the other agency representatives. Twice she had taken mobile satellite phones out to the provinces and on both occasions these had been confiscated by security forces. Mary Jo had been unable to replace the expensive equipment and now depended on others to assist. Her photographic coverage of events was frustrated by these communication difficulties. On occasion she sought the help of other foreigners working with Aid agencies or foreign missions but these had diminished in number with the outbreak of civil war.

International communications outside major provincial cities had broken down more than six months before and, at best, her stories were now filed from wherever she might be in the country via Jakarta, and then forwarded to her editor in the States. Mary Jo was determined that this story should be wired to New York as expediently as humanly possible. Although the chances were now slim, Mary Jo believed her report might just prevent the catastrophe looming along the beaches of Pelabuhan Ratu.

In her mind, she had already written the story of the children who had been deserted and left to certain death by their parents. She stared out through the darkness towards the floating city in the distance, her anger burning deeply as she considered the parents who had fled, leaving their children behind. Tomorrow, she would walk amongst those people, taking their photographs without knowing who amongst their number had left their loved ones behind to die.

They returned to the Samudera Beach Hotel where Mary Jo completed writing her story, checking this before calling Anne to her room and then settled down to wait for a connection to be made to Jakarta. After several hours had elapsed, she left her assistant with this task, deciding to go down to the lobby to see if she could encourage the staff to expedite her call with a handful of American dollars. Mary Jo climbed into the lift and was no sooner under way when the power failed, sealing her inside the dark, airless space between floors, where she remained for more than two hours while the engineers worked to repair their generators.

Rattled, angry and saturated with perspiration when the lift doors finally opened at the ground level, Mary Jo's mood was volatile. She stormed across the lobby to where one of the staff continued to snuff candles placed along the reception desk when the power had failed, and vented her spleen on the astonished employee. She snatched the house phone angrily, phoned upstairs to see how Anne had fared, then instructed her to come down to see if they could find something to eat before the lights died again. While she waited, Mary Jo walked outside and took stock of the scene overlooking the salt-water pool. Waves breaking on the adjacent beach reminded her that she had not bathed and Mary Jo was tempted to return to her room and change out of her sticky, soiled clothes.

As her eyes adjusted to the moonlight, she could see that someone was swimming alone, and assumed this to be one of the staff from the deserted hotel. Her eyes roamed further, the silhouetted coconut branches moving gracefully to the soft, sea-breeze catching her attention. Suddenly, she frowned then moved closer to the railing and peered through the stand of trees, convinced that the natural lighting was playing tricks with her sight. A cloud crossed, hiding the moon, and Mary Jo felt a chill standing there waiting, goose-bumps appearing as the evening breeze gently touched her skin. She crossed her arms, listening to the sounds of darkness, the waves crashing as they broke along these timeless shores. In that moment, the moon escaped its cover and she glanced back through the trees, startled by what was there. Mary Jo hurried down the steps through the pool area and towards the heli-pad. She stood with hands on hips, staring at the helicopter parked there, confused by its presence.

'Looking for a ride?' she heard someone call, and turned in time to see the swimmer climb from the pool. The voice obviously belonged to a foreigner. She frowned and tilted her head, then moved slowly towards the tall visitor as he stood, toweling himself. As she approached, Mary Jo suddenly hesitated, deciding the light was playing tricks again. She faltered, then moved forward again disbelieving her eyes.

'Hamish?' she called, her voice reflecting her shock.

'Mary Jo?' he replied, just as surprised. 'My god! What are you doing here?' For a moment they stood facing each other, lost for words. Then Hamish stepped closer and placed his cold hands on her bare shoulders, sending a shudder through her spine. She started to say something, then stopped, glancing back towards the helicopter.

'Yours?' she asked, turning back to him. Hamish nodded in the moonlight, releasing Mary Jo as he did so. He felt the cold and wrapped the towel around his shoulders.

'I'm here with some others. We're on U.N. business, Jo,' he explained.

'My god,' was all she could find to say, shaking her head slowly. 'How long have you been here?'

'We arrived earlier today and will head back to Jakarta before lunch, tomorrow.' Mary Jo could not see his worried expression in the dim light. 'What are you doing here, Jo?'

'Same old thing,' she replied, lightheartedly but Hamish detected a flatness in her voice. 'We came in today, as well.'

'I saw the aircraft earlier,' he said, 'but I had no idea that it had landed. Where's your pilot?'

'My pilot?' she repeated, her mind suddenly elsewhere. 'Well, he wasn't too pleased with the prospect of staying on.'

'You have no way out of here?' Hamish asked, astonishment in his voice.

'Something like that,' Mary Jo attempted nonchalance but disappointment was evident instead. 'Seems that the *Mufti Muharam* will be here soon.'

'Come back with us, tomorrow,' he urged.

'Great!' Mary Jo shrieked, thinking that events could not have worked out better. Then she frowned again. 'Is there room for Anne, my assistant?' she asked. 'You remember Anne don't you Hamish?'

'Sure, I remember Anne,' he answered, his tone warning Mary Jo that there was a problem. She glanced back at the helicopter. It was a Bell Jet Ranger. She looked back into Hamish's eyes, unable to see clearly in the soft light.

'Is there a problem?' she asked, sensing there was.

'That chopper carries five, including the pilot. We have three on the team, and an interpreter. That makes five. Let's talk to the pilot and see if he can carry seven.'

'If there is a problem, Hamish, perhaps you could arrange to have them return for us,' Mary Jo suggested. He considered this and nodded.

'I don't think it will come to that, Jo. Let's wait to see what he says.' She nodded, looking up to the poorly lit lobby windows where she thought she could see Anne standing. A thought suddenly crossed her mind.

'Where did your people eat?' she asked, having missed all meals that day.

'We brought some canned food. There's nothing much here and you can forget going outside,' Hamish warned. 'The rest of my group are probably asleep already,' he added, looking up at the seven storey structure to see if any of the rooms were lit.

'God, I'm starving,' she said, worried also for Anne. 'Why don't you meet us in the coffee shop. I have to go. Anne is waiting up there now,' she said, waving at the shadowy figure upstairs. Hamish agreed, promising to catch up when he had changed. They walked back up to the lobby level together, Anne's mouth falling in surprise when she saw Hamish as he flashed through the lobby on his way to the lift.

'The staff have rice, rice, and more rice, Mary Jo,' Anne told her, forcing a smile. 'You can have it fried, steamed or served like porridge.'

'There's nothing else?' she asked, dismayed.

'There's a few eggs left. And some very suspect seafood,' Anne said. Mary Jo settled for the fried rice and eggs, the offer of a lift the next day lifting her spirits in spite of the food. As they ate, Mary Jo outlined how she saw their movements for the following morning.

'I won't have too much time,' Mary Jo informed her assistant. 'Whoever takes me out to the fleet must agree to get me back in time for Hamish's departure. I think it wise that you wait for my return, Anne.'

'And if we don't get through to Jakarta tonight?'

'Then we will leave it until we return to the capital,' Mary Jo answered.

Her priorities had not changed. It seemed most unlikely that they would be able to make contact with Jakarta now, considering the complete breakdown in communications. Besides, she would be able to file her story, together with the startling imagery, directly from the capital. New York would have everything they needed to inform the world as to what was happening in this quiet corner of Java.

'Then I can come with you tomorrow?' Anne asked.

'No,' Mary Jo replied, snappishly.

'Why not ask Hamish if he would lend us the money for me to go with you?' Anne suggested. It made sense. Mary Jo thought about this for a moment and promised to do so.

'Sure. But if he can't, then we stand by the original plan. Okay?'

'Okay,' Anne agreed. She wasn't particularly keen to accompany Mary Jo but would do so if Hamish could assist.

'Have you organized transport for the morning? We won't have much time to play with,' Mary Jo cautioned.

'I've already made the arrangements,' Anne promised. Mary Jo knew that her assistant sometimes considered her naïve. There was still no guarantee that they would be able to secure passage out to the fleet. In fact, the more she thought about this, the more unlikely it appeared. But at least she would give it her best shot.

'Tell the driver we want him on deck around four,' Mary Jo insisted. 'If we can hit the beach before sunrise, we will have at least three to four hours to play with. Anne nodded, but Mary Jo sensed some reticence.

Even after two years together, she knew that her junior quietly questioned her brash, aggressive behavior, often falling into pensive, uncommunicative moods when they were traveling together through difficult and often dangerous situations.

* * * *

When Hamish returned, Mary Jo flashed a warning look at Anne which she failed to understand. Several steamed dishes arrived and the two women hungrily devoured the bland food, while Hamish McLoughlin looked on amused. When they had finished Anne awkwardly excused herself, aware that only a few hours remained before they would need to be prepared to leave again.

'Wake me early,' Mary Jo warned.

'Goodnight Hamish,' she said, tired to the bones. 'And thanks for the lift back,' she added.

'We'll do what we can, Anne,' he responded, uncomfortably. He had still to discuss this with the pilot. 'Catch you in the morning,' he said.

'Will you return to the camp?' she asked, rising to her feet. Anne hoped this to be true, unhappy with having to remain alone while Mary Jo visited the fleet.

'Just briefly,' he answered solemnly. As there was no organized refugee camp per se, their mission had been purely fact finding in nature. Their pilot had insisted that they remain overnight as night flying conditions, under current circumstances, were extremely hazardous. Hamish expected his team would depart well before lunch and return to the capital, following the same circuitous route as before to avoid flying over the trouble spots. They had carried additional fuel for this purpose and Hamish was concerned that this may be the only hitch regarding taking on extra weight.

He expected that once his associates were aware of Mary Jo's predicament, none would object to accommodating the additional passengers, providing, of course, the pilot agreed. His eyes locked with Mary Jo's, the flickering candle-light casting playful shadows across her face. She was still beautiful, he thought, and realizing that he had been staring, dropped his gaze, embarrassed.

'Do you still travel with a bottle of whiskey in your case?' she asked. Hamish's face immediately broke into a grin.

'Of course,' he laughed, identifying the hint. 'Care to sit out on the balcony upstairs and reminisce?' Mary Jo did not hesitate. She could taste the whisky already and stood, looked around for service, but the remaining staff had slipped out quietly and gone to bed as soon as the meal had been served. There had been no senior management around this hotel for months, the local staff now treating the premises as their own.

'Don't expect any ice,' he said. 'Besides, you wouldn't want to drink anything here that hadn't been boiled while you were watching.' They caught the lift up to Hamish's room, Mary Jo recounting her earlier experience when caught in the blackout.

They settled down on rusting, plastic-covered deck chairs, placing the full bottle of Chivas on the table between them. Hamish poured two neat shots of whiskey, passed one to Mary Jo, then raised his glass to hers.

'Here's to the end of this madness,' he said, swallowing most of the contents in one gulp, the warm, soothing sensation inside immediately raising his spirits. 'What have you been up to since Kuala Lumpur?' he asked, topping up his whisky.

'Aging, considerably,' she responded, holding out her own empty glass, 'and adding a few more calluses.' Hamish tipped the Chivas in her direction.

'Where to next?' Mary Jo thought about this for a moment, before replying.

'I hadn't given it much thought. Indonesia is not exactly the place right now to be making plans about one's future.' She looked out across the shimmering sea, the waves breaking on the beach below caught by moonlight as foamed crests rolled over the sand. 'Right now, I just want to get out of here and file my story. After that, I think it's time I took a long break away from Indonesia and what these people are doing to each other.' Her mind was filled with the terrified faces of children left to fend for themselves.

'Well, we'll do what we can about getting you back to Jakarta in the morning.'

'Don't be in too much of a hurry, Hamish,' Mary Jo said, looking at him. 'I plan to make a dash out to the refugees' main fleet before leaving.' She could see his frown growing. 'It is very important to me. And to the refugees,' she added.

'There's nothing you can do, Jo,' he said, critical of her intentions. 'If anything, you'll most probably only aggravate the situation. Do you have any idea how they would have reacted to your pilot's flying over their boat colony?'

'They would know we were not from the military,' she said lamely.

'No they wouldn't,' he argued. 'and my guess is, you would be unwelcome out there.'

'I'll be back before eleven,' Mary Jo stated, and he recalled how obstinate she could be. 'If that's too late, then, I guess we'll catch up in Jakarta.' Hamish remained quiet, not wishing to antagonize her. It was obvious that she was determined to go.

'Are you taking Anne?'

'No,' Mary Jo replied, surprising him further.

'Why?' Hamish asked, his concern growing.

'Firstly, I can communicate well enough without her,' she said, without boasting. 'Secondly, I doubt if those bastards ferrying refugees out to the main body of ships would take her without screwing us to death.' Hamish was surprised with her vehement response. She glanced over in his direction again, then stretched out, placing one hand on his forearm. 'It's okay, Hamish, just venting some of my anger over what I saw today.' Mary Jo went on to describe her encounter with the deserted children.

'What can you achieve by going out to the fleet? Surely you're not thinking of confronting these parents?' he asked, alarmed.

'No, Hamish, I'm not. It would be impossible to identify those responsible, anyway.' She finished her Chivas and, without waiting, poured herself another shot. 'I want to get some coverage of conditions out there. I want to know what drives people to abandon their children. I want to see the looks on their faces and capture this to show the goddamn world just what these people have been reduced to. Perhaps, by exposing what is really going on here, we can orchestrate some intervention. Someone has to do something Hamish. This country's turned into a cesspool and it's the children who are paying the ultimate price.'

Hamish knew precisely what Mary Jo meant. Having visited many of the refugee camps as far as Irian Jaya and witnessed first hand, the result of man's inhumanity towards his fellow being, Hamish had lost the desire to remain in Asia much longer.

'Do you want me to come with you?' he asked sincerely, and could see that Mary Jo was pleased with his offer.

'No,' she replied, jokingly, 'you'd most probably scare the hell out of them.' She patted his arm and smiled. 'Don't worry, Hamish. I'll be okay. It couldn't be any worse than Beirut!'

'You were never in Beirut,' he challenged.

'See, just goes to show how smart some dumb blondes can be,' she laughed, the whiskey having the required effect.

Hamish was still unsure but knew Mary Jo well enough to let it go. The last thing he needed right then was an argument. For a moment he remained quiet and Mary Jo followed suit, each deep in thought about the other. Then, almost simultaneously, they both spoke.

'Mary Jo..'

'Hamish..'

'Sorry, you first,' he said.

'No, it's okay. Go on,' she urged. Hamish finished his drink and placed the empty glass down without refilling it.

'Can we talk about what happened in Jakarta?'

'It's a long time ago, Hamish,' she answered, with a touch of sadness in her voice.

'This is the conversation we should have had in Kuala Lumpur,' he suggested, casting his mind back to their abrupt parting. Mary Jo leaned slightly in his direction and looked directly into his eyes.

'Why did you really leave without contacting me again?' She had asked this very question a thousand times before, wondering why she deserved such shabby treatment. They had been close, perhaps even in love. Mary Jo had to restrain her rising anger. She had never really forgiven Hamish for his past behavior.

'You know I was called to Geneva. I really did try to contact you that night, Jo. Things were confused, and I just ran out of time.'

'That's it?' she asked, indignantly.

'No, it isn't,' he answered, defensively. 'What ever happened to your friend, Fieldmann?' At first, Mary Jo did not understand and thought she had misheard.

'Eric? Eric Fieldmann?'

'Yes, Jo.'

'What's Eric got to do with anything?' she asked, mystified.

'Jo, listen,' Hamish said, 'I tracked you down that night, anxious to let you know what was happening.'

'And?' she waited, now perplexed by whatever he was suggesting.

'I phoned his room and you answered,' he explained, now feeling a little foolish.

'Eric? And me?' Mary Jo's mouth opened wide. 'My god, Hamish! Did you think we were getting it off in his room?'

'And you weren't ?' he demanded, the old wound open now, memories of her naked with someone else flowing through his mind. Mary Jo's thoughts flashed back to that time, her memory of what really transpired clouded by the excessive amount of alcohol she and her associates had consumed earlier in the evening. She looked at Hamish, slowly shaking her head.

'Would you believe me now if I said nothing happened?' Mary Jo observed Hamish closely for his reaction. His eyes dropped momentarily, then returned to hers.

'Did it?' he asked, annoyed with himself immediately for doing so. Mary Jo leaned back, withdrawing her hand from his arm. She knew that even with the truth the question would always be on his mind, like a minute particle of poison, slowly eating away at his confidence and trust.

'I guess you earned the right to ask that question,' she said. Hamish waited uncomfortably, wishing now they had not got into this. He wanted Mary Jo to deny his allegations, while firmly believing the worst. 'Does it really matter any more what happened?'

'Yes Jo, it does,' Hamish replied.

'And if I tell you that nothing happened, would you accept me at my word?' she challenged. Hamish's mind raced. He had visualized this discussion many times before. Could it be possible that nothing really did take place between them?

'Yes, that would do it,' he said, not entirely sure that it would. Mary Jo rose to her feet and leaned over the stone balustrade to the pool below.

'Feel like another swim?' she asked, redirecting the conversation. Hamish looked up surprised, believing then he had his answer. He rose to his feet and placed his hand gently against the small of her back.

'Sure, why not,' he agreed, an emptiness forming in his stomach. 'The sun will be up shortly,' he added, then felt a little foolish as he turned and went inside to change. They could always be friends. He turned as she entered, removing the shorts he held from his hand, throwing these casually back onto the wicker chair.

'You won't need those,' Mary Jo moved into the bedroom, heading for the door.

'Skinny dipping?' Hamish hesitated, looked down at his damp shorts, and shrugged, then followed Mary Jo to the lifts and down to the saltwater pool. There, in the early morning hours they both undressed under the soft moonlight and plunged into the tepid, unguarded swimming pool together.

Chapter Twenty-three

Hani

'Try and eat something,' Budi insisted, holding the bowl of steamed rice for her to accept, but Hani merely shook her head.

'I can't, Budi, can't you see, I can't!' she sobbed, her rib cage sore from dry-retching for hours. He tried to force her to sit up but she slapped at him wildly, barely missing his head.

'If you don't eat, it will be worse,' he insisted. Hani could not see how this might be possible. Why did she feel like this?

'No, Budi, please!' she pleaded, nausea dominating her mind. She pushed his hand out of the way and leaned over the side of the perpetually moving deck.

'Hani,' he coaxed, *'I promise. Just take a mouthful and you will feel much better'.* Budi half-filled the ceramic spoon and moved this towards her mouth. Her eyes were partially glazed and he knew she was dehydrated. Hani attempted to take the small mouthful of steamed rice, the starchy smell sufficient suggestion to cause her to choke. Budi wrapped one arm around her, worried that if she felt this way now, how could she possibly cope with the open-sea crossing.

Unbeknown to the new arrivals, cholera had broken out in the camp days before, many already stricken with the deadly disease, and it was this which concerned the others aboard the ship. The locally prepared food Hani had consumed on the beach had only contributed in part to her condition. She was more than two weeks late.

'Tell her to sit up, and watch the shore,' one of the others suggested, annoyed with the young woman. Budi turned and glared at the woman, sitting bunched amongst a number of others chewing on a strip of *dendeng,* the local bully-beef. Hani felt slightly delirious. She thought she could smell *ajam gule,* her mother's favorite dish of chicken curry, spiced to burn

one's stomach. Her mind wandered, images of her father carrying home one of the half-meter mountain *kalong,* the bats cooked in a steaming pot as an asthma cure for her brother. She shivered, half-conscious now as her fever continued to ravage her weakened body, shadows playing with her mind. Within the hour, her condition deteriorated even further.

'Hani?' Budi called, shaking her gently, his concern growing when she did not respond. His father shook his head, one finger across his lips. Let the girl sleep, the message read. In her mind, demons chased each other as she slipped further away.

Suddenly, she cried out, *'Budi!'* as childhood stories returned to haunt her weakened state, the imagined outline of the *kuntilanak* ghost appearing, striking her with fear. As this apparition continued to transform from one persona to another she screamed, her mother's face appearing before her to warn that this evil would steal her baby's blood, then change into a beautiful woman to further deceive. Before mid-morning, Hani's condition caused fear amongst her fellow travelers, many of whom whispered that she should be thrown overboard without delay.

Deep inside her womb, and barely two weeks into gestation, the minute embryo which had contributed to her nausea was lost forever and Hani commenced bleeding profusely.

* * * *

Mary Jo & Hamish

She kept her body immersed in the pool, just below the water-line. Even though the water was lukewarm, the gentle sea-breeze still chilled as it brushed softly across her face. They had splashed around for almost an hour, like children without a care in the world. Then, as they tired, Hamish indicated that he'd had enough.

'Come here, first' she invited, and Hamish swam closer, stopping short of touching. He could see her breasts through the water and, although tempted, he kept his distance.

'Let's finish that conversation now,' Mary Jo offered.

'I thought we'd been down that path already,' Hamish replied, a touch churlishly. Mary Jo stood, exposing her body, and brushed her short hair back. He could see her erect nipples, his reaction instant.

'The answer to your question is no, Hamish. I did not sleep with Eric on that occasion.' She moved slowly towards him. 'But you should know, we were once an item and very close.' He had guessed as much but remained silent. 'I had not seen him for some time and, to be honest, at the time I was both angry and pleased to see him, but I guess that's natural enough. Don't you agree?' By now Mary Jo had positioned herself within reach and her hands moved to the back of his neck.

'I don't know what to say, Jo,' he tried to apologize but it sounded hollow. 'It just seemed……' he attempted to continue but Mary Jo pulled his head down to accept her warm mouth. She kissed him tenderly and she could tell immediately that he was aroused. As they embraced, he pulled her closer, and Mary Jo's hands found their way, guiding him inside, crying out as he lifted her knees and lunged forward before she was prepared.

They continued to kiss passionately, oblivious to their surrounds, the warmth of their bodies lost in the near-weightless conditions as they moved together, their thrusts gentle at first, then faster as the moment built, Hamish's hands pulling roughly under her thighs. Mary Jo pushed harder against his body, her fingers interlocked behind his back as his excitement grew, his hot breath against her cheek, punctuated with rhythmic grunts of pleasure. Suddenly, she felt his uncontrollable spasm and Mary Jo cried out, her own climax sending waves of sensuous pleasure through her entire body.

For several minutes they remained locked together, each slipping back slowly from their heights of ecstasy as the sky overhead became brighter with the first traces of false dawn.

'Thanks, Jo,' Hamish said, softly, and they kissed, this time tenderly and held each other as lovers do after those moments of release. Mary Jo slipped her arms around his firm waist, moving her body teasingly against his.

'What do you think, cowboy?' she asked, laughingly. Her hands moved to encourage Hamish but this was not to be so. Mary Jo turned, startled, when she heard her name being called.

'Mary Jo,' Anne's voice pierced the early morning silence, 'the driver's waiting. You'll be late!'

'I'm coming,' she called back, with nowhere to turn. Hamish spotted the Indonesian woman first as he climbed out of the pool, cursing for forgetting to bring a towel. He heard Mary Jo giggle, then follow.

'Wait for me upstairs,' she shouted across the pool. Anne had been too embarrassed to approach any further, having been informed by staff where Mary Jo might be. The early starters were all standing in the shadows on the second level, discussing the foreigners, having observed them from the moment they first entered the pool. Anne had checked Mary Jo's room, then downstairs, becoming agitated when she had not located the woman as it was already well past four.

The couple dressed quickly and hurried up to the foyer where Anne waited, equipment at hand. Five minutes later, after a brief exchange, she left Hamish standing alone in the foyer annoyed that she could still consider venturing out to the refugee fleet alone.

* * * *

Haji Abdul Muis

Abdul Muis examined the report received not minutes before, exhilarated by its contents. His *Mufti Muharam* now controlled all of Sukabumi and its surrounds, their successes paid for in the currency of life and blood. With General Praboyo's death, the Moslem army had easily destroyed the remnants of his final stronghold in hours. Having occupied Bandung, they then drove General Winarko's troops back to Bogor and onto Jakarta. With more than two-thirds of Java now under his control, Muis' forces concentrated on cleaning up isolated pockets of resistance, consolidating their positions in preparation for the final assault on the capital.

In Sumatra, all of Aceh and most of the south had fallen to friendly forces. The Christian Batak soldiers had offered fierce resistance and Muis had sent word to the Moslem factions to delay, until he could send reinforcements from Java. As for the rest of the Indonesian archipelago, civil war continued to rage between opposing ethnic and religious groups, and Abdul Muis was obliged to admit silently that, at the end of the day, the *Mufti Muharam* might be obliged to be satisfied with control of just Java and Sumatra.

Fighting along Bali's shores had been swift and bloody. The *Mufti Muharam* had been unable to secure a foothold on the island, even with air support. Across the string of islands to Irian Jaya, the story had been the same. Christian militia had taken control over Timor, Ambon, Flores, and Jayapura. In the north, control over Menado continued to change hands as the opposing forces there battled on and along the coastal reaches of Kalimantan, most mosques had been torched by Dayaks with tens of thousands of Moslems unaccounted for in these southern districts of Borneo.

It was Muis' intention to return to contest these areas once the two major population centers of Java and Sumatra had fallen into his hands. Then he would mobilize in the east with his massive following and retake the delinquent, breakaway Christian strongholds, taking the fight as far as the Philippines, when the time was ripe and Islamic Indonesia was adequately armed to stand against those who would see its destruction.

He would rebuild the economy and the country's infrastructure. Petro-dollars would be utilized to strengthen the military and advance the Republic, providing advanced technology and skills to the Indonesian people in their quest for better lives guided by the hand of Allah, The One and True God. The children of Indonesia would grow in mind, body and spirit and become as one, safe from the adulterated mix of Christian-spawned beliefs.

Now, as his dream approached reality, Muis became impatient to take the capital, the last bastion to afford shelter to his enemies. The government's forces were still significant in strength and although tainted with the Suhapto brush, international support remained with the quietly spoken general who had recently assumed the role of President, and now stubbornly refused to consider the possibility of defeat. Muis' forces had been most unfortunate not to capture Praboyo's wife and children before they fled Bandung. He had hoped for this leverage against Winarko, now guardian over both the Suhapto and Hababli families, whose fortunes were essential to the Moslem leader's long-term strategies.

Muis' one remaining question was whether General Winarko was prepared to commit his remaining forces in a fight to the end, or would he compromise and deal with the equally powerful *Mufti Muharam?* Winarko still controlled the navy and most of the air force. Army divisions loyal to the General were of sufficient strength to carry the fighting through another year. The question was whether many of the soldiers would want to continue their war against fellow Muslims, and Abdul Muis was counting on mass defections once his troops had occupied Bogor and the smaller but heavily fortified towns of Serang and Purwakarta. He firmly believed that once his army was in a position to threaten Jakarta, Winarko's remaining forces would crumble quickly.

Then, and only then, could his dream of an Islamic state be realized. In the meantime, his forces would continue to crush any remaining resistance, driving those not of his faith into the surrounding seas.

* * * *

Mary Jo & Hamish

The phone's incessant ringing finally woke Hamish from a deep, satisfying sleep. He groped for the receiver, struggling to read the bedside clock. Once Mary Jo had disappeared in her jeep he had decided to catch up on a few hours before meeting with Peter and the others in the UNHCR team.

'Is that you, Mister Hamish?' The shrill voice belonged to the U.N. interpreter. 'The pilot has received your message and wishes to talk to you. Can you come down? He says it's urgent.'

'Is Mister Peter there?'

'No, Mister Hamish. I have just spoken to him and he asked me to wake you all.' Hamish rolled his wrist, checking his Seiko against the bedside clock. It was past eight o'clock. He had slept for more than three hours but from the gritty, sour taste in his mouth, he knew his body needed more.

'Okay, I'll be down in ten minutes,' he said, replacing the phone. Hamish rose, stretched, then walked to the windows and opened the curtains. The morning sun's reflected brilliance blinded, forcing him to shield his eyes. Hamish lowered himself to the carpeted floor, easing slowly into his customary, early-morning calisthenics and, having completed these, hit the shower. Fifteen minutes later he swung by his associate's room and the two men rode down to the lobby together, providing Hamish with the opportunity to brief Peter concerning Mary Jo and her assistant Anne.

'It's okay by me,' the other man had said. 'Pity we hadn't known yesterday. Had she taken a quick ride out to the boats in the afternoon, we might have been able to get away a little earlier. Still, I don't mind waiting the few extra hours.' As team leader, Hamish was obliged to clear this request with him, before discussing the matter with the pilot.

They entered the coffee shop where the others were waiting, the mood amongst the team obviously pensive from their somber expressions.

'What's up?' Peter asked. One of the other men nodded in the pilot's direction.

'Better ask him,' he answered, then folded his arms and leaned back to listen.

'First of all, we could take the two additional passengers, providing they don't have any luggage. It's a bit tight but we burned off enough fuel getting here to accommodate the extra weight. Are they ready to leave?' he asked.

'Not until eleven, perhaps twelve,' Hamish replied. The pilot's face became more serious.

'Where have they gone?' he asked, looking directly at Hamish.

'The American lady has gone out to the fishing-fleet,' he said, his concern rising. 'Why? Is there a problem?' The pilot breathed in heavily and nodded.

'Most of the hotel staff have disappeared. Their families came about an hour ago, lifted whatever they could, then left.' Hamish did not quite understand the significance of this, waiting for the man to continue. One of the others in his team jumped in.

'Tell him the rest,' he snapped, looking at the pilot.

'We should leave as well,' the pilot advised, agitated. 'According to the staff, Pelabuhan Ratu is in danger of being overrun by advancing troops. I have just been out to my radio listening to traffic. Seems they are right. The *Mufti Muharam* rebels are occupying the fishing port area as we speak.' For a moment his statement hung in the air before cold realization struck.

'If you want my vote, we should leave now.' This from an unshaven member of their group who, until that moment, had remained quiet, listening. 'As for waiting for the others, this is, after all, a U.N. team effort and shouldn't be compromised.' Hamish glared at the surly faced man, then turned to the team leader.

'Peter, let me go out in the chopper and see if I can get Mary Jo to return now,' he asked. But while Peter was considering their dilemma, the pilot interjected.

'Mister Hamish, I'm sorry, but we don't carry any slings, we wouldn't be able to lift her out of there. Even if we had floats, I still couldn't land out there. It's a lot rougher than you'd think that far offshore.'

'We'll drop her a note warning her of what's happening.'

'Christ, Hamish, you'd never find her amongst that lot!' Peter added.

'How about I give it a try, anyway,' he pleaded. 'I'll fly out with the pilot and see if we can spot her and get her attention. She's sure to realize something's wrong and return immediately.'

'What do you think?' Peter asked the pilot.

'If we go now, it might be okay. My suggestion is you all wait out there by the heli-pad and we'll take a run out to the fleet and back.' The pilot then looked Hamish directly in the eye. 'Where is the Indonesian girl, Anne?'

The realization that Anne would be waiting somewhere along the beach amongst a multitude of panic-driven refugees suddenly struck Hamish in the pit of his stomach.

'She'll be waiting somewhere along the beach, wherever Mary Jo caught her lift.'

'Does she have transport?' Peter asked.

'Yes, they had a jeep and driver.'

'Then, unless she's smart enough to get out of there and return within the next thirty minutes or so, we'll have to leave her behind,' Peter declared and Hamish knew the man was right. His mind raced, looking for a solution.

'If we're going, Mister Hamish, we should leave now,' the pilot warned and Hamish nodded, rising to his feet.

'Okay,' he said, 'let's go,' rising to his feet. 'We won't be long, Peter,' he promised.

'We'll be waiting outside when you get back.'

'Fine,' Hamish said, then turned and placed his hand on the pilot's shoulder. 'I just need to get something from my room,' he said, and hurried out into the lobby.

'I'll wait in the chopper,' the pilot called. Hamish cursed the hotel staff for having left the generators unattended as he jogged across the marble floor. Hamish started the grueling climb back to his room, via the fire stairwell. He took the steps, two at a time, the punishing effort sending his heart racing wildly, breathless before he reached halfway. He reached the top floor and staggered into his room. He grabbed a few items, wrapped these inside his swimmers and ran back down the concrete steps to the lobby and outside to where the pilot waited, the helicopter's blades already turning slowly in readiness.

He climbed inside the Jet Ranger and they were airborne within seconds, heading out to sea towards the fleet anchored some fifteen nautical miles to the east of the Samudera Beach Hotel where, half an hour before, all hell had broken loose when word arrived that the port of Pelabuhan Ratu had come under attack.

* * * *

Mary Jo

'Where are you going?' Mary Jo yelled after the ferry as it sped away from the fleet. During the past hours, she had scrambled from one ship to another, visiting more than thirty vessels, talking to refugees in her broken but effective Indonesian. The huge fleet was tied closely together, permitting unrestricted movement within the floating community.

She was amazed at how quickly the people had adapted to their conditions. Charcoal fires housed in clay pots created a market atmosphere as women sat hunched over their cooking, while children played within their confined spaces under the watchful eyes of all. Mary Jo was convinced that many of these ships were not sea-worthy - that their owners, having recognized this opportunity to divest themselves of their aging boats, did so knowing that should their boats be lost, there would most likely be no survivors to deal with anyway. The panic driven refugees knew little of the fishing boats' seaworthiness. They were just thankful to be on board.

Earlier, Anne had taken her to the fish markets where a broker happily accepted her dollars and arranged for a small tender to ferry Mary Jo out to the fleet.

'The boatman will wait, Mary Jo,' Anne had explained, 'but please don't stay too long,' reminding her that they were to return to the hotel before eleven. With a wave, Mary Jo had climbed into the rickety boat and was taken out to the fleet. The journey took no more than twenty minutes and as her ferry approached, Mary Jo was struck by the magnitude of what lay before her, wishing she had more time to spend amongst the floating city. She checked the time, noting that it was already past six o'clock and decided to remain until ten, then return to the harbor. She instructed her boatman to pull alongside the closest ship and wait.

When Mary Jo climbed aboard the first vessel, she was greeted with a stunned silence as more than fifty passengers stared at their visitor, her fair complexion so out of place, her height towering above them all. She had quickly put them at ease, sitting on the deck, speaking to the children as she recorded the historical event. Mary Jo continued to make her way from one vessel to another, climbing over ropes and under makeshift washing lines, around drums of stinking diesel fuel, dry stores and bedding, conscious that not all those aboard appeared to be happy.

When Mary Jo spotted a number of young couples sitting alone, staring forlornly towards the shore, she was reminded of the children who had been abandoned and wondered how parents could cope with the guilt of such actions. As she continued to take stock, Mary Jo realized just how young most of the refugees were, the absence of elderly amongst those she had seen, distressing. During the short time she had been in their midst, she had noticed the constant flow of smaller vessels carrying produce out to the flotilla and the ongoing process of transporting new arrivals to the already overcrowded vessels.

Towards nine o'clock, her attention was drawn to the increase in activity around the fleet, with orders being shouted in a dialect she could not understand, apparently instructing captains to maneuver their boats into new positions. She imagined that this was caused by changing tides or rising weather conditions. Mary Jo looked up at the clear sky then back towards the shoreline, the buildings in the distance barely visible to the naked eye.

She sensed a noticeable change of mood in the air, the fleet suddenly coming alive as people scurried back to their own boats. Alarmed when a number of diesel engines coughed, spluttered, then rattled noisily through the fleet, Mary Jo returned to where she had first landed, stunned as she witnessed her ferry depart.

'Come back!' she screamed, with her hands cupped around her mouth, almost losing balance as the deck moved under her feet. *'Come back!'* she yelled again, as loudly as her lungs would permit, her panic rising when she realized that the fleet was moving and she had been deliberately left behind.

* * * *

Anne

The rattle of automatic weapons from across the paddy fields punctuated, occasionally by the evidence of rocket-launched grenades, confirmed the refugees' worst fear. Pandemonium followed shock when the refugees lining the shore recognized the familiar sounds of approaching gunfire as the first wave of *Mufti Muharam* poured into the coastal town, firing indiscriminately to clear the congested road. Within minutes, a roar passed through the tens of thousands lining the beach, their faces covered with fear when word spread that the murderous rebels had arrived.

Anne was at a loss as to what to do. She bit her lip anxiously, calling out in anger as someone ran past carelessly, knocking her off balance. She had but two choices. Remain and wait for Mary Jo or run with the others, hoping her driver still would be where they had left him earlier. Another volley of shots echoed overhead, sending the panic driven mass fleeing in shocked confusion. An approaching helicopter caught their eye and they reeled back, turning to escape what they believed would be an aerial attack. Possessions were lost, or discarded as the terrified population attempted to flee their attackers. Men, struggling to get free of the crowd, screamed abuse at each other. Women and children were knocked to the ground in the melee, while others ran into the sea in one last, desperate attempt to board fully laden ferry boats departing at that moment. As the swirling mass moved first in one direction, then another, Anne was knocked to the ground. She tried to get up and was cruelly kicked in the side.

'Help me!' she screamed, but her pleas fell on deaf ears.

'Please, someone, help me!' Anne attempted to lift herself up and was kneed in the head, the impact sending her crashing to the sand. She cried out weakly, the crowd smothering her now muted voice as they pushed in

her direction, their feet trampling her broken body into the sand. Within those few, brutal moments, the air was crushed from her lungs and as Anne surrendered to her last breath, the words 'Mary Jo' formed on her silent lips and she died.

* * * *

Hamish

'Over there!' the pilot indicated the fleet, surprise written across his face.

It took a few seconds for Hamish to realize that the ships were steaming further out to sea, his nervousness reaching climax when he identified the movement.

'What in the…!' Startled by what he saw, Hamish looked back towards the coast hoping to identify smaller vessels heading back to shore. 'They're already under way!' he shouted, observing the formation of ships strung out below. 'She's most probably already on her way back. Can we run back towards the beach and check out any of those boats down there?' The pilot nodded, turning the helicopter towards the coastline. They flew low over a number of returning, smaller boats but she was nowhere to be seen. As they came closer to the sprawling camp, they were shocked by what they saw.

'Get down lower!' he shouted, the pilot immediately shaking his head.

'Too risky!'

'We'll never be able to spot her if you don't,' he argued. They continued to hover for some minutes but it was impossible to see anything with any clarity amongst the teeming mass below. Hamish peered up the beach in the direction of the fish markets, recognizing immediately the cause for the panic below.

'We're too late!' the pilot yelled, pulling away quickly as he spotted the soldiers aiming their rifles at the Jet Ranger.

'Go back to the fleet,' Hamish ordered, and the pilot looked at him as if he were mad.

'Five minutes, okay?' he offered, expecting those ashore to report their presence. They sped out to sea, Hamish praying that Mary Jo was, in fact, still aboard one of the fishing boats and had not been caught back there on the beach. They arrived within minutes, flying over the ships as these headed south, Hamish's spirits falling, faced with the formidable task of spotting one person amongst such an impossible number of ships.

'That's about all I can give you, Mister Hamish, sorry,' the pilot said, tapping the fuel gauge with his fingernail.

'Give it a few more minutes,' he pleaded, now uncertain that Mary Jo had not returned to shore. The thought that she might already be back in the hotel had occurred to him but Hamish was reluctant to leave, knowing there would not be another chance.

The helicopter drifted slowly across towards the centre of the fleet, when something caught his eye.

'There!' he yelled, excitedly, 'she's over there! Look, over there to the right!' he pointed and the pilot's feet touched the left pedal lightly, bringing the helicopter into line. Hamish nodded, raising one thumb and smiled, but Mary Jo could not see much of either of them at that distance.

'I can see her,' the pilot nodded. Hamish took the note he had written on the way out, changed the instructions and placed this inside the empty Chivas bottle, screwing the damaged cap back on as tightly as he dared. Her earlier instructions were to return to shore. Not only was that now impossible due to the danger there, the handful of smaller craft attached to the fishing fleet were far from where Mary Jo's own vessel was positioned.

It was most unlikely that she would be able to convince any of the captains to surrender one of their tenders, now they were well under way. He had told her to have her own ship's captain pull away from the other ships and, when clear, dive overboard. Hamish planned to stand out on the helicopter's skis and lift her from the sea.

'See if you can get alongside that boat,' he asked, waving again in Mary Jo's direction. The pilot attempted to do so, pulling back at the last moment.

'This is about as close as we get,' he shouted, pointing at a number of masts wobbling dangerously close and in line with his rotors. The pilot then positioned the Jet Ranger so that Hamish could have a better chance of lobbing the message as the fishing-boat approached. They both watched as Mary Jo raised her hand to shield her eyes, Hamish holding the bottle outside for her to see. She waved, acknowledging that she understood. Hamish wrapped the bottle inside his swimmers, reached out and threw the bundle towards the boat below.

Mary Jo had pushed her way forward, warning those nearby to move back. She watched as the package fell, spinning towards her and she leaned forward, reaching out to catch the falling bundle as the ship rocked under her unsteady feet. The bottle struck with a distinctive thud, glancing off the ship's high, solid wooden bow before falling into the sea. For a moment Mary Jo stood there, a look of disbelief clouding her face. Then she looked up and saw Hamish as he too stared down into the sea, the helicopter hovering alongside her vessel.

'Sorry, Mister,' the pilot said, 'but now we have to go.'

'No, wait!' Hamish yelled, unbuckling his belt.

'What are you doing?' the pilot shouted, with one sweaty hand ready on the helicopter's collective controls.

'We can't leave her!' he snapped back. 'Take me up ahead, I'm getting off!'

'You can't!' the pilot shouted, again, 'we should go back and tell Mister Peter.'

'I don't expect you'd understand this but Mary Jo has a much greater chance of having someone come to help her if I'm on board,' he tried to explain, the noise inside the cabin making this near impossible.

'What will I tell Mister Peter?' the pilot worried, moving away from the fishing boat.

'Just tell him what happened. He'll know what to do!' Hamish then pointed ahead, thrusting his hand forward, indicating he meant business. Reluctantly, the pilot flew several hundred meters ahead and hovered dangerously close to the rising sea. Hamish removed his shoes, climbed out and hung onto the side of the helicopter with one hand, while waving for the approaching boat to stop. Twice he attempted to have the fisherman slow and was both times ignored. He climbed back inside, frustrated by what had happened, overcome by a feeling of helplessness.

On board, Mary Jo pleaded for the captain to stop but he refused. In desperation, she ran to the side but balked at the last moment, realizing that if she jumped, the following vessels would surely cross her path before she could swim out of harm's way.

'If we don't return now, we won't have enough fuel to reach Jakarta,' the pilot warned. 'Sorry, mister, but now we must really go.' Hamish could see Mary Jo's distinctive shape moving around the vessel. He continued to stare, wishing there was something he could do. To jump now would be folly, he knew. The captain had made his intentions clear.

'Then let's say goodbye,' he said, a knot forming inside his stomach. The pilot flew alongside and Hamish leaned out and shouted to Mary Jo as they hovered above.

'I love you!' he called and waved, his words lost to the surrounding noise.

Mary Jo stood, staring up at Hamish's face, unable to comprehend. She shouted for him to hurry back, then blew him a kiss as the helicopter pulled away, and then they were gone, Mary Jo watching the Jet Ranger disappear out of sight behind cloud-touched peaks, leaving her alone to come to terms with her precarious situation.

* * * *

Chapter Twenty-four

JAKARTA

General Winarko stormed into the Department of Defense offices, furious that Admiral Sudomo had failed to respond to his earlier calls. Unable to locate his most senior officer, the President thought he might have been betrayed by yet another close friend.

'He's waiting, inside, General,' an aide advised, opening the door into the large, operational office buried deep inside the ABRI complex. Sudomo did not bother rising when Winarko entered. This was not a sign of disrespect, the Admiral was physically exhausted.

'Where have you been?' Winarko demanded, his anger evident as he threw his peaked cap down carelessly.

'Believe it or not, out at sea,' he replied. Winarko raised an eyebrow questioningly. 'It's true,' the Admiral continued, 'and we have some major problems brewing amongst the junior officers.'

'What's happening?'

'Half of our captains have absconded with their ships. That's what's happening,' Sudomo announced, not at all enjoying the look of concern which then spread across the Chief of Staff's face.

'Impossible!' Winarko rejected the idea.

'They've already sailed,' the Admiral confirmed.

'Where?' General Winarko asked, shocked by this revelation. *'Have they gone over to Muis?'*

'No,' the chubby Admiral answered, *'nothing as simple as that. Had they simply sailed across to join the others in Surabaya then the problem would not be as serious.'*

'Where are they headed?' Winarko wanted to know. If he lost the navy, the air force might follow.

'From what I managed to glean from the remaining captains, those who left have piracy on their minds.'

'I don't understand. Piracy? Surely they're not considering attacking shipping in the Straits of Malacca?' The possibility that Indonesian warships might attack international shipping sent a shudder through his spine. That would be the end surely as the British and Americans would not hesitate to enter the fray.

'No, no, nothing like that,' Sudomo explained, *'eight ships are steaming through the Sunda Strait, their destination the refugee fleet which set sail from Pelabuhan Ratu.'* Sudomo observed General Winarko frown and continued before the man could interrupt him again. *'They'll most likely return to formation once they discover that those involved in the mass exodus under way down there, don't have hoards of gold with them. I don't know how it started but rumor swept through the fleet that the large number of fishing boats are all loaded to the gunnels with Chinese gold.'*

The existence of the large number of boats was no secret to Winarko and, he guessed, to Indonesia's neighbors. Although Australian authorities had offered to send their own navy further into Indonesian waters to assist deterring the ever increasing numbers of refugee ships, he had declined their offer. It was difficult enough with the American Seventh Fleet maintaining a presence in the country's east, south of the Philippines, but he did not wish to create a scenario which permitted the Australians to build up any defence presence, believing that they had designs on Indonesia's eastern provinces, such as Timor and Irian Jaya. As a number of provinces in that area were demanding recognition of their independence declarations, Winarko believed that the Australians would welcome the opportunity to provide support to these resource-rich territories.

Acting on advice from his own officers, Winarko permitted the flow of refugees to continue, acknowledging that this kept the limited Australian navy fully occupied and out of his way. In the meantime, one third of his navy was loosely spread out from north of Java to the western coast of New Guinea, to contain the warships under Muis' control out of Surabaya. Of these, Muis had managed to convince the captains of some six corvettes and three frigates to follow his cause. Armed with Harpoon and Exocet surface-to-surface missiles, Winarko did not wish to risk losing any of his own ships in a direct confrontation, unless this became absolutely necessary. He knew that his strength lay in his ground forces and counted on the remaining, serviceable AURI aircraft to maintain the capital's integrity from aerial attack. Winarko was aware that more than two thirds of the air force had been destroyed in the prolonged fight against Praboyo, most of these belonging to the ambitious upstart's forces. Better these were destroyed than have Abdul Muis' arsenal enhanced with F-4's and F-16's, he thought.

'Which ships have sailed?' he asked, his thoughts returning to the problem at hand. It was not all that serious, he believed. If anything, he could probably claim responsibility for sending the ships there, to prevent their escaping for Australian shores.

'Corvettes five, Frigates three,' he answered, holding fingers in the air.

'Have you been in contact with their captains?' Winarko asked.

'We've tried, but we're being ignored.'

'What do you want to do about them?' Winarko pressed. It was, after all, the Admiral's problem. The overweight officer shrugged.

'Let them go. Who knows, maybe they'll get rich,' he attempted a smile but was too tired to enjoy his own joke.

'When will they arrive?' the Chief of Staff asked, more out of curiosity than any strategic reason.

'Well, they broke formation about four hours ago. We've been tracking them. They should reach their destination in two to three days. Their quarry will not be making much more than five or six knots.'

'We should inform the Australians,' Winarko advised, then added, *'and the Americans.'*

'They'll find out soon enough,' Sudomo quipped. General Winarko nodded sagely, perhaps he could claim credit after all.

'Where is the American fleet?'

'Still holding off, north in the Celebes Sea.'

'Warn them, anyway,' he ordered. The ships' passage would be through international waters but it would be to his advantage to pre-empt any rumors that these were renegade captains. After Sudomo departed Winarko paced the floor. He had more pressing problems to consider.

He opened the letter delivered surreptitiously that morning. It was from Abdul Muis and written in his hand. General Winarko read through its contents again, wondering if the man was bluffing or would really risk losing everything and attack the capital as he had inferred. Then there was the powerful Muslim leader's veiled threat to issue a holy letter of condemnation. This, he knew, could easily be construed by any of the *Mufti Muharam* zealots as an execution decree.

Winarko placed the letter carefully back in its envelope, his Javanese heritage influencing his thoughts. He would not refuse to discuss the matter with Muis. Consensus and discussion had always been part of their culture and perhaps they may be able to find a solution to the impasse they had both reached. Somewhere in the distance he heard the magnified cry calling the faithful to prayer and he checked his watch. He was late. Summoning his aide, Winarko hurried out to the waiting staff-car and went directly to the Istiqlal Mosque, where he prayed in silence that Haji Abdul Muis would not carry out his threat to issue a holy *fatwah* bearing Winarko's name.

* * * *

EAST JAVA REFUGEE FLEET

Lily

Lily looked up at the dark, cumulo-nimbus cloud bank with its promise of rain and whispered a silent prayer. It was hot. Humidity had reached debilitating levels as the sun climbed to its zenith, the absence of wind typical before the turbulence of storm.

She tied a soiled handkerchief loosely around her forehead to prevent salty drops of perspiration from falling into her food. She leaned forward over the small, ceramic bowl and scooped the hardened rice into her mouth. Rationed carefully, their food supplies might last another two weeks. Lily's eyes passed over the mound of unhusked coconuts to her left, accepting that when these were finished, they would be totally dependent on rain to quench their thirst. The fleet had left Grajagan Bay before final stores could be taken on board. Their fishing boats had been fired upon from the shore and the refugees had sailed south, to wait for the West Java fleet in open waters. Now, more than one hundred miles from the inhospitable south Java coastline they drifted, their vessels tied together to conserve valuable fuel.

Occasionally, a wailing cry would pierce the quiet somewhere within the fleet when another of their number died, the sound now all too familiar to her ears. Since escaping the Balinese onslaught, cholera had swept through their fleet, the tragic results no longer evident as bodies were quickly cast into the sea. Lily prayed that her god would not remain an absentee landlord, as she continued to live with the fear of death.

A brief puff of wind across the calm sea gently brushed their faces, the suggestion that rain would follow raising hopes. The refugees made ready with plastic buckets to catch the precious drops, while others ignored nature's signal, having experienced such false promises many times in the past. Lily moved towards the wheel-house and looked up inquiringly at the man who had been appointed captain over her vessel.

'Will it rain?' she asked, hopefully. The well weathered seaman smiled at the young, resilient woman. He enjoyed talking to her. She seemed keen to learn.

'Perhaps, perhaps not,' he answered, a twinkle in his eye.

'Someone back there said you could tell by sniffing the air,' Lily had overheard someone suggest this. The refugees had little else to do but gossip. *'Can you?'*

The man displayed a yellow-toothed grin and breathed deeply for show. *'Once you have learned how to listen to the wind, understanding will follow,'* he said, reciting something he had learned from his father. *'For even the most powerful storms commence with but a soft whisper.'*

She held her hand out, palm facing towards the sky, closed her eyes and breathed in slowly.

'It's raining!' someone cried, and suddenly Lily could smell the distinctive change in the air. At first, only a few drops fell, the refugees all holding their breath, praying for more. Then, as the wind increased and the surrounding sky darkened, the heavens opened sending sheets of stinging rain across the sea. Lashed by growing wind the ocean's waves swelled in size and, within minutes, what had previously been a moderate sea turned into a swirling, threatening cauldron, sending fishermen scurrying to start their engines.

The storm lasted no more than an hour. Tropical skies quickly cleared and the sun broke through. Hot, sticky conditions which had preceded the storm monotonously reappeared, blanketing the fleet with an air of listless despondency. Another day passed and they waited, impatient for word that the great fleet would soon pass by.

* * * *

Hani & Mary Jo

Two hundred miles south of Pelabuhan Ratu, the fleet turned to the east off Christmas Island and set a new course which would take them into the lower latitudes. The lead ships would not normally have traveled this far south before turning towards Northern Australia but radio intercepts had influenced those in command to take these measures. Surprise soon turned to concern when they discovered that Jakarta had sent a number of warships in pursuit, and they monitored the airwaves to determine why the Indonesian Navy had suddenly had this change of heart.

Mary Jo waited, impatiently, for some sign that either Hamish or Anne had found some means of rescuing her but as the day wore on and the distance back to the coast grew with each hour, her hopes started to fade. The fleet moved slowly through the deep blue water, the late crimson sky blurring at sunset against a background of purple haze as the refugees loaded their clay cookers with charcoal and commenced preparing their last meal in Indonesian waters.

Mary Jo watched as children were fed first, then the men and finally the women. Although the meals were basic, Mary Jo felt the first pangs of hunger, willing to try the rice porridge or even the greasy fish cakes should any be offered.

The pungent smell of *sambal* paste assailed her sense of smell, her empty stomach reacting to the drifting aromas as sizzling sounds teased, her eyes observing one woman dropping prawn crackers into a pan, then seconds later retrieving the cooked, crispy wafers which had more than trebled in size. Mary Jo smiled at the woman but was ignored. Embarrassed, she made her way towards the stern and watched the other ships as their passengers gathered around their own pots, preparing to eat.

Amongst the crowded ship, she suddenly felt desperately alone and, for the first time in many years, vulnerable.

* * * *

After the first day at sea, Mary Jo's lips were chafed, her sunburned arms, neck and feet now quite red and beginning to cause her some pain. She craved a cigarette, tempted to ask one of the men for one of their *Ji Sam So kretek* cigarettes. She had checked the contents of her soft, leather equipment carryall and discovered that apart from the many rolls of exposed and unused film, and several partly consumed packets of peppermint and gum, there was little else which could be of any use to her, stuck out there.

As the coastline had slowly disappeared from view, Mary Jo had looked back wistfully, unaware of the horrific blood-bath she had left behind, and wondered why neither Anne nor Hamish had come to her aid. Throughout her first day, she scanned the sea for signs that she might be rescued but as the hours wore on, and the mountains high above Java's dangerous coastline gradually blurred with the ocean, she unhappily came to terms with her predicament. She checked her equipment, determined to make the most of the situation.

By the end of the second day, Mary Jo already knew a great deal about those aboard her vessel. She spoke to them, inquiring about the fleet's destination, the duration of their voyage and their expectations upon arrival. Most seemed receptive to her presence, although the boat's owner cum captain did not appear all that pleased. Then there was the problem of food and drinking water.

Mary Jo was conscious that the passengers had been limited in what they might take on board. Money, what little she carried, was useless out there on the ocean. She had gone without food for the first day, believing she would be rescued. An unopened roll of peppermint lifesavers had done little to stave off hunger. When clay-pot charcoal fires were started again, late afternoon on their second day, Mary Jo reluctantly avoided the cooking area, moving away so as not to impose. But the aroma of food was too much and, as Mary Jo looked wistfully over at the fires, she was observed. At first, she had been embarrassed when asked, but Mary Jo knew she would have to eat to survive and was relieved that someone was willing to share their food.

'Would you like to try this?' the man kindly offered, holding a bowl filled with rice cakes for her to try. In spite of her hunger, Mary Jo was cautious not to take too much, accepting the food with her right hand as she had been coached by Anne.

'Terima kasih,' she smiled, thanking her benefactor. *'Is she your daughter?'* Mary Jo asked, looking in the sickly young woman's direction.

'No,' he replied, bending down to offer the girl some dried beef, *'but she will be when we arrive in Australia.'* For a moment Mary Jo was confused by his response, then she realized what he meant and looked at the boy sitting alongside his fiancee.

'You are the son?' she asked, and Budi nodded, embarrassed by this talk in front of all the others. *'What is your name?'* Mary Jo kneeled down to speak to Hani. She could see that these three were quite different from the others on board. Even the captain treated them more deferentially and Mary Jo was curious as to why.

'I'm Hani.' the frail Indonesian girl answered, Budi assisting her into a sitting position. It was obvious that she was quite ill and had a fever. Mary Jo watched as she was offered the *dendeng* beef but she refused, asking for water to quench her parched throat instead. Mary Jo sat on the hard, wooden deck beside Hani and held her wrist. Her pulse was weak and Mary Jo could see from her pallor that she did not take to sailing too well.

She reached into her leather bag and found the half-eaten packet of lifesavers and extracted one for the girl. Hani placed this in her mouth, smiled weakly and closed her eyes.

'What's wrong with her?' she asked Budi.

'Sea sick, that's all,' he replied, uncertainly. Mary Jo placed her hand against Hani's forehead for several moments, then patted her hand reassuringly.

'Are you a doctor?' Hani asked. All she could really make out was the foreign woman's silhouette against the brilliant sun. Her eyes hurt, so she kept them shut.

'No, I'm like a reporter,' Mary Jo answered, *'and when you're feeling better, I'll take your photo.'* Hani smiled again, her hand unconsciously moving across her untidy hair.

Mary Jo rose to her feet, stretched, then scanned the horizon ahead between the thirty or so fishing-boats which had moved into position ahead of her group in the overall convoy.

On either side, the fleet was spread out over half a mile or more, whilst behind she could no longer see the end of those which brought up the rear. She had been told that there were more than eight hundred fishing boats in the fleet. No one seemed to know for sure just how many passengers had been taken on board but Budi's father had suggested that the floating population would be in excess of fifty, and possibly as many as seventy-five thousand.

Mary Jo was staggered by these figures and, as she looked out across the amazing spectacle, wished she had brought more equipment to capture this incredible drama in which she now played a part. Mary Jo recalled that her prestigious alumni from the Rochester Institute of Technology now boasted seven Pulitzer prize winners in photojournalism. Her own work had always met the highest standards and, considering the imagery she had captured already and the photo-opportunity which continued to unfold, Mary Jo was confident that her coverage of this epic would be well received and highly regarded by her peers.

During late afternoon on the third day they witnessed the most incredible display when a swordfish appeared and danced across the top of the waves.

'Isn't it beautiful!' Hani had exclaimed. She was now feeling considerably better, delighted with the visitor as the huge fish leapt into the air, its long sword dangerously close to the ships as they advanced. Children raced to the sides of ships to watch in awe as the magnificent exhibition continued, the beast not disappointing any as it danced across the huge swells, thrashing its tail-fins for elevation, the choreographic display part of the ritual mating game.

'Can you eat them?' Budi asked, imagining large, tasty slices cooked over charcoal for dinner.

'Yes, of course,' his father replied, Mary Jo noticing traces of mirth around the man's mouth for the first time. *'But you'd have to catch it first.'*

'Miss Jo, Miss Jo,' Hani called, with childish exuberance, *'would you photo that for me, please?'* and Mary Jo did so, catching the swordfish in all of its natural splendor.

Later that day, Mary Jo noticed a significant change in the sea's conditions, the waves much larger than before and the wind stronger than they had experienced since leaving port. Towards evening and at the time most would be tending to meal preparations, the weather deteriorated dramatically, casting a cloud of fear over them all. Waves taller than any they had yet seen slapped at the fishing-boats, white foamed peaks standing well above the wheel-house where their captain fought to maintain any semblance of speed through the turbulent sea. Lightning flashed, followed by rolls of deep, terrifying thunder, bringing drenching rain. The refugees huddled together, lashed by rain one moment, and salt spray the next, their ships tossed around like oversized cork toys as they endured the tropical storm. Then, as quickly as it had appeared, the threatening weather was gone, leaving the refugees with a taste of things to come.

* * * *

Mufti Muharam

A suffocating stench of death pervaded the narrow, coastal strip running from Pelabuhan Ratu, through to Samudera Beach. Bodies lay where they fell, their grotesque features evidence of the horror cast upon the refugee community, as wave upon wave of screaming, blood-thirsty soldiers invaded their camp, spraying the panic driven crowds indiscriminately with lead.

The elderly, the young, women and children, none were spared in the slaughter. Fierce *golok*-wielding raiders sliced through everything in their path, decapitating those caught short-footed in the melee.

Shrill, bloodcurdling cries of *'Allahu Akbar! Allahu Akbar!'* filled the air, as flashing swords slashed through the multitude, the massacre continuing until none were left standing.

A group of terrified orphans discovered hiding under an upturned outrigger were hacked to death, their bodies left to rot under the midday sun, the blood stained sand immediately attracting plagues of flies. Mothers gathered their children, only to be cut down in their tracks as they attempted to flee. Without any real resistance, the carnage continued the slaughter accounting for thousands as the *Mufti Muharam* ran amok, sweeping all before them as they made their way along the narrow beach corridor towards the hotel.

When evening finally descended upon these fields of horror, there remained no sign of life. Their objective achieved, the soldiers had retreated back into the hills as ordered, where they regrouped, waiting for confirmation of their next target.

* * * *

AUSTRALIA - THE NORTHERN TERRITORY

Darwin Meteorological Station
Tropical Cyclone Warning Center

'The coastal areas of the Northern Territory, Western Australia and Queensland have always been subjected to tropical cyclones. It is for this reason that three Tropical Cyclone Warning Centers were located in Darwin, Perth, and Brisbane. Each of these centers is staffed by experienced specialist scientists and technical support staff. They have access to radar, satellite and computer systems, as well as the Bureau's network of automatic weather stations, some of which are located on offshore islands and reefs.' The resident specialist paused, looked at the school children, then continued.

'Now, you will ask, why is a cyclone dangerous?' He looked down at one of the young faces and smiled. 'Well, cyclones produce extreme wind conditions. Some of these exceed two hundred kilometers per hour.' One of the children towards the back whispered something about drivers in the Darwin to Alice Springs Cannonball road race reaching speeds in excess of that, and the specialist waited for the sniggering to die out before continuing.

'These winds can cause extensive damage. In fact, we know that people can be killed during such conditions.' He looked towards the inattentive child at the back and asked, 'Can you tell me the name of the cyclone which wiped out Darwin in 1974?' But before the child could answer, there was a response from the others. Almost in unison, they yelled, 'Tracy! Tracy!'

These children had been raised to understand cyclones. When Cyclone Tracy devastated the city during Christmas in 1974, many lives were lost, the damage to property - the worst in Australia's history. Had it not been for the U.S. submarine which mysteriously appeared from the trenches off

East Timor, and tying alongside Darwin Harbor the following day, there would not have been any power for weeks.

'That's right,' he responded. 'Does anyone know why we give these powerful forces, names?' He looked around the group, not really expecting an answer. Receiving students from different forms was one of the duties he enjoyed. 'No? Well, I'll tell you. We call them tropical cyclones and give them names when the winds reach gale force. Now that's pretty powerful, in anyone's book.' He continued to smile at the small sea of faces. 'We only get really worried about these when they threaten coastal or island communities. That's when we start a cyclone watch.' He could see that they were quickly losing interest.

'Then, when the winds build, and we think there is a chance that any of our communities might be affected, we issue a cyclone warning. By then, the cyclone has a name, we know how powerful the winds are, and everyone should know which way it's going.' The child at the rear of the class had, by now, totally lost interest and was distracting some of the others. He lifted his voice and moved towards the back of the room. Immediately he had their attention.

'You kids all live in the most affected zone in Australia. That's why you're here today. Cyclones can bring heavy rainfall, flooding, and even incredibly high tides.' He carried on, finishing on a high note when promising that at least one of their names would be given to a cyclone in the coming year. He always did this, and never missed to impress.

Towards the end of the afternoon, the specialist checked with the other Met offices in Exmouth, Onslow, Port Hedland and Broome. Satisfied that the coming weekend would not see him called out again, he left his Casuarina offices after picking up another case of beer and headed home where he knew his wife would be preparing their customary Friday barbecue for neighbors and friends.

* * * *

JAKARTA

Hamish

'There's nothing further we can do, Hamish. I'm sorry.' The U.N. senior representative for Indonesia apologized. 'Our hands are tied. Had she been a member of an United Nations' team we would not have had this difficulty.'

'What did the Indonesians say?' Hamish asked.

The senior officer became even more serious. 'To put it bluntly, they have much greater problems on their minds than to concern themselves with a missing American journalist.'

'Any suggestions?' Hamish asked, addressing the group sitting around discussing Mary Jo in the U.N. Jakarta offices. They had been helpful, making calls to Indonesian officials and offering advice. As an independent, apolitical body, Hamish knew that there was little else they could do except make inquiries on her behalf.

'Speak to someone at the American Embassy. She is, after all, a U.S. citizen.' He opened a directory and started searching for a number. 'I'll make the call for you if you wish,' he offered. Hamish nodded affirmatively, thanked the official and waited while arrangements were made. He then left the U.N. offices and drove to the U.S. Embassy where, having been cleared through security by well-armed Marines, he was escorted upstairs and introduced to a State Department liaison officer.

'We can't do much either, I'm afraid,' Hamish was told. 'In fact, I doubt if you could really claim that she is missing.' Hamish struggled to control his temper.

'Would it help if I gave you my statement on UNHCR letterhead?' This prompted a more favorable response. The career bureaucrat stopped tapping his fingers on the glass-topped table, and leaned forward as he spoke.

'That's not necessary. Miss Hunter is an American citizen and we do care.'

'Then why don't you do something!' Hamish snapped, the feeling of helplessness clouding his judgment.

'Mr. McLoughlin, I am not unsympathetic but try and understand our position. The country is teetering on collapse as we speak. Our Embassy has instructed American citizens to leave Indonesia. There's an army of murderous cutthroats pouring down from the hills threatening Bogor, and that's less than an hour from here. Miss Hunter is God knows where, out on the Indian Ocean, on a fishing boat you yourself have stated she boarded willingly. Mr. McLoughlin, what would you suggest we do?' There was an absence of sarcasm in the man's voice and Hamish knew that he had been unreasonable.

'I'm sorry,' he said, rising to his feet slowly. Everything ached and he desperately needed some rest. Hamish extended his hand, thanked the official and returned to his hotel to gather up the remainder of his personal effects. Following the advice issued by most foreign missions in Indonesia, he too left for the Sukarno-Hatta Airport and boarded one of the many aircraft charters organized to repatriate foreign nationals from the capital as it came under siege.

Chapter Twenty-five

Indian Ocean Joint Refugee Fleet

Lily

When the cheer went up piercing the noonday torpor, Lily cupped her hands around her eyes and peered in the direction others were pointing. There, on the horizon, she could see the advancing fleet, tears immediately filling her eyes with the sight.

'There are so many ships!' one on her boat cried in amazement.

'Even more than we first started with,' another said, the level of excitement continuing to rise as the first ships steamed to within several hundred meters. They watched as a smaller but faster craft broke away from the main body of ships and headed towards Lily's fleet. Several men jumped from the speed-boat and boarded the fishing boat belonging to her group's leader where they remained in conference for some minutes before returning to their own fleet.

There was an air of apprehension as Lily and her fellow travelers watched these activities, praying that all was in order and hoping that they would now join with the larger fleet. Lily heard what she thought to be a horn blast emanating from somewhere amongst the other boats and her heart lifted when she recognized that this had been the signal for her own ships to merge with the others. Within minutes they were under way, sailing parallel with the larger fleet, waving happily to those they had joined.

They were now less than six hundred miles west of Broome and would be standing on Australian soil before the end of the week.

* * * *

Mary Jo & Hani

Mary Jo watched with interest as a much smaller group of ships assumed position along her own fleet's port side. This far south, those in charge of her flotilla had all agreed that they were now out of danger, reasonably confident that the Indonesian Navy had discontinued their pursuit.

'*East Java fishing boats,*' she heard someone mutter, loudly.

'*They look like they have been waiting a long time,*' Hani said, now well enough to stand by herself and walk around the fishing boat unaided. Mary Jo continued to peer across at the closer ships. Their markings were quite different, and she could see that a number of the vessels had been subjected to fire. As they came even closer, Mary Jo observed the general appearance of the newcomers, concluding that these refugees had already been through some difficult moments. She waved and was rewarded with a number of lethargic responses. Mary Jo had taken photos of the new arrivals, using her telephoto lens to confirm her suspicions that this group had been at sea considerably longer than her own.

'*They're all Chinese,*' Budi said, matter-of-factly, and Mary Jo looked puzzled with the statement.

'*How can you tell?*' she asked, but Budi just smiled, then looked at his father. Mary Jo tried again. '*Are there many in our fleet that aren't Chinese?*'

Budi shook his head. '*Most of our group are also Chinese,*' he answered, and although she could tell that he was not comfortable with these questions, Mary Jo pressed ahead.

'*And you don't like the Chinese?*' she asked, her voice lowered.

'*They're all right,*' he replied, looking around to see if they were overheard.

'*Did you have any Chinese friends back in Sukabumi?*' Mary Jo noticed that Budi avoided her eyes when he responded.

'*Not many,*' he said, his voice becoming sullen. She looked at Hani, then back at Budi's father, and decided to let it go. But then Hani offered an opinion.

'*They are not liked,*' she said.

'*Why?*' Mary Jo asked, genuinely wishing to know more. She had discussed Indonesia's ethnic and racial differences with Anne in depth over the past two years and had always sensed that her assistant had held back. On other occasions, whenever Mary Jo had raised the issues with Indonesians of varying ethnic and social backgrounds, she had found considerable resistance to any open discussion regarding racism.

'*The Chinese control the shops, the businesses, everything!*' Hani replied, emphatically. '*We resent the power they have over us and their wealth. It is because of them that Indonesia now suffers as it does.*'

Mary Jo was surprised by her candor. *'Did you have any Chinese friends, Hani?'* she asked, curious when the young woman shook her head, shrugged, then said nothing more. There was an awkward silence and Mary Jo decided to let the subject drop, recognizing that Hani's small family of three were not all that comfortable amongst the others, experiencing for the first time in their lives what it was like to be part of a minority group. Later, Mary Jo broached the subject again when Hani asked about her work as a journalist.

'Do you think people outside Indonesia care about what's happening to my country?' Hani had asked. Mary Jo had given her some background, filling in time as the long, monotonous hours dragged by, each the same as the one before.

'I'm sure they do,' she replied.

'Why didn't they come and help us?'

'They did, in a way,' Mary Jo answered. *'They gave loans, billions of dollars in fact.'*

'No, I meant why didn't they come and help us stop the fighting?' Mary Jo squinted in the sun as she raised her head to look the younger woman directly in the eye.

'Whose side would they have taken, Hani?'

'Side?' she said, *'they shouldn't take sides, just stop the fighting, that's all.'* The naïve response brought a mirthless smile to Mary Jo's lips.

'But that wouldn't resolve anything,' she parried, *'would it?'*

'Why don't the Americans come and help,' she asked, sidestepping the question.

'Why should we?' Mary Jo challenged.

'You sent your soldiers to fight against Saddam, when he attacked other Moslems. Is it because of the oil?

'That was different, Hani,' she decided to explain, difficult as it was with her limited vocabulary. *'Saddam Husein has dangerous weapons, weapons that can kill many, many people. And it wasn't just the Americans who fought against Saddam. It was the United Nations.'*

'Isn't that the same thing?'

'No,' Mary Jo managed, mirth creeping into her response, *'but I agree that it often seems that way.'*

'Are you going to write about us?' Hani asked, changing the direction of the conversation again.

'You bet,' she smiled. *'The world is going to know all about you, and the others on these boats, I promise you,'* Mary Jo answered, emphatically.

'How?'

'Believe me, I'll make sure.'

'How will that help us?' Hani wanted to know.

'It probably won't. But at least it will help others.' Hani looked around at the other refugees.

'Why help them?' she asked, dropping her voice. 'They're Chinese!'

'Seems to me, Hani, they are the ones who really need the world to know what is happening.' Wishing to explore further, she took control of the conversation now. *'Their churches have been burned, their homes and shops destroyed, and many have been killed. How do you feel about that?'* Hani thought for a moment, then shrugged.

'Why should I feel guilty about what's happened to them? It was they who corrupted the nation.'

'How can you say that and believe it?' Mary Jo challenged again.

'Because it's true. At least they won't have any trouble when we arrive in Australia. Do you think we will also be permitted to stay?'

'I don't know, Hani, perhaps. Why do you think that you might have trouble?'

'If we were Chinese, they would let us stay,' she answered, confident that this was true. Hani waved to Budi and his father, standing at the far end of the vessel talking.

'How do you know that for sure?'

'It's true, Mary Jo. Many of us heard about the Australian Prime Minister's statement on radio. When the riots first broke out in Jakarta, the foreign press made it appear that only Chinese shops and people were being hurt by what was happening. He said that Australia would accept any Chinese from Indonesia who wanted to stay in Australia. Do you think that's fair?'

'Are you sure he really said that?'

'Yes. I'm sure. That's why we worry that, when we arrive, they will send us back.'

'I'm sure that if the others can stay, so will you, Hani,' Mary Jo tried to reassure her but could see from Hani's uncertain expression that she would remain troubled until after their arrival in Australia. Mary Jo felt disturbed by Hani's obsession that Chinese in her country had been given preferential treatment over the indigenous peoples. From her travels, she knew this to be untrue, for in every small town and village she had visited, Mary Jo had witnessed for herself the number of Chinese whose lives remained a difficult struggle. And now, having been at the sharp end of the murderous vigilante attacks, they were still to be blamed for being what they were.

She glanced around the overcrowded boat, uncertain as to who on board might fall into this category.

But try as she may, Mary Jo could not determine, simply by looking, who amongst those on board were of Chinese extraction, and who were not. Everybody had black hair. Although some may have commenced the voyage with slightly paler skin, exposure to the harsh conditions had soon remedied that. Deciding to let the conversation go for the time being, her energy sapped by the shortage of food and sleep, Mary Jo did as the others and slept during the midday heat, dozing off as the fishing-boat, in harmony with hundreds of others, hummed along slowly, making its way towards the Australian coast.

She slept, only to be awaken when someone shouted, warning another vessel that it was in danger of coming too close, alongside. Mary Jo stirred, climbed to her feet and went to the rear of the boat to wait her turn to use the open toilet which, by now, she had mastered carrying out her ablutions without embarrassment or shame.

Then, she inspected her equipment, noting that the scribble-pads were full and now had nothing left on which to write. Hopefully, they would reach landfall soon. Mary Jo cast her eyes ahead, hoping that their captain's information was accurate and that they would arrive at their destination in less than a week. Then she looked back at Hani and the others, pondering what might await these people who had fled their homeland, in search of racial and religious tolerance in Australia.

* * * *

Canberra - Australia

The Prime Minister considered the statement, then directed his question to the Defence Minister.

'Where is the American Seventh Fleet at this time?'

'Still steaming around south of the Philippines,' the politician replied. 'They will not intervene unless we make a specific request for their help.' Those at the meeting had always believed that, when tested, the ANZUS Treaty might prove embarrassing to the Americans, considering their vested interests in countries to Australia's north.

'What do we have in Darwin?'

'We have two frigates already standing by off the Northern Territory. These are the 'Darwin,' and the 'Melbourne'. As for destroyers, well the 'Hobart' will arrive some time today but the 'Perth' and 'Brisbane' will not get there until the end of the week. The Prime Minister knew that these ships were all equipped with state of the art guided missile systems. 'As for patrol boats,' the Cabinet Minister continued, 'we now have eight stationed permanently in Darwin, four on temporary duty in Broome and another two operating from Port Hedland.' The Fremantle Class Patrol Boats had been more visible than other Australian navy ships, as these were deployed to patrol Australia's extensive northern coastline, and Economic Exclusion Zone.

'How do they stand up against the Indonesian ships?' the Prime Minister asked, wondering how the country could afford such a fleet, when even Australia struggled to maintain such a small navy.

'Well, satellite intelligence shows that the Indonesian fleet consists of three frigates and five corvettes. The latter are all part of the former East German Fleet purchased after the Soviet collapse. These are not equipped with any surface-to-surface missile systems but the frigates are a different story. We have identified all three ships. Two are former Van Speijk class from the Netherlands. They are armed with Harpoon surface-to-surface missiles and the third is a former Yugoslav Fatahillah class ship armed with Exocet missiles. We all know from the Falklands what these can do.' He turned and looked at the others present, as if soliciting support for his next statement. 'I believe that the Indonesian ships are well enough armed to represent a real threat but our ships could deal with them if a confrontation occurs.'

The majority of those present nodded sagely in concurrence, believing that had it been the Indonesians' intention to threaten, then they would have sent their entire fleet.

'Then you agree with the Director, here?' the Prime Minister asked, indicating the security chief. His earlier assessment suggested that the Indonesian warships, identified by satellite as traveling towards Australia, had been deliberately delayed until the massive refugee fleet was closer to Australia's shores.

'Yes, I'm afraid that I do,' the Minister confirmed. 'The picture would be clearer if only we could determine what's really happening between Muis and Winarko. If these ships are under Abdul Muis' control, then we have a most serious problem. If they're not, then what are they up to? Winarko certainly would not have sent them down in our direction without first alerting us as to his intentions. That's why I believe that these warships are part of some ploy Muis has initiated.'

'But why only send less than half of their ships?' the Foreign Affairs Minister interrupted.

'Because they don't want to show their hand,' the intelligence chief offered.

'Let's face it, we're not about to send our navy out to destroy the refugee ships en masse, are we?' he asked, rhetorically. 'It would be unwise for us to ignore the possibility that there could be a significant number of well armed, devout *Mufti Muharam* followers amongst the refugees. If the warships are, as we believe, under Abdul Muis' orders, then we must assume that he has decided to take advantage of the mass exodus, to gain a foothold on Australian soil. We estimate that the refugees could number as many as one hundred thousand in this wave. What if Muis has been able to disguise say, two or three thousand of his faithful followers amongst the others. I doubt if all those on board are Chinese. It is my department's assessment that the Indonesian Navy ships are there as escorts, that with the landing of such an incredible number Abdul Muis would have established a foothold without so much as firing a shot. He is very clever, and we should not underestimate this man.' He looked around to see if they had understood and, from their grim expressions, it was clear that they had. For many years Australians had been relatively ignorant regarding their neighbors in Asia. When the man on the street finally recognized that they lived in a Moslem world, with the largest Islamic population of almost two hundred million breathing down their necks, they panicked.

'Then we agree that a full blockade is the only answer?' the Prime Minister asked, seriously concerned with the possibility that fundamentalist Moslems now threatened Australia's security. He had graphic images in his mind of how far the militant Moslems could go once they had established a foothold on Australian soil. The events of the past year had demonstrated that the *Mufti Muharam* had little respect for other than their own. The last major blood-letting during the mid-Sixties had resulted in some half a million Indonesians being killed during the anti-Communist sweeps. Conservative estimates had the *Mufti Muharam's* running toll at in excess of three million, most of whom were of Chinese descent.

His Cabinet agreed unanimously. The country's military would immediately go to full alert, with the navy being directed to fire upon the approaching refugee fleet should it ignore warnings to return to Indonesian waters.

* * * *

Darwin Meteorological Station

Tropical Cyclone Warning Centre

The resident specialist looked out through the haze, pleased to be inside the comfortable air-conditioned offices in Darwin's northern suburbs, protected from the Territory's sweltering conditions. On his way from the parking lot he sensed something in the air, his senses suggesting that conditions were changing, his empiric knowledge warning not to assume anything until the data had been reviewed. The Darwin T.C.W.C. had been tracking the rapidly changing conditions which had originated well out in the Timor Sea. The storm build up had then moved to the east, away from his sector, into the Indian Ocean where it had gained momentum.

A Cyclone Watch had been issued to coastal and island communities earlier in the day, and had now been upgraded to a Cyclone Warning, as gales were now expected along the western coastline within twenty four hours. These warnings would be updated at three-hourly intervals, and would also be closely monitored by Australian defense establishments in the area. The specialist had observed the increase in military activity over the past twenty-four hours, assuming this to be somehow connected with the sudden influx of Indonesian fishing boats carrying refugees from the strife torn islands. For a few brief moments he reminisced, recalling the holidays he had spent in Bali, just two hours to the west, wondering if the holiday destination would manage to sustain their culture against the onslaught of Java's determined Moslems.

His thoughts returned to the matter at hand. He was aware that the navy's patrol boats had been working overtime to discourage the continuous flow of Indonesian boats entering Australia's exclusion zone, with R.A.A.F. Orions maintaining aerial reconnaissance to support their efforts. With the possibility of a cyclone developing, it was imperative that aviation and shipping be kept aware of any changes in wind and sea conditions.

He turned as one of his fellow officers knocked on the open, glass-paneled door and entered.

'This one's getting serious, Ross,' the woman said, handing him the hourly update. 'Upgraded and coming back our way.' The word 'FLASH' was emblazoned across the top of the message, an alert issued when major changes occur such as the unexpected movement towards the coast or rapid intensification of tropical storms. She knew that the contents of this message would no doubt require station staff to be retained on duty around the clock to broadcast cyclone information.

'Perth?' he asked, and she nodded. The Tropical Cyclone Warning Center in the Western Australian capital was responsible for coverage of the Indian Ocean, west of the line where the Darwin T.C.W.C.'s sector ended at 125 degrees longitude. He read the report, a sardonic smile crossing his lips.

'Cyclone Pauline?' knowing that the naming of cyclones were not at all random. The Meteorological Bureau prepared lists which were followed explicitly. Then, as he read on, he whistled softly.

'Category Four?' but his associate knew that no response was required. Categories of cyclones range from 'One' for weak cyclones, to 'Five' for the most severe. The devastating Cyclone Tracy which had struck Darwin at Christmas more than a quarter of a century before had been rated 'Four'.

'Yes,' she replied, 'and turning back towards Dampier.' Tropical storms in the Australian region always exhibited more erratic paths than cyclones in other parts of the world. This, coupled with the fact that these dangerous conditions could change at any time turning sharply, sometimes even following a looped course, made forecasting more than a science. They walked to the wall map together, tracing the newly named threat with their fingers. Both knew that Cyclone Pauline would bring very destructive winds and dangerously high tides. Another phenomenon they would have to consider was the almost certain threat of a storm surge. These raised domes of water which measure from sixty to eighty meters across, and up to five meters higher than normal tide levels, were of immense danger to low lying coastal areas, should they occur at the same time as a high tide.

'Okay then,' Ross sighed, returning to his desk, 'tell the others,' then went about preparing the text of the cyclone warning for his own sector.

Across the city, and deeply engrossed in their own activities, Northern Command communications officers busied themselves alerting navy ships and boats to the changed conditions, recalling the entire fleet. Patrol boats were ordered to their closest ports, warships were instructed to sail further north, and all R.A.A.F. aircraft were grounded. In Canberra, the general consensus amongst senior military officers had been that the Indonesian ships would be in complete disarray, trapped in the cyclonic conditions. They also agreed that the Australian blockade would most probably now fail, given that the tropical storm would no doubt spread the huge fleet across an area impossible to police once conditions permitted. Signals containing their new concerns were flashed to all northern military stations, ordering immediate resumption of aerial and sea reconnaissance following Cyclone Pauline's abatement.

* * * *

THE REFUGEE FLEET

Mary Jo slipped then fell crashing her knee against the wooden deck as the ship pitched forward, then sideways, the captain unable to maintain speed in the rough conditions.

'Hold on!' she heard Budi call, catching a face full of sea water just as another wave crashed over the side. Mary Jo was frightened. The fishing boat did not seem that seaworthy as it bobbed around, tossed in all directions.

The weather had changed quickly, catching the inexperienced off-guard. Before the storm, humidity had been exceptionally high, most passengers electing to remain sitting propped wherever they could find a comfortable position amongst the over crowded vessels as they proceeded through the calm seas. Mary Jo watched disinterestedly, as the ships cut their way slowly through the water, the low, oily swells lulling all into a false feeling of tranquillity. Out of the corner of her eye, she noticed Hani and Budi dozing, their arms wrapped around each other, oblivious to the heat.

Following daybreak, high, feathery cirrus clouds passed overhead and, a few hours later, Mary Jo observed the build up of dark, thunderstorm clouds on the horizon, alarmed when these approached with noticeable speed. Seas began to rise, whipped into greater motion by strong winds and the captains widened the distance between the vessels in the interests of safety. Then, as the weather deteriorated further, the skies darkened, the winds increased in intensity and waves of incredible heights towered threateningly over the fleet.

'Tie everything down!' the order went out, and amongst the frenzied activity possessions were swept overboard, lost forever in the turbulent seas. As the winds increased in velocity, blinding rain lashed the fleet, reducing visibility even further. Mary Jo heard Hani cry out in fear when a wave crashed over their vessel, lifting those on board, before tossing them back cruelly onto the hard deck.

'Budi! Help me!' Someone screamed and Mary Jo turned in time to see Budi grab for his father's hand, the older man struggling under the deluge of sea water swirling through the boat. Mountainous, white crested waves climbed to fifteen meters and more, before crashing over the fleet, extracting their deadly toll. Fishing boats ruptured, breaking up upon impact, while others were spun out of control, crashing against each other, spilling their terrified passengers into the raging seas.

'Look out!' Mary Jo cried out but she was too late. A wall of water collapsed against their ship throwing her cruelly against the wheel-house, then dragged her along the deck as receding water threatened to carry all overboard.

And so it continued. For more than eight hours, the fleet was buffeted cruelly by the cyclonic conditions, with winds reaching two hundred and twenty kilometers per hour. Twenty-meter waves continued to savage the fleet, washing many to their deaths, their cries drowned before others could come to their aid. Temperatures dropped and the beating continued, Mary Jo's vessel badly damaged when struck by another, tossed together by the giant seas.

Then, mysteriously, it seemed that the refugees' prayers had been answered. The wind fell, the waves sloshed around in a confused state and rain ceased as the fleet entered the cyclone's eye. Sunlight streamed down through the funnel briefly, highlighting the black, swirling mass of clouds strung all around the horizon. Believing they had been delivered from the threat of a watery death, the bruised and battered survivors clung to each other unaware that they were still in peril.

'Look! Over there!' Someone shouted but most were too exhausted to care.

'It's a warship!' the cry swept through the fleet. Mary Jo rose wearily to her feet, and peered across the still turbulent sea, her eyes focusing immediately on the tall, gray, steel hulled warship as it ploughed through the scattered flotilla.

Screeching, tearing screams of timbers being torn asunder cracked across the foam tipped waves, as the first of the three thousand ton frigates came into full view. The Indonesian warship drove through the center of the fleet, carving a deadly path directly across Mary Jo's ship's bow, sinking more than twenty of the wooden hulled fishing boats in its path as it attempted to slow. The frigate's captain signaled the other warships in his group which were still wrestling with cyclonic bands, more than twenty miles astern. The remaining frigates and corvettes changed course accordingly, swinging wide to avoid the danger of collision.

At first, seamen aboard the fishing boats assumed that the Indonesian ship was from the Eastern Fleet and had stumbled across their flotilla by accident. But later, when almost an hour passed and the remaining warships came into view, they realized that they were doomed.

In total disarray, those in control of the refugee fleet panicked, breaking away from the main body of ships. Within minutes, and without the benefit of the more experienced seamen, many of the fishing boats lost direction amidst the fear and confusion. Once again, the sky became dark and the fierce winds returned, lashing all with blinding rain as the cyclone's eye passed over the fleet, and Mary Jo feared that they would all die, trapped in nature's devastating cauldron. The cyclone returned with a vengeance unparalleled to anything she had ever witnessed before that day, the towering walls of water smashing, crushing, then sweeping terrified refugees into the unforgiving sea where they perished, many trapped between the timbers of pilot-less ships.

As the powerful winds dispersed the ships in each and every direction, the storm tossed warships kept their distance, their captains recognizing that they were already at risk and could achieve little in these dangerous conditions. Without exception, none of these officers had ever experienced such gigantic seas and were astonished with the severity of the cyclone's force. Centered around the equator, most of Indonesia's thirteen thousand islands lie only a few hundred miles to the north of the primary cyclone zone. Although the country experiences storms in the extreme, the powerful forces which unpredictably ravage Northern Australian communities between November and April every year rarely occur in the archipelago. Incidences of freak cyclones occurring in the easterly areas surrounding Timor and Flores had only been evidenced twice in more than twenty years and there were none amongst these crews who had witnessed either event.

Naval captains struggled to maintain control over ships and crews. As mumbling amongst the lower deck grew, the threat of outright mutiny finally forced six of the warships to turn for home. Recognizing the futility of the exercise, another followed within the hour, leaving the frigate which had earlier burst through the refugee fleet standing alone. Although as weary as any in the crew, the captain maintained watch through the night, fearful of losing his ship in these unfamiliar waters. The frigate continued to roll dangerously, the high seas challenging even the most seasoned sailors on board. But the crew remained loyal, anticipating even greater rewards now the other ships had withdrawn. When weather permitted, boats filled with armed sailors would be lowered into the sea, the defenseless refugees unable to prevent what would happen next. Their minds filled with gold, those aboard the frigate waited for the winds to subside, impatient for the slaughter to begin.

The cyclone's fury continued, the nightmarish conditions already too great for many in the fleet. Inundated, and unable to recover as wave after wave beat upon their ships, almost half the fleet was destroyed before morning, the darkness blanketing the thousands of bodies swept before the churning sea.

Mary Jo's boat was driven under by one freak wave, then rose up again only to be hit by another. She lost her footing countless times, slipping and sliding as the deck underfoot suddenly disappeared, then slammed back with brutal force, driving her to her knees. She knew the likelihood of being swept overboard, as had most of her fellow passengers was increasing, her strength now beginning to fade. Mary Jo crawled towards the stern, clinging frantically to a well-secured rope. She wiped the stinging spray from her eyes and saw a couple struggling to keep hold of each other. The third member of their family, Budi's father, fell heavily, and cried out.

'Get into the wheel-house!' she shouted at Hani, but the young woman was too terrified to move. Mary Jo slipped as the boat swayed dangerously, regained her balance, then grabbed Hani by the arm and dragged her into the one man wheel-house just as a thunderous wave crashed onto the deck, washing Budi, then his father, overboard. Hani tried to scramble after them but Mary Jo held her back.

'Help them!' Hani screamed, but in that instant they were gone. Both men were doomed by the weight of their gold belts, sucked down into their watery graves before either could release the weighty metal tied around their waists. At that moment, her attention distracted, Mary Jo fell forward, crying out in pain when her shoulder struck the engine controls.

'No!' Hani choked, realizing that Budi was gone. Mary Jo positioned herself on the loose boards set directly above the diesel below, then lowered herself into position, bracing herself with both feet against the timbers. Gritting her teeth in pain when the boat rocked savagely under the weight of another crushing wave, she tugged at the smaller woman, forcing her close to her side.

'Stay here!' she ordered, shaking Hani with one hand.

'Mary Jo, let me go!' Hani shrieked, her head banging savagely against Mary Jo's as the boat jerked, then dipped, before being tossed aimlessly into a deep trough.

'They're gone, Hani! They're gone! There's nothing you can do!'

'Let me go!' Hani cried again, struggling to free herself of Mary Jo's firm grip.

'Stop it!' Mary Jo shouted, her command lost when another dreadful blow sent a shudder through the badly damaged ship. Hani made another attempt to break free but Mary Jo's open hand flashed, striking the terrified girl sharply. Stunned, her mouth fell open, her eyes wide, then she burst uncontrollably into tears while clinging fiercely to Mary Jo.

'We're going to die!' she whimpered, her choking sobs buried against the other woman's chest.

'We're not going to die!' Mary Jo admonished, squeezing Hani closer. Below, she could hear the terrifying noises of timber beams groaning. Like others in this fleet, these ships had been designed for coastal waters and more moderate seas. *'It's okay, Hani, I've got you now,'* she said reassuringly, still holding her firmly.

'I'm cold,' Hani complained, and Mary Jo knew this was not just the shock. She too had begun to shiver. Wet, tired, and the temperature below

what they had become accustomed to, Mary Jo knew they might not have much longer. Her shoulder ached and when she attempted to lift her right arm, bolts of excruciating pain flashed through her body.

'Shh!' Mary Jo whispered hoarsely, while stroking Hani's head. Then she whispered again, her attempts to console the Indonesian girl failing as Hani quietly slipped into shock.

More than eight hours passed before Mary Jo dared climb from the battered enclosure to inspect her surrounds. The cyclone had diminished in intensity during the darkness of night, and turned towards the Australian coastline and Broome, high on the Western Australian coast. Deeply distressed, Mary Jo refused to believe that there were no other survivors on board their battered vessel. There had been more than sixty commence the voyage together on this boat. Amongst them there were eight children. A thought crossed her mind that some may have taken refuge below, in the small hold where supplies had been stored. Then she discovered that the hold cover had been smashed away, the tell tale sounds of water swishing around below giving rise to new fears. They were sinking, she knew, then wondered how far they might be from help.

Mary Jo's body ached all over but her earlier fears that her collarbone had been fractured or even broken could now be dismissed. She inspected the injury, grimacing in pain as her fingers touched exposed bone, grateful that her fall had not been more serious.

Morning arrived, bringing with it choppy seas and gray skies, the wind strength sufficient to cause discomfort. Mary Jo climbed painfully to her feet, relieved to find that Hani was conscious although uncommunicative. Mary Jo knew it was imperative that they take stock of their situation, then decide what course of action they might take. Without food or water, she knew their chances were slim. As her now rudderless ship spilled from one wave to the next, she caught occasional glimpses of another vessel and decided to signal for help.

An hour later, when she found herself with Hani standing in ankle deep sea water with waves washing precariously over the deck, Mary Jo fought rising panic. She screamed out, her voice carrying across the waves to the solitary figure she could clearly see on the other ship but, incredibly, her pleas for assistance were ignored.

'Can you help us?' she tried again and again, each time with a similar response. Mary Jo refused to give up. She brushed spray from her face, mystified by the unresponsive soul standing almost statuesque in pose, not one hundred meters away. It was as if the other person was deaf or perhaps traumatized by the cruel passage.

'Please! We need your help!' she called again, her voice fading with the effort. Mary Jo knew she could not depend on their boats drifting closer together. If anything, she feared that the distance would grow, the possibility of deliverance fading with the strong currents.

'Hello!' Mary Jo screamed, one more time. *'Please help us!'* Then, suddenly, the other figure waved, and Mary Jo yelled with delight, waving her left arm furiously.

* * * *

Lily

Bloodied from numerous falls and disorientated from being knocked unconscious in the wheel-house, Lily remained huddled inside the seriously damaged ship, recognizing that she was alone. In the dark, storm filled night, as crushing seas relentlessly beat down upon her flimsy vessel, Lily had managed to find temporary refuge inside the compact, partially protected quarters. She was grateful to the old seaman who had dragged her inside the three-sided wheel-house, acknowledging that she owed the man her life. Now, he was gone as well, washed overboard while attempting to salvage something from the hold.

Deprived of food and water, her mind became clouded with the knowledge that her vessel must surely sink, having taken on far too much water during the fierce storm. Exhausted, her will to continue weakened by the punishment her body had endured, Lily curled her bruised and aching limbs under her chin and prayed. As wave upon wave crashed down upon the fishing boat tossing her body cruelly around the cramped space, she cried out in anguish, pleading that her ordeal would now end. The storm progressed, her mind drifting in and out of consciousness, carrying Lily through the dark morning hours to when she awoke, startled to discover that her nightmare was terrifyingly real.

While she slept, the tropical cyclone which had so ravaged her fleet, had moved on, now dumping record levels of rain across the barren north-western areas of Australia. The rough seas and fierce winds continued to abate through the early morning hours, providing Lily with the opportunity to drag herself to her feet inside the wheel-house, where she stood groggily staring at the gray, misty world outside.

She felt cold but remained inside, still uncertain as to what she should do next. Lily placed her hand on the greasy, engine controls, then peered down into the compartment where the four-cylinder diesel stood, awash in sea-water. She checked the battery as she had observed the seaman do so many times before, her heart falling when there was no response. She checked for supplies and found these spoiled. Apart from a number of near empty water containers floating around inside the ship, Lily had no remaining rations to keep her alive.

By mid-morning, visibility had improved dramatically and Lily was shocked to see that her ship had either drifted away from the main body of the fleet, or very few others had survived the storm. She watched as another fishing-boat floated aimlessly nearby, concerned when she saw the two survivors on board. Alone, Lily felt vulnerable. The rain water sloshing around in the twenty-liter, plastic jerry-can out of sight in the hold would, Lily knew, keep her alive for but a few more days. They outnumbered her and, in her weakened condition, she would not be able to defend herself in the event they attacked.

Gradually, their ship drifted closer and Lily became even more anxious, fearing that they might board. When the taller of the two began calling out, she refused to acknowledge, convinced that she would be better off alone. Besides, she could see that the other vessel was dangerously low in the water. This would mean that they would soon disappear altogether and that would be that.

But when their vessels drifted even closer, Lily rubbed her weary eyes and stared at the distressed survivors on the other ship again. She could clearly see that the larger woman had fair hair.

'Please help us!' she heard the voice call again, and this time Lily waved in response, stunned with the discovery that there were foreigners amongst the refugees.

* * * *

DARWIN -AUSTRALIA

Hamish

Hamish McLoughlin remained inside the MGM Casino Hotel, looking dismally out across the wind swept sea as tall palms swayed to and fro in the foreground, bending excessively under the gale force winds. The high-wire fence strung along the beach around the hotel to prevent the intrusion of crocodiles stood unyielding, and Hamish turned from the turbulent scene, sick to his stomach with the thought that Mary Jo was out there, somewhere, and he could do nothing to help.

He went to the bedside phone and dialed the number again, his sense of frustration further exacerbated when connected to a recorded message at the

Bureau of Meteorology. Hamish slammed the receiver down heavily, cursing systems which interfaced machines with those in their time of need.

He had arrived late the evening before, having boarded a flight from Singapore. There, he had been advised by the British High Commission's Defense Attaché that satellite surveillance had, indeed, established that a sizable fleet of fishing boats had been identified, heading for the north Australian coast.

When pressed, the British colonel had contacted his counterpart in the Australian mission and confirmed that this was the very same fleet which had departed from the area identified as Pelabuhan Ratu on the south Java coast. His spirits lifted, Hamish had jumped on the first plane for Darwin, acting on advice given by the consulate authorities in Singapore. There, he had expected to charter a plane and go looking for the fleet himself and, once within striking distance, intended to persuade one of the deep-sea charter captains to take him out to search for his woman.

But Cyclone Pauline had interfered with these plans and now Hamish was grounded in Darwin, depressed by the impotency of his situation. He turned to the television, played with the remote control until finding the CNN broadcast, then slumped unhappily into a cane wicker chair. The repetitive news program with obvious American bias continued its global coverage of current events, with Hamish almost missing the comment regarding the Indonesian warships. Immediately, he became more attentive, his face becoming grim with what he heard, his thumb punching the volume button as he listened to the CNN presenter.

> "And to confirm earlier reports, it seems that the massive exodus of refugees attempting to cross from the Indonesian island of Java to Northern Australia has been intercepted by warships. Information bulletins, based on unconfirmed satellite reports, suggest huge losses amongst the refugees. Cyclonic weather conditions continue to hinder rescue attempts, adding to the catastrophe which has some analysts now lifting earlier estimates to more than fifty-thousand lost when the cyclone struck. Viewers may remember that more than twenty-five years ago, that part of our globe was subjected to another devastating cyclone which hit the Australian coastline..."

Hamish sat staring at the television screen, numbed by this news. He leaned forward, grasping his head in despair, fighting the turmoil inside as images of Mary Jo fighting for her life, cluttered his mind.

* * * *

INDIAN OCEAN - WEST OF AUSTRALIA

Satisfied, the Indonesian captain passed the binoculars to the officer alongside. It was apparent that the main body of the refugee fleet had not weathered the cyclone too well. This would make their mission far more difficult and time consuming. He had hoped to find at least three, even four hundred vessels in close formation. Instead, the group off his starboard numbered considerably less than that.

'Boarding parties?' the captain inquired. The frigate had located a string of fishing boats, obvious survivors from the original refugee fleet.

'Boarding parties all mustered, sir.' The sailors had been assembled for at least an hour, waiting for the order to lower their boats.

'Away boarding parties!' the captain ordered.

'Aye aye, sir. Away boarding parties,' the officer of the watch repeated. A number of Gemini rubber dinghies and Zodiacs were swung out on davits and lowered into the sea. Each of the small craft carried six, well armed sailors, all eager for their share of what lay hidden in the ships ahead. Within minutes, they were making their way through the calm water towards the scattered fleet.

They boarded the first vessel, quickly dispensing with the unarmed passengers once rings and other valuables had been surrendered. The sounds of automatic fire carried for miles across the sea, striking fear in the refugees' hearts as one by one, the Indonesian sailors boarded their vessels, dealing brutally with those on board. Within the first hour, more than thirty fishing boats had been left in bloody disorder, the raiders swiftly executing the entire complement of each ship they attacked, having relieved those on board of everything of value. Bodies were left where they fell, the few who threw themselves into the sea in desperation were shot as they attempted to swim away.

The viciousness of the sailors' actions grew from their disappointment in the value of their haul. For most of the past week, ship-board gossip had estimates of the bounty they might find grossly disproportionate to what, in reality, many of the refugees had carried on their journey. Incensed by the discovery that there were but few gold bars to be found, the boarding parties showed no mercy, murdering all without exception. Ear rings were ripped from lobes, ring-bearing fingers hacked from hands and, on one ship, an old woman's gold teeth were bludgeoned from her mouth with gun butts as she lay dying. Unarmed, the refugees could offer no resistance, most dying, cut down by automatic fire within the first moments as they kneeled in prayer, some bludgeoned to death while terrified children looked on. Then, their turn followed, the seamen leaving none behind who might bear witness against them.

By dusk, more than one hundred fishing boats had been raided, their silent, bloody cargoes, evidence of the brutality inflicted that day. More than a thousand refugees had been slaughtered, the booty recovered in no way commensurate with the frigate captain's expectations. Disillusioned by the results, he issued orders that raids were to continue with first light, determined to fill his ship's coffers before rejoining his own command.

* * * *

Chapter Twenty-Six

Mary Jo & Hani

Not twenty miles to the east of the Indonesian warship, Mary Jo's boat was starting to founder as it took on more water. She raised herself to full height, winced painfully, then looked out across at the other vessel.

'Hani, can you swim?' Mary Jo asked, shaking the young woman slightly.

'Swim?' she replied, her mind elsewhere.

'Our boat is sinking, Hani. We must swim over to that other ship.'

'Swim?' she muttered, distantly. Hani stared at Mary Jo as if she were mad. *'No. I don't wish to swim,'* with which, she brushed her hair back with one hand. Mary Jo frowned. The distance between the two boats had grown marginally and, judging by the condition of her own vessel, she knew that little time remained for any attempt to swim to safety. She looked up at the late afternoon sky. It would be dark in a few hours and Mary Jo knew that it would be better to take their chance now, while they could still at least see the other vessel. Her shoulder still hurt like hell and she was not all that confident that she could make it to the other ship with Hani in tow. Mary Jo called out, across the widening gap, to the other survivor.

'Can you swim?' she shouted, but when there was no response she knew that they were now out of hearing range. Her eyes scanned the horizon. There were other ships but these were impossibly out of reach. She turned back to Hani, again.

'We must swim to the other boat, Hani.' Mary Jo insisted, taking her by the hand. They had nothing which would support their attempt. The fishing boat was devoid of anything except what was left of the battered hull and twisted wheel-house. Her cameras and film had been lost, her

photographic records dating from when she first set foot on the fleet, washed away before she realized these were gone. Hani stared at Mary Jo vacantly, permitting her to take her hand.

'Hello!' she shouted again, ensuring that the other person understood her intentions. Satisfied that they were being watched, she took Hani forward and plunged into the sea before Hani realized what was happening. She screamed in terror as her head went under, immediately fighting to escape Mary Jo's firm grip on her wrist, thrashing around in fear.

'Let me go!' she spluttered, salt water filling her mouth. *'Let me go!'* she managed again, this time striking with her free hand, hitting Mary Jo on her injured shoulder. Shocks of pains caused her to gasp, swallowing enough salt water to make her choke but she maintained her grasp on Hani's arm. By now, their boat had drifted and when Hani became aware of this she screamed as panic took hold, and started kicking as she had once been shown.

The current was strong and Mary Jo's energy was soon sapped as she struggled to drag Hani behind without the aid of either arm. She kicked, and continued to do so, soon recognizing that they were making very little headway. The ocean swell lifted them up, then down, then up again and she caught the outline of the other boat ahead. Mary Jo set her mind swimming now with her legs kicking in frog-like motion, similar to what she had practiced a thousand times before, when breast-stroking through her college pool.

A small wave caught them unawares, causing both to swallow water. Hani struggled and for a moment she managed to break free. Mary Jo grasping her by the leg, then the waist, slapped her face with as much force as she could muster, then grabbed the stunned woman under the chin, gaining more freedom of movement as she returned to her challenge. Another few demanding minutes passed and Mary Jo was forced to rest, treading water while holding tightly onto her charge. As a wave lifted them again, her heart fell when she saw that the other ship was no closer than before, and for the first time Mary Jo was tempted to let go and save herself.

* * * *

Lily

As fatigue set in, tempting Mary Jo to go it alone, Lily watched the foreign woman struggling with her companion. She judged the distance from her boat, and although she believed that this would be an easy swim for her, Lily was certain she would also perish if she attempted to save both. Lily could see that they were in extreme difficulties, expecting one or both to go under at any moment. When suddenly they stopped, then disappeared, her heart was pricked by a twinge of guilt and Lily prepared to lunge into the sea. She lowered the end of a short length of nylon into the water, checking first that this was still firmly tied to the cast-iron bollard, before feeding the rope through the hole in the bulwark.

She paused, picked her moment, then threw herself out, hitting the water with confident strokes, taking her to the desperate couple within minutes.

'She can't swim,' Mary Jo shouted, overcome with relief.

'Can you swim alone?' Lily asked, taking the Indonesian woman from the foreigner's grip, holding her head as the other had done.

'Yes, I can swim. But I have injured my shoulder.'

'I'll take her; you swim alone,' Lily yelled, kicking hard as she commenced the difficult swim with another in tow. They kicked and pulled their way through the unkind sea, Mary Jo resting from time to time, waiting to catch the outline of the ship to ensure they were swimming in the right direction. Finally, when they reached the battered vessel, Lily insisted they swim around to the other side, to take advantage of the ship's list. There, Lily passed Hani back to Mary Jo and climbed aboard, using the rope for leverage. Then, reaching down, she dragged the water logged Hani up in stages, finally falling heavily to the deck with her arms around the other's chest. She left her there, face down, returning to help Mary Jo.

'Here, take my hand,' Lily called, leaning down as far as she could reach. Their first attempts failed, as Mary Jo was just too heavy for the smaller woman.

'Put your foot here,' Lily indicated the hole where the rope passed through the bulwark. Mary Jo understood, and placed one foot on the well-worn, wooden hull, while waiting for the swell to lift her body. Then, when she felt herself being lifted, Mary Jo mustered her remaining reserves and pulled herself up and over the bulwark, collapsing painfully onto the deck. Exhausted, Lily held her head between her knees and threw up. Minutes passed and she looked up, then over at the women she helped save, lying curled on the deck.

'Terima kasih,' Mary Jo thanked Lily, having recovered her breath. *'My name is Mary Jo. And we both owe you our lives.'* She crawled over to where Lily sat, crouched on her knees and placed her good arm around the young Chinese woman, kissing her gratefully on the forehead.

'My name is Lily,' she said, pleased now with what she had done.

A groan caught their attention and Lily looked over, catching the eye of the other survivor who, with great difficulty, was struggling to her knees. For a moment Lily stared, then her mouth fell open in shock, her eyes locked with those of the woman she had just saved.

'Wha...?' Lost for words, Lily could not continue. Her face smothered with disbelief, she moved forward, then pulled back as old superstitions suddenly filled her with apprehension.

'What's wrong?' Mary Jo was surprised by the sudden change in Lily's expression, as the air suddenly cracked with hatred.

'No! It can't be true!' she said, shaking her head.

'What is it?' Mary Jo tried again.

'Hani? Are you Hani Purwadira?' Lily challenged, using the more familiar Jakarta dialect. She waited for some sign of recognition, now almost certain that this puffy-faced woman she had just dragged from the ocean was General Purwadira's daughter. *'Is it really you, Hani?'* She asked again. Mary Jo watched with growing concern, looking first from one, then to the other, unable to follow what was taking place.

Hani tilted her head to one side, her face covered with quizzical expression.

'Who are you?' she asked, the curtains covering her mind suddenly lifting, the shock of near drowning jolting her back to reality. Hani rubbed her eyes with wet hands, then looked again.

'What's going on?' Mary Jo interrupted, observing the exchange between both young women closely. Again, she was ignored.

'Hani, it's me,' Lily said, confused by what she now felt. Bitter memories came flooding back and she recalled, with great clarity, the events which had followed the last time they had seen each other and the resulting recriminations.

'I'm... sorry, but.. I don't understand.' Hani responded. Then, as signs of recognition triggered her own memory, Hani's hands went to her face in shock. *'Is that you, Lily?'* Hani asked, searching the other's face for verification. Lily sucked in a short, quick breath, startled by this confirmation. She looked at Mary Jo, then back to the woman who had once been her friend.

'My God,' Lily said, her voice but a whisper, *'it really is you?'* and climbed unsteadily to her feet. *'What are you doing here?'* Mary Jo was now completely puzzled by what was taking place.

With great difficulty, Hani rose also, shakily holding to the side of the ship.

'Lily..?' she whispered, confused and bewildered by the other's presence. The physically demanding ordeal of past weeks had taken its toll. Hani started to waver precariously as she staggered towards Lily, reaching her as she fainted, falling dead weight into her rescuer's surprised arms.

It was then Mary Jo became aware of the ship's list and the cause for the way the vessel sat so low in the water. She crawled across to the open hold and looked down, then back at Lily.

'Yes,' she said, softly, and without emotion, *'we're also sinking,'* with which she moved out from under Hani's seemingly lifeless form and crawled across to sit beside the American woman.

* * * *

Hamish

'But she could be anywhere, for chrissakes!' the voice at the other end of the line argued. 'Sorry, love to take ya money, mate,' the charter captain offered, 'but I really don't think you're gonna achieve much without something more definite.' Satellites crossing the disaster scene had difficulty identifying anything due to cloud.

'I realize that there's no way of knowing which group of boats she might be with,' Hamish tried, desperate that this owner would agree. He had worked his way through the registered charter companies, none willing to venture out even though conditions had improved. 'Couldn't we just give it a try anyway?'

'Sorry, mate,' the man replied without hesitation, 'why don't you leave it to the navy? If she's out there, they'll find her,' he added, encouragingly.

Hamish thanked the skipper and hung up. Having run out of options, he felt the disappointment of defeat. He had phoned every government agency even remotely connected with shipping and aviation in his attempts to galvanize the authorities into action.

'Search and Air Rescue is under way,' he had been told. 'We have a number of Australian Navy ships on their way out there as we speak,' another officer advised. 'The search area covers an area greater than England, Scotland and Wales,' a miffed bureaucrat suggested officiously. By the time Hamish had finished his phone around, everyone in town knew of his presence and short temper. In the end, there was nothing else he could do, but wait. Hamish stepped through the open, sliding-door leading out onto the balcony, immediately regretting this decision. The temperature had climbed back to uncomfortable levels, the sticky conditions causing perspiration to appear within seconds. He looked up, shielding his eyes from the sun, feeling some comfort from the bright, cloudless sky, pleased at least that the cyclone had turned away from the refugee fleet, raising his hopes for Mary Jo's successful rescue.

* * * *

Mary Jo & Party

Mary Jo had never been one to be frightened of the dark but out on the ocean, the only sounds were those of slapping waves against their boat. She decided to encourage her new friend to talk. This had not been all that easy, Mary Jo sensing the younger woman's reluctance to enter into conversation. Finally, after some hours in close company, it became impossible for Lily to avoid responding to her questions. They talked, Mary Jo about how she became stranded on the trawler, while Lily listened, finally concluding that her own terrifying experience had been far more traumatic. Hani's presence on the boat had unsettled her considerably, confused by what she felt and angry that she had re-entered her life in such a manner.

Mary Jo had pressed on, hoping to pass time and reassure the young Chinese woman that they were of no threat to her. When Lily had explained her limited reserves of drinking water, Mary Jo had immediately understood her concerns. As a diversion, she engaged Lily in conversation, hoping this would ease whatever still bothered the young woman.

'So that's how you knew each other?' Mary Jo was responding to Lily's explanation regarding her relationship with Hani. Lily had not gone into any great detail and Mary Jo suspected that there was more to the story than had been told.

'Yes, we attended the same university.'

'Were you friends?' Mary Jo had asked, but when this received no response she tried again. *'Lily, were you friends at .....'*

'Shh!' Lily interrupted, *'what is that?'* Lily heard the strange, mixture of sounds coming towards them through the darkness, first. All three women were bundled together for warmth, with Hani placed safely in the middle.

They were immersed in mist. The wind had died and the sea, an eerie calm since night fell, provided the opportunity for Mary Jo and Lily to talk in whispers whilst Hani slept.

Mary Jo listened, the distant, mechanical hum immediately raising her hopes.

'It's another ship!' she shrieked, awakening Hani. *'Quick, get up!'*

'What's happening?' she asked, still groggy from her deep sleep. She sat up, assisted by the others, confused in the dark. *'Where am I?'* And then, *'I'm thirsty.'*

'You're safe. We'll get you some water in a moment.'

'Do you remember anything, Hani?' Lily asked, wishing they had some light.

'Lily?' Suddenly, it all came flooding back. She reached out to touch the shape which was Mary Jo. *'Mary Jo?'* she asked, finding her hand, fearing the tales of the sea goddess might be true.

'Yes, Hani, it's me. I need you to be fully awake, okay?'

'What's that noise?' Hani cocked her head in the dark, the engine sounding more prominent now as the frigate approached.

'It's a ship,' Lily answered, still straining to see if she could determine how close it might be. They all listened, the chugging sounds growing louder as the three thousand ton warship's massive propellers chopped their way through the night.

'It's definitely coming this way,' Lily said, her concern that they would not be seen now overshadowed by another and far more perilous threat. *'My god,'* she cried, suddenly afraid, *'what if they hit us?'* The thought had already crossed Mary Jo's mind. All three sat listening, trying to discern from which direction the danger might come.

'It's getting very close,' Mary Jo had to raise her voice, Hani's hand finding hers in the darkness. Suddenly, the fear of collision became very real as they were engulfed by an incredible noise and they strained, searching the darkness for lights, for the shape of the ship, anything which might tell them what was happening.

Without warning, the frigate was upon them, steaming dangerously close to the shipwrecked trio as it passed to within fifty meters. Rocked unexpectedly by the warship's bow wave, the women panicked, fearing they would be swamped by the sea.

'Help me!' Hani cried, terrified in the dark, the wave easily washing over the half-submerged boat. Mary Jo grabbed her arm and, in doing so, lost her own footing.

'I've got you!' she heard Lily shout, wondering if they would now go under. They waited and for a moment it seemed they would be safe.

'Hold on!' Mary Jo yelled, when the boat rocked violently, tossing them around in the passing warship's wake. It seemed that the nightmare would never end, the deck now listing at an alarming angle.

'We're sinking!' Lily shouted, scrambling higher up the inclined deck,

gripping a bollard with one hand, while hanging onto Hani with the other. *'Climb up here!'* Mary Jo's arm touched someone's feet and, using these as her guide, she pulled herself up to the others.

'Just hold on!' she insisted, spitting water between breaths. Caught off guard, she had almost lost contact with the boat in the darkness. Now, holding the nylon rope once again, her confidence returned as she managed to pull herself out of the water.

'We'll be okay,' Mary Jo spluttered, pain shooting through her shoulder. *'Just don't let go!'* Her feet found the raised, wooden lip running around the hold and she used this to support her weight. The ship groaned underneath, Mary Jo certain that it would slip under, she willed the broken hull to remain afloat.

When dawn arrived, the women's confidence was given a boost when they discovered a number of other fishing boats in their area. They watched these drift ever so slowly towards their own vessel, bewildered when it became apparent that these ships had been abandoned as at this distance with the bodies of those slaughtered by the Indonesian Navy hidden below the bulwarks, they could see no signs of life.

'Do you think they have already been rescued?' Lily asked, her heart sinking with this thought. There were now at least a dozen ships within view, all floating aimlessly, occasionally slapping into each other, the sound of groaning timbers adding to the weird spectacle.

'It's possible,' Mary Jo agreed. There was no point in giving the other two false hope. They continued to watch, praying that one would come to within striking distance of their water-logged vessel and, several hours later, they were given this chance.

'We can make it,' Lily assured them both. *'We could use the empty jerry-cans to keep you and Hani afloat.'* Mary Jo now understood why their own boat had not already sunk. These containers had provided some semblance of buoyancy inside the hull, although she doubted that they would keep the ship from sinking too much longer. The weight of water in the hold must eventually drag the structure under. It made sense that they should attempt to swim to the more sea-worthy fishing-boat, drifting listlessly not more than a hundred meters across the calm sea.

'Do we have to?' Hani pleaded, fear building inside.

'If we remain here, this ship will sink under us. If we wait too long, we might miss the opportunity.'

'Can we just wait a little longer, please Mary Jo. Perhaps that boat will move closer,' Hani's grip was hurting and Mary Jo moved to reassure her.

'We can wait a while longer.' At that moment, she felt the boat move

under her, catching Lily's signal that they should move immediately. She watched Lily tugging at the plastic containers, dragging these from inside the hold.

'I can only get one,' she said, after a short time, the others firmly stuck, pressed into place by rising water. Lily raised the jerry can and unscrewed the lid. *'Here, drink,'* she instructed Hani, tilting the cumbersome container carefully, while balancing with her back against the bulwark. Mary Jo watched, concerned with how little water remained.

'You first,' she said, when Lily offered her the tepid water.

'It's okay,' Lily tried to smile but her lips were sorely cracked. *'You can go next,'* with which, she tilted the container again, allowing Mary Jo to drink.

'Enough for one more drink,' Lily said, savoring the few drops she had taken. She screwed the lid back on and passed the near empty jerry can to Mary Jo. *'If you keep hold of this with your good arm, I'll take Hani.'* Mary Jo nodded, not entirely happy with the arrangement but pragmatic enough to agree.

'Are we ready?' Lily asked, taking the reluctant Hani by the arm.

'No, wait!' she begged, pulling away from the other's grasp.

'We have to go,' Mary Jo encouraged, holding the plastic container firmly in front.

'Yes, come on. Let's do it now,' Lily added, taking her by the arm again.

'No, wait!' Hani shouted, pointing across the water. *'I can see a ship! No, two ships!'* she cried, and the others turned, skeptical of her ruse, their eyes following the direction of her outstretched arm.

'My God, she's right!' Mary Jo exclaimed in surprise. In the distance, she could clearly see the outline of a large ship and further out another, and perhaps a third. Something else caught her eye, and she continued to watch for a few moments fearing what she saw to be a seagull or some other bird. Then she was sure.

'There's a plane!' she yelled, *'over there!'* The others searched the sky, Hani spotting the Orion before Lily.

'It's coming this way!' she shouted excitedly, and all three watched as the aircraft continued in their direction, flying low across the ocean as it approached. Mary Jo waved the empty container through the air, while Hani and Lily both waved their arms to attract the crew's attention.

'Down here!' Lily screamed, waving furiously. The pilot banked sharply, circled the abandoned fishing boats several times, then turned away.

* * * *

'Any survivors?' the Broome Coastwatch centre wanted to know. The civilian contractors had been requested to deploy additional aircraft to the area, the fleet now supported by four Britten-Norman Islanders and two de Havilland Dash-8's for electronic surveillance. Darwin station monitored the exchange, recording the information for Canberra.

'Negative,' the pilot answered, ignoring the half-submerged wreck off to port. His two observers continued to check the sea below through the large, bubble windows. Both men indicated that they could not see any survivors. 'The pattern is the same as the others,' the pilot reported, referring to similar scenes detected earlier from the air. 'Just a few bodies scattered around the decks.'

The Darwin Coastwatch then interrupted, seeking further information. He listened, then confirmed again what he had seen.

'Negative, can't identify any movement down there.' The pilot listened as further orders were given and then acknowledged. 'Roger that, Darwin,' he responded, turning the aircraft to the east, pleased to be heading home.

* * * *

For a moment there was a stunned silence, the women astonished that they had not been seen.

'Do you think they saw us?' Hani asked, still staring after the aircraft as it winged its way back to the coast.

'Of course he saw us,' Mary Jo promised. *'How could he have missed?'* They watched the Orion disappear across the horizon and Lily leaned across and touched Mary Jo's hand.

'They were only interested in the other ships,' she said, looking across the water. *'Even if they did see us, there's not much they can do. We should still try and get over to that other ship.'*

'No!' Hani could not believe her ears. *'I'm staying here until they come to rescue us,'* she shouted, defiantly. Mary Jo looked at her sadly, shaking her head.

'Nothing's changed, Hani. This boat is still sinking.'

'I'm not leaving!' she spat, clinging to the ship now with both hands.

'Then we'll leave you here,' Lily snapped back angrily. *'Mary Jo? Are you coming?'* she asked, turning as if ready to jump into the sea. When the American did not respond, she looked back and was startled to see how ashen the woman's face had become.

'I think we'll have to stay with Hani,' she said, her voice filled with uncertainty. Lily frowned, then followed Mary Jo's gaze across the calm

sea. At first, she did not understand. Then, when she saw the distorted shadow move under the surface, she gasped.

'Sharks?' she whispered hoarsely, knowing this to be true.

'What's that?' Hani wanted to know, peering over the side. When she saw the shape, she instinctively pulled back, overwhelmed with what she saw.

'What will we do now?' This, from Lily, now trembling as she recalled how close she had been to diving into the ocean.

'We stay here until it goes away or the ship sinks.' Mary Jo was more terrified than the others. She had photographed sharks and their victims and had suffered many sleepless nights as a result.

They fell into silence, not speaking for fear that this might somehow contribute to their vessel sinking even faster than it already was. The minutes trickled by slowly, the women conjuring up in their minds the terrifying possibility of being eaten alive by sharks.

Chapter Twenty-Seven

DARWIN

Hamish

'It's on CNN now,' the Coastwatch officer informed Hamish. He immediately dropped the phone, cursing when he could not locate the remote control. Seconds later, he sat transfixed, watching the satellite broadcast live from the United States.

> "...and confirmation has now been received that the Indonesian warship is aground in an area known as Scott Reef, some one hundred miles north of the Western Australian coastal city of Broome. The Australian Government has requested United Nations intervention, charging the Indonesian Navy with acts of piracy and intrusion into Australian waters by a foreign warship. Earlier reports that fire was exchanged between the Indonesian frigate and Australian ships has now been corroborated by authorities in Canberra. No casualties have been reported but the Australian Government claims that the Indonesian Navy is responsible for the deaths of tens of thousands of refugees will, no doubt, increase tensions in an already hostile environment. State Department officials have denied claims that the United States Seventh Fleet is steaming into the area, while humanitarian groups worldwide have called for war crimes tribunals to be established to try those responsible for what is now being declared as one of the worst acts of genocide since the Second World War. And now we cross to..."

Hamish watched the end of the bulletin then flicked across the other channels to see if there was more. Then, remembering that the refugee centre over in Port Hedland had reported an influx of more than six thousand new arrivals over the past twenty-four hours, he went back to the hotel operator to see if they could hurry his call.

* * * *

Mary Jo & Friends

Mary Jo lifted her head and looked up, immediately realizing her mistake when her eyes were struck by the sun's brilliance, painfully blinding her vision. The temperature was even hotter than the day before and Mary Jo knew that she had to keep her mind occupied. The wind had dropped, the timbers on that part of their vessel which floated above the water line, scorched. She peered at Hani and Lily wearily, her throat dry, resisting the temptation to ask for water then, knowing that only a sip remained. Her mind wandered and for a moment her head was filled fleetingly with images of her father. Mary Jo knew she was losing it. She had to keep herself conscious - she had to make the others talk.

'Lily,' she called, her voice barely audible. There was no response. She tried again, *'Lily, let's talk.'* This was also greeted with silence. *'Lily?'* she whispered louder, concerned she might have slipped into unconsciousness, dehydrated by the unrelenting heat.

'What is it?' Lily answered hoarsely, her speech slightly slurred. She had been dozing, her body resting against the ship. *'Is something wrong?'* Had their circumstances been different, Mary Jo might have broken into laughter. There they were, floating around the Indian Ocean in a water-logged, storm thrashed fishing trawler and Lily wanted to know if there was something wrong.

A wry smile threatened to crack her lips and Mary Jo's mind suddenly snapped back. She knew she had to keep talking or at least avoid sleeping during daylight hours, their only chance of sighting another vessel. She kept telling herself that as long as they were alive, there was still hope. Slowly, she scanned the horizon and her hopes fell - only nothing. During the night their boat had drifted further, the large ship they had spotted before, in their minds perhaps a figment of their willing imagination. She could see a few deserted trawlers floating around aimlessly in the distance. Mary Jo looked back at Lily, deciding it would be in both their interests to get her talking.

'We've got to try and stay alert.' There was silence for a moment, then Mary Jo watched as Lily came slowly to life, leaned forward and rubbed her dry face.

'Let's finish what's left, now,' she suggested, moving cautiously to where the jerry-can lay, propped alongside the hold.

'We should wait, if you can,' Mary Jo warned. Lily paused, thought about this, then sighed.

'I know,' she said, but there was no sign of desperation in her voice.

Mary Jo followed Lily's eyes to where Hani lay asleep. She did not look well.

'What will you do if they let you stay in Australia?' Mary Jo asked. When there was no response, she glanced over to see if she had heard the question. *'Lily?'*

'In Australia?' Lily looked at her hands, the thick black line of dirt under her broken nails the least of her worries. She wondered how her hands had suddenly become so old. She then looked over at Mary Jo. *'If they let me stay, I will get a job. If I'm able, I would like to finish my studies.'* She tried to clear her throat, without success.

'Did you have a boyfriend back home?' Mary Jo tried to encourage the conversation with difficulty. She moved her tongue around inside her dry mouth, wishing she had kept the peppermints till now.

'I didn't have time for a boyfriend,' Lily said, her voice coming and going. Her tongue searched for saliva. She needed to spit.

'Tell me about you two,' Mary Jo tried. Exhausted as she was, Lily came alert, viewed the foreigner suspiciously, then glanced across at Hani. Seeing that she was asleep, Lily nodded wearily.

'There's not much more to tell,' she lied, now wary. *'We met at college, like I said. That's all.'* This exchange caused her to cough harshly, the lining of her throat felt scratched.

'Lily, I would like to ask you about your story,' Mary Jo tried to put the younger woman at ease. *'It will help keep us awake. There has to be another ship come by soon.'*

'My story?' Lily seemed confused. She tried to clear her throat but there was nothing there but the feeling of sandpaper. *'I don't have a story.'* She looked longingly at the distant horizon, wishing she could see land. *'Why?'*

Mary Jo tried to smile but her cracked and swollen lips prevented this. For a moment she thought of discontinuing the attempt, fighting the overwhelming fatigue which threatened them all. *'Because I would like to understand what it might be like, to have been in your position,'* she said. Again, there was no immediate response. She could see Lily was also desperately tired.

'My position?' Lily squinted, then coughed, imagining that her tongue was swollen. If only she could spit!

'Yes, Lily,' Mary Jo coaxed, her voice as hoarse as ever. *'what it was like to be Chinese, in Java?'* Lily stared blankly, as if she had not heard. Mary Jo made one final effort to engage her. *'It's okay, Lily, you don't have to talk to me if you don't want to.'* Minutes dragged by, and Mary Jo hoped from

her silence that Lily was considering the question. She rubbed at muscle twisted nerves, moving her head painfully from side to side, then forward as her hand gently massaged her sunburned neck, finding no relief.

'You want me to tell you what it's like to be Chinese in Indonesia?' she heard Lily ask. Mary Jo responded by leaning over and placing her palm on Lily's arm.

'Only if you're up to it.' She looked at Lily, her eyes filled with pain. She nodded again. Somewhere behind seagulls announced their presence, distracting both. They stretched their necks to look but could see nothing.

'Will you write about what I tell you?' Lily's voice was but a whisper, glancing over to where Hani lay sleeping.

'Yes, that's what I'd like to do.' Mary Jo knew she would most probably forget most of what might be said. She felt so goddamn tired!

'And then everyone would know?' Lily asked, drawing on reserves to force herself to crouch. Her legs had gone to sleep.

'No one would know that what I wrote came from you.'

'Why?' Lily countered, now curious. She wriggled her toes and fingers slowly to restore circulation.

'Because I would not mention your name unless you said it was okay.' Mary Jo followed suit, moving her toes ever so slowly, discovering for the first time how badly bruised her ankles were. Unconsciously, her hand touched the ugly purple skin but she felt no pain.

'I don't mind,' Lily said, after a few moments, *'but I don't think you would understand.'* Lily hesitated but not from the strain of talking. *'You are a foreigner. How could you possibly understand?'*

Mary Jo thought about this for a minute or two before replying, mustering as much energy as she could to keep the conversation flowing.

'If you mean I don't know what it's like to live as a Chinese in Indonesia, I admit that is true.' She paused, catching her breath. *'Would you like to try to tell me something more of your family and your life before you left?'* She then waited, exhausted from the effort.

'Okay, Mary Jo,' she agreed, extreme weariness evident in her tone. With considerable effort, Lily moved closer so as not to be overheard and to preserve her voice, reduced already to but a hoarse whisper.

* * * *

Somehow, through the following hours, they found the words to communicate together, breaking to rest their parched throats, stopping when it was obvious that one or the other had lost track of the conversation either from fatigue, the debilitating heat or Mary Jo's limited vocabulary.

This story varied dramatically from what Lily had said before, when she had dragged them from the ocean and kept Mary Jo company through their first night. Lily started, her words staggered but coherent, her voice struggling to finish the story she wanted Mary Jo to hear. But she recounted nothing of her final days in Jakarta, for these had been permanently locked behind the window to her mind, the dark terrifying memory of her near death and rape, too personal, too shameful for Lily to relate. Finally, when her voice gave out, she simply stopped, tried to clear her throat again, then rested.

In that short time, Mary Jo came to understand something of the hardships faced by Indonesian ethnic Chinese who had managed to survive in the face of adversity, at the wrong end of the economic spectrum. She listened, as Lily told her story from childhood, from when she was raised in the small East Java town of Situbondo, recalling her earliest memories of school, family and friends. But unbeknown to Mary Jo, this rendition had been deliberately softened, as Lily was not about to reveal all to someone she had only just met.

Mary Jo's heart went out to Lily when she heard part of her story, amazed at the resilience of this young Chinese woman and her family. Mary Jo suddenly wondered why she had not taken the time, nor made the effort to approach the Chinese situation from a more personal perspective before. It just seemed that from the first moment she had stepped foot inside this country, there was just no time to sit and consider what the country's problems were really all about. The initial explosion of violence was political, not because of racial tensions. How did it all go so wrong?

Lily finished her story by relating some of the events leading up to when her uncle in Jakarta had offered to provide for a higher education. There were no such facilities in Situbondo, she had explained.

'It was my only opportunity to escape,' she said, resting her voice before continuing. *'My parents were not wealthy. I was very lucky to have an uncle to help.'* She paused, turned her head, just to make sure that Mary Jo had not fallen asleep. *'Chinese families are like that,'* she said. A few minutes passed before she continued. *'We just try and help each other because no one else will.'* Lily was now dreadfully tired but that was not the reason she had no desire to continue.

Mary Jo heard every word and from the corner of her eye she could see Lily looking at Hani as she spoke.

'I think we should rest, now.'

'We should drink, Mary Jo,' Lily suggested and, without waiting for a

response, dragged her bottom slowly down the sloping deck to retrieve the plastic water can. She gripped the handle and pulled the almost empty jerry can back up to where they had been resting. '*Hani, can you hear me?*' she called, while unscrewing the cap, passing this to Mary Jo to hold as they had done before. She waited for the gentle swell motion to pass, then held the container with both hands, pouring what amounted to a spoonful of water into the cap. '*Hani,*' she called, this time louder with a hint of annoyance in her raspy voice.

Mary Jo waited as Hani slowly raised her head, and stared groggily around.

'*Water?*' she asked, her voice shaky, verging on delirious. Mary Jo slid down gradually and held the half filled cap full of water to her lips with one hand, while assisting with the other. The ache in her shoulder had lessened and for that much Mary Jo was grateful. Both Lily and Mary Jo then each took their ration of water and once the cap had been screwed tightly back on Lily held the can up with one hand to show the others that it was now all gone.

Mary Jo sensed that now Lily might have regretted having saved them. Alone, the water would have lasted her days. She knew that this must have crossed Lily's mind as well and moved to thank her again for what she had done.

'*We'd both be dead now if it hadn't been for you, Lily.*' This was followed by an echoing silence. Lily did not believe Mary Jo's words required a response.

'*I'm tired now,*' she said, '*we can talk again later.*' With which, Lily moved away from where she had been sitting and rested, her throat not as dry as before. Mary Jo followed suit, noticing that Hani had fallen back to sleep again, suggesting that of the three, her condition was the most serious. With no respite from the torturous, burning mid-afternoon sun, they conserved what energy remained, an occasional lethargic movement the only indication to the birds gliding with the thermals in the sky high above that there was still life aboard the half-submerged trawler.

* * * *

Lily rolled to one side, exhausted. She knew that it was imperative now, to conserve energy. Her eyes wandered. The sea lapped at her feet, tempting her to swim. She looked up, momentarily blinded by the sun, then closed her eyes. She could still see the huge, bright shape burning through her eyelids. The sea was windless, her head ached and her thirst demanded that she soon drink.

An image of her mother intruded and for a lingering moment she thought it real. Someone coughed. Lily's lips attempted a sickly smile when she realized that it was she who had made the dry, barking noise. Saliva stuck to the roof of her dry, tongue-swollen mouth and she tried to avoid thinking about her thirst. She heard Hani groan, wondering how long it would take her to die without water. Her mind clouded even further by the stifling, dehydrating sun's effect, she leaned back considering how far she would have to swim to save herself.

Lily caught some movement from the corner of her eye as Hani came into focus and her heart hardened. She had made a mistake. She should have left the two of them in the water to drown. In her debilitated state, her mind skipped and she found herself talking out aloud. But no one listened. Later, in a more lucid state, she looked over again at the prostrate form of the West Javanese girl and shook her head with what little energy remained, the question on her mind what would Hani have done had their roles been reversed?

She looked out, her eyes floating with the moving horizon, again tempted to slip into the ocean and cool her sun-scorched body in the sea. Suddenly, her mind was alert. She sat upright and glared at the listless form, half-floating on the partly sunken deck. In that moment, Lily wished she had the energy to push Hani down the ship's side, to punish her as an act of retribution for all those who had filled her life with so much pain.

In the mists of her mind, she imagined seagulls, wondering if this meant they were close to land. Again, someone coughed. This time, Lily knew that it was Mary Jo. With considerable effort, she raised herself on one arm and checked to see how the American woman was faring. Her light, sunburned skin was covered in blisters. Lily could see that her lips were cracked, unconsciously touching her own as she peered at the foreigner's sun ravaged face, pieces of their discussion, coming to mind.

Lily wished she had been strong enough to explain what was really in her heart but their condition and language barriers prevented her from doing so. Because she was a journalist, Lily wanted Mary Jo to understand how the indigenous Indonesians refused to acknowledge that the ethnic Chinese had as much right to preserve their culture and heritage as any of the two hundred minorities throughout Indonesia. Lily wished she could have explained but did not know how to do so. Words such as 'frustration', 'rage' and 'betrayal' had come to mind but she had avoided their use, suspecting that Mary Jo would not have understood.

The hypocrisy of Indonesian politics had left her people permanently scarred. The application of racial and cultural tolerance embodied in the *Pancasila* and Constitution were never applied to her race.

Lily remembered what it was like to be constantly ridiculed by the young, handsome, *pribumi* boys, with their deeply-held prejudices and their snide, cutting remarks suggesting that she and her friends were cold that they could not enjoy the intimacy of a sexual relationship unless money was involved. The more she thought about what she had wanted to say but could not, the more angered Lily became with what had happened to her in Jakarta. Her eyes fell on the sleeping form not meters from her feet and Lily's heart turned to stone, annoyed again that she had not let Hani Purwadira drown.

* * * *

Mary Jo had been first to identify the sounds of gunfire. She pulled herself up into a sitting position and peered out wearily across to the warship, unaware that this was the very same vessel which had threatened to sink them when it passed perilously close in the darkness of night. Every bone in her body ached and she wished desperately for a cigarette.

The Indonesian frigate had been prevented from further acts of piracy by navigating directly into the reef area, aground and now under fire from an Australian destroyer. As the three women looked on from afar, a number of naval patrol boats scoured the area for survivors. Aerial reconnaissance reports had not been encouraging. Coastwatch aircraft had been joined in the search by R.A.A.F. Orions, crews scouring the sea for what was left of the devastated fleet had reported many of the fishing boats as being abandoned. The Norman Islander crew which had flown the area the day before, reported sighting bodies strewn around the decks on a number of boats, resulting in the Australian Navy's two hundred ton patrol boat being dispatched to investigate. Her throat on fire, Mary Jo felt herself sway as she tried to hold herself steady, struggling to focus clearly on the scene before her.

'We're over here!' Mary Jo willed the distant ship silently, wondering if her eyesight was playing tricks again. Then, she thought she saw movement and rubbed her eyes before looking back. Was that a ship coming towards them? At that moment, Mary Jo imagined movement under her feet and was suddenly struck with fear. She looked slowly around the trawler and closed her eyes. Don't sink now, please don't sink now!

How their trawler managed to remain afloat was almost beyond comprehension. The heavily water-logged trawler's deck was now barely visible, the light ocean swells reaching more than half-way to where they clung for dear life. Mary Jo noticed the fingers of her left hand as these gripped the side of the boat. The nails were all ripped and torn, her hand swollen. Her shoulder still ached and her mouth was dry. None of them had eaten for days. She wondered how much longer they could hold on. She looked out again, the reflections of sunlight dancing across the sea blinding her vision. Mary Jo rested her eyes momentarily, then tried again. There. She saw it again!

Hani's hand moved across and touched Lily's. *'Lily,'* her voice was barely a whisper. *'Lily, I'm sorry,'* she managed, her head dizzy now. Lily squeezed the other girl's hand, her mouth far too dry to carry on further conversation.

'Don't talk,' Lily croaked, releasing her grip.

Hani coughed, her tongue felt swollen. Lily remained quiet, hoping Hani would do the same. *'Thank you, Lily,'* the words came slowly, her hand searching for Lily's again.

'Just rest,' Lily replied, incapable of carrying on further conversation. The question of whether she would have saved Hani's life had she known who it was beforehand had plagued her mind since the event. Now, she was just too damn tired to care.

Then, from Hani, *'Mary Jo,'* she called weakly. *'I can't hold on much longer.'*

'It won't be long now,' Mary Jo whispered comfortingly through dry, cracked and swollen lips. Her head had started to swim, her head ached, the dehydration now playing with her mind as she thought she could hear engines somewhere. She glanced wearily towards Lily, who now lay half floating with her legs dangling back across the deck, partially under water. There it was again! Mary Jo raised her head groggily, wishing she had the full use of her other arm. She waited for her eyes to become accustomed to the glare again, then squinted, concentrating on the shape she could see moving through her line of sight. It was a boat. She turned to Lily and called out, her voice barely more than a hoarse whisper.

'Lily, there's a boat coming.' Then, to Hani, *'There's someone coming to help us. Hold on!'* Mary Jo then stared back at the approaching Australian Navy patrol boat and tried to smile but her eyes filled with tears instead, clouding her view, when she identified the flag and knew in that moment that they were saved.

* * * *

Darwin Harbor

'You have nothing to fear now,' Mary Jo said, misconstruing Lily's contemplative look as she sat, leaning forward, her chin resting comfortably on

her hands peering across to the welcome sight.

'I'm not afraid, Mary Jo,' Lily said, rising from the seat. She moved to Mary Jo's side, and took her hand in hers. *'I was just thinking how wonderful it would be if they let us stay.'* This, while looking down at Hani, totally preoccupied with the sailors running around the wharf, preparing for the patrol boat's arrival. They had not been transferred to the larger Australian ships due to the possibility of further conflict with the Indonesians. Instead, they had steamed back along the coast, arriving in Darwin late the following day. The twenty-two officers and sailors had gone out of their way to make the women as comfortable as they could. Having rested, they were treated to their first real meal in more than a week, for Lily even longer. At first, Hani and Lily were worried that they would be locked in some cell but this was not to be. Both the Indonesian women were treated civilly, their concerns soon swept away by their rescuers' friendly manner.

'I'm sure they'll let you remain, Lily,' Mary Jo suggested, reassuringly.

'What about me?' Hani turned, playfully pouting while hiding her apprehension. Mary Jo smiled at them both and shook her head.

'After what you have both been through, how could they possibly send you back?'

'Would you speak on our behalf,' Lily asked, embarrassed that her knowledge of English was so limited. Mary Jo nodded.

'Sure,' she promised and wrapped her arm around Lily, kissed her on the forehead, turned to Hani and repeated the gesture.

At that moment, all three lost balance when the two hundred and twenty ton patrol boat's twin, sixteen cylinder engines suddenly slowed, as the ship came alongside the wharf and stopped. They were ushered on deck, then assisted onto the wharf where immigration officers waited to take them away.

'Not you, Miss Hunter.' Mary Jo turned to the official dressed in shorts and long socks.

'I'm sorry?' she asked, frowning.

'These two ladies will be processed at the camp facilities. You're being cleared through immigration here.'

'Why?' she asked, taking Lily by the hand. Detecting that they were in trouble both Hani and Lily moved closer together.

'Because they're illegal immigrants and you're not,' was the man's response. She had wanted to argue but was just too damned tired to engage the official any further.

'What's happening, Mary Jo?' Lily asked, intimidated by the presence of officialdom.

'They want you to go to the camp with all of the others for processing.'

'Will you come with us?' both pleaded, fearing deportation.

'I can't,' she answered, angry that she could do nothing.

'But why not?' Hani demanded but Mary Jo was lost for an answer.

'They'll take good care of you, I promise,' she said.

'Will you come and visit us, Mary Jo?' Lily now close to tears, pulled her hand from Mary Jo's, taking Hani's instead. She did not want to cry. It was just that she felt so alone. Mary Jo was overcome by the emotion of the moment, tears welling up inside.

'I promise to come and visit, wherever you are,' she said sincerely. And then turning to the two officers waiting impatiently for Hani and Lily to follow, she added in Indonesian, as if they could understand, *'and if anyone makes either of you unhappy, I will take their photos and have these put in the newspapers.'*

'Come on, ladies,' the more senior of the two officials insisted, stepping in to shepherd the Indonesian women away. Hani sobbed, tears flowing freely down her cheeks and, as Mary Jo watched the two small frames walking away, dwarfed alongside the Australian men, her eyes blurred, and she took a step to follow.

'No, Miss,' the official warned, not unkindly, 'better to let them get on with it.' Filled with sadness, she watched as they were led away and ordered into a waiting pickup.

'Follow me, please Miss,' she heard her escort say and Mary Jo looked back for one final glimpse of her companions as they were driven away. Suddenly they were gone, an emptiness enveloping Mary Jo as she gazed after them.

With her eyes fixed dejectedly on the over sized rubber sandals she had been given on board the patrol boat, Mary Jo followed the officer, her legs still wobbly from the time spent at sea. They entered a small, air-conditioned office where she was offered coffee and instructed to wait. Moments later, as she stared down at the floor Mary Jo heard the door open, then close, her thoughts still preoccupied with what might happen to Hani and Lily.

'Even dressed like that, you're a sight for sore eyes,' she heard someone say, and looked up, astonishment flooding her face when she saw Hamish McLoughlin standing there. Then, she frowned. Her heart awash with a flood of mixed emotions, Mary Jo rose slowly to her feet, images of the suffering, the grief and sacrifice she had witnessed over the past days suddenly clouding her mind.

'Hamish?' as Mary Jo started to rise, he stepped forward to take her arm, unprepared for the stinging slap which followed. 'Bastard!' she cried, swinging with deadly accuracy. He rocked back on his heels, staggered by the force of her blow and the venom behind it.

'What in the….!' Hamish yelled, stepping back out of striking range, one ear ringing loudly from the attack.

'That's for not coming back to get me,' she said, her voice trembling. Mary Jo took another step towards Hamish, her hand flashing through the air again. 'And that's for…' she started, cut off in midair as Hamish leapt forward and caught her by the wrist, forcing both arms behind her back.

'Jo! Stop it!' he shouted, holding her tightly, then pulling her roughly to his chest. He heard Mary Jo gasp in pain, and Hamish immediately let go, startled that he might have hurt her.

'Jo, are you okay?'

Fighting tears, she clenched her teeth and gripped her injured shoulder, her anger spilling over. 'What happened to you, Hamish?' Her voice was filled with bitterness, unaware of events surrounding her unexpected voyage from Pelabuhan Ratu. She pulled away and stepped back, suddenly spent, and slid into a chair. Out of the corner of her eye she caught a glimpse of an immigration official approaching from one of the inner offices down the hallway. 'I could have died out there,' she said, with a glaring look. 'And I've lost all of my film and equipment.'

'Jesus bloody Christ!' he swore, 'of all the ungrateful…'

'Ungrateful?' she exploded, struggling to stand, 'why didn't you commandeer a goddamn boat and come back out to get me?' She flopped back into the chair. Embarrassed, the immigration officer had stopped in mid-step, remaining in the hallway until the quarreling had finished. It then dawned on Hamish that Mary Jo had no idea as to why she had been trapped on the fishing boats. He started to explain.

'Jo, I'm sorry. It's obvious you don't know what happened back there. I just assumed that the others on the fishing boats would have told you.'

'Told me what?' she snapped, her shoulder throbbing painfully.

'The whole place was overrun. That's why the fleet set sail with such urgency.'

'Mufti Muharam?' she stared up at Hamish, skeptical. She forced herself upright in the uncomfortable seat. 'They were that close?'

'They swarmed all over the place while you were out visiting the ships. They even managed to get a few shots off at our Jet Ranger,' he explained. 'There wasn't a boat anywhere to be found by the time we returned to the hotel. We did everything possible Jo, but in the end the U.N. team leader ordered us to get the hell out of there before it was too late. I had no control over the situation.' They exchanged glances, Mary Jo dropping her eyes.

'And Anne?' she asked, wondering why he had not mentioned her name. Hamish shook his head, Mary Jo immediately expecting the worst.

'She didn't return to the hotel Jo. It's obvious that she waited for you, and missed the flight. We took a run at the beach but it was in total chaos. There was just no way we could have picked her out of those crowds.'

'And you've heard nothing since then?'

'Only that the entire area fell to Abdul Muis' forces. I'm sorry Jo but I wouldn't hold out too much hope for Anne now.' Mary Jo nodded silently, not wishing to speculate on what might have happened to her assistant and friend at the hands of the Moslem rebels. She had witnessed enough suffering for one lifetime, most of it within that week. She put Anne to the back of her mind, promising to attend to her whereabouts as soon as she could get to a phone and contact Jakarta.

'I guess I owe you an apology,' she said lamely, offering her hand to Hamish for his assistance. He hesitated, then helped her to stand.

'You're hurt?' he asked, pointing to her shoulder.

'Yes, but at least I'm alive,' she replied, emotionally drained and suddenly extremely tired. Hamish attempted to wrap an arm around her waist, perplexed when Mary Jo resisted, wondering what had altered the chemistry between them. She pulled away again.

'I'm sorry Hamish, but I need some time to myself. I'm not even sure if I'm still the same person you left in Samudera Beach. A great deal has happened over the past week and I'm going to need some space.' She reached over and touched the distinctive, red welt on his cheek. 'Am I forgiven?' she asked, without warmth to her smile, and in her eyes he could see the scars of others.

Hamish's free hand went to the side of her face, gently touching the tender, sunburned skin. He could see that she had been deeply affected by her terrifying experiences, the coldness in her manner silent testimony that these had brought change. He would have to give her time, and the space she demanded. Hamish gave her fingers a reassuring squeeze and returned her smile recognizing, sadly that their relationship might never be the same again.

* * * *

Chapter Twenty-eight

INDONESIA

President Winarko stood looking out the window of his old office, across Merdeka Square towards the national monument, observing the American flag as it moved under the morning breeze. The official palace offices had been destroyed in an aerial attack.

A line of black, official limousines drove out of the U.S. Embassy, turned left into Jalan Merdeka Selatan and followed the military escort. Winarko knew these would be filled with the remaining diplomats' families, on their way to the airport. He looked up at the gold tipped flame atop the magnificent obelisk in the centre of Merdeka Square, his thoughts filled with concern for his own family. He checked his gold plated Omega and, although not normally given to displaying any emotions, the general's heavy heart caused him to sigh as he turned to the aide standing patiently behind, waiting.

'It's time, General,' he heard the colonel say.

'I know,' he answered in his customary, quiet voice. Winarko walked slowly towards the door, followed by his aide, leaving the command office unattended. They went directly to the heli-pad where a Super Puma had been waiting on stand-by, with its precious passengers. They were airborne within minutes, the pilot flying the President to the air-force field at Halim Perdanakusumah. There, standing on the tarmac, its starboard Rolls Royce engines already turning slowly, an air force VIP Boeing 707 prepared for departure. When General Winarko's helicopter landed, a well rehearsed team of combat hardened soldiers raced to the aircraft and formed a protective shield for those alighting.

First to step down was Nuri Suhapto with her husband and children, followed by Tuti and her youngsters.

'Quickly! Quickly!' the women called, hurrying towards the Boeing with their families in tow. Amongst the fleeing group, the man who would be

king - former President Hababli - scolded one of his grandchildren for stepping on his toes, as he too made his way to the air-force passenger jet. One by one they boarded, leaving General Winarko standing anxiously on the tarmac watching, silently urging them all to hurry. His wife and children climbed the stairs to the aircraft, turned with tears in their eyes and bade him farewell.

The President stepped back, covering his ears as the jet's four screaming engines' deafening pitch filled the air, his face grim as he caught one final glimpse of his wife waving goodbye. Winarko watched the aircraft take off, then re-entered the helicopter with a dozen or more of the hand-selected soldiers. Within minutes the Puma was airborne again, but it did not return to the city. Instead, General Winarko sat back counting off the minutes before he and his guard, would arrive at his enemies' lair. Having placed those who still controlled much of Indonesia's wealth out of Abdul Muis' reach, Winarko would now sit down and negotiate his peace with the *Mufti Muharam*, confident that the former First Families would provide for his own wife and children, in the appropriate manner, should he not succeed.

* * * *

SYDNEY

Mary Jo

Mary Jo handed her new passport to the immigration official, waiting patiently in line until he had punched the numbers and other information into his computer.

'Did you enjoy your stay in Australia?' the smiling officer asked.

'Sure,' she lied, 'could have stayed on.' She accepted her travel documents then proceeded to the designated waiting lounge, where she flopped into an empty space, preparing her mind for the long flight home. Mary Jo looked down at the cheap Kodak camera she had purchased with funds borrowed from Hamish and smiled, wondering what they would say in New York if she were to walk in with a five dollar throwaway like this. Her eyes dropped to the photograph of the two Asian women.

She had remained in Darwin until the U.S. Embassy in Canberra had forwarded a new set of travel documents. Mary Jo acknowledged that she was fortunate to have had Hamish as a friend. He advanced funds, assisted with her arrangements and stood by quietly without making any demands.

Mary Jo was grateful and wished she could have demonstrated this to Hamish in a more physical way but she could not stop hurting. He had left, returning to Switzerland, promising to keep in touch.

The following morning Mary Jo had visited with Hani and Lily, undertaking to do whatever was in her power to assist with their applications to remain in Australia. Unfortunately, this proved to be of little significance the government already swamped with requests from more than one and a half million refugees. They had been tearful and, in spite of her assurances to the contrary, both believed they would be deported, sent back to face the horrors of living in Indonesia. Some scars would heal but she knew theirs would not.

Mary Jo had made arrangements to return to New York for a long, overdue break. Although surprised, the chief of staff had promised she could return to Asia and this pleased Mary Jo, more determined than ever to maintain her coverage of refugees, their plight and society's attitudes towards the millions of displaced people who remained in camps around the globe.

Her flight was called and Mary Jo boarded the Qantas 747, destined for Los Angeles and New York, where the new equipment she had ordered would be waiting, ready for her next assignment.

* * * *

Indonesia

Bogor Palace - West Java

There had been no warmth in Abdul Muis' smile when he exchanged greetings with General Winarko. His troops had expected the Acting President's arrival by helicopter and now stood with weapons raised, pointed directly at Winarko's soldiers standing guard over the Super Puma.

'It seems we have reached an impasse,' Muis admitted, surprised with Winarko's revelations regarding those he had helped escape. The General had not said, but Muis expected that Winarko's own family would have accompanied the others. They sat opposite each other in the hastily prepared setting. It had been more than six months since they had spoken and, although surprised with the request to meet in this particular location, Abdul Muis was receptive to the suggestion that they sit down together, in a neutral zone. He looked around, sniffing the decay which had permeated this room inside the Bogor Summer Palace.

Muis had observed his opponent when Winarko entered, surprised that the general had put on weight. They shook hands with guarded politeness and took their seats in what had become a museum dedicated to the first President, Soekarno. One of Muis' security officers poured the lukewarm tea into miniature sized cups, then stepped back. Winarko observed that both men wore side arms. He was concerned, not offended.

'I still don't think you can take the city,' the General challenged, not wishing to mince words.

'We could, in time,' Muis replied, not arrogantly. Winarko silently agreed.

'It's time to call an end to the fighting,' he declared. These were the words Abdul Muis had hoped to hear but showed no sign that this was so.

'You will have to step down,' Muis insisted. Winarko had not expected less.

'And my position after that?' he asked, feeling the guards' eyes boring into the back of his head. He glanced over in their direction, hoping Muis would take the hint.

'Vice President, if you want it,' Muis answered, knowing he no longer had anything to fear from this man. The threat of Winarko living the rest of his days with a *fatwah* hanging over his family's head had, the Moslem leader believed, resolved the leadership question. Winarko seemed to have surrendered, accepting the inevitable. Muis was immediately elated with the outcome and had difficulty hiding his pleasure. He moved his head slightly, indicating to his two white clad bodyguards that he wished to be alone with his visitor.

'Then it is time to re-establish peace in our country,' the General proposed, and Muis nodded, eager to proceed. He would be President before the sun had set across the white domed Istiqlal Mosque in Jakarta. They would return together, he as the victor, to declare Jakarta as the capital of his Islamic state. He would hold his prayer sessions there, that night. He beamed at Winarko, clasped his hands together and raised them to his face as a gesture of salute to his new ally. Then he closed his eyes and uttered the words *'terima kasih'* in gratitude for what had just transpired.

With a rehearsed movement, General Winarko swiftly extracted the weapon he had concealed inside his vest and, placing the point of the automaic directly at the Moslem leader's forehead, fired once. Haji Abdul Muis' head snapped back, his eyes opened wide in shock and disbelief as the false prophet fell dead to the floor.

The room exploded into activity as Muis' personal bodyguards poured back into the room, their guns raised as they ran to their leader's side.

'You killed Abdul Muis?' one of the men screamed, hatred filling his eyes as he pointed his weapon at the President. Winarko braced himself,

expecting to die at that moment. He stared back at the soldier, his face like granite. Outside, the air erupted as automatic fire was exchanged by the opposing troops standing guard around the helicopter. Momentarily distracted, the first guard fell dead when Winarko fired, the second caught as he rose to his feet from checking the body.

'General!' Winarko heard the officer outside and did not hesitate. He ran from the building out onto the lawn where the fire fight continued. The General was rushed to the Puma, its huge rotor blades already cutting a path through the air.

'Go! Go! Go!' the NCO screamed to those of his men left standing, and they too ran to the helicopter as he covered their retreat. The pilot did not hesitate, the powerful twin engines lifting the French designed transport into the air at his command. The helicopter rose, its four bladed rotors dangerously close to tree tops as bullets continued to thud heavily into the aircraft's fuselage. One of the commandos screamed, a bullet hitting him low in the back, another falling silently as he too was struck. The Puma beat its way into the air quickly distancing the President from ground fire and Winarko looked at the young officer and grinned, raising his thumb in the air as he did so.

His subterfuge had worked.

In a world dominated by forever changing political alliances, General Winarko had made his choice. Whether his stance against Moslem sectarianism might be perceived by the American people as a positive step really was of no consequence to the Javanese General. His people had dominated these islands for more millenniums than any European state had been in existence. The responsibility for maintaining the nation's cultural core was far more important than any religious issue. Winarko now accepted that Java was, although the dominating force, not representative of all Indonesia. He would initiate changes which would reflect the country's multi-ethnic community. Even the smallest state would have representation. The nation's cultural passage through time had produced a vibrant, talented community. Although diversified, under his guidance, the country would remain unified.

The United States had undertaken to leave the American Seventh Fleet on temporary duty in Indonesian waters as a buffer against the threat of outside aggression. In turn, Winarko had undertaken to strike the *Mufti Muharam* while their leadership was in disarray and to totally destroy the militant movement before Beijing considered the opportunity to occupy Indonesia, too tempting to resist.

* * * *

Washington D.C.

The Chairman of the Joint Chiefs of Staff sat pondering the assumptions outlined in the final assessment, the thick file document now lying on his desk. In a few more months he would retire, the complicated issues raised in the submission would then become the responsibility of others. For this, he was grateful. Past recommendations made by the Joint Chiefs to the President had not always been without heated debate, nor had these been unanimous for even amongst his peers, politics played an important role in the decision making processes.

The Admiral's thoughts returned to the final numbers suggested by his analysts, annoyed with the uninformed who still maintained that U.S. foreign policy had been mainly responsible for what had happened. It was easy to apportion blame without understanding all of the facts. Now, the pendulum had swung too far in the other direction. In the years since President Suhapto had stepped down as President of Indonesia, more than ten million had died in Java alone. Most, he knew from intelligence reports, had been Christians and Buddhists, many of these of Chinese descent.

He considered the events which had required the Administration's manipulation of IMF and World Bank bail out packages for Indonesia and asked himself in their efforts to curtail the rapid growth of China's influence across the Asian and Middle East regions, had the United States provided the catalyst for this bloody outcome? Had President Suhapto been permitted to serve out his term, or even left to die in office, would Indonesia have continued on its path of stability as it had for more than thirty years or would the endemic corruption on which the American supported Indonesian dictatorship thrived, ultimately have produced the same disorder and civil unrest? These and other questions continued to occupy his mind, as he worried that there may never really be any solution to the inherent problems which faced resource rich countries such as Indonesia.

The United States had embarked on a more militant road in response to international terrorism. U.S. forces' strikes against Sudan and Afghanistan marked the beginning of his country's stand against Moslem extremists who, unlike Saddam Husein, had taken their war to the Americans by bombing diplomatic missions in Africa and the Middle East. These incidents had stirred strong passions amongst the American people. Although the actions had the negative effect of uniting the extremists, at least his nation had demonstrated its willingness to retaliate when American life and property were threatened. In hindsight, he now believed that the United States should have struck and destroyed the very source of the problem while they still had the chance. China's belligerent, highly confrontational support for Iran and Iraq would undoubtedly result in Israel being attacked with Chinese produced ballistic missiles, launched by militant Moslems. He admitted silently that had the United States initiated preemptive strikes against Abdul Muis' *Mufti Muharam* while in its infancy, the lives of millions would surely have been saved.

In the meantime, the Admiral knew that the United States had to be content that at least one major objective had been achieved, albeit at the expense of the many who had died during the *Mufti Muharam* reign of terror. Indonesia would not, he firmly believed, become a nuclear threat - at least not in the foreseeable future, leaving the United States to consider how to protect the archipelago from its militant neighbors.

* * * *

Israel - Tel Aviv

Major General Shabtai Saguy sat motionless, listening to the intelligence briefing presented by the United States officer. The threat against Israel had not diminished in any way as a result of their ally's determined response to Moslem militancy. If anything, the threat had grown. Iran's ICBM capability was now widely known amongst intelligence agencies. Why the Americans continued to refuse to target these facilities was the question which continued to plague his people.

He knew that Israel's interests were so closely aligned with those of the United States it would only be a matter of time before both would become embroiled in a nuclear confrontation with one of his country's aggressive neighbors. As for the Far East, he disagreed with his American counterparts that the Moslem dominated Republic of Indonesia was no longer a threat. Shabtai Saguy had been an intelligence officer too long to disbelieve that by simply changing the country's leadership the national psyche would follow. He would reserve judgment and wait to see how this fellow Winarko behaved, before making any further recommendations regarding Mossad activities in the world's largest Moslem nation.

* * * *

Epilogue

Mary Jo - New York

'Way to go, Mary Jo!' her chief-of-staff whistled. 'Listen up everybody, got something to say.' He stood with a huge smile creasing his chubby face, the paisley tie loosened around his neck hiding undone buttons. Mary Jo turned when she heard her name, raising her eyebrows.

'What's up Pete?' she asked.

'What's up, my dear? You might very well ask that question.' He leaned against the doorway, waving a sheet of paper at the staff. 'Seems we have an extremely talented young lady working amongst us,' he grinned mischievously.

Her curiosity aroused, Mary Jo sauntered over to her editor and removed the paper from his hand. The communication was a faxed copy of a news bulletin released by Columbia University during a three o'clock press conference. She read the first two lines almost disinterestedly, then stopped, her eyes wide and stared back at her boss.

'I've won?' she shrieked incredulously, and then again, 'I've really won?' while the editor gave a conspiratorial wink to his staff. It was he who had submitted the entry for consideration.

'Yes, ladies and gentlemen, I give you Miss Mary Jo Hunter, this year's recipient of the Pulitzer Prize and I quote, "For a distinguished example of reporting on international affairs, including United Nations correspondence, Five Thousand dollars!"'

The room erupted with cheering. 'Drinks on you!' a colleague yelled.

'Wait everybody, wait,' he called, 'there's more. The announcement goes on to say, "Awarded to Mary Jo Hunter for her compelling, comprehensive and compassionate reporting from Indonesia of the refugee crisis in Indonesia, and her contribution to journalism with her coverage of the UNHCR resettlement camps throughout South East Asia."'

The office broke into thunderous applause, several of her associates rushing up to congratulate Mary Jo on her success.

'Drinks on me, everyone!' she laughed, tears of joy streaming down her cheeks, then went directly to the phone to call Columbia University to thank the office of trustees responsible for awarding the Pulitzer Prizes. She remained on the phone, the number of incoming calls congratulating Mary Jo seemingly never ending. Western Union called and read her official notification from the Pulitzer Prize Board. Then, with a nod from their chief, half the editorial staff downed pens and swept Mary Jo away to the local bar where celebrations continued through the rest of the afternoon and, for some, well into the night.

Later in the quiet of her apartment, while savoring the moment of her success, Mary Jo's thoughts crossed to those who had influenced her decision to dedicate the past twelve months to her study of Asia's lost tribes — the refugees.

Upon her return from Australia, and good to his word, Mary Jo's chief-of-staff approved her request to conduct in-depth coverage of those displaced by the Asian turmoil. With new equipment in hand, she had flown to Singapore, using the stable city as her hub. From there, Mary Jo visited camps throughout Malaysia, northern Australia and Indonesia's newly created provinces which now enjoyed autonomy over all matters except defense. By then East Timor had achieved independence. In Aceh, Mary Jo was on hand when yet another gruesome grave site containing more than seven hundred bodies of women and children had been uncovered, victims of Javanese oppression.

First on her agenda, had been to determine what had happened to Anne. Mary Jo returned to Indonesia, her heart heavy when she learned of the seaside massacres, Anne's family reporting that they had not heard from her since she left with Mary Jo for East Java. Mary Jo revisited Pelabuhan Ratu, still scarred by violence, conflicting emotions tearing at her heart when she saw the skeletal remains of the gutted Samudera Beach Hotel, standing as silent testimony to the *Mufti Muharam's* destructive forces.

Following the loss of their leader Abdul Muis, the movement had floundered in the ensuing leadership vacuum and, with General Praboyo's former forces now firmly behind him as well, President Winarko had struck a decisive blow amidst the confusion, the threat of American intervention forcing the warring factions to the negotiating table where accommodations were made and compromises placed Winarko firmly in control. The *Mufti Muharam* collapsed as a movement with the emergence of a number of charismatic scholars who divided the remaining party into three, after which Winarko's forces easily disarmed them all.

As Mary Jo continued with her ongoing assignment, she gradually acquired a greater understanding of the racial, ethnic and religious issues which still dominated life at village level, everywhere she visited. She was deeply affected by what had happened to the culturally rich archipelago nation, saddened when it became evident that the wounds opened by the conflict remained festering, unlikely to heal.

Mary Jo made new friends, occasionally crossing paths with old acquaintances as she traveled the region extensively, filing reports regularly, her stories earning accolades around the globe. She was aware of her nominations. In fact there had been two, her head swimming with excitement when she learned that her black and white study 'Children, The Real Victims of War', had also been acknowledged by the trustees at Columbia. And now her work had earned her the highest accolade her profession could offer, A Pulitzer Prize.

She opened the bedside drawer and extracted a bundle of letters lying there, tied in ribbon. Mary Jo opened the first, a lengthy letter, the child like handwriting on lined paper was written in Bahasa Indonesia. It was from Hani, and as she started to read the familiar contents for the umpteenth time, her eyes became misty, recalling how the two waifs had first appeared in her life.

Dear Mary Jo,

We must move to a center in some place called Port Hedland, Lily says that I should try and speak more English, but I don't care to.

Mary Jo's hand came to her mouth, unconsciously touching her lips, remembering what followed:

Lily says she doesn't hate me anymore and that's something, although she also said we could never really be friends again.

I try to understand what happened, Mary Jo, what I did to make her feel this way but I can't think of anything. I feel sorry that so many people were hurt. Lily says she read in the papers here that Indonesians like her (that's Chinese Mary Jo, I don't know if you knew this) have left the country and taken all of their money with them. Now, she says, they are all too frightened to return. If this is true, then I can't say that I blame them. If you can believe what Lily says, a lot of Chinese were killed. But I'm not sure about this either.

You've got to understand, Mary Jo, but ever since I can remember I have never seen any of her people poor. Not like us. I guess this is why there is so much bitterness. They always had fine clothes and plenty of money to buy the things they wanted. I don't understand why it was like this, it just seemed to be the same everywhere at the time. There are lots of others here who are like Lily. Some of them have small bars of gold which they keep hidden from the security here. I saw one a few days ago but when they saw me looking, they sent me away and told me to mind my own business. Oh yes, and Lily snapped at me yesterday. She said I was lazy. I don't think I am. Do you think I'm lazy Mary Jo? I am trying very hard to stay here in Australia. I don't want to go back to Indonesia. My family are all dead. Did you know that my father was a General, Mary Jo? It's true. He was killed. So was my brother. I don't know what happened to my little sister, I just hope she is safe somewhere and remembers me. There are lots of others here who are like Lily. I feel so lonely here. Please come back soon to help me, Mary Jo.

Goodbye, your friend, Hani Purwadira.

Hani had obviously saved this letter, as a second had been commenced half-way through the first. They were dated a fortnight apart.

Hi Mary Jo,

I don't want to forget my own language, Lily refuses to speak to me in Indonesian anymore. She is always in a bad mood with me. I don't know what is wrong. Perhaps she still blames me for what happened to her. Lily told me a long story yesterday. I'm not sure she didn't make it up. I asked her if it was really true and she became very angry so maybe it really happened. I don't know. I told her some of my secrets as well but she didn't seem interested so I stopped. Did she tell you that she lived in a very large apartment before, Mary Jo? If she did, it's a lie. I went to visit once and it was nothing. That's the truth. If she writes to you and tells you things like that, please don't believe her. Fancy telling people you had a swimming pool! I can tell you for sure that her place was always very dirty. I only went over to see her once or twice because she was in some of my classes. Did she write and tell you any of this Mary Jo?

Please don't tell her what I write.

Your friend, Hani.

And, a month later:

Hi, Mary Jo.

I have been sick. The doctor here says I can't go with the others because I am still not well. I don't understand why Lily won't stay with me. She is going to move somewhere, I can't remember the name. Lily says that she was told by the office here that she will be able to remain in Australia. I think it's because she is Chinese. It's always been like that, Mary Jo. They get everything they want. I asked if she would stay with me but she has stopped talking to me now. I think she really does hate me for the way she was treated. Has she written to you, Mary Jo? I hope she has not said bad things about me. If she has, then she is lying. Did she tell you that she was once raped? Lily has other friends here. I think that's why she doesn't have any time for me anymore. All her friends are like her and if I go up to them they all stop speaking until I leave. I am very lonely here, Mary Jo. I wish you could come to see me as you are my only true friend.

Hani

Finally, her first letter from Lily arrived. Now, as she read this, Mary Jo bit her lip, the memory of its contents still as fresh in her mind as the day she first read the brief communication.

Dear Mary Jo,

I write to you in English. Please understand and forgive me for mistakes. I am sorry Hani is dead. I am sorry also not writing to you before now. She die from something wrong in her stomach. They took her body away and we did not see her. I am very sad for her, even she tells so many stories.

If you write back to me like you write to Hani I promise to answer. They take me to another place soon. I can do some study there.

Goodbye,

Lily Ong. (Here, in this country, we are free to use our own names)

And then, six months later when she returned from her last trip through the desperate camps of East Timor and West New Guinea, Mary Jo found this letter waiting at her office.

Dear Mary Jo,

I am writing to tell you I have a job. I am very happy here in Australia. I work at an office every day but on the weekends I also help at the Golden Galleon restaurant. At night, I study. Next year I will have my degree. Then I will have a better job.

Mary Jo, I have seen your name in the magazine. Did you take those photographs? I am very proud to show this to all my friends. Would you send me one with your autograph please? I want to show it to them so that they believe me better. But there is something I want to tell you also.

That is another reason for my letter. It is about Hani. I want to tell you that I did not hate her even though she thought I did. It is difficult for me to explain but I think that as you have been in Asia a long time, you will understand. I sometimes think of going back to Indonesia. After all, it is my country where I was born. But I am afraid. In Australia I feel safe but it is not the same. My memories of what happened are still in my head and sometimes I still have terrible dreams. Hani was once my friend. One day she and others turned on me. Even now I do not understand why this happened that way because I really did like her. Some of the bad things which happened to me I don't want to tell you. These would only make you sad. When I go to church I pray. This is true, Mary Jo. I pray that one day I can go back to Indonesia and visit, and no one will attack me or hate me because I am Chinese. Do you think that day will ever come? Or will it never change and, because we are different and our culture or religion is not the same, we must be afraid to go back there?

* * * *

It was always at this point in Lily's letter that Mary Jo ceased reading, folded all the letters and placed them back inside the drawer. She leaned back to rest her head on the soft pillow, permitting her thoughts to wander. She had replied to Lily's last letter, unable to offer her any solace, for Mary Jo was convinced that such deep rooted racial animosities would always exist, particularly in an environment such as Indonesia's. Its kaleidoscope of ethnic biases seemed to naturally nurture discrimination.

No, she thought, turning off the bed lamp and sliding snugly down into the soft cotton sheets, it was unlikely that racial tolerance would ever exist anywhere in this imperfect world. Not in her lifetime.

She sighed forlornly, unintentionally disturbing her partner.

'Better get some rest, Jo,' the muffled voice alongside suggested. She smiled and leaned across to kiss Hamish tenderly on his forehead, then lay in his arms, soon drifting into a deep, satisfying sleep.

* * * *

Author's Note

When I read the Indonesian transcript of a twelve year old Chinese child's statement to Jakarta police in which she related the horrors of home invasion, gang-rape, and murder, I cried unashamedly. I am no stranger to violence, having lived in some of Asia's less attractive destinations for more than thirty years, and would be dishonest if I did not admit that the young girl's horrific experience still haunts me, even today.

The question must be asked as to why the authorities in Jakarta, and many other Indonesian cities, failed to prevent the tragedy which occurred during ten days in May 1998; the rape, murder and torture of Chinese women, whose ethnic group had been specifically targeted for political gain.

The Republic of Indonesia now lives in danger of becoming an economic dust-bowl, inflicted with poverty and pestilence, the number of unemployed and destitute reaching catastrophic proportions because of the self-serving interests of those entrusted with the country's leadership.

I find it most ironic that, as Indonesia slid into chaos and more than twenty million citizens' incomes fell to impoverished levels, the United Nations awarded President Soeharto, the architect of this disaster, an award for his fight against poverty.

During the period Lieutenant-General Prabowo Subianto, President Soeharto's son-in-law commanded the Kopassus Special Forces or influenced their role as a result of his relationship with the First Family, the following acts of genocide were recorded:

> Aceh, North Sumatra, approximately 3,000 killed, their bodies thrown into mass graves, 1988 - 1998.
>
> East Timor, approximately 200,000 killed, or died as a result of the Indonesian occupation, 1975 - 1998; and the killing continues.
>
> During the period now known as Ten Days in May 1998, there were 1,198 people killed, 437 reported cases of rape, 40 shopping malls and 4,000 shops razed.

That Indonesian ethnic Chinese have suffered so cruelly without international indignation bringing those responsible to justice is a clear indictment of our 'trade before human rights' mentality. Not all Chinese are wealthy. That they are perceived to be so was, perhaps, the genesis for what now must be deemed as the greatest of all Indonesian tragedies.

We have seen, and mainly ignored, the systematic eradication of Christian places of worship in Indonesia over the past thirty years. We have also witnessed the ethnic cleansing by powerful, militant Moslem factions of weak and isolated Christian communities in that country.

Statistics relating to the number of churches damaged or destroyed during President Soeharto's reign, are as follows:

1966-1974	(Soeharto consolidates power)	46
1975-1984	(Soeharto invades East Timor)	89
1985-1994	(The annihilation of Christian Separatists)	132
1995-1998	(Re-emergence of militant Moslem groups)	134

Total number of Churches severely damaged or destroyed during the Soeharto Presidency, 401. (Churches continue to be attacked under the new Presidency)

* * * *

It is most unlikely that the ethnic Chinese will be easily encouraged to return to Indonesia. And one would ask, why would they wish to? Legislating against racial discrimination is not enough but it may lead to a greater understanding of the racial undercurrents which continue to flow through Asian cultures, dominated economically by Chinese minorities.

This story is a work of fiction based on my personal observations of events, and is not meant to denigrate any individual, ethnic group or religion in any way whatsoever. Although some readers may associate my characters with those in real life, that act would merely be a product of their own imagination.

* * * *

ACKNOWLEDGEMENTS

I find considerable pleasure in acknowledging those who have assisted with my research for *The Fifth Season.* It was not until I commenced researching cyclones and their incredible impact on our lives, that I began to understand our dependence on weather forecasting and the frustrations of unpredictability which confront those who work in this field. I wish to express my gratitude to Ross Evans, the Cyclone Liaison Officer in Darwin, Northern Territory, for his advice.

I wish also to thank John Lee, Nico J. Tampi, the office of the United Nations High Commissioner for Refugees in Canberra, and John Pike, the Federation of American Scientists, for assisting with information concerning missile strike capabilities. I recommend to my readers that they visit web site http://www.fas.org/ to appreciate the Federation's contribution in keeping us informed, as to matters relating to the proliferation of weapons of mass destruction.

There are others I wish to mention here; Andrew Karam, MS,CHP, RSO, University of Rochester, for his friendship and support; Nancy Stuart, Interim Associate Dean, College of Imaging Arts & Sciences, Rochester Institute of Technology, New York, for her assistance with my research; Tim Coy for the technical assistance and Internet backup; Claudia Stone Weissberg, The Pulitzer Prizes, Columbia University; Rob Dix (R.A.N. retired); Sinta Collison, Fay Hyde and Terry Bibo.

To the many readers who have written, with warmth and encouragement, the radio and television presenters who have supported my work by providing air-time for interviews and the amazing number of editors, journalists, book shop owners and managers who have assisted with my promotions, thank you all, for your wonderful support.

K. B. Collison Melbourne - Australia

To order an autographed copy of *Merdeka Square*, *The Timor Man*, *Jakarta*, *Indonesian Gold*, *In Search of Recognition*, *The Happy Warrior* **or** *The Fifth Season*, photocopy this page & send it along with your cheque, by mail to:

Sid Harta Publishers
P.O. Box 1102
Hartwell - Victoria 3125
AUSTRALIA

Prices:	**Australia**	**Outside Australia**
Merdeka Square/Freedom Square	A$16.95	US$7.95
The Timor Man	A$16.95	US$7.95
Jakarta	A$16.95	US$7.95
In Search of Recognition	A$16.95	US$7.95
Plus A$5.05 postage within Australia		US$6.05 P&H
Indonesian Gold	A$24.95	US$12.95
The Fifth Season (Pancoroba)	A$24.95	US$12.95
The Happy Warrior	A$24.95	US$12.95
Plus A$5.05 postage within Australia		US$6.05 P&H

Other best-selling titles by Kerry B. Collison

Readers are invited to visit our publishing websites at:

http://www.sidharta.com.au

http://www.publisher-guidelines.com/

http://temple-house.com/

Kerry B. Collison's home pages:

http://www.authorsden.com/visit/author.asp?AuthorID=2239

http://www.expat.or.id/sponsors/collison.html

Asia Times current affairs site for travel warnings and other information with a focus on Indonesia: http://asia-times.net

email: author@sidharta.com.au

Also from Sid Harta Publishers

New Releases

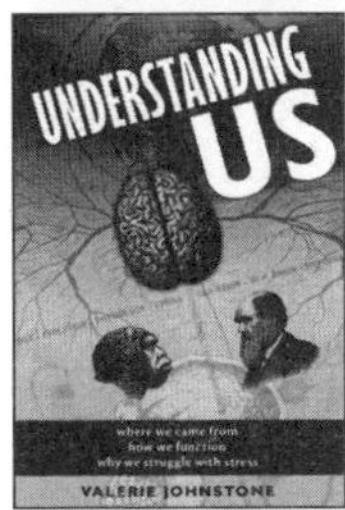